TALES *of* RAVENS NEST

ALSO BY JOSEPH COLWELL

Canyon Breezes:
Exploring Magical Places in Nature

Zephyr of Time:
Meditations on Time and Nature

Sands of Time: A Flight of Discovery
and Search for Meanings of Time

TALES *of* RAVENS NEST

A Life, A Place: Stories and Reflections

JOSEPH COLWELL

Lichen Rock Press
Hotchkiss, Colorado 81419

Editing and photography: Katherine Colwell
Book design and publishing services: Constance King Design

Lichen Rock Press
Hotchkiss, Colorado
ColwellCedars.com

ISBN: 978-0-9962222-2-8
Printed in USA

Contents

PART III: JAKE'S REFLECTIONS

Editor's Introduction to the First Edition

This is a collection of works written by Jake Collins. I gathered his writings after he passed on to his next life. I have previously published three books of essays and poems written by Jake. I had no part in those other than a final edit and proofread, with no comments or introduction by myself. Here, the novella *Tori's Dream* documents in fictionalized form his later years, including the arrival of Tori Reynolds and myself. You could call it historical fiction but to me it is closer to autobiography. He wrote the first four chapters with instructions to me to finish the story. However, the story will never be complete. As with any true ecological story, it is continually evolving, never ending. That was one of Jake's legacies to me—an understanding of the natural world. I have given instructions that either my wife Tori or someone else take the story of Ravens Nest past the time I leave the scene.

I knew Jake dabbled in writing, but he always deferred to me, intimidated by my professional standing. I earned my living writing, and Jake did it for fun. While living at Ravens Nest with Jake and his wife Rachel, I never knew he had written the works in this collection. He rarely showed me his work nor did I ask to see what he had written. Whenever I would encourage his writing, he kept saying he couldn't write. Many of these are very personal and most are to some degree autobiographical, in the nature of the short story genre.

Creativity was the moving force of Ravens Nest, both the

retreat and institute it evolved into. Jake was creative with his writing, but also with his thinking. His wife Rachel was an accomplished artist. My wife Tori is a world-renowned singer, songwriter, and musician; unknown even to her most devoted fans, she also is gifted as a gardener, spiritualist, and ecologist. I have been a writer all my life and like to think I too, am creative at what I do.

But the essential creativity that permeates Ravens Nest is what Jake and Rachel instilled in the land and the people who have lived here. Tori and I were city people who knew nothing of Colorado or the West, and even less of nature and its wonders. On a lark, Tori and I visited Ravens Nest a lifetime ago, on a journey to discover the American West. We found Jake and Rachel, who took us under their wings and adopted us as their own. Little did we know at the time what would come next. The world opened up to us as we were mentored by these two special people. Their lifestyle, philosophies, their whole beings, set an example that we and countless others they touched have learned from. We are part of this world and we need to live with it, learn from it, nurture and nourish it as all of life nourishes us.

After we were absorbed into the world of Ravens Nest, my writing and Tori's music reflected this. Tori's countless gold records, music awards and reputation are based on her unique, nature-oriented world view. My Pulitzer and other awards are similarly the result of what I discovered and have tried to publicize about how humanity needs to live as part of the natural world.

Long after this is published, I do not know what Ravens Nest will have evolved into. I know the Institute will be run by the Northern Ute Nation, with covenants and restrictions to protect the values we live by. Since Jake and Rachel had no children, they bequeathed it all to Tori and me. We are childless as well, so we have decided to return it to the hands of those who nurtured it and protected it for millennia. Regardless of how long the Ute, or Nuche, lived here, whether hundreds or thousands of years, they represent the beliefs and humble spirituality of members of the natural world. That is what we all want.

Many of Jake's stories are, in general, autobiographical, although he did change names, locations, and agencies he worked for. Others reflect his views and beliefs on various subjects. Jake led an eventful life whether working for the Division of Wildlife, the Forest Service or the Park Service. He jumbled details, and he created fictional children and grandchildren. As far as I can tell, his only reference to the actual Ravens Nest is in the novella *Tori's Dream,* about Tori and me.

I never dreamed that being executor of his estate would also mean being his literary executor as well. There were no introductions or descriptions to most of his writing. Knowing some of Jake's history due to living and working closely with him for many years, I recognized most of the adventures he wrote about. He cast his own experiences as that of different characters, under different names, jobs and locations. The first five are mostly autobiographical, although Jake changed details. He cast himself working in the Forest Service in most cases rather than the Division of Wildlife. Although I knew that he worked the first half of his career with the Forest Service before moving to the Division of Wildlife, I was surprised he didn't write much about his career with Wildlife.

I searched in his files for stories that were about that phase, but either they don't exist, or he kept them separate from all the others. This is the biggest of Jake's mysteries. He did talk about some experiences with me that did not make it into his writing. It appears his writing was slowly working through his career and had made it halfway when Tori and I entered the scene. He may have stopped writing once we took up so much of his time. I greatly regret that, if it is really the case.

As for his stories and reflections, *Paradise* was intended to describe the 60s. In discussions with Jake over the years, he recounted how he met Rachel at Mt. Rainier in 1968 and claimed it the highlight of his life. Living and working on a trail crew at the Mountain for two summers was something he said changed his life. Jake and I had several great discussions about the 60s. I missed living them, but have written several articles about that period and the effects of the war and the turbulent times three decades later. I envied Jake and Rachel and their time on the Mountain. I recently took a trip there and found Paradise Lodge relatively unchanged from the time of the story. It and the Mountain that tower over it are magical places.

I am guessing that *Fire on the Mountain, Memories of a Wilderness Cabin,* and *Alpine Thunder* are based on experiences in his very early Forest Service career. *Elk Peak* seems to have been in his late career, but his placement and his main character were a mystery to me. It might have been one of his later writings where he was experimenting with characters and synthesizing cumulative experiences. *Finding Janet,* in my opinion, is strictly a fictional account, but based on his fire experiences. He did write a full memoir about his fire adventures, including years as a Fire Information Officer.

With one exception, the final six stories were written late in Jake's life, reflecting his focus on end-of-life themes. Although I did not know the young Jake, I do know that in his last years, he reflected more and more on death, life-after-death, and more melancholy, yet realistic themes. Jake lived an active, future-oriented life, reaching for dreams, living adventures, taking challenges. When the careers were complete, the dreams met, the adventures more in the telling and re-telling rather than the living, then his focus became legacy: what the meanings of life and career were about. Discussions Tori and I had with Jake tended more and more on reflections and conclusions. He liked to tell stories with meanings, to pass on his accumulated experience and wisdom.

Tori refers to this last group of stories as the tear jerkers. Jake had a way of bringing happy tears. They reflect sad situations that leave good thoughts rather than negative ones. To me, that reflects Jake's entire outlook on life: a circle that happens in an amoral natural world.

Jake once gave me an assignment to write my own obituary, and we had conversations several times similar to *The Obituary*. The story was in response to a comment from a high school classmate that a particular obituary of a former classmate was poorly written. *Soledad's Journey: The Voices and The Spirit* deals with life after death and may have originally been two separate stories. Knowing Jake's views on what comes next—we discussed this many times—I believe *Soledad's Journey* sums up his perception of what happens after death. Jake was not religious, but both he and Rachel were very spiritual. He said many times that there is no God, but each of us is a god, determining our own future and life.

Included in a book of Jake's essays that I compiled and published, *The Secrets of Time,* is an essay called "Byron's Poem." This is about an inscription in a book of Byron's poems Jake found in a used bookstore. The story *Blue Gentians and Columbines* is based on that essay. *Dedicating Daddy's Lake* is the first short story Jake ever wrote; I learned this from early drafts and reviews by a writer (a childhood friend of Jake's) who led a writers' workshop retreat at Ravens Nest before Tori and I entered the picture. It is about a young couple who deal with the death of her mother and father and the young couple keeping the memory and legacy alive.

Drifting does not fit any category. It combines stories from early in Jake's life, but through the eyes of a grandfather. Neither Jake nor Rachel talked about the fact they didn't have children. I saw them around children who came for classes at the Institute and they gave much attention to young people. This story is an adult conversation on a stormy evening between a grandfather and granddaughter. *White Bison* is the last thing Jake wrote. It was found on his desk, dated and printed the day before he and Rachel left us. I believe he intentionally left it incomplete, leaving me to add the last few paragraphs. He and I had talked often during his last weeks about his ideas on death. Since he had written earlier of a granddaughter, he chose to close his series of stories in the same vein.

I found it an honor and a pleasure to complete Jake's works and assemble them in this book. As I look up in the night sky, I can see and feel Jake out there. Maybe his hand will reach out to me when my time comes. I welcome it. Peace, old friend.

Alistaire Corey

PREFACE TO THE SECOND EDITION

It has been several years since Alistaire Corey published this collection. I have added two chapters to *Tori's Dream,* per instructions, to bring the story of Ravens Nest up to date. I tried to keep the writing in the same style, since it continues the story begun by Jake years ago, using Tori's notebooks and diaries as well as my personal knowledge of Tori. In publishing this second edition the only changes are those two chapters and this preface.

After the publication of *Tales of Ravens Nest,* Al received several letters from old friends of Jake and Rachel, confirming that many of the stories in the book are more autobiographical than Al realized.

After Al passed, Tori continued with the evolving saga of Ravens Nest, solidifying her place on the mesa as well as her place with her world-class music. She brought me on as an intern, then hired me as manager. I basically took the place of Tori and Al as the adopted heir to this marvelous place. Just as Jake and Rachel did not have children, neither did Al and Tori. I didn't know Al very well since he passed not long after I came to Ravens Nest. I served as Tori's helper, then confidante, and came to love and adore her as a mother, a mentor, and the keeper of the flame.

Tori is gone now as well and I continue with the help of the Northern Ute Nation in keeping alive the spirit of Ravens Nest. I will not do the same as the others in bringing on an adopted heir. The Nation now has a presence here, including a large conference center and housing for several managers. The original Ravens Nest has stayed the same, with Jake and Rachel's house serving as a library. New housing has been built on adjacent properties that the Institute acquired over the years. Both Jake and Rachel as well as Al and Tori would see little change from what Ravens Nest looked like in the early years.

This closes the chapters on Jake and Rachel, Tori and Al. I will write no more but the story continues, in cycles and circles beneath the endless blue sky where we all will meet again.

Bernice Sanderson

PART I

TORI'S DREAM

CHAPTER 1

RAVENS NEST

"It's not what we want anymore. We don't like what we are becoming. We have found something out here that both of us need. We feel so good with it."
Tori Reynolds

RACHEL PUT HER hand over the phone and shushed me, motioning me to go away. I had just finished washing the supper dishes and wandered into her office, wondering who she was talking to this late in the evening. After pronouncing our name several times, she patiently guided the caller to log onto our website. I made a funny face as she spelled out the name, and she shushed me again.

We live on one hundred acres in western Colorado where Rachel and I developed a small retreat. We feel at home living with the trees and hills, the birds and streams. We don't watch TV or read newspapers, and basically leave the outside world where it belongs—outside our lives. But we do invite people into our lives.

Our preferences are guests who appreciate what we offer—quiet and solitude—savoring the peacefulness of our natural setting. Many inquiries don't pan out, but we are not a bed and breakfast or dude ranch. Our amenities are the bounties of nature, not fancy furnishings or food that people seem to expect from upscale lodgings popping up in rural settings like this.

I had given up waiting for her to finish the phone call and was starting to get into bed when she came in to tell me about the call.

"You won't believe the conversation I just had."

She paused as if she expected me to say something. I waited for her to complete her tale. Finally, realizing I wasn't going to say anything, she continued.

"It was a lady from New York City. Sounded young. I would guess maybe in her early thirties. She wants to take a trip out west and, in her words, see the real America. She couldn't log onto our website. She for some reason had the wrong name and kept getting some place in Canada. She knew we were in Colorado and she knew our phone number. Someone had written our information down for her but got the name wrong. She was searching for 'Raven Retreat' instead of Ravens Nest."

I smiled. "Well at least she got through to us. Another one we will never hear from again?"

"Not sure. She seemed interested, but she was getting frustrated she couldn't find us. So she just called instead. I walked her through and she got the site." Rachel disappeared into the bathroom and shut the door.

I stood staring at the door, wondering if that was the end of the conversation. Why tell me just enough to have me interested, then stop the conversation? Surely there was more than that! I waited patiently.

When she came out of the bathroom, she gave me a puzzled look. "You waiting to get in? I thought you were done."

"No, I'm waiting for you to tell me more about this mysterious phone call. You tantalize me with hints of it, then you just drop it. What!?"

"Oh. I thought I told you all of it. She wanted information about Ravens Nest. I gave it to her."

"And?" I was still waiting for more details.

"She's some flaky musician from New York City. Said she doesn't even know how to drive. She and her second half as she called him, have traveled abroad and visited places like Paris and London, but she hasn't really seen her own country. A friend suggested they come out to Montana or Colorado and see what the West is really like. She liked the idea and the friend gave her a list of websites for small retreats and guest ranches. Ours was one. She said she would ponder it, to use her words, and let us know."

I had never been to New York City and had no desire to see it. I was skeptical of anyone from a big city. I knew we would never hear from her again. I wasn't sure I would want to even be around someone who had never been outside New York except on a cruise ship or tour group. She probably wouldn't even know what a tree was. I love spending time exploring our little wilderness of juniper and aspen, gurgling streams and small waterfalls, but I like our guests to at least know the difference between a raven and a chickadee.

Several days later—a scorching August afternoon—after I had forgotten about the phone call, and as Rachel was taking a nap, the phone rang. A female voice with a mild New York accent was on the other end. She introduced herself as the person who had called earlier, and after realizing I wasn't going to wake up Rachel, she decided to talk to me. She said she and second half wished to come for a visit. Her preferred dates in September would work for us so I asked her which rooms she wished to reserve. She said she didn't need a kitchen as long as they could eat in our dining hall. After a polite chuckle, I told her we had no dining hall. We were fifteen miles from town where the nearest restaurant was. Silence on her end meant she was rethinking her decision.

I told her we were not fancy, but offered seclusion and interaction with the outdoors. If I remembered right, she couldn't even drive, which might present problems. How would they get out here?

More silence, then a hesitant voice replied, "If we stayed for a week or two, could you guide us around? Al can drive but rarely does. We don't own a car."

I was used to guiding guests for hikes around our one hundred acres, but the thought of guiding a couple city folks, showing them what I wanted them to see, intrigued me. "Where would you want to visit?" I hesitantly asked.

"You are familiar with your part of the country. Drive us around to areas of interest and explain your lifestyle to us. You may think us naïve city folks. Maybe we are. But we want to get a feel of what it is like to live out West. Drive us around, explain things, give us a taste of Colorado and the West.

Silence on my end of the phone sat heavy for several seconds. Finally, she asked if I was still there.

"Yes, I'm here. Your request is intriguing. I am thinking about it. There is a lot to see from right here, but if you want more than that, we would have to rent an SUV since my pickup only seats two comfortably. I envision several trips to the high country and we would need a four-wheel drive. Then maybe a trip to a place like Moab. Maybe even the Grand Canyon. That would be nearly a full day drive, but it certainly would expose you to something you may not be used to. Miles and miles of nothing, but a very enchanting nothing."

Silence once again on her end.

I quickly added, "of course it would all depend on your budget as well as your objectives." I added as almost an afterthought, "yes, I would love to do it."

"Budget isn't a concern. We would just need to know how much to set aside."

That comment at first flew past me, although it hit me as I started talking. An unlimited budget? Wow, I thought quickly to myself. I said, "I would have to propose an itinerary. I think the best thing is to agree in principle, then when you get here, sit down with a map and go over each item. We could easily spend a few days right here while you get acclimated to the elevation."

I could hear her talking to someone in the background. I caught a man's voice saying "you told him we had an unlimited budget? Are you crazy? He will take us to the cleaners." After that the voice stopped, probably by a tighter hand clamped over the phone. In a few seconds she came back on and apologized. She said this was a very interesting idea that she and Al had not discussed yet. Could she call me back once they decided what to do. She did say they wanted to come out and stay a week in any case. We agreed on the dates and decided she would call the next day at 6 pm my time.

As I hung up the phone, I must have had a look of total disbelief because Rachel walked in and stared at me. "Now it's your turn, huh? What gives? Our New Yorkie again?"

"Now it's my turn to say, 'you won't believe this.'" I sat down at the kitchen table and repeated the conversation to her. She said it was getting weird and she wasn't sure we would want to commit to something like that. I told her it was me that was committing since I would be the one to ferry them around, not her.

"What if it turns out they are total flakes and obnoxious and you can't stand them?" she asked.

"I've dealt all my life with flakes and people I don't really care to be around. You have too. For enough money, I can put up with anything for a couple weeks."

She opened the fridge, hefted out a watermelon, and started cutting it up. "What would you charge them? And if you are gone traveling around, do we charge them for the room they won't be in?"

"No idea," I said as I grabbed a chunk of melon. "Sounds to me like they have money and she isn't worried about it."

"This is getting stranger by the minute. You want to do it, fine, but I don't have a good feeling about it." She had a habit of slicing the watermelon into small pieces rather than eating it with her fingers like I did. As I picked up my piece to eat it my way, it slipped out of my hand and fell on the floor. YoYo, our border collie mix, was quick as lightning as she ran over to grab it, but then she gave me a stare and walked away. "Thanks," I said to her as lay down with her back to me, obviously disgusted that I hadn't dropped something more to her liking.

"I guess I will think about what to charge and maybe a first shot itinerary and see what she says when she calls tomorrow." I washed off the melon and quickly ate it before I could drop it again.

Since I was retired and had no job other than tinkering around on my own property, I couldn't place a value on my time. I wouldn't have to pay anyone to do what I would be doing while I was ferrying city folks around the country. I would probably be chopping firewood or cutting brush, which was turning into a lifetime job as it was. Besides, it might be a nice vacation for me, with someone else footing the costs. Although I had not done this professionally, being an interpreter or guide was something I was good at and enjoyed. I had a nice gift of gab, but without being obnoxious. Too many people told me that for me not to believe it was true.

Victoria Reynolds according to the caller ID, but Tori as

she referred to herself, called at 6 right on the nose. She said she and Alistaire had talked it over and decided to do it. She liked my voice and felt they could be comfortable with me. She said they would fly into Montrose and pay for a proper rental vehicle for two weeks if I would drive them from there. They wanted the apartment, but would pay an additional $75 a day for us to cook their meals, plus $250 a day for my guide services. While traveling they would pay all food, gas and lodging costs.

Although this was probably very inexpensive for them in relation to what they would pay for some first-class cruise, it seemed more than fair to me. I thought later I could probably have bargained up for more, but why be greedy? I wanted to show them the earthy hospitality they were looking for. I said it sounded good to me and I would work on a detailed list of what to do. I did say we would spend some time in the high country around Silverton and Gunnison, with a side trip to Moab and the slickrock country. She didn't know what slickrock was and I told her to wait and see. I said she would love it, so different from Manhattan.

I gave them a list of what they needed to bring, such as good hiking boots and proper clothes. I was afraid to think what a fancy place like Abercrombie and Fitch might consider good boots. Since they would be coming early September, we could encounter all types of weather, but at least they would catch us at a great time of year.

Although I developed an extensive list of places to visit, I did not finalize anything. I wanted them to make those choices themselves. I needed to get a personal feel for what they were like and what they might enjoy. I was afraid they would be too delicate for any extensive hiking. For the next few weeks, Rachel said very little about my upcoming adventure. I know she thought I was taking a big risk with these city folks, but she let me do my thing.

On an early Friday afternoon, I met the once-a-day Continental flight from Houston to Montrose. I had a nice four-wheel drive rental all lined up and parked out front awaiting them. I told them I would be wearing a Hawaiian shirt; they thought that a great idea and said they would also. I had to laugh when I saw a young couple come into the terminal from the plane wearing what I considered good old fashioned cowboy flowered shirts. They fit right in in this western environment. Much more than my genuine glow-in-the-dark palm tree and parrot shirt.

Tori was not at all what I expected. She was tall and very thin, almost anorexic. Her long blond hair was tied up in a bun. She wore glasses and had a very attractive face. Al was shorter than Tori, but didn't weigh much more than her. His jet black hair was cut short. As they walked together, he seemed to follow Tori, letting her make the decisions. She seemed very much at ease being in charge. Although they were dressed to fit the West, they both had the air that said "city folks." I couldn't place exactly what it was, but when they spoke, it became quite obvious. They were New Yorkers in speech. Al had the city accent that I found irritating, but Tori was more moderated. Tori talked fast, Al very slow and deliberate. All my preconceived notions were confirmed. Both seemed very nice, although it seemed Tori wore the pants in this family.

I asked them how their trip was. Al mumbled something about it being long, but Tori started a ten minute monologue. Even though their connection in Houston kept them in the airport, she was fascinated by Texas. I didn't catch many good things she had to say about Texans; she was fascinated by a class of people she found interesting but in their own world. I didn't disagree with her take on that.

Rachel had driven me to Montrose but let me off at the airport where I got the rental and she drove on home. She didn't feel she needed to meet our guests while they were probably tired and worn out from the flights. On the hour-long drive home I learned a lot about Tori and Al. They also learned a lot about me. We hit it off, although I found Al very quiet. Whether he was just tired, or he was totally overwhelmed by his more extroverted wife, I wasn't sure. I guessed them to be in their mid-thirties, but it was getting hard for me to judge people's ages.

Tori was an accomplished violinist and cellist, who substituted for both the New York Philharmonic as well as the Metropolitan Opera. She also took on students at her home. Al was a staff writer for the *Atlantic Digest,* but recently spent most of his time researching his latest book. His research often took him out of the country, mostly Europe. He did admit he had a driver's license, but Tori was correct that they had never owned a car and she really did not know how to drive.

Tori let it slip that her father was the Reynolds of New York financial circles. I of course had never heard of him, but what did I know about Wall Street? The family had been on the stock exchange for five generations and constituted what is considered "old money." They owned an entire floor of a high-rise bordering Central Park. Tori was brought up mingling in the exclusive circles of the city. However, she didn't seem at all snobbish to me.

Although Al was raised in the city, his family heritage was slightly less impressive than hers. His family was in the textile trade, whatever that meant. I assumed he might be Jewish, but I didn't consider that relevant to anything so never asked. Both had spent some time in Europe, Switzerland mostly, in schools, but their degrees were from Bryn Mawr and Princeton. My work was cut out for me to get them past their upbringing and the world they were ensconced in and into the laid back, uncultured (probably

to them) civilization of the wild west. I wondered if they would label us in the Rocky Mountains as a subclass like the Texans they found "interesting."

My tourists found the ride from Montrose to the North Fork awesome. They couldn't believe the desolate landscape outside Delta and the surrounding forested mountains, lightly dusted with the first snow of the season. As I pulled into our long driveway, with its birds-eye-view of mountains and valleys, Tori was bubbling with descriptive adjectives. I told her we try and not take the views for granted. Even Al said it was grand, worthy of a story.

As they got out of the vehicle, YoYo pounced all over them, despite Rachel's efforts to restrain her. Tori would not obey our requests not to pet YoYo until later. Although Tori had never had a dog, she connected with YoYo immediately. They would become fast friends over the next couple weeks. Although we called her YoYo because of her bouncy nature, Tori thought it was in honor of Yo-Yo Ma, her hero. I didn't correct her.

We sat on the deck after a supper of buffalo burgers, which came from a bison ranch a mile down the road. Al was hesitant to eat buffalo, but Tori liked the idea of eating local food. She was interested in our large garden, which was almost finished for the year.

"I just cannot comprehend this," Tori said after staring off into the distance. "All of Manhattan island would fit down there in that valley. This much space where I live contains millions of people. How many live there?" She waved her arms from horizon to horizon.

"There are only about 30,000 or so in the entire county. Everything you see from here. Actually you are seeing 70 miles to the San Juan Mountains there on the horizon and that is about two counties away." I pointed out the mountain ranges and wilderness areas, where no one lived.

"I cannot get my mind around that one," Al broke in.

"Wait a few days till I take you over to Utah," I said. "There is a place where you see an area that is larger than about six or seven states. And less than a thousand people live there. All slickrock desert of southern Utah. I've never gotten *my* mind around that one."

"How do people make a living here? It looks like a lot of farms. Do you get all your food here? And what do they do for entertainment?" asked Tori.

"Living here in the fresh air and open spaces and blue skies is all the entertainment we need," Rachel said as she stood up to go inside. She returned in a minute with a bowl of fresh peaches, from the orchards down below. "Last of the season," she said as she passed the bowl around. "Ever have any right off the trees? And yes, we try and eat locally as much as possible. "

"I wish we could eat from our own garden. Actually I wish we could have a garden." Tori picked up a peach and looked at it. "It's all fuzzy. Do you eat that?"

Al laughed as he took one and picked up a knife Rachel held out for him. "You peel it Victoria. Don't tell me you've never eaten a fresh peach?"

"Well, yes, but I've never peeled one."

I grabbed one and started peeling it. "That's okay, Tori, I can't stand the fuzz either. But lean over as you eat it. You will have juice running all down your blouse otherwise. You can help me can some tomorrow."

Then I explained that the view below used to be all fruit trees, but each year, whole orchards were being uprooted. Growers couldn't find pickers, or else they were being undercut by China or other countries. Plain economics I said.

Tori looked at me with a disbelieving look.

"You want to see the immigration debate first hand,"

I said, "just drive around down there. You can't find any local Anglos to work here. Either in our orchards, or the ski resorts in Vail and Aspen. We have to have migrant or at least local Hispanic workers. But then people say they are stealing our jobs. Bull. It's that or nothing. You go to any hotel or resort around the West and you will be lucky if anyone there speaks English. They are not stealing our jobs. They are the only ones willing to work in hard jobs like that."

Al looked up from his peach. "I did an article last year about the problem in New York with hotel and restaurant workers. Yeah, big problems and no one is dealing with the issue. Politics gets in the way."

We sat quietly, watching birds flitting to and from the bird feeder. An eagle was soaring high above, making its not so regal chirping sound. Tori screwed her face and asked what that noise was. I looked up and pointed with my eyes at the bird. "Not your majestic screech you hear in the movies is it? It's a golden eagle. They are here year round."

She stared into the blue sky, and whispered, "a real eagle."

We sat around the kitchen table that night making plans for our trips of exploration. Short hikes on the Ravens Nest trails would be a good break-in for Tori and Al. They were puffing after a short uphill walk. I was too, but I had a good excuse: sixty-four-year-old lungs. Their excuse was elevation, which they would get over soon. We decided to start with day trips up on to Grand Mesa and along the North Rim of the Black Canyon. Our first priority a morning spent picking peaches from a local orchard, then processing two canner loads, while Rachel made a peach cobbler. Although Al said he had watched his grandmother can apricots, Tori had never even seen a canner, much less peeled or canned any type of fruit; her culinary experiences involved restaurants and meals prepared by her housekeeper.

Short trips the first several days worked perfectly for all of us. Rachel was free to do whatever she wanted during the day, while Tori, Al, YoYo, and I hiked and drove into some of Colorado's finest country. They marveled that it was all within a couple hour's drive from where I lived. They asked how much time I spent up there. I was a little embarrassed to say not much. They said they would spend all their time up there if they lived here.

They were amazed that my career was spent in the wild country as they called it—thirty years with the Forest Service, and ten with the state Department of Wildlife and federal Fish and Wildlife Service as a biologist. They could not conceive of the fact millions of acres of mountains belonged to them as American citizens nor had they even considered there was a science of wildlife management. They felt sorry for the deer and elk and didn't realize all those animals were destined to die, if not by bullets, then by disease, starvation or predators. They were horrified when we drove through an active timber sale. I told them that if humans didn't cut down the trees, then the trees would die from disease or fire. Tori said it wasn't fair. I spent one whole afternoon talking population biology. Her emotions said she didn't agree with any of this, but her intellect agreed to the facts of science. Al was mostly quiet, although he took a lot of notes. He finally said he smelled an article, if not an entire book on this fascinating topic.

It was past our normal monsoon season so I felt safe enough on Wednesday to climb to an exposed rocky knob on the Continental Divide near Cottonwood Pass east of

Gunnison. But clouds started building late morning and now were blackening the sky above us. I knew we had better head for the truck, but Al was engrossed in his writing; he had taken a lot of notes on our high country trips and seemed to be putting them all together. Tori was trying to feed the chipmunks and Steller's jays, but I told her she was talking too much to get customers. We quickly ate a light lunch as I nervously eyed the sky.

With the first rumble of thunder not far to the south, I quietly told them, "you may not be familiar with high country thunderstorms, but I have been caught too many times above timberline waiting for lightning to part my hair. Stay here if you want, but don't move. I will know where to find the charred bodies." With that, I got up and started scrambling down the slope, YoYo bouncing beside me.

"Jake, wait, we're coming," yelled Tori as she stumbled over Al's outstretched leg. They quickly followed me down to the scraggly trees marking the transition to timberline. I didn't even stop to point out the marmot scolding us as we went by its rock field. We were about a mile or so from the vehicle and I knew we would not make it before the rain. Tori had stuffed her cap in her pack, and the wind was whipping her hair.

We made it far enough down the slope to ease my concern, but I still didn't like being exposed to storms. The spruce tops were swaying in the now steady winds. Drops of rain started hitting us as we walked briskly, just short of a run. Thunder was closer and louder. Finally I stopped at a large rock outcrop. There was a small overhang on its north side, so I said we should hole up in there 'til it blew over. Tori was excited, but I think Al was frightened.

"We will be safe here," I calmly said as a bolt of lightning flashed directly overhead. I didn't even count to four before the thunder shook the air. "Enjoy the mountain symphony.

I don't know what it's like for the thunder to reverberate in the canyons of New York City, but you are in for a treat up here. A clap of thunder will bounce around for minutes in these canyons."

Another bolt flashed nearby and the explosion was almost instant. Then we listened to the echoes mingling with echoes as they bounced from ridge to ridge.

"Wow," was all Tori said as she leaned out to feel the raindrops, now splashing wildly off the rocks.

"It just goes forever, doesn't it," Al mumbled as he pulled his notebook out of his pack.

"Nothing like it," I said, and described several occasions when I was caught above timberline on horseback in lightning storms. All I could do was tie up the horse, hope he didn't pull loose, then I laid flat on the ground and waited. I got soaked of course, then almost covered by hail as the storm blew past.

"You got paid to do that kind of thing?" Al said as he quickly scribbled in his rain-splattered notebook.

"Every day. We are sitting in what was essentially my office for over 30 years. Of course I didn't get to be out in it every day. Way too many days indoors at a desk, but I got out into settings like this as much as I could."

"And I thought I got a thrill going on stage before a thousand people. Boy, I'd trade that in a New York minute," Tori laughed as she said the words New York with an exaggerated accent.

It only took fifteen minutes for the storm to pass. We could track where it went by the sound of the thunder, fading into the distance north of us. It was now bouncing off Collegiate Peaks, heading past Mt. Harvard. We sloshed the mile back to the vehicle through pea-sized hail and water flowing down the trail.

Another day, we spent an entire afternoon playing in

last year's snow fields above Silverton. Tori wrestled YoYo on a particularly steep snowfield, both sliding down a hundred yards to the bottom. On a safe stretch of an old mining road, I let Tori take the wheel of the truck. She raced up and down, bouncing me and Al and YoYo every which way as she hit every rut. Al got the hang of four-wheel drive and I let him drive us up one steep and rocky piece of road above timberline. Tori was white knuckled as she held onto the door and chided him for every rock he bounced over. I sat quietly in the back seat.

One night as we sat around the dinner table, eating fresh vegetables from the garden and finishing a bottle of Chardonnay from a North Fork vineyard, I told them we needed to agree on an itinerary for the final few days of their stay. I was thinking of the slickrock country around Moab. The weather was cool, with highs only in the seventies and nights in the low forties. After looking at pictures I had taken of our latest trip to Arches, Tori said, "Let's go."

They agreed to camp in my 18-foot travel trailer, after spending a test night in it at Ravens Nest. I figured this would really give them a feeling for the West. For some reason, the idea of using an outhouse appealed to Tori. By now, Al had gotten used to the fun of just going behind a tree or rock to pee. Tori said she was jealous, especially since the first time she tried it, she peed on her feet. I smiled and said some things you just had to get used to. That was the first time I heard Al snort as he laughed.

As we came down the grade into Moab on Highway 191, both were speechless at the red cliffs. They wanted to visit Arches, but I told them we would do it on the way back. We stopped at two tourist shops on Main Street, and Tori bought a pair of moose hide moccasins. Then we headed south of town and turned onto the road to the Canyon Rims area. My favorite campground was Windwhistle, on BLM land. The campground was only half full at 3 pm. We set up the trailer, then looked at each other. Who was going to do the cooking?

Rachel couldn't come, although I knew this was one of her favorite places. We had guests coming to stay in one of the small cabins and she needed to be there for that. I knew she was enjoying both Tori and Al, but she said she had things she had to do and I decided not to argue. The guests had stayed with us before and probably could have gotten by without us, but Rachel said she couldn't do that. Besides, this was my project and I needed time doing something fun like this.

I said, "How about before we deal with food, let's drive on out to the Needles Overlook. You have had a preview of this country, but let's go see the real thing." I was anxious to see their reaction to the view from the cliffs. I wanted to see if they could get their minds around the views from these overlooks.

When we pulled into the parking area, there were no other cars. The vast expanse of the plateau we had just driven across was a pleasant change from the rugged alpine areas of the past week. Miles and miles of sagebrush and dried autumn grass with views that never ended was something neither of them had ever seen.

I did something I had always wanted to try. I blindfolded Tori—Al refused to cooperate with this one—and led her to the first real overlook. Al gave an exclamation as he stopped, mouth open.

"Oh, let me see, let me see", Tori whined as we stood with hands on the metal railing.

I touched her shoulder, then said quietly, "First I want you to listen."

No one said anything for several seconds. "I don't hear anything," Tori said.

"That is what I want you to hear. The sound of nothing. But it is something. Just listen."

Thankfully for me, a raven flew up out of the depths, squawking as it flew over us. The breeze through its feathers was the only other sound.

As I slowly removed the blindfold, I told her, "Okay. Tell me the first thought in your mind."

She looked out over the miles of canyons and plateaus, nothing but rock and space. "Oh God!" she almost screamed. "Al, can you believe it?" She grabbed Al and stepped back from the edge. "I can't believe we are still on this earth! Oh Al." She stood there holding onto Al, who was still mesmerized by the view below us.

"This is a different world," Al finally said. "It's unreal."

I smiled. "Yeah, pretty awesome, primeval earth. It would probably look the same if we were standing here a million years ago." I shielded my eyes from the autumn sun low over the Maze.

We were on the edge of the plateau, looking over an expanse of desert far below us. The Colorado River was down there, hidden in the haze of rock and sky. The quiet was explosive in its impact. There was no sign of humanity anywhere. For miles and miles. A huge chunk of earth and time had been lifted away, or floated away on a river that had roared and flowed for millions of years on its way to a distant sea. How could anyone grasp this the first time they saw it?

Tori looked at me with the question in her eyes. She didn't even need to speak it. I knew the question, but not the answer. I smiled, then drew her eyes back into the abyss with mine.

"I wanted you to get a view of it now. We will spend more time up here tomorrow. There is a great spot further up the cliffs to walk along the edge. I will let you think about this overnight. Let's go back and make something to eat."

"Can I just stand here for a while?" Tori asked, still holding onto Al. He had been toying with his camera, but hadn't taken any pictures.

"How can you capture this?" he finally asked. "There is no way."

"I know. It's like the Grand Canyon. First time you see it, you want to start snapping pictures. Most people do. When they get home, they look at the feeble attempt, then hit delete. There is no way to capture it. This is one time the old saying "you just had to be there" is really appropriate. Not like New York City is it?"

That evening was the first time Tori had cooked since I met her. She turned out to be a very good cook, especially given the limits and confines of the trailer. It was equipped with a full kitchen, but since we were on the road, we were pretty limited on the raw ingredients for a meal. She made a stew out of fresh veggies from our garden, rice, and chunks of roast pork Rachel had sent with us. She still marveled over the fact we knew where most of this food was grown.

Later, we sat comfortably by a campfire, in the brisk night air of the Utah desert. Of course I pulled out marshmallows, soda crackers, and chocolate bars. They had never heard of s'mores. They loved them—the slow twirling of marshmallow over the coals, the sudden flaming marshmallows, the crisp and gooey and sweet and salty sensation of eating, and the marshmallow taffy.

Although both had been seeing the Western starry sky for several nights, it seemed to be especially brilliant. The Milky Way painted the blackness with a billion stories. We shared stories of our own lives as the campfire flickered and danced, throwing shadows onto the ghostly branches of the nearby junipers.

Tori told of her time in the Swiss boarding school. Of

all the time she spent there, she had not gone hiking in the Alps. Most of the time she spent in the towns and cities. She was well versed in the music and culture of old Europe, but surprisingly short on her time with nature. She said she was learning more in the past week than she had in all her previous thirty-some years.

Before he met Tori, Al had done some hiking in Austria and France and spent one summer on the rivers and canals of France on a river barge. But as was his fashion, he shared very little with me. I was having a hard time figuring him out. I knew there was something deeper there that I would eventually coax out.

We were up early in the morning, and at breakfast Al read aloud an essay he wrote by the fire long after I went to bed. I was surprised at his grasp of what he was seeing and feeling. This guy was a writer. I had not had a chance to hear Tori play the cello or violin but I sensed she was just as talented. I felt like a midwife giving a new life to two adult children. Two people who were being exposed to a life and environment they had previously been sheltered from. I didn't know their world, but I sensed they were finding mine preferable to theirs. Most people from the cities and suburbs found this type of setting nice, but were usually glad to get home. I wasn't sure about Tori and Al. They were loving this.

With water, lunch, dog snacks, and a bottle of a North Fork Vineyards Merlot efficiently stashed in knapsacks, we drove further out the road to the Anticline Overlook. This gave a totally different—but just as impressive—view from the Needles Overlook the night before. We watched a few Jeeps crawling up the trail hundreds of feet below us. Tori wanted to do that and I told her we could do it later that day or the next. I had opted, with Tori's money of course, to get extra rental insurance, so we were covered in case we got intimate with any rocks or cliff faces in the brand new vehicle.

I explained the settling ponds for the huge potash mine visible below us. I felt it appropriate to toss in mining as an issue to discuss, especially in a place like this. We had seen old mining ruins near Silverton and above Gunnison, but most of them were just that—historic ruins from a much technologically simpler time. On this subject, it wasn't Tori who objected, but Al. He thought it sacrilege to despoil a place like this to get something basic like potassium. Tori thought the ponds attractive in their azure blues and greens, in stark contrast to the reds and oranges surrounding them.

Tori wanted to hike along the edge of the rim, but I told her to wait. Our next stop was further south, between this overlook and the previous night's overlook. We accessed it along a rather tame 4x4 road that took us to a remote section of this same meandering cliff wall. I let Al drive us to the end of the road, and instructed him to turn the truck and park headed out. We donned our knapsacks and started ambling down a trail that paralleled the rim.

"Oh, Jake, you keep finding new surprises for us," Tori said as she grabbed my arm. "This is so austere, yet so beautiful. I am composing music to accompany it in my head already. How can something so simple and stark be so beautiful and complicated?"

This area was typical of the slickrock country I had fallen in love with years ago. The ground was mostly exposed sandstone bedrock, interspersed with reddish orange sandy soil, and the vegetation typical to this country. Juniper and pinyon lifted their stubby heads a few feet above the ground, while cliff rose, chokecherry, Indian ricegrass, cactus and other plants speckled the red background with greens, tans, and browns. Very little was in bloom this time of year, so I gave them an account of the glorious colors they could find here in April and May.

"Not like Central Park, is it Al?" Tori said as she squeezed his hand.

Al took off his cap and fluffed his short hair. "It has a different story to tell. It gives me a strange feeling, but I admire this more. Each plant has to struggle. Back east, there is so much green. Trees and flowers have it so easy— they overwhelm you. Here," he paused as he looked around, "here, life isn't easy. There is no soil. Just rock. Earth. Primeval earth with life in a struggle to exist. That is the theme of life out here isn't it?" He looked at me. "That has been what you have been trying to get across to us in your subtle way. Not just with the environment, but people as well."

I smiled. "Great minds think alike, huh?"

We walked further down the trail, stopping to admire the shapes of rock, the grains, swirls of patterns and colors. A juniper snag, old and gnarled, twisted and grayed with age, stood sentinel on the brink of the cliff. It belonged to a bygone era, as did the rock a thousand feet below. Tori stopped and stared at it. None of us said a word. I found the tree a work of art. Tori and Al did as well.

"This tree sums it all up for me," Tori said as she walked over to stand by it. "Al, take my picture," she said as she reached to hug the tree.

"Good grief, Tori, be careful. It's right on the rim," Al said. No sooner did he finish his statement, than Tori screamed and disappeared in a cloud of dust.

My heart fell through my shoes as I envisioned her falling. I raced the few feet to the edge, where the slab of rock had broken off. I didn't hear any screaming voice fading far below. As I looked over, I saw Tori sitting jammed against a rock on a wide ledge ten feet below us. She looked up and laughed and cried at the same time.

I don't think I had breathed the entire time, which actually couldn't have been more than ten seconds. The ledge was about five feet wide. Below it was another ledge, stair step style. Then the cliff gave way and it was a good thousand feet straight down. The ledge disappeared about 100 yards further along the rim. If Tori had been standing at that point, she would still be falling.

"God, Tori, do you realize..." Al's voice trailed into silence. He reached down and grabbed Tori's hand as she stood on top of the rock. I held onto Al's belt as he helped Tori scrabble up the rim.

Tears streaked the red dust on her face. She was holding her wrist which had blood on it. She looked down at her bare leg, where blood was running down from a long scrape on her thigh. "I didn't want to see it that close up," she laughed as she wiped her face. "Now we have to get a picture of this tree." She stood a foot in front of it as Al reluctantly snapped her picture. He zoomed onto her bloody leg and took a picture of that as well.

We walked a few feet inland and sat on a smooth sandstone slab under the shade of a large juniper. No one said a word for nearly a minute. We just looked at each other. In all my years of scrambling along cliffs and rocks, I had never come close to anything like this. I had stood many times on the edges of precipices and never seen a rock break like that.

I took off my knapsack. "I don't know about you, but suddenly I am hungry. Maybe I better try one of your Manhattan sandwiches while I can still compliment you on it."

Tori laughed as she poured water on her scraped leg. "It's just a scratch. Do you think it would have been much worse if I had fallen all that way? Probably not much more blood."

Al groaned as he shook his head. "No problem for you. What would you have cared? We would have been the ones

to scrape up the body two days from now when we finally got to you. God, Tori, is my hair white yet? Feels like I aged about fifty years."

We finally laughed as we dived into lunch. I was eating my Snickers bar when I heard the first canyon wren of this trip. "Now there is music you can use to compose your main theme. We can call it the "falling symphony." Falling notes and falling rocks. Sit back and see yourself falling through the clouds."

Tori sighed as she took a bandage Al handed her and put it on the mangled skin. "Too bad it's not deep enough for a good scar. That would be worth telling people about."

"I don't think I would like you showing that much thigh," Al said as he put away his little first aid kit. He looked at me as if to say "you quit looking, too."

We sprawled on the rocks and sand under the tree after eating. The bottle of wine didn't last long. Tori wanted to leave it in the tree as a gift to the rock gods, but I nixed that idea. The wine and excitement did a job on me as I quickly fell asleep. When I awoke about twenty minutes later, the two weren't sitting with me. I looked around, but didn't see them anywhere. After a while I heard voices from near the rim. I got up and crept towards them. They were sitting safely on a large rock about five feet from the rim. I could tell they were arguing about something. Tori was quite animated, with Al his normal hesitant self.

"But you can write anywhere. You said yourself you want to take time off to do the two books. Now you have said you could do a book on the ideas you have got on this trip." Tori was massaging her wrist as she shifted on the smooth concave surface.

"This is new to you. And I know you well enough by now. You get excited over new things, then settle down after getting used to them. Remember that time on the island off

Greece. Which one was it, Lesbos?"

Tori looked at him with a frown. "No, it was Mikonos. How could you forget that. That was the night we did it six times. Not a wink of sleep."

"Well regardless of that," he said with a twist of his lips, "you wanted to move there and start your own recording company. A week later, you couldn't stand it there. What were your words? Insanely provincial? Or something like that. Look how isolated it is out here."

"You know something is missing in the city. I certainly feel like I am missing something. It's the same old thing. We talk about it all the time. It's like being in a big prison." The way Tori was waving her arms around, I was concerned she might fall off the rock. I crept back towards our lunch tree, then made noise as I stood up and looked around.

Al saw me and yelled that they were over there. I walked over, pretending to be half asleep. "You not get enough of the edge, yet?"

Tori jumped off the rock. "You were sleeping so soundly. We were discussing a project. I write the music to a documentary that Al writes. Sound good?"

"You know, I still haven't heard you play music. How do I know you are any good?" I wondered what their argument was about, but I wasn't going to say anything. It had obviously been discussed before.

The next day we drove to Moab, then up the river road. Tori wanted to hike up to Corona Arch, even with her sore leg. She was limping noticeably by the time we got back, but even so, she couldn't stop talking about how cool the arch was. Then we drove down the Hurrah Pass Trail to look above and see where we stood the day before. That was a long day of driving, even though we took turns with Tori behind the wheel for a few miles of level road.

Earlier we had talked about a side trip to the Grand

Canyon, but both Al and Tori were getting restless. I knew their argument was still going on, some of it in cryptic language in front of me. The next day, we hooked onto the trailer, and after making a side trip into Arches, where Tori and Al hiked to Delicate Arch, we headed back to Ravens Nest.

Tori and Al changed their plane reservations to go back to New York earlier than planned. Tori's wrist was hurting and Al thought they should get back and x-ray it. Since it would be another day before they could get seats on the plane out of Montrose, we spent their remaining time at Ravens Nest. Knowing a cold front was moving in, I decided it was time to drain and winterize the landscape irrigation system. I was pleasantly surprised with Al's help including his knowledge of mechanical things. The air compressor gave us trouble, but he was able to tinker with it and fix it. When I asked him where he got that handyman skill, he shrugged and said he learned a lot from his summer on the river barge.

While Al and I were struggling through a drizzling rain, Tori tried to help Rachel clean the house and cook a chicken dinner, but was limited by her aching wrist. Rachel marveled at her enthusiasm about cleaning and cooking.

That evening I started a fire in the wood stove in the lodge building. Tori and Al lounged on the bison robe as they recounted their favorite adventures of the past two weeks. As we enjoyed another bottle of local wine, the rain turned to a light snow. It didn't stick but it hinted of things to come. Finally Tori looked at Al and both nodded slightly at each other.

"Jake and Rachel, we have had the time of our lives. We have never experienced anything like this and the amazing thing is, it is a normal life for you. We are in love with it. Is there any chance you could sell us a small piece of land that we could build a house on? We wish we could live right here the rest of our lives." She looked at Al as if to say, 'there, I said it.'

I don't know what expression I had on my face, but whatever it was, it caused Tori to burst out laughing. I looked over at Rachel and she had a look of surprise as she looked at me. I didn't know what to say.

Al spoke up. "Tori and I have spent a lot of time talking about this. Of course we could look for a place in this area, but we feel that Ravens Nest is special and right for us, and want to be associated with it. We're sure you don't want to sell any of it, but we wanted to ask. We have come to feel connected to both of you as well as to this place. That may sound kinda weird, but that's how we feel."

I started to say something, but Al interrupted me. "I want to finish before you say anything. This has been a very tough thing we have been wrestling with. We are from the city and have both felt for a long time that something is missing in our lives. Tori is an established musician and I am a good writer. You probably know this already, but we have plenty of money. Tori has a trust from her father of over $3 million right now. She is an only child and is set to inherit about $10 or 20 million more. I will inherit some of my own. We don't like having the money and if we stay in New York, I'm afraid we will turn into the type of people we don't like."

Tori cut in. "Everything is so impersonal in the city. Oh sure, we have friends and there is so much to do, but it's, well, I don't know..." She drifted off, staring at the fire. "It's not what we want anymore. We don't like what we are becoming. We have found something out here that both of us need. We feel so good with it.”

“Well, I’m speechless,” I finally said when she paused. “You have seen a lot of the attractions. But this is so different. What would you do? There are none of the things you are used to.”

“And that is what we like,” interrupted Al. “We’ve realized we don’t need them. We can do what we are good at here. Work that is.”

I looked at Rachel and mentally asked her if I should bring up what we called The Subject. She looked back with a slight nod. She and I had talked for years about this, but had never had to chance to seriously propose it to anyone.

“We would not sell even an acre of this to you or anyone else.” I waited for a few seconds for a resigned show of disappointment to appear on their faces. Tori started to say something but I put up my hand.

“We would not sell it to you, but we might think of giving you the whole thing.” As Tori’s eyes popped wide open, I quickly continued. “Someday. Not now. We have talked for years about finding someone to adopt and leave the place to. As you know, we don’t have children. This is a problem of who to leave all this to. It’s nothing like you have, but it is a lot for us. We feel that Ravens Nest is special, too, and we don’t want it to go to just anyone. We have only known you for a short time, but we both find you very special people. You are like children we never had.”

Rachel took over. “We are starting to edge up there in years and before you know it, we won’t be able to do the things we can do now. What do we do then? I would love someone to cook and Jake could always use help with all the work he does on the place. We would build a cabin or small house for you.”

“Or let you build something bigger, on something like a

50 year lease, for, oh, let's say a dollar a year," I added.

"I'm sure you both could do your own work from here and still keep your national and international connections. Build your own music or recording studio. Teach classes. There are a couple spots you could build, close to the water and electric. We would expect work from you, though. Menial things like cooking and cleaning as well as hard physical labor around the property. You've both shown you can do that, but the question is would you be happy doing it? Before any permanent decisions are made we would expect you to come back and stay in the apartment for a few months first. Get the feel of actually living here before committing anything. We should both get to know each other better. For your and our protection."

Now it was Tori and Al's turn to sit there with their mouths open. Finally Tori stood up and came up to me. "You are not kidding us are you." This came out as a statement and not a question. She turned to Al. "Oh I know it would work. You are such wonderful people and true in your hearts." She leaned over and hugged both of us. "This feels right. Al?"

I sensed Al was more a power in this family than I thought. His look turned serious as he commented. "Yes. We both judge people and I can't think of many people we would have spent two weeks with and not come away complaining about them. Let's sleep on this and talk more tomorrow. The plane doesn't leave until late afternoon."

Tori lifted up her wine glass, nearly empty, and said, "Then let us toast to a good future. I know we were meant for each other."

"Now Tori, this is not a proposal of marriage," I laughed.

"Maybe it is more than you realize," Rachel said as she lifted her glass.

We both saw them off at the airport. Tori hugged me very tight for quite a long embrace. Al even put his arms around me. They waited until the last minute before they went through security. We hung around the terminal until they boarded, then turned in the rental. Tori had given me a large envelope with money in it to pay for the SUV as well as the payment for my time and their food and lodging. When I opened it before I paid for the rental, I let out a noise that made the agent ask me what I said.

I leaned over to Rachel and showed her the stack of $100 bills. There was way more than what we agreed to previously. Rachel said maybe it was the wrong envelope. I said no, I think that's what they wanted to do.

"It may be a down payment on the rest of our lives," I sighed as I took out a few bills to pay for the rental. The agent said, "Your kids? Nice looking family."

Rachel smiled and looked at me. I just nodded and whispered, "yeah, good kids."

CHAPTER 2

METAMORPHOSIS

THE RINGING PHONE jolted us both out of bed the next morning. I looked at the clock as I reached for the handset. It was half past 6. Normally we would be up by then, but we stayed up late discussing the past two weeks. I looked at the caller ID before I picked up the phone. Victoria Reynolds. "What the hell?" I muttered.

I answered it cheerily, then asked if she forgot the time difference. She apologized, but said she wanted to call and let us know they got home all right. She and Al had talked non-stop all the way home and she was so buzzed, she couldn't sleep. Then she asked, meekly for her, if it was all a dream.

I laughed as I handed the phone to Rachel and stumbled into the bathroom. I then took YoYo out to do her chores and when I came back inside, the two had just finished talking.

Tori's wrist was still hurting and she was sure she had a broken bone. She would get it x-rayed that afternoon, but she said it was a badge of honor and the doctor would be impressed how she did it. I rolled my eyes when Rachel told me this.

After we were both up, Rachel scrambled eggs for breakfast as she related Tori's conversation. They would start closing things down back in the city and planned to be out here by Thanksgiving. I wouldn't have been surprised if they had said they would be back next week.

Events had jumped us like a springing cougar. I still wondered if we had done the right thing by bringing two city folks we had known only two weeks to be our adopted heirs. That was a little beyond my fantasies of the past several years. I liked both Al and Tori and they seemed to glow at the thought of living here. But in my work over the years, I had seen people move from the city to a small ranchette or property in the mountains, only to realize after the first hard winter or the first nearby wildfire that they had made a mistake. It took a special kind of person to enjoy the lifestyle out here. If you grew up with it, that was one thing. Knowing only the city and all that went with that life, well, that was a whole different animal. Yet I was a small town boy and Rachel was a suburban California girl and we managed quite well. It did take a little getting used to, though.

Over the years, both Rachel and I had acquired discriminating judgment of people. So now we talked a lot about Al and Tori and found them to have their faults, but nothing monumental. I liked Tori. Al was a little hard to judge, but he seemed to be grounded more so than Tori. He was more serious while Tori had an impish streak I liked. It didn't hurt that she was a very attractive lady and flirted with me as much as I flirted with her. Rachel found both to be level-headed and not full of bullshit as she put it. They didn't put on airs, which did not fit with my idea of rich city people. Maybe that in itself was a plus in their favor. I wondered how they judged us, but evidently we had passed their scrutiny.

Rachel touched my arm to get me out of my thoughts. I had been playing with the scrambled eggs on my plate until they were cold. "Quit thinking it to death," she chided me. "You will worry yourself sick over it. We made a decision and so did they. Either it works or it doesn't. There is a reason we are insisting they live here a while before committing to anything. If they break all ties with the city, then have to move back, well, that was their choice. We both gave them ample warning about what they will be getting into. They are grown adults. You are the one who keeps talking about consequences. They will learn a big lesson. Let's hope it turns out for the good." She looked at my eggs. "You want me to heat the eggs up?"

"No, I live with my consequences," I said sarcastically. I slipped some of the eggs off the plate into YoYo's waiting mouth, as Rachel turned to put dishes in the sink.

We didn't hear from either Tori or Al for over a week, but went ahead with a little remodeling in the guest house to make it more of a full-time apartment. There were no other guest reservations scheduled for the apartment, so we took it off the vacation rental market for the time being. The refrigerator was nearly twenty years old; it was the one we used to have in the house. I ordered a new one from the appliance store in Delta, along with more kitchen shelves from the lumber yard.

The day they delivered the new fridge, we got a letter from New York. Tori's handwriting was something like you see from the 1800's, exquisite in its penmanship. Along with the short letter, was a check for $5,000. Tori said the money was to go for a new refrigerator and she specified the type. I stared at the letter as I read the brand and model she wanted, then I looked up and read the exact same words on the front of the new fridge. It was quite spooky, I thought. Could we read each other's minds? Or maybe she had said something about what we should get and I didn't remember it. No, I would have remembered that.

She also asked if I would use the money to extend the concrete driveway to where they would park their new car. If that wasn't enough money, she would send more. I hesitated to keep accepting their money. I knew they were rich, but somehow it didn't feel right to me. Rachel said, "Do it." So the next week, we hired a contractor to pour the small parking pad, then I went ahead and put a roof and three walls over it. I made it big enough to store a few things since our garage was getting full and we needed a little extra weather-proof storage space ourselves. This was an expensive project for the small amount of time they would be using it since if they did end up staying, their new house would be several hundred yards away.

Tori started calling about twice a week. Al was in France finishing the research on an article (or was it a book?) he was writing and when he got back, he planned to start packing. I didn't understand this since there wasn't much they needed to bring. The guest house was fairly small and already furnished so I wondered if they were already planning their new house.

I was getting as excited as the kids as I started calling them. Rachel told me to stay out of details, let the youngsters deal with that. All we were to do was provide guidance as asked. I wanted this to be one of my projects where I did more than wait until asked, thus I came to the conclusion this was probably going to be harder on me than anyone else. Expectations usually got in the way of my letting life happen.

The autumn weather held as November started with 70 degree temperatures. During October, I completed my defensible space chain-saw work, was nearly finished with my annual trail maintenance, and was mentally making a list of projects for Al to help with. That I would have to keep to myself since I needed to let them plan their own time until they got used to their new life. Rachel's advice was sinking in—mostly.

On November 6, Tori called and said they were leaving New York the next day since Al had rented a truck and they had it packed, ready to roll. They would wait and buy a new vehicle out here based on my recommendation they not buy anything in New York. I suggested this for several reasons, the major one being it would be cheaper out here. Plus the vehicle would already be tuned and adjusted for high elevation. With Al doing all the driving, it would take them the better part of a week to get here. I smiled at Rachel as we discussed this. We knew Tori would end up driving some, after gaining confidence with her western driving lessons. She said she hadn't gotten a driver's license, but I knew that wouldn't keep her from getting behind the wheel on the Interstate.

I was chopping firewood just after noon on the 11th, when I saw a mid-size rental truck coming down the long driveway. I called for Rachel, who was inside cooking lunch. As Tori drove the truck to the apartment and parked it, she lay on the horn. She jumped out and ran over to Rachel and gave her a big hug, then turned to me and grabbed me. Of course YoYo was all over everyone barking. Al was slow to climb out the passenger side. He came up and shook my hand, saying "God, I've just spent five days cooped up in this with a crazy woman. She talked and sang the whole 2000 miles."

I laughed and asked Tori, "Did you abuse your poor husband?" Then, after I noticed the changes in her, I said, "Tori, what have you done? Your hair." Tori had a pony tail tied up with flashy tie-dye fabric, had on no makeup, and was wearing a brilliant red and yellow Hawaiian shirt (a real one this time) with really short shorts.

"We are starting a new life, totally unconstrained and I'm ready to live it," she smiled and punched Al. "And I did not talk the whole way."

Al looked different as well. He had grown a mustache and was letting his hair grow. They really were changing their lives.

"I don't know what you've got in there," nodding my head towards the back of the truck, "but I doubt if we have room for it."

"Oh, not to worry," Al said, looking at Tori. "I did something without telling you. Really, I was going to ask first, but I got such a bargain."

Tori put her arms around me. "We are having one of those storage containers delivered. You know, the kind on cargo ships. Al was surfing the Internet one night and saw them advertised. He called a friend in the shipping business and wouldn't you know it, they just delivered one to a guy in Denver who backed out at the last minute. We got a super bargain price on it."

I stepped back from Tori's embrace. "And you didn't even think to mention it to us?" I was ticked and showed it in my voice. "Where is it going to sit? How big is it? Does it need a foundation?" I was starting to get animated. It didn't help that YoYo was jumping into the cab of the truck, vacuuming up spilled peanuts or chips or whatever.

Al seemed indifferent to my questions. "It can be temporary if you don't want it here. After we build the house, we can sell it. I bet there are a dozen neighbors who would love it."

"Damn it Al, I've thought of getting one myself, but remember the agreement. We have not finalized anything yet. You may think this is a done deal, but we need to test it first." I looked at Tori and she was doing a pouting thing with her lips. With her pony tail and outrageous shirt, I couldn't help but laugh. She quickly reached over and put her hand on my arm.

I looked at Rachel who was smirking, then muttered to her, "Do they have us outmaneuvered or what?"

We unloaded the truck the next day, putting everything in the lodge building until the storage container was ready. The truck was full, mostly with packing cartons, but with some furniture, including a piano, taking up much of the space. With a catch in her throat, Tori explained that her grandmother had died five years ago and the piano was a present from her grandmother for her tenth birthday—the one thing she couldn't part with.

When I followed them into town to return the rental truck, we stopped at the car dealer, where they laid out cash for a brand new four-wheel drive SUV. The dealer only had one in stock and both Tori and Al were pleased with the style and color. From there, they went to the courthouse, registered the SUV, and took their drivers' tests. When they returned to Ravens Nest several hours after I got home, they waved their new drivers licenses and spent the next hour describing all the features of their new vehicle.

Three days later, a truck with a large flatbed and attached crane came down the lane. Al and I had spent the previous morning clearing and leveling a spot near the gate at the entrance to our property. It was mostly hidden from the road and only required us to cut three trees to get decent access for it. After the container was set up, Al spent the next two days cleaning the inside, painting the outside, and bolting in shelves. Once again, I was surprised by his handyman skills.

The cargo container was fully enclosed, watertight, and

to my delight, chipmunk- and mouse-proof. We didn't have electricity to it, but Al arranged to hang several battery lanterns that lit it nicely. We had it full of both their and some of my stuff within a day. After this initial flurry of activity, I left them alone to get settled.

We had all planned to go to Grand Junction the Tuesday before Thanksgiving, but we woke up to 6 inches of snow. I took Tori along with me as I plowed snow off the long driveway. I had rigged a snowplow blade to an electric golf car with ATV knobby tires. It had always worked great plowing the small amounts of snow we usually received, but I discovered 6 inches depth was its limit. I made the first run, taking off about 4 inches, then I let Tori plow the remainder. She was as excited as a little girl as she learned the delicate touch of the winch button to raise and lower the blade. Her training as a pianist and cellist must have given her that very light touch.

She shocked me during the excursion when she made a comment that Al had to go back to France for a week. His mistress wanted him there for some high society event. I thought she was kidding, but she explained that she knew about the woman for years. Al met her before he married Tori and had continued his affair. Al didn't think Tori knew, but she learned about it the first year of their marriage. She thought it would end, but as it continued, Tori accepted it. She said Al had overriding qualities that she felt outweighed his indiscretions.

I was uneasy as she told me this. I was disappointed with her for putting up with this behavior, but she said that Al was good to her and their relationship allowed each other plenty of space. I looked at her and asked if she responded in kind. I knew that was none of my business but she put her hand on mine and said, "No." She was happy with her music and now she would put energy into cooking and cleaning for us. She knew her life had been pampered and she looked forward to joining the common people. I told her we were about as common as they came. She apologized if she offended me. I said, "No, I am proud to be common as dirt."

As Christmas approached, I learned that neither Al nor Tori were religious. Al was Jewish, but didn't practice his faith. Tori said she was brought up Episcopalian, but quickly lost interest as she realized the poverty and injustice in her city. They had never celebrated the winter solstice, so we held an informal ceremony in the lodge. Al was motivated to do research on the solstice and wrote and read aloud a short piece about the event: antiquity and spiritual meanings of what were the original celebrations that turned into Christmas, Hanukkah, Saturnalia and many pagan rituals.

Al was in France all of January. One night at the end of the month, during a warm spell, I set up the telescope outside. Rachel was finishing an artwork for a looming deadline, so Tori and I sat under a star-filled sky looking at the constellations.

"You are quiet tonight, Tori. Everything okay?" I asked as she sat staring up at the North Star.

"Oh, I'm fine. Just pensive I guess. I feel like I missed half of my life. We never saw this from the city." She scanned the sky from horizon to horizon. "And I guess I was too busy studying or socializing to notice while I was away at school. Last September was the first time I really noticed the sky."

"It's sure brilliant this evening. And look at the Milky Way." I was always amazed at the millions of stars that clouded the sky. They were especially clear in the cold January air.

"Most people are missing so much, Jake. With your star chart, I have been able to see the constellations I never even knew existed. But you realize," she pointed her finger at me, "you have created more questions for me. You told us the more you know, then the more you don't know. I never thought about the sky and what's out there. Now, I am fascinated by it. What is up there? What forms of life? There has to be life out there. Don't you agree?"

"Oh, I'm sure there is life. I wonder about what is out there, but there is enough mystery right here on earth to keep me occupied thinking about it. I guess I am more interested in the physics of outer space, not the biology."

"But you are a biologist. I would think you would carry that to the next phase." She pointed with her eyes to the heavens.

"Oh, but I do. I held a dove in my hands today that something was wrong with. It looked at me with its eyes, trusting I would not kill it. It couldn't fly. I carefully carried it to the ground under the bird feeder and laid it there so it could at least get food. Within an hour it died. I put it on the woodshed roof so a hawk would be able to take it."

"Oh, Jake, that is so sad. Do you think it felt pain?"

"Maybe. But all creatures are meant to live and die. Everything dies. That makes me wonder what exactly life is. What happens that one minute something is alive, looking at you with large eyes, thinking something. Then a minute later, it is dead. Life left it. What does that mean? What is it that is the difference between being alive and being dead?" I waited a few seconds, then continued. "Life is precious. For anything. You and I, a deer, a dove. We suddenly are created when a sperm connects with an egg. In every living thing, at least above an amoeba. Then it's gone. Does it go somewhere? Maybe out there in the universe to reorganize and then come back here. Or stay out there?"

"Jake, you think of things I never ever thought of. My god, I don't know the answers. No one can know them. I think you have just succeeded in keeping me awake all night thinking of these questions. Thanks."

I looked at her in the darkness, not seeing much except a young woman bundled from head to toe. "Odds are something is out there. I have given it a lot of thought. Sounds like you are just now thinking about it." I had given it much thought throughout my life. The night we camped outside Moab we had talked about infinity and eternity and life, so Tori knew these ethereal and philosophical questions were one of my favorite subjects.

"Oh, I started thinking last fall over by Moab. That is when it really hit me. Then, I started coming outside at night, especially after Al left a month ago. I never thought about infinity. I do now."

"Kinda lonely at night now, isn't it?" I knew I might be treading on thin ice.

"Al? No, I am used to it. We both need our space. Sometimes I wonder if I am losing him. I never had all of him anyway. But what I had was enough. He likes it here. I think he is torn now. Wants both the cake and the icing. He may have to choose. I can live with either choice."

That answer surprised me. I had always thought they were the perfect couple, but now I was seeing the delicate relationship that really existed. Ever since she told me about his other life in France, I was angry at Al for how he was treating Tori. He obviously loved her, but just the fact he was splitting his time showed a subtle contempt for her. Or a selfishness on his part.

"But that is here. I am interested in out there." Tori held her hand to the sky. "You are right to ask if heaven is out there. Do we go there after we die? Or come from there when we are born? There are so many questions that I never thought of before. I feel like I lived in a cave and now can see the sunlight." Then she laughed, "or the starlight."

"How is this adventure working for you?" I changed the subject, and tried to see her eyes in the darkness. "Is it what you thought?"

"At least on my end, you couldn't pry me out of here. I love it. You are so free up here. The big question for me is it working for you? You are the one giving away your life."

"No, we are sharing our lives. I wish we could do it for more people. I wish we could open the eyes of everyone that there is so much to life they are missing. I feel good that you are so happy." I hesitated for effect. "And yes, it is working for us. You are taking care of us more than we deserve. Damn, you are a good cook. Where did you learn that? Haven't you had servants most of your life?"

Tori laughed again. "Servants? Slaves? We call them domestic help. You watch too many old movies. I watched our help work and only got shooed out of the kitchen when Mums was home. She thought it demeaning. You have never met my folks. They are what you call old school. Moneyed old school. I loathe it."

"Yet you spend their money." I realized that came out too quickly and bluntly.

"Touché. Yeah, you are right. It is there, and I try and put it to good use. And for my comfort. Why not. You are benefiting as well."

"Touché for you. And I wish you wouldn't. But we do appreciate what you have done here."

"So it is working for you?" Tori asked, shifting in her chair. She didn't wait for my answer, but stood up to look through the telescope. "You know, binoculars work just as well as this. This doesn't make the stars any bigger."

"You need a huge, expensive one to really make out anything. I would love to see the Horsehead Nebula sometime. I think it is in Orion, but I'm not sure. Is it working? You haven't seen my mean ugly side, yet."

"And I won't. I don't believe you have one. Both of you are so nice. You are different. Old fashioned, but not like my folks. I think you are living a way of life that is gone for most people. Or never existed. You are holding on to something valuable. We want to be part of it. How long is our trial period?"

"We just don't want you to commit to something without really knowing what you got into. It's for your own protection. Have we seen your mean ugly side?" I smiled.

"How about I throw a tantrum so you can see it, then get it out of the way?"

"I worry a little about Al. He seems to enjoy it here, but, well, you know."

"Al is Al. We take what we get. He likes it here, but he is like a little boy and can't decide what he likes better. He has always come back to me. Hopefully he will get Monique out of his system and realize what he has here. I am here regardless. To stay."

"You decided yet where you want to build your house?" I started to get into specifics, but at that moment, Rachel came out with a tray of hot chocolate and the cookies Tori baked that afternoon.

"You night owls enjoying sitting out here in the cold and dark?" she said as she handed the tray to Tori.

"Rachel, you shouldn't be out here. You need to stay focused on your deadline." Tori handed me the tray and stood up and gently nudged Rachel back to the house.

"Quit mothering me. I just needed a bit of fresh air. What are you doing sitting out here? You will get a cold or pneumonia."

I couldn't take their bantering. I had spent days on end in weather colder and nastier than this. "Both of you quit it.

Are you having a mother hen contest? We were sitting here discussing the universe and origins of life and why YoYo's nose is black. Satisfied? And it's not that cold. I once hiked ten miles in 40 below temperatures."

Rachel interrupted, "Yes we know and you swam the Arctic Ocean chasing polar bears. It's a wonder you are still alive. Drink your chocolate before it gets cold. Won't take long out here."

With that, she turned and walked back into the house.

"I get a kick out of her. She has put up with a lot, hasn't she?"

"What, you mean putting up with me? Keep it up and you will see my mean streak." I held the cup in my hands, warming them up.

"We were thinking of building up by the garden. Or maybe over on Cougar Ridge. Can't decide. What do you think?" Tori continued the discussion as if we hadn't been interrupted.

"Will take more water line to get over there, plus you will have to improve the road. We don't want to see the house from our windows. That is our only requirement. Yeah, I think keeping all the buildings here on Deer Ridge would be better."

"I like the view from out there, but in a way, up by the garden seems more secluded to me. It is more on the edge of Badger Basin." Tori giggled. "Sounds like we are living in a zoo. Who would guess you were a wildlife biologist?"

"We didn't just pick names. There is a story for each one. Have I told you?"

"Well, since it appears you have named every tree and rock, I would think you would run out of names. No, you haven't told me, but do we have time tonight? The sun will come up in, what, 10 hours?"

"Cougar Ridge is where we saw the mountain lion one

morning right after we moved into the house. I heard this horrible screaming and knew it had to be a big cat. I walked over there with Blanca, our previous dog, on a rope. I could see fresh tracks heading down the ridge. We didn't follow, but heard screams all that day and the next night. I'm guessing she was still training her cubs, but we didn't see any more tracks."

"So I've decided to live in a place where there are things that want to eat me?" Tori handed me another cookie.

"Tough world out there. Eat or be eaten. Badger Basin had a couple badgers digging up the hillside several years ago. Fox Ridge was where a bunch of magpies were chasing a poor fox one day. They were screaming and dive bombing this poor critter as he ran trying to get away. I'm sure he was trying to get at a nest of eggs or chicks. You can always tell when magpies or jays are ticked off at a coyote or an owl or a bobcat."

I had to smile as I thought of all the adventures we had had on this property. Seems like my whole life was about the environment around me.

"You really pay attention to things don't you?"

"Eat or be eaten. Sure, we pay attention to our surroundings, but most people don't. Life is in seasons and cycles. You will pick up on that. I suppose life in the city is just one day after the other."

"Pretty boring compared to this. But excitement on another scale. All artificial, though. I never thought of that before. Oh look, a shooting star! Did you see it?" Tori pointed to the east, over the apartment roof.

"Sorry, I was contemplating my hot chocolate. Should we name your new house 'shooting star'?"

"Hmmm, maybe, but don't change the subject. Go on about cycles."

"Nature is cyclic. Seen any rabbits since you've been here?"

"No, should I?"

"Three years ago, you couldn't walk from the house to the lodge without seeing about twenty rabbits. Now, nothing. They go in cycles, ups and downs. We used to have a titmouse who would eat out of our hands. Would follow us on hikes, begging sunflower seeds. Then we went about five years without seeing or hearing one. Saw a couple this year. Cycles. Part of nature. You pay attention to your surroundings. Our ancestors had to recognize all this. Their lives depended on it. "

"How will I ever learn all this?" Tori sighed.

"Pay attention. It's easy," I said. I was looking forward to passing on my accumulated knowledge to this young woman, so eager to learn.

A week later, Al called Tori to arrange for her come get him at the airport. He was in New York, visiting her folks and would leave the next day to fly out. I was surprised to see how excited she was. Her husband abandons her for over a month to shack up with his mistress in France, but Tori can't wait to have him return. I didn't know if this was a generational thing, or some quirk of their personalities. It's not what I would condone, but I was trying hard to stay non-judgmental about these potential heirs.

Al was glad to be back and quickly jumped in and helped me finish my burning for the winter. I found the burning meditative and relaxing, since most of the time was spent watching the fire. Al had never been around fire and found it interesting, but still thought it dangerous. He was amazed at how fast and furious a juniper branch with dried needles would burn. I told him it was as safe as it could be since by burning a pile this way, I could control the height of the flames. One five-foot-long branch, much smaller than a standard Christmas tree, would throw flames fifteen feet in the air.

I had perfected the chore to a routine. I should have—I had been doing it for years, reducing the wildfire danger from extreme to relatively safe. Living in a juniper forest on a hillside had advantages, but threat of wildfire was not one of them. The routine began in late summer, with chain sawing of individual trees and areas of brush and trees that were potential hazards; then piling the accumulated slash. Each winter, I would have 25 to 50 piles scattered over the property. Once there was snow on the ground, every morning (and some afternoons) I would select a pile, start a small fire in a nearby open space, then chuck in the limbs and branches that were good and dry by now.

Al soon got the hang of it and would have spent all day starting fires if I'd let him. He quickly learned the ecology of wildfire and became active with the local fire department. He had a hard time understanding our fire protection with an all-volunteer force. When he returned from the first fire he was called to—a local farmer burning ditches on a windy day in March—Tori wouldn't let him in the apartment until he totally stripped off his smoke-covered clothes, even down to his underwear. By the time I called Rachel to the window to observe the scene, his bare behind was entering the door, a pile of clothes left lying on the sidewalk.

By March, Tori had chickadees and nuthatches eating sunflower seeds out of her hand, and had named all the deer that frequented the yard. There was usually a herd of 15 to 20. The big bucks stayed to themselves, but a few spikes hung out with the does. Tori tried to hand feed some of the herd, but I kept discouraging her. I told her these were not tame deer and we needed to keep some fear of humans in them. One morning, I saw her get within five feet of a doe. She sat down in the snow and held out an apple. Frustrated the deer would not make that final effort, Tori finally tossed the apple, which the doe actually caught mid-air. I had never seen anything like it.

In April, the four of us sat down in the lodge and had a serious discussion of our relationship. We were all in agreement that this thing was going to work out alright, so we picked out their home site and agreed on their house plans, which Al had an architect friend draw up. I was pleasantly surprised the house would be fairly small, only 1500 square feet and one story, but with a full basement with one side a walk-out since it was on a hill. That would be Al's writing den and Tori's music studio. They decided on a log construction for the upstairs, even after my warnings about the maintenance issues we discovered with the lodge. Logs were nice, but needed a lot of diligent, tender care such as caulking and varnish on the inside and stain on the outside.

We had the backhoe work done by May, excavating for the basement and putting in septic tank and leach field. Several trees had to be removed to punch in a couple hundred yards of new gravel road. Al decided to put in a carport and not a garage, but I bet him within two years, he would wall in the carport and make it a full garage.

The big news of the summer was publication of Al's new book: *Political Reform in the Euro France.* He still remained a roving editor for *Atlantic Digest,* but put his energy into another book he tentatively called "The Ethics of the New West." He was using a lot of my philosophy, but traveling closer to home talking to mostly the urbanites in places like Denver, Salt Lake, Bozeman, Flagstaff and Santa Fe. It seemed to me that he and Tori were cementing their marriage in this new home.

Tori split her time between doing our cooking and cleaning, and forming new relationships with local musicians. She was pleased to find the diversity of musical talent and groups in the area. She teamed up with a Celtic/New Age combo group in Montrose, who did some touring within a couple hundred miles. They were putting together a CD and Tori's experience was the factor that helped them accomplish this. Without even advertising, she had six high-school students—three pianists, a cellist, a guitar player, and a violinist—she was tutoring once a week in the lodge. She turned down requests from the local school district, as well as the college in Grand Junction, to teach part time. We hadn't realized the extent of her reputation, and felt privileged and somewhat humbled that we had two rather famous people who had chosen to live here.

After listening in on one of her student's lessons, I sat down with her at the piano, which was still in the lodge. I thought she was mostly interested in classical music, but she said she was interested in creating her own music. She liked artists like Enya and Loreena McKennitt, who were creating their own styles, using regional music as a starting point. Her goal, she said, was to not fit into any category. When I asked her if she sang as well as played, she sang one of her songs as she played the piano. I had never known this side of Tori. I had nothing to say after she finished. She laughed at my expression, which was some combination of surprise and amazement, with quite a bit of admiration thrown in.

"I never guessed you were so talented. How do you have any room in the creativity department to be doing the ecological transformation you have been doing?"

"You should know as much as anyone, Jake. Creativity feeds on itself. The more you express, the more room you open up to learn even more. You have opened up a whole side of my brain that lay dormant."

"Don't get melodramatic on me, Tori," I said as I rubbed the piano top with my hand. "You cannot motivate employees, you only allow their own motivation to emerge. Same with creativity."

Tori smiled. "Yes. And did you hear my words? I said you opened the door. You didn't lead me into it. That is true teaching: you allow and encourage the person to learn."

She ran her hands across the keys and back, then said, "I haven't been idle. Remember last fall over by Moab? Al and I wanted to partner on something to capture the spirit of the canyons. Listen to what I have come up with so far." She played a composition that had me closing my eyes and seeing red rock and green junipers. And I heard the call of the canyon wren. After she finished, she said it was better on the cello, but she wanted to record it with both. "I'm still polishing it," she said, as she stood and walked to the window. She stared off into the distance. Neither of us spoke for several minutes.

"Al told me he's never going back to France. He guessed that I knew about Monique and says it's over with her. He wants to be here, with me." She turned to me, with tears in her eyes. She came over and hugged me, sobbing on my shoulder. Her tears brought tears to my eyes.

Rachel walked into the room at that point. She started to say something, but Tori saw her and ran to her and hugged her as well. I quietly retreated and walked outside, figuring those two could communicate emotionally better if I was out of the way.

Even before Al and Tori came to live at Ravens Nest, I had a habit of daily walking on the trails. I continued that, but many days, either Tori or Al joined me. Of course, YoYo was always with us, spending more and more time with Tori. Tori seemed to have a special connection with animals of all kinds. This connection was growing as she tuned in with nature, something she had never had the opportunity to do before. She began to feel and see energy in trees, rocks, and animals.

One morning we were sitting along Dragonfly Creek in a group of large, lichen-covered rocks and very old junipers. I was staring at the cattails that filled the creek drainage. Since it was early autumn, the cattail fluff was just starting to release and drift in the breeze. Tori had witnessed this the previous winter, including her first experience pinching a mature cattail catkin.

"The energy is really up this morning," Tori said as she stared at the treetops.

"For you maybe," I replied, "but I didn't get much sleep last night. My energy is still asleep."

"No, not my energy. The energy out there." She pointed at the hillside and the sky.

"What are you talking about? What energy?"

Tori looked at me with that questioning look I was familiar with. "The energy of the land. The trees."

I stared at her, then looked around me. "No comprendo. Better explain that further."

"You don't see the energy field?"

"I guess not. I see you and blue sky and green trees. What do you see?"

"I can't believe you don't see it. You are the nature boy. The energy of life. Earth energy." She still stared at me with amazement.

"I'm not a shaman or medicine man. Hate to disappoint

you. I talk to the birds, but I don't understand what they say back."

"You don't see it. That surprises me. Of all people, I would have thought you saw and felt it."

"Tell me what you see."

"Oh my god, Jake, I see waves of a whitish light or vibration coming off the trees. It—I guess emanate is a good word—it emanates from things. It can be rainbow colored, sort of flickers like a campfire. Some trees have more, some rocks have it. The stream really has it, sort of like an electric current. I can sometimes hear a buzzing like a light bulb. I hadn't seen it until a few months ago—very faint at first, but now, especially today, it is way powerful."

She almost seemed hypnotized as she talked. She looked at me, but I felt she was looking through me. It scared me a little. "You have a power, then. A gift. I am envious. Do I have to start bringing you sacrifices now?"

"Don't kid, Jake. I am serious. This is powerful. I can see it coming off you now. That's the first time I have ever seen it on a person. Oh wow." She stood up and backed away from me.

I stared at the tree tops, but still didn't see anything. I had heard of people who could see auras of light or color on some people. I had tried to see it, but was never able to. I didn't understand what it was, but obviously some people had another sense or something that allowed them to see or feel energy. Usually these were traditional shamans or holy people, especially native people. I had never heard of someone all of a sudden gaining these powers, unless trained by a tribal elder or shaman.

"Go stand by the tree there," Tori pointed to a large juniper at the creek's edge, one that had to be hundreds of years old.

"Will it transport me somewhere?" Tori didn't appreciate

my lightness about the subject. She frowned.

"Okay, okay," I got up and put my arms around the tree. It felt strange as I stood quietly with my hands and arms against the shaggy bark.

"You don't feel that?" Tori almost shouted as she backed away. "You are glowing."

I shut my eyes. "I do feel something like a slight vibration. But that might be some trick like the aspen thing I used to do in environmental education workshops, with students pressing an ear to an aspen to hear gurgling as water went up the trunk." I explained to her that it was real, but I had never been convinced it wasn't just the wind blowing the leaves and that was the noise we heard transferred through the trunk. And it might be water or it might be energy vibrating this old juniper. Tori laughed and rolled her eyes as if to say, "believe what you want!"

The first spring and summer they were at Ravens Nest, Tori and Al were hypnotized by the hummingbirds. Black-chinned hummers would show up like clockwork every April 21, only a few at first, but within two weeks, we had dozens. At sunrise and sunset, they swarmed the feeders and it was truly a swarm. There was no way to count them. We figured in the twenties, but it was like trying to count mosquitoes as they darted and jumped around. Tori and Al easily got them to sit on their fingers as they fed. This led Tori to study native plants for wildlife, and her expansion of the Ravens Nest flower gardens to attract even more birds and insects. And of course, she wrote a song called "Hummingbird" and Al wrote an essay that was published in *Audubon Magazine*.

By late fall, their new house was finished and Tori's folks came out for what Tori called the christening. She asked her mom to break a bottle of champagne on the deck. I told her that was a big waste of champagne not to mention the broken glass. It didn't matter since they couldn't get the bottle to break. Her dad said he once attended the launching of a nuclear submarine and they had the same problem. The First Lady tried to smash the bottle, but only succeeded in smashing her finger.

This was the first time we met Daddy and Mums as Tori called them. I was a little nervous at finally seeing what old wealth was like, but I learned they were regular people. I got along fine with Russell. We walked the trails and he actually knew some of the birds. He was very knowledgeable on many things and wanted to know all about my career. He wasn't that much older than me and we told stories of our college days. Rachel got along well with Mums, but needed Tori there as a buffer. Mums was accustomed to the high society crowd, which Rachel always termed the do-gooders. Mums was very interested in what we had to do to cook at this high elevation, although I doubt if she ever did much cooking herself.

One afternoon, Tori and Al took Daddy and Mums for a drive up onto Grand Mesa where the fall colors were prime, with the temperature in the low 50s. I had a fire going in the campfire circle when they got back about sunset. Tori had cooked a spaghetti dinner that morning so Rachel heated it up. We ate at a picnic table by the fire circle which was certainly a new experience for Mums.

"What do you think of our little piece of the world now that you have seen some of it?" I asked Mums.

"Well, you are certainly isolated way out here. Lots of empty space. But beautiful," she quickly added. "I know Victoria certainly has fallen in love with it. She has talked of nothing but it since I have been here. I guess she has left the city behind." Her voice carried a hint of sadness.

I got the feeling Mums was being polite. I could tell she didn't connect; this was so alien to her, I'm sure she was uncomfortable with such a wild environment. I know I would not be able to connect with her lifestyle, even though I had never been within a thousand miles of New York City.

I noticed Mums winced as she sat upright on the bench. I asked her if she was feeling alright. "Sometimes this high elevation takes a little getting used to," I added.

"Oh, I'm all right. I've had a little pain in my side for a week or so. Maybe my age is catching up to me."

Russell, quietly staring into the fire during the conversation, added "Oh, don't talk that way. You are as old as you feel and I find this trip has invigorated me. You should come for a hike with me in the morning. That will ease out those aches and pains. Right, Jake?"

"You bet. I haven't taken you down into our wilderness yet but we can go there tomorrow. No trails, just a lot of wet hillside. I'm not sure that would be a good place to take Evelyn, though. Maybe Tori could take her out to Fox Point. That is an easy walk."

Mums smiled and touched Tori's hand. "Maybe. We will see."

Daddy and Mums stayed for almost a week, but he had to be back in Washington for a Congressional hearing, so Tori took them to the airport one snowy morning. I was surprised they didn't come by corporate jet. I found out later they would have, but it was scheduled for a meeting of foreign business leaders in Australia. Daddy could have gone to that but he opted to be with his only daughter.

Al and I had started burning our brush piles after that snow. I was burning one pile down in Badger Basin while Al was ahead of me doing a little more chain saw work to clean up one area. I was meditating by my fire when I heard the chain saw stop, and the silence was immediately filled with frantic yells—Al screaming for help. I dropped everything and ran the hundred yards to find Al lying on the ground holding his leg with a lot of blood staining the fresh snow. He was fumbling to remove his belt.

"Jake, I think I did it big time. I hit an artery. Help me do a tourniquet."

I didn't panic, but I started feeling very queasy. The chain saw had ripped through the edge of his chaps and sliced his right leg below the knee, blood flowing freely. I pulled off my sweatshirt and shirt while he managed to free the belt. I wrapped his leg as tightly as I could, then tried to tighten the belt above the wound, but it was too long. I was almost ready to panic, when I remembered the rope dog leash in my pack. Luckily I hadn't taken off the pack when I started burning. The rope worked to stop the bleeding, and Al began to turn white and actually passed out at one point, but I rubbed snow on his face and he came to.

Usually I carried a two way radio, but hadn't put one in my pack that day.

"Al, we stopped the bleeding for now, but I know we shouldn't leave a tourniquet on too long. I don't want you trying to walk back up the hill. Can you stay right here and not move? I have to run up and call 911, then I will be back."

He nodded his head. I loosened the rope for a few seconds and blood started seeping out. I tightened it again and ran up the hill. It took me a couple minutes to get up to the house. I was breathing so hard, I could barely get my breath. As I ran in the house, I yelled for Rachel, finding her and Tori upstairs. When Tori saw me, she evidently read the panic in my expression. The blood on me gave her another clue. I croaked "call 911. Now!" Tori screamed, but Rachel calmly picked up the phone and hit 911.

"Ambulance," was the best I could get out. Rachel was still very calm when she explained to the dispatcher that I had run in the house, unable to talk because I was breathing so hard. But she ordered an ambulance and gave the location. By the time she got that out, I could talk. I grabbed the phone.

"We have a person who cut his leg in a chain saw accident. Bleeding very bad. I put a tourniquet on. He is laying down the hill in the snow. Don't want him to walk up the hill to the house."

They told me what to do until they arrived. By that time, Tori was out the door, without even a coat or boots. We could hear her screaming for Al as she followed my tracks all the way down the hill.

"Get a coat and boots for Tori, get dressed yourself and follow her down. We need to keep Al still but keep him warm. He will be in shock by now so I will get some hot water and a blanket for him. The ambulance should be here in about twenty minutes. I will stay up here to lead them down. In the meantime, keep Al laying down, with his leg elevated and his head down."

Rachel was out the door before I finished. When I heard the siren out by the road, I went out to the road. I met them and they pulled out the litter along with a kit. Luckily there were three of them. They half skied and tumbled down the hillside. Al was unconscious when we got there, Tori cradling him in her arms. Rachel had emptied the gasoline out of the chain saw and had started a fire with some of the branches Al had been cutting. She had found matches in my pack. The ambulance crew quickly inserted an IV in Al's arm and had eased him onto the litter, then ripped off his pants and put a proper bandage on the wound itself. Rachel was very calm, but Tori was in near hysterics. She was sure Al was already dead.

Ernie, one of the EMTs, stayed with Tori by the fire. He told her she needed to calm down. Soon, another EMT had arrived to help with the evacuation. By the time they had Al up the hill and in the ambulance, Ernie said Tori could go up and ride in the ambulance. He was afraid she was in almost as much trouble as Al, gave her a sedative injection, and reported the additional patient to the hospital. His relief was evident when Tori was able to tell them Al's blood type. Ernie reassured her that Al would be okay although he had lost a lot of blood. He said our tourniquet had probably saved his life.

Within a few minutes, Tori was calmed down so Rachel and I walked her up the hill. When we got there, the ambulance had turned around and was ready to go. We helped Tori inside and it raced off, siren blaring.

Rachel and I stood there holding each other. I don't know if we were trembling more from the cold or from fright, but I know I wasn't that far from going into shock myself.

Calmly, Rachel said, "Let's go in and you wash up. You have blood all over you and your face is covered with it. I will change clothes and drive us into the hospital. They said they were going to Delta and didn't think a life flight was needed. They will have blood ready. Tori will probably be sedated to the point of being helpless, so we can stay with them as long necessary. Is the fire okay to leave?"

"Yeah. It's safe," I mumbled. "Let me sit down for a few minutes. Then I will take a shower. There is no big hurry for us to get there. Probably best to wait a while anyway. I feel like I am ready to throw up. That run up the hill almost made me sick."

By the time we reached the emergency room, Al had already been taken to a private room. He had a leg full of stitches and a pint or two of new blood. Tori was still in emergency, heavily sedated, but not in any danger, so Rachel and I helped with all the admissions. Rachel then stayed with Tori and sent me to be with Al.

I wanted to find out exactly what had happened, but I had to wait a day before I could talk to Al. I knew he had learned to be very good and very careful with the chain saw. In all my own sawing experience, I had never had any type of chain saw accident and I taught Al well. He later described how he had done everything right, but the saw bound up on a tightly bent limb, the limb broke, and the saw kicked back and bounced off a tree trunk. The chaps had saved Al's life, as did the tourniquet we applied.

There was some lingering muscle and tendon damage, so Al had a slight limp ever after when he used his legs a lot. From that point on, Tori accompanied Al whenever he did chain saw work, just one indication Rachel and I noticed that they seemed closer than ever. And, Al had the scar that Tori wanted from her cliff fall. Tori was oddly jealous of the scar.

CHAPTER THREE

INTERVENING YEARS

*We have talked about the concept. Simple, fitting in
with what our overall goals are, but, well, elegant and
dignified is the best way to put it.*
Tori Reynolds

Tori AND AL established themselves as caretakers of the
land as well as our buildings. I continued to write, Rachel
continued to design and create stained glass and other art
commissions, and we both hiked our secret hideaway for
inspiration. We still took in guests at Ravens Nest Retreat,
but this consumed less and less of our time. Tori ran much
of the business as well as keeping us fed and being the
daughter we never had. Although Al was gone much of the
time doing research for his articles, books, and stories, he
was more like a brother to me than a son.

I never gave much interest to the business aspect.
Luckily, Rachel did. She was meticulous in record keeping,
including the taxes. Now, she counted Tori as an employee,
as well as herself. Al and I did the physical labor around the
property, content to disappear into the forest and along the
streams. Just as Al found mechanical things easy, Tori found
the detail work of cleaning, planning meals, growing food,
keeping books, all to her liking. Rachel, by the nature of
her work, was a perfectionist. It turned out that Tori, by the
nature of her music skills, was just as much a perfectionist.

Al and I called them the left-brain-right-brain twins. They called us the scatter-brain brothers.

We four were creative in different ways. My work had been scientific, Al's was journalism. We both dealt in facts, digging beneath the obvious to find out why things worked the way they did. The girls, as we called them, much to their displeasure, created new things out of imagination, structured in minute detail. Al and I floundered around with the big picture. I don't understand how we didn't drive each other crazy, but it helped that each of us had a partner to our own liking. And each of our life partners counterbalanced each other.

Two years after Al and Tori moved in, we noticed a For Sale sign on a neighbor's ranch. Todd and his wife didn't live there full time, but stayed in Pueblo where both were retired doctors. Todd intended to move here eventually, but soon after he bought the ranch ten years earlier, he was diagnosed with a rare form of cancer. He didn't want to live so far away from the Front Range medical facilities, so they leased the grazing to another neighbor and settled into visiting every few months for a week at a time. We didn't see them very often, although they were friendly, but at a distance.

When Tori drove by the ranch the day the sign went up, she came back all excited. I immediately called the real estate agent, who said that Todd had passed away and his wife put the ranch on the market the week after the funeral. My first thought was who would we get as a new neighbor. Tori didn't even let me express my thought.

"Jake, we can buy it. It will go perfectly with Ravens Nest. No one can make a living off that small an acreage; it will just be subdivided. Do we want half a dozen new neighbors fresh from the city?"

I answered so fast, I forgot who I was talking to. "Fine,

let's just buy a couple ranches. For crying out loud, Tori, do you know how much they are asking?" The agent told me what the asking price was. I knew it was double what Todd had paid for it years before.

"Oh, Jake, you are so naïve. Of course Janet is asking a big price. I bet if we made an offer about two thirds of the asking price, she would sign right then and there. The market is down right now and I know she never had a love for the ranch. It was Todd's dream, not hers. I'm surprised she didn't give it to her children, but didn't you tell us none of them are interested? She wants to just get rid of it fast. If we snap it up right now, we keep it from some developer."

"I guess if you have the money. I sure don't." I knew as soon as the words came out of my mouth, it was a done deal. Of course Tori and Al had the money. I was well aware of Daddy's last visit, when he told Tori he would sure love to move out here someday. She was keeping her eye out for just the right property and money was not an issue.

After a phone call that afternoon, Marsh Madison, the agent, was sitting at our kitchen table. Even before Marsh arrived, Tori had called Daddy. With one more phone call from his daughter, Daddy would wire $500,000 to the local bank. No fooling around with earnest money or deposits. A week later, Ravens Nest owned the yet-to-be-named addition to our little empire. I wasn't sure why they didn't buy it in their own name. I had nothing to do with it, but it would become an integral part of Ravens Nest. Tori started to explain it had something to do with taxes and gifting. I was lost before she started so I motioned for her to stop right there. They were the financial experts and if Daddy wanted to do it this way, then that was his decision. My property taxes would skyrocket, but I also knew they would be paid before I even got the annual bill.

The 150 acre property, an old ranch, with falling down

barns and corrals, was adjacent to Ravens Nest. The house itself would best serve everyone by being bulldozed, or used as training for the fire department. At one time, the ranch had been much larger, but during the Depression, it was split up, with all the sub parts unable to support profitable operations. Current owners of the sub parts were hobby farmers and retirees, trying to grow hay and raise horses or cattle or llamas, but their main effect was to overgraze the pastures. Alfalfa or native hay was about all that was grown at this elevation, although at the turn of the century, apple orchards were planted all over the mesa. All had been cut down decades ago. This entire area had a history of dirt poor owners, with a succession of families trying to make a go of it and none of them succeeding, to the surprise of no one. Rachel and I hated what we saw happening to the wildlife, as dogs and domestic cats and houses slowly eroded the value of the land as winter range.

Three of the pastures of the ranch were watered by irrigation, but prairie dogs were more numerous than alfalfa plants. The southern portion was sagebrush and pinyon-juniper forest, a mirror-image of Ravens Nest. Once this new addition was securely in our name, Tori asked Daddy to fly out and plan for what to do with it. He sat with us one afternoon in the middle of the prairie dog field, as I called the twenty acre pasture along our lane.

Russell Reynolds was wealthy for a reason. He was smart, sharp and perceptive, and willing to let others talk while he listened. I liked him the first time we met, but I still had an instinctive and cautious mistrust of him due to his money and power. The first thing he did was ask me what I thought would be the best use of this property.

"Jake, you know the land. What the hell do I know about such things? Central Park is the wildest piece of land I know. You are the professional here. What is the health of the land? What is it good for?"

Tori winced as he asked the last question. "Oh god, Daddy. What is it good for? What am I good for? What is Reynolds Financial good for? Is that all you think of?"

"Oh, settle down princess. You know what I mean. I didn't buy this for you in order to make a profit. If I wanted to do that, I would call in a developer tomorrow and build million dollar condominiums and triple my money in a month, selling them off to Dallas and Los Angeles investors. I meant what is the best use to put it to for the land itself—isn't this what you've been bending my ear about? This number of acres in Iowa would be good to grow corn on. In Alabama, to grow trees on. What kind of soil is it?" He reached down and picked up a handful of the reddish brown, dry dirt. He tossed it in the air, then looked at the red dust on his fingers. "What will this climate allow? What do you want to do with it? Just leave it be? Continue to grow alfalfa? Marijuana?"

Tori rolled her eyes. "Yeah, we will be the country's largest medical marijuana grower. Did you know this area was famous in the Sixties for Rocky Mountain High, a special variety of pot? A lot of hippies lived up here and did quite well growing the weed until the narcs really cracked down. Lot of property confiscated. Some of the hippies are now respectable ranchers, contractors, local business people. Put that in your pot and smoke it."

I chuckled, then looked at Tori. "How did you know that? I never told you that."

Rachel smiled. "I've been educating her on the history of the mesa. You already know all that."

"Of course I do, but..." I stopped as a golden eagle swooped down and caught a prairie dog about a hundred yards from where we sat. It lifted up, with the dog wriggling as it dangled in the bird's talons. By the time the eagle was over us, the dog hung limp, the life squeezed out of it. Rachel and Tori both clapped as Al shook his head and said "way to go big guy. There, Russ, this may be the best use."

I watched the bird soar off with its afternoon snack. "Al may be right. What is the best use of Ravens Nest? Just what you see—a retreat from all that you are used to, Russ. A quiet place where you can come and refresh yourself. Watch the deer and eagles be free in their own element. A place to get away from crowds, noise, the turmoil you are used to every day. No offense, but you need this, just like your city needs Central Park."

Tori, becoming animated as usually happened when she turned on her passion, started a speech. "It will be incorporated into Ravens Nest. We will build more trails. But we will reclaim the land itself. It is overgrazed. We will plow it up, replant with native vegetation, graze a few animals, but on a sustainable basis. Some of it is potentially good agricultural land once it gets reliable water. We can grow our own food on a bigger level. Jake knows exactly what to do to make it better wildlife habitat. With the water, we can do way more than on the original Ravens Nest. This pasture up here is not wild like the forested areas on our slopes." She looked to the south and nodded. "The south part will remain just like it is. This north part, we can use it to demonstrate what sustainable grazing and ranch management can do. It will be a model."

She looked at Daddy as she adjusted her cap. "And, here is the repayment of your investment: we build a lodge for you to use for meetings. It will be where you bring your boards of directors, your political friends."

I looked at Tori. "We are not turning this into a small scale Aspen or Telluride."

Daddy started to say something, but Tori put her hand on his and turned to me. "No, no, Jake. Not at all. We keep it low key, small, but elegant. Rache, you agree with me on this." She looked at Rachel with pleading eyes. "We have talked about the concept. Simple, fitting in with what our overall goals are, but, well, elegant and dignified is the best way to put it."

Everyone looked at Rachel. She looked past Russell, to the southern edge, where the trees sloped down to the mesa's edge. The view was breathtaking, even to those of us used to it. The outline of Black Mesa bordered the view, with Uncompaghre Peak thrusting its pointed top above the near horizon. "The best use is to educate, to enlighten, to stimulate creativity. That is in our mission statement for Ravens Nest. This becomes part of Ravens Nest. We have a small lodge already. A bigger one, within limits will fit in. So will everything else," Tori said.

Al picked a small white flower from a weed near his knee, and stood up. "Do you realize how much work this involves? Good lord, just look at the sorry state of the corrals, the house, the fences. There is no decent road in here. The prairie dogs have taken over. The fields are nothing but weeds." He threw his hands in the air. "I can't do this and Jake can't either."

"Who says you have to?" Russell said as he reached into his shirt pocket and pulled out a packet of breath mints. He offered them to everyone. Tori was the only one who took one. "This is a big investment. Big investments require even more investments. You hire the work out. You supervise it. Don't tell me there aren't people here to do physical labor. Tori, you take a lesson from what Jake and Rachel hopefully taught you. They brought you on to help them. You bring others in to help you. Or hire them."

Storm clouds had slowly been forming over the Black Canyon, with the first rumble of thunder. We walked back to the Ravens Nest lodge, with YoYo chasing a rabbit as soon as we got to the trees.

Tori did hire others, including a planner to negotiate and work within the county regulations on expansion of use for the land, as well as navigating the paperwork and inspections of the buildings to confirm they were asbestos-free.

So, within two months, we tore down the old house and the largest of the barns. The corrals were nothing but rotting old aspen slabs, and came down easily with a slight nudge from a backhoe. After the first snow in November, we torched the huge piles. The fire department helped us by using it as a training exercise.

The next spring, Russell came out to help break ground for the lodge. We carefully located it on the south edge of the property, with a view that equaled our own. Tori and the architect worked all winter, in collaboration with Rachel, to make sure the lodge would not be what she called obscene opulent, but have a subtle and gracious quality. Rachel called the result natural elegance: ten guest rooms on the second floor of one wing with a large commercial kitchen and dining room beneath; another wing of small conference rooms and art studios; and the main lodge blending log construction, sandstone fireplace and mantle (with energy efficient insert), lichen lava rock gathered from Ravens Nest, vaulted ceiling with skylights, and two-story passive solar windows on the south side. The architect worked with a wildlife-consultant to incorporate bird protection technology into the window wall design.

Tori's Mums had passed away soon after her first visit, but Daddy remained strong and hardy until after the new lodge was complete. He visited more often, and stayed with Al and Tori longer each time, particularly while the building was being constructed. After it was completed, one evening he passed away in his sleep on the sofa in front of the fireplace in the main lodge. Tori found him there the next morning. The doctor said it was a massive stroke. Tori was relieved that it was quick and painless, unlike Mums, who succumbed to a fast growing pancreatic cancer. She loved her Daddy and missed him, but now she had the full responsibility for his fortune. Tori had always been sensitive to the label of rich city girl, and now you would never guess that by seeing her lifestyle—most summer days, she was in the garden, hands and face streaked with the reddish brown soil, and summer and fall she canned and dried fruits and vegetables, often donating much to the local food banks.

Tori had continued working on her music while at Ravens Nest, devoting all her spare time to composing and sharpening her skills with more instruments. So, the next year, she built a music studio with professional recording facilities near the lodge. Over the years, she performed locally and became well known in the region with her unique style blending Celtic harp and fiddle, South American and Native American flute, Asian instruments, voice, and the classics: cello, piano, harp, violin. Her solo concerts for Denver and Salt Lake City audiences were the most distant, and she was known simply as Tori.

After completion of her first CD—dedicated to Daddy—it was almost a year for national fame to hit. Al's contacts in the publishing industry helped in leading her to the right people. Her music filled a niche that found popular appeal, and was soon labeled environmental optimism, due to its hopeful feel like the music of John Tesh, yet the serious and contemplative feel of Enya.

As she became more well known, Rachel and I encouraged her to spend less time on domestic duties, but she still insisted on caring for us as much as she could. Rachel and Tori worked together to find, hire and train two young women who filled Tori's shoes when she was away—a fifth generation local of Scottish descent and a recent immigrant from Guatemala. Tori didn't like doing tours or concerts, although the demand was high for her appearances. She didn't do it to make money, although she was paid well, but to spread a message of environmental awareness, respect for nature, and peace with our fellow creatures. If she had been of my generation back in the 60s, she may have been a flower child with guitar. Something was different fifty years later, but her passion was no less than hippies I knew in my time.

While Tori was becoming known for her music, Al was plugging along doing his unique journalistic writing—completely freelance, with an eager audience in several national magazines. I told him his writing felt like fiction. He spent weeks researching a story, then told it in a folksy, personal way. He once told me the stories were out there waiting to be told, but I disagreed. He had an investigator's knack for sniffing out stories.

"Jake," he told me one night, as we relaxed in the new lodge, "I could write an entire book just on stories within a 30 mile radius of Ravens Nest." He looked at me with a strange smile, almost challenging me. "You could do the same. You write well and you have a nose for digging for facts. You may not be aware, but Rachel showed me a couple of your stories."

"You are on. I have a hundred dollar bill that says you could not make even a short book."

"Jake, sometimes you are so naïve. You are on. And I

challenge you to write a couple of stories yourself. Another hundred dollar bill on that."

So I did—an article about the bison ranch down the road. A rancher from Steamboat Springs sold out several years ago when the price of open ranchland skyrocketed, making him a millionaire. He used that to buy a thousand acres west of us and raised bison and elk, marketing locally and statewide. He advertised and sold the elk antler velvet for its arthritis benefits. We bought bison hamburger from them and they sent out-of-state customers to us for housing. I found it easy to write, spending only two hours interviewing him and several of the local outlets for their meat. I bought another bison robe and deepened the story by expanding on historic native use of bison for robes, tepees, and clothing. The twenty page article I sold to *Outdoor Magazine,* and Al framed the $100 bill he presented me.

I in turn framed my hundred to him when he published his book, *Secrets of the North Fork*. This collection includes stories on local wineries, the Mennonite population and their business enterprises, the aspen mill in Delta, scenery changes due to Sudden Aspen Decline, fly fishing in the Black Canyon of the Gunnison with famous fishermen such as Jimmy and Roselynn Carter, the expansion of organic farming in the area, and local water companies using small hydro as part of their supply systems. I had to admit there were a lot of fascinating stories right under our feet, and came to the conclusion Al could write for the next hundred years and not cover all the interesting things surrounding us.

I asked him why he didn't dabble in fiction since he wrote his nonfiction in such a story-like way. He grinned the way he did when he knew he had a secret he was about to share. "Why invent fiction," he said, "when the real world is much more interesting. You don't need violence and sex to write an engrossing story." He was right.

Walking with Al along the creek one hot afternoon, I suggested he lead a writers' workshop at Raven Ridge. He threw it right back to me. "You could do it just as well as me, Jake. You can write fiction. You are a good teacher." He stopped and picked a watercress leaflet, put it in his mouth, chewed a moment, pulled it out of his mouth and looked at it. "I had no idea what this was when I first saw it. I just assumed it was a weed that grew in the water. You gave me a five minute lecture about how it's used in fancy restaurants. Right then I wanted to harvest basket loads and take them up to Aspen and Vail to sell to restaurants. Remember what you told me?"

I walked over to uproot a thistle that was growing by the water. "Not really. How could I lecture you for five minutes on that?" I didn't remember that conversation at all.

"You said you didn't want to bother. If I wanted to, then I should go ahead and do it since it was not of any interest to you. You pick and choose what you are interested in. You said if you stopped to explore everything of interest, you would never get anything else done. You have to prioritize. That is one of your mantras: prioritize." He reached down and picked another bit of watercress.

"There is too much information out there, you always say. Your brain would explode if you learned everything there is to learn. Jake, you are basically intellectually lazy. And I say this thinking that you are one of the smartest people I know. Your depth of knowledge, your curiosity, the quest to know the answers to questions most people can't even think to ask. The problem is you don't want to learn something that doesn't immediately interest you. I still am learning. That is why I write nonfiction. Look at how easily I wrote the last book. Everyday things surround us that are fascinating. Watercress. Just a weed. Yeah, but look at how much people pay for this on a salad. Why? I want to know.

Maybe your brain is full at this point in your life, but I don't think so. You are so engrossed in listening to the silence, you are missing all the noise waiting to be heard."

He handed me a piece of watercress. "Taste it. Close your eyes and tell me what it tastes like."

I frowned at him. "You know I don't care for it. It is too peppery." He stared at me, holding the green leaf.

"Oh, all right." I took it and put it in my mouth. "Now what?"

"Do you deny that you could spend five minutes describing the feel, the taste, the sensation, what it brings to mind?"

"Sure, I could ramble on, but so what?"

"You are creative. Most people would just say it tastes peppery. Or something drab and simple like that. You can conjure up images. I do it with facts and background, you do it by telling a story. You paint with words, just like me, but in a slightly different way. You would not only say how it tastes, but the setting it grows in, how it grows, what it looks like, and on and on. You are perceptive, original, creative."

He had me there. He was right about not spending time if I wasn't interested. I used to want to know everything but now I was prioritizing. Some things weren't important to me, yet I did want to know how and why everything happened. I looked at Al, then spit out the fragments of the watercress.

"Okay, but what the hell did all that have to do with you not teaching a writers' workshop?"

"It had everything to do with the fact you could teach it as well if not better than me."

"But I don't have any training in writing. I write but I don't know any of the basics."

Al backed his butt up to a tree and leaned against it. "Good grief, Jake, you know more than many bestselling authors out there today. Quit selling yourself short. I don't have any training in biology or defensible space or geology or ranching. Do you claim I couldn't teach someone else about what I have been doing, under your tutelage by the way, for the past few years? Of course not. You don't need the formal training. Most university education is a bunch of bullshit anyway. Highly paid welfare. Most professors don't know squat about how the world works. They spend years telling students how things ought to work, then the poor students get into the real world and have to learn how the world actually works."

"Boy, I lit a burr under your ass, didn't I?" I started to walk on down the trail. "I still wouldn't know how to teach a class."

Al hurried after me as I kept walking. "How did you teach Tori and me about all this wild west ecotopia? You share your experience, you describe what works for you."

"You have the name. My name wouldn't draw anyone. I haven't published any books. You have. Your name alone would draw participants here, not mine."

"Okay, I put my name on the announcement, then I turn everything over to you. You know my thoughts on celebrity. Half the bestselling authors out there write trash. Trash sells, good literature doesn't. The general public doesn't know quality. They know fast-paced, shoot 'em up violence, sex, mystery. That is not good writing. That is good selling." Al mumbled to himself, but meant for me, "here we go again on the quality argument."

"Oh, all right, I won't go there. We all agree, whether it is music, literature, journalism, art, anything creative. Talent goes unrecognized while mediocrity…"

Al interrupted as he waved his walking stick at me, "goes rewarded. Sermon number twenty five. End of discussion."

We didn't need to elaborate on the subject. All four of us had beat this one to death. We had become a family of

Artists, and had the good fortune to be able to create for creativity sake, not for the necessity of selling. Rachel and I had been discussing this for decades.

Tori was now creating, producing and performing music that satisfied her, not necessarily the buying public. Fortunately, the public was satisfied and now buying it and making her in great demand. But she did everything on her terms and did not do music to make money. If she didn't want to make any appearances, she didn't have to. She pushed herself, but she would do that even if she sold nothing. Al was writing also on his own schedule. If he never sold another book, he would still write. And of course I wrote for my own satisfaction. I didn't even try to sell anything I wrote.

Not a lot of people had the luxury of creating their own works of art just for the sake of their own creativity. We were all very fortunate and we knew that. Our work on the ranch fell into the same category. We did what we wanted for its own sake and for our own education. That is why all of us were committed to sharing what we had.

We advertised a writers' workshop with nationally known author and Pulitzer prize winner Alistaire Corey. Seventeen people registered, with several more turned away due to space limitations. Al led them through basic writing styles, then turned it over to me for fiction writing. It was a success.

Our plans for the restoration of the ranch took us about two years to implement. Earlier, Daddy, along with his friends in major nonprofit organizations, had assisted with another aspect of the ranch restoration—creation of Raven

Ranch Foundation to oversee the multiple facets of the plan as a research and demonstration project. On the overgrazed pasture land, we brought in a half dozen bison, which required building stout fencing. We didn't want to keep out the deer and elk, so we kept the fence low in order to mimic multiple herbivores grazing the way they did centuries ago, keeping the bison herd less than ten animals. We grew hay on thirty irrigated acres, but left the rest as native pasture. Even on the hay acreage, we went to a native grass mix. The goal was not to make money—rest assured, at first we did not—but to demonstrate what a native ecosystem might look like. It was amazing how the former sagebrush and rabbitbrush fields converted to bluebunch wheatgrass, stipa, Indian ricegrass, and an assortment of native wildflowers that surprised even me.

Public groups increasingly requested I give presentations on the Raven Ranch Foundation, and the difference between Raven and conventional ranching was we were not pressured to make a profit early on. We eventually would, but we initially kept grazing pressure low in order to restore the ecosystem. Once there, our capacity would be greater than those operations who had to push grazing pressure in order to pay bills. I always emphasized that Raven Ranch was primarily a research and demonstration project, and our experiences could be useful to other ranchers.

The new buildings were totally solar and wind powered, plus an experimental small hydro installed in one creek. When we eradicated the tamarisk and many of the cattails that lined the creeks, the increased water flow was available for pumping by hydraulic ram to further water the native plant gardens. We were able to legally use this water since we made an agreement with the rancher who owned the water rights below us. We increased the flow from the springs and in return, we used that increase in water. In keeping most of the creek drainages natural, more wildlife-friendly native vegetation returned, such as willows and berry bushes. Eventually, our efforts made the Denver news, helped along by the articles Al published in several national magazines. We were getting more fame and exposure than I was comfortable with, and it kept us all busy.

I often sat at the end of Fox Ridge on sunny afternoons and gazed across the valley. I took a pack with snacks and a blanket or pillow, and our current pup. These moments often gave me ideas for new short stories or poems, but more often they were filled with remembrances of my life. I thought back to my early days in the different agencies, and the joy of wandering the back country of mountain and plain. I was lucky to do what I did and the time I did it. Things have changed beyond recognition since those heady days. I grew up and started my career in a time of excitement, the environmental movement, nature still on its own terms. Now, it seems no one has the freedom to live life the way it was meant to be. My theory has always been that all problems come down to too many people. As a biologist this is my understanding of basic population dynamics. Too many of any species crowded into too small a space will make anyone crazy. I am convinced this is what is happening. Of course technology is separating us from nature as well, but that is a whole different subject.

Most days I would fall asleep as I sat either in the sun or shade, depending on temperature. This was my time to be in contact with the earth as I sat on a lichen-covered boulder, or stretched out on the soil, feeling the spirit of the land. On days when she was home, Tori would often walk Ravens Nest until she found me, then sit next to me, or sometimes lay her head on my shoulder or outstretched leg. We would talk philosophy or ideas for the ranch or about past experiences. She always wanted to hear my stories, but

I was just as interested in her days in the cities. And I often told her that the scene we were looking at was the same as viewed by the native peoples centuries ago. Without of course the buildings and roads.

Al was home less than Tori, but he would seek me out, too. We would talk about his latest article or research. He bounced ideas off me and I was always glad to give my opinions. Whether he really used these or not, he always acted like I had solved a tough problem for him. I appreciated that.

I reflected on my childhood, thinking that as a youngster, I would never have guessed my final years would have been like this. But then, who does really know how they will end up? So many of my childhood friends led what I consider uneventful lives, often never living more than a hundred miles from where we all grew up. I find that sad, but to each his own, right? Usually a thought like that pushed me over the edge into nap time. The clouds drifted by and the seasons followed, adding to years.

CHAPTER 4

SUNSET

*It is the land. That's where it all starts
and ends. Know the land, respect it, and
you will be alright.*
Jake Collins

As THE ECONOMY spiraled into the Second Depression over the next ten years, we were able to buy more adjacent ranches. When the one hundred acre parcel to our west came on the market, I told Tori to buy and pay whatever our neighbor's family wished; she had been nearly as reclusive as Rachel and I. Her property was similar in topography to the original Ravens Nest—nearly all forested, and steep drainages sloping downhill to the next mesa below. The west edge was sagebrush, without any irrigation water. My main purpose for picking this up was to set us up to purchase the large irrigated fields to the west. That ranch had been on and off the market for several years. The owner could never get what she asked, then would take it off the market and lease it for a few years, then put it up for sale again. She was asking at least double what it was worth, but its south edge was prime for upscale housing with a view. If that edge were developed, it wouldn't affect us, but I knew what it would do to the wildlife winter range, so I figured we would do what we could.

As we were buying the last pieces of property for

our expanding operations, Tori set up a new nonprofit foundation called Raven Ridge Institute—which we all referred to as Tori's Dream. We transferred all the property to this foundation, and worked through the paperwork to put all the parcels in conservation easements. At the start, all four of us were directors, but Rachel and I insisted that Tori and Al take total control, providing for their future. They enlisted two other musicians who were part of Tori's Raven Ridge Music group. Rachel and I were then satisfied that our dream would continue in good hands. Ravens Nest and the expanded Raven Ridge Institute would never be subdivided and developed further, and would provide the model for land stewardship. We made sure to allow for minor buildings necessary to manage the land, but these would be minimal. Although I took an interest in the additions to the property, I focused most of my time and passion on our original Ravens Nest acres.

We abandoned the original driveway into Ravens Nest and constructed a new, paved lane that snaked through the new property. From Bison Lodge, it wound several hundred yards through the trees to Ravens Nest. I had helped Al lay out trails on the new portion of the property when I was still able, but he and our ranch employees did all the construction. Since the flats on the new property were accessible to vehicles, Al brought in large equipment to thin some of the juniper for defensible space. That was also part of the effort to increase forage for the bison, which took on the appearance of a lightly wooded savanna. I guessed this was how the whole country looked five hundred years ago.

With the added grazing land, we expanded the bison herd to over one hundred head. The business was still not making money since we increased our expenses by hiring two former ranchers to administer the grazing and the improvements. But we were nearly self-sufficient ourselves since Tori had expanded our vegetable garden into a twenty-acre truck farm. It was obviously more than we could handle ourselves, but she worked with Colorado and Utah college and university agriculture programs, bringing in student interns, March through October. We provided housing and food, with a minimum wage stipend. The students were so enthusiastic about the set up, they nearly always gave us far more than we compensated them for. We sold organic produce through the regional food producers' hub, and were getting demand from the Denver markets. Al created a compost business, using waste clippings and vegetation from locals. While we spread and pulverized the bison chips in our own fields, we collected manure for the compost from recently certified organic feed yards in Montrose and Delta. We devoted nearly ten acres to this facility and were starting to satisfy demand from as far away as Denver.

I was helping with the green bean harvest one August afternoon when one of the interns brought me a jug of lemonade.

"Jake, you should take it easy on a hot afternoon like this. Sit down and tell me more about Raven Ridge."

"You aren't one for telling someone else they are working too hard. It's Amanda isn't it?" She seemed surprised I knew her name. "I've seen you out here at 5 in the morning. You don't get paid enough for those long hours."

"I have learned more this summer than in the last two years at the University. You know the old saying, Jake, that you don't become a farmer to make money."

"Sort of like working for the government then. We do it

for love." I smiled as I handed her my empty glass for a refill.

"Tori told me about your career and what you have done here on Raven Ridge. I can't believe your magic touch. Seems like you have found a niche for about everything you do. Should I call you Mr. Midas?" Amanda refilled my glass and pulled a granola bar out of her apron pocket. "Like to share this?"

"No thanks. Miss Tori is the one responsible for all this. I was just living a peaceful retirement in seclusion when she came along and started throwing money at me. Do they teach you in ag econ that money makes all the difference? You grab whatever opportunity comes along, but it helps to have a dream before you start grabbing. You work hard and dream. I can see you meet the first challenge. What is your dream?" I liked this girl. She didn't seem to be over 18, but had maturity well past that.

"I've talked a lot to Tori. What a down-to-earth wonder she is. And so famous and talented. I can't believe she is out here in the dirt with the rest of us. And you, too."

"You realize then, that Tori and I and the others around here are a drawback to a past time. We rely on virtues that are all but gone nowadays." I looked past her at the view and pointed with my head. "It is the land. That's where it all starts and ends. Know the land, respect it, and you will be alright."

"I grew up on a farm in Iowa. I agree with you. My dream is to have my own farm, just like this. I don't care if I make a lot of money." She laughed. "I don't think I need to worry about that, do I?"

"You just might. I think things are turning around. More people are going back to the land. You grow decent food, organic of course, and be smart with what you do with the land, you might be surprised. This right here was a prairie dog field just a few years ago. The soil is good. You just need to treat it right. And by doing that, you automatically treat people right. And that, my young friend, is the compilation of all my years of accumulated wisdom." I laughed and patted her shoulder as I got up. "If anyone here is not treating you with respect, you come let me know personally. Deal?"

"Deal. You take care. You don't worry about me." Amanda set the lemonade jug and glass in her electric cart, climbed in, and drove back to the main barn.

I picked a few more beans, then wandered back to the lodge. I gave the beans to Rachel for the evening meal. She scolded me for being in the sun too much, but I said I loved being with the kids on the ranch. I told Rachel and Tori that was what kept me young. Tori said I flirted too much with the girls. I replied that's what kept me ornery. Truth be told, Tori still flirted with me as much as I flirted with her.

I was getting unable to walk the trails as I had done daily for years. My knees and ankles, which I had always bragged were sound, started to give out, as did my lungs. I could still make it down to the bottoms of the creeks, but less often and with more pain. I was out of breath walking up the hills, unable to make it without resting. Rachel said it was just age, but I knew it was asthma compounding the years.

Rachel's eyes were giving out as well as her short term memory, but the macular degeneration was just another challenge; learning braille was possible even with arthritis. She and I spent much of our time sitting in the large common room of Bison Lodge. It was painful to me to watch her memory slide, but she remembered enough to recall most major events in our lives.

Rachel and I had remodeled four small rooms in the lodge into a small apartment. We spent more and more time there rather than being alone in our large house. One evening after Rachel had gone to bed and Al was in Denver for an editorial meeting for a new book, I was sitting in front of the fireplace in Bison Lodge with Tori. She was playing the piano when I asked her to come and sit next to me on the sofa. I saw her now as a grown up daughter, as close as any natural child I could have had. Her hair was long and had started turning white a couple years before. I kidded her about us causing her to prematurely age. She said she was what kept us young. She wore bifocals that highlighted the expressive wrinkles around her eyes, but still looked like the young woman who joined us so many years ago.

"Well, Tori, it's been quite a ride, huh?"

She looked at me with a puzzled expression. "What have we ridden? You still trying to hop on some of them bison?"

"You being here. The past twenty six years. Remember that night you first called from New York to ask about Ravens Nest? It was just a shot in the dark for you wasn't it? You knew nothing about us and we knew nothing about you." Her smile was the same, but wrinkle lines spoke of a subtle wisdom.

"Good Lord, Jake, you are on a real memory trip aren't you? Of course I remember." She squeezed my hand. She had always had a habit of touching and holding, which I never failed to enjoy. "What made you think of that?"

"Get my age and you start to relive a lot of things. I was thinking of how all our lives changed because of your phone call that night. Your trip out, those first visits to the high country and the desert. Your moving here, buying your first car, building your house, taming a wandering husband, then the Big Bang of the ranch and the foundation. Now this, sitting here and watching it all end. Was it what you wanted?"

"Wait a minute," Tori said as she moved to the edge of the sofa and turned to face me. "I don't like where this is leading. It is not ending."

I winced. "Sorry, bad choice of words. Ending for me, not you. You know a lot of the old cultures valued the elders. But they also realized when they were not productive and needed to move out of the way for the next generation. Same with wildlife, actually. Old ones went off to die. Nature isn't compassionate. It's quite amoral, you know."

Tori went over to put another log on the fire. She came and sat very close to me, putting her arms around me. "Jake, we are not the old culture. And when the elders had children, those children took care of them. The old ones were honored."

"Tori, we have had this discussion in the past. Remember that time sitting down at Wild Plum Grotto? The future is about young people. We have been through a tough period the past fifteen years, with the Depression, continuing recessions, the war, the riots. Look at the old ranches the foundation picked up for a song. How many acres do you control now? I've lost track."

"You know what we have." She emphasized the word we. "You helped pick out the best ones to buy. You paved the way and led us by the hand, two city people who knew only the city life. You transformed us. It was your brains and my money. What a combination, huh?" Tori laughed and gave me a squeeze.

I smiled. "What a choice. Money without brains or brains without money. I guess that is what has ruled the world. Those with money, with help from those with brains. Lucky for me, you ended up with both."

"Whatever I have, you have and vice versa. That's the way you planned it all along."

"One thing I have never gotten a good answer from you on." I looked at her as she perked up, expecting some gem of wisdom.

"Well what?"

"You never explained why you kept your maiden name. Victoria Reynolds. Why didn't you take on Al's when you got married?"

Tori burst out laughing. "Oh, Jake. Sometimes you really crack me up. You think I would have ever made it to first base with you if I had introduced myself as Tori Corey? You would have hung up the phone on me right away." She started laughing again, so hard that it got me going. We got to giggling so hard, we had tears running down our cheeks .

I tried to regain my composure. "I thought maybe you wanted to keep the Reynolds name in the public eye. It does have quite a pedigree doesn't it?"

"I think Tori Corey would have lit up the public sky even more."

"You could have gone by Vict Corey." That set her laughing again.

"Jake, you think you are so serious and dignified, you are just as impish as a little fox pup. Yet, wise like an old fox."

"Dignified, huh? You know who I see as dignified? The elders. You have brought some of the tribal elders out here. There is only one word I would use to describe them. They exude dignity. They are quiet, steeped in tradition, humble, but dignified."

"Right about that. I love being with them, yet I feel the outsider even here on our own land. But then, their ancestors lived here much longer than us."

"Well, put a feather in your hat for bringing them back. This land will eventually return to them won't it? That is your plan?"

"My plan? No, Jake, don't try and weasel out of your responsibly in all this. You knew what you wanted all along and you got it. You just used me." She smiled.

"I do have one serious question. I have noticed you for

years pulling out little notebooks and scribbling. Sometimes a word or two, sometimes sentences or paragraphs. I never said anything or asked to look. Well, now I'm asking to look."

Tori studied me with a quizzical scrunch of her eyes. She just stared for several seconds, then said slowly, "Jake, you old fox, why have you waited all these years to ask that question?"

"Dunno. An old person just gets to thinking. Maybe I finally got through my list of thoughts to think about."

Tori let out a combination squeal and laugh. "God, Jake, you will always keep surprising me. For how many years have I been keeping a journal, writing down thoughts for songs, lyrics, even melodies for my songs. Ideas for Al to write about. Projects for me to do. Questions for me to ask you. I didn't think it was private, although no one ever asked me about it. I just assumed people knew it was personal, just scribbles."

"Got your little secret book with you now?"

She reached into her vest pocket and pulled out a ragged and torn notebook, the size of a large deck of cards. "This here old thing? You think I am writing about you?"

"You are a talented artist, creative, innovative. You must have good stuff there. Read me a page."

"You are kidding, aren't you?" Tori looked at me, then at her book, then back at me. "No you are not."

She opened the notebook about halfway through, looked at the pages for a few seconds, turned a page, then slowly read. "The sunset breaks through a wall of clouds, painting the sky a salmon orange. The winds drift shapes of fingers and loops of kaleidoscope oranges and reds, purples, then grey blues. The lingering light of a dreaming sun keeps the secrets of the night away. But only for awhile. The blue black of midnight comes stealthily overhead, covering all with a protective blanket."

All that sounded somewhat familiar to me. I asked to see the page. Tori handed it to me, not saying a word. "Scribble is right. I can't even read this. A foreign language?"

"No, silly. This is my own secret language. It's not meant for your eyes or anyone else's. Those words became my song *Nightscape.* You said you loved it. It made you think of the Alaskan sky. Or Colorado sky. Or Utah sky. Don't remember which. It was a sky you taught me to look at, admire, wonder about. So I wondered—and caught it in a song. The melody came first, then I crafted the words to fit. Mostly the cello, but with a flute as background. Tough recording that way. You know I played all the instruments, at least on the recording. On stage, I had to have backup musicians."

"So you always carried this, putting thoughts down right when they hit you. For years. How many notebooks?"

"Who knows. A dozen or so. Al does the same thing with his ideas. But his are more literary."

"This seems pretty literary to me. I never knew how you came up with your music. For years?"

"Yeah, Socrates, for years. You cannot tell me you never wondered or wanted to know. You always wanted to know everything else."

"Guess some things I liked the mystery of. Your music is so mysterious, so sacred to me, I suppose I didn't really want to know. Some mysteries should go with you to the grave. Guess I am now ready. Go sing me *Nightscape* again. Or do you have scribblings for a new song in there?"

Tori got up and walked over to the grand piano in the corner. "Speaking of a new song, I have been working on one just for you." She sat down and started playing—slow, melodic, and very mournful. As I listened, I thought the music blended exactly with how I was feeling. Hopeful, yet sad. An ending and a beginning. The past blending into the future. I closed my eyes. She shifted to the cello, then back to the piano.

When I opened my eyes, Tori had come back to sit next to me again. "I wrote this for you. I wasn't ready to play it for you yet, but I felt I needed to now. Still needs a little work. I will call it *The Journey.* It's your song. Yours and Rachel's.

I patted her arm. "Thank you. It was very nice. It does seem to summarize our journey. A nice way to end it."

Tori touched my face and turned my head to her. "Jake, quit it. You are scaring me. End what? Nothing is ending here."

"Everything comes to an end. The secret is to know when to end it. Too many people try to stretch good things past their lifespan. Athletes, politicians, maybe even musicians and writers."

Tori turned away. When she looked at me again, there were tears in her eyes. She couldn't speak, but just stared at me, then the fire.

"Remember Bruce and his long life, and your recognition of his coming end?" I asked. For fifteen years Bruce had been the lead bull of the herd. And in spite of his age we could not kill him for meat or for his hide. He could hardly walk. One winter day, he went off in the thickets and we couldn't get him out. He lay down under a large old juniper and didn't get up. We found him one morning covered with snow, his old eyes closed, his heart stopped. Tori took the loss hard. She had been able to walk up to Bruce and pat him on the head. None of the rest of us would dare try this. I would always get a lowered head, a snort, pawing of the ground, and a wild look in his eyes. Not Tori. She could talk with Bruce. She felt his energy and said he was a kindly old man. I thought she was losing it when near the end she told me that Bruce was ready to go. He had conveyed to her that he was tired and needed to rest. She always knew what animals were thinking, and I often wondered if she knew what I was thinking.

"You're not Bruce. You aren't going to go lay in the snow and die." Tori laughed, but was crying at the same time. She threw her arms around me. "Quit talking like this. You are not that old. Sure you are slowing down. You deserve to take it easy. Do we mistreat you?"

She pulled one of Rachel's grandmother's embroidered linen handkerchiefs from another vest pocket and wiped her eyes. She moved to the piano again and began playing one of my favorite songs from her first CD.

"You didn't answer my question," I said as she slowly trailed off her song.

"I don't remember a question being in there," Tori sniffed.

"Now you are mistreating an old man. You think I can remember what I said five minutes ago?" This made her laugh.

"Well if you don't remember it, then how can you ask me if I answered it. Of course I answered it. Silly." She got up and stood by the fire with her back to me.

"Was it what you wanted? Or expected? You two had no idea what you were getting into. City kids coming to live in the wilds of the West. You both would have still been famous if you had stayed in New York. And probably richer. Al would have still been a Pulitzer Prize author. You would have been lead cellist for the New York Philharmonic. Tori Corey, famous cellist."

She turned to face me, her hands behind her like a schoolgirl saying her part in a Christmas play. "We had good judgment. We recognized a wise couple when we met you. You have to give us credit for that. Maybe we were naïve and city stupid, but we knew we were going to be well taken care of and given instruction in how to live a new life. Yes it was what we wanted. We weren't happy in the city and you know that. Life is about more than being rich or famous. You know we are giving away all our money. Look at what we do with the Raven Ridge Institute and how it helps locally. We didn't know the details of how things would turn out, but overall, yes, we wouldn't change a thing. I would call it perfection. And will continue to be for years, with your guidance. See this little book? It is still half blank. You need to give me more ideas, more wisdom for my work."

I just smiled and closed my eyes.

Tori continued, avoiding what she knew was really happening. "You taught us well. You showed us how to live as part of nature, not apart from it, how to respect nature, how to learn from nature. We are living the way all people should live, but don't. I see nature's energy because of you. I can capture that energy in my music. Al sees it for his writing. I would have been nothing more than a music teacher and second string cellist if you hadn't steered me in the direction I took. You want to read all my notes?"

"I steered you? I don't know anything about music. And I cannot even read your handwriting."

"Remember that first trip we took?" Tori shot back, ignoring my last comment. "You had just learned to play a native flute. Were still learning actually." She smiled. "You really were stumbling along but you continually got better. Nothing fancy. But it was haunting. It captured what I was looking for. It was nature, the environment. I was not familiar with native music so I started listening to professionals— Native American, Incan, Peruvian. That got me interested in a whole different style. I was able to weave that and other aboriginal music into my own work, a Mozart with Andean flutes and Chinese drums. And the time was right for it and it took off and look where my music is now."

"You would have gone that route anyway. You are

always telling me we are guided by a force of nature. No coincidences, right?"

"Yes, but it takes wisdom to know how and when you are being guided. You are the wise elder. So is Rachel. You are like the king and queen in the fairy tales. We should build a monument to you, right out on Coyote Point, overlooking the valley."

"Now you are getting silly. We are not gods, just ordinary people. Ordinary old people whose time is fading. What is that old saying about the student becoming the teacher and the teacher becoming the student?" I stared into the fire. "Go turn out the lights. Let's just watch the fire." I didn't want her to see my eyes misting up.

There was so much I wanted to say, but over the years I had said it all. I didn't know the pride a father could feel over a child who grew up and succeeded in life. But I did know the pride I felt in watching Tori mature and thrive in a new life that I helped her find. I didn't know all the answers and I had been asking questions all my life. What was life all about, what was important, how could we survive as a part of nature and not apart from it? I guess I would never learn the answers; neither would Tori or anyone else, but life was about trying to find out.

I had no regrets about my journey. I started simple and kept to the basics. I loved the outdoors and spent my life working with nature. My decades with the Feds and the State as a wildlife biologist let me explore Colorado as few people got to do. I had walked the prairies, climbed the peaks and ridges, discovered red rock canyons, floated rivers large and small. Then another ten years with the U.S. Fish and Wildlife Service gave me priceless opportunities to wander Alaskan wildernesses larger than half the states of the Union. But throughout it all, the Valley and Ravens Nest was my adopted home. The bluebird skies over the golden aspen autumns, the roiling and boiling thunderheads of July, the quiet snowfall of winter. Every season had its joys and surprises.

But now, I was unable to enjoy what I always had looked forward to. I had what most people only dream of, but dreams always end. I thought of Bruce and his departure—the subject Rachel and I had always kidded about.

My thoughts returned to Tori and Al. They were humble, respectful, and students of life. They had skills and used them to further themselves and others. There was nothing more I could do. My time was past and I felt good about what I had done as well as what the kids had accomplished. In a way, I felt a stranger in this room, in this building. It was not part of my original dream, but my dream merged into that of Tori and Al. They would carry on quite well. I wanted this moment to last forever. Maybe it would.

We sat in the darkness, watching the flickering light of the fire. I watched Tori as she sat still as a pillar of sandstone. Tears left trails like dew on her cheeks, glistening in the reflected firelight. I thought I heard the hoot of an owl nearby as I fell asleep—her head on my shoulder, her hand in mine.

CHAPTER 5

ALISTAIRE'S VIEW

*"Sunsets and sunrises," I can clearly hear
Jake say. Native peoples knew the cycle of life.
No beginnings, no endings.*
Alistaire Corey

IT HAS BEEN over a year since Tori and I said goodbye to Jake and Rachel. They departed together, I know as they planned for a long time. Their passing has been harder on Tori since she, in her prescient way, knew what was going to happen and couldn't change it. She had seen the energy aura around them weaken and dim, nearly fading out the last day we saw them. It wasn't easy on me, either, but I saw the natural side of it easier than Tori. I miss them, but it seemed right, in the way Jake would have seen it— they weren't able any longer to live the life they loved. It was time. The torch had passed. Tori and I accepted it with grateful tears.

Once in a while Jake would read me one of his poems or a short story, but he felt he couldn't match a professional writer like me. I told him he had talent, but he always thought I was just saying that to make him feel good. He never accepted that I really meant it. Although he did write the bison ranch story on my bet, he felt more comfortable writing fiction. Yet Tori and I knew that most of it was more

autobiography than genuine fiction. Even knowing that, I was surprised how much of his life I didn't know. It has taken me a long time to read through his full oeuvre: essays and poems, short stories, and even two novels. Sadly, he never tried to publish any of them. Now, I fully understand his genuine and simple talent. His writing needs polishing by a top-notch editor, but I am pleased and proud of the depth of his work. I've edited a collection of his poetry, which was published late last year. And I am currently guiding his first novel in the final stages toward release with a major publishing house.

What has surprised me most was finding this story of which I am a part. He took our adventure and made a novella out of it. He embellished some things, altered a few details, but the essence is intact. It is the story of part of my life and the climax of a full life of his. A large part of his earlier life adventures are fictionalized in several of the short stories. They are autobiographical and filled with his wisdom and philosophy as well as exciting adventures. In this novella, he left a note for me to add this chapter. He ended his story with the scene of him and Tori in the lodge. Soon after, the real story came to its end.

Like Bruce the old bison bull, he and Rachel did the equivalent of laying down under the trees and passing onto their next adventure. As Jake said numerous times near the end, "This is true with a lot of wildlife. They know their time is up so they just lay down to die. Animals can do this. People, too. Listen to stories of an old person dying and very soon after, the spouse dies as well. We can will ourselves to die when we think the time is up."

Jake and Rachel were tuned into nature. They had almost shaman-like powers. This gets to Jake's philosophy that many aboriginal peoples had powers we nowadays consider magical. They were more a part of nature than most people today. So, for Jake and Rachel, there was no need for a pill. No need for a bullet. No need to jump off the cliff. The life they knew and loved was no longer possible, so they willed themselves to end it. I envy them that ability, but Tori and I dedicate our remaining years to fulfilling their passion and dream. He called this story *Tori's Dream*. It was his dream all along.

Early in the morning following Jake and Tori's philosophizing by the fire, she called me, her voice nearly in a panic. I had a hard time understanding through her sobs. I came home the next day, leaving my editorial meetings early. Everything appeared normal to me, although Jake seemed to be more distant than usual. He had been turning quite retrospective; Rachel was quiet as well. They seemed to look at each other with questions in their eyes every day. Neither could do what they spent their lives doing. The enjoyment they got from watching the sun rise every morning was over. I told Tori to let nature take its course. We enjoyed those last few days as we all sat in the lodge and talked about how our lives turned out.

Jake said the acquisition of the new property was his biggest surprise. He kept saying he was a simple boy at heart and had no business playing with big money. Yet he guided us well and enjoyed the metamorphosis of Ravens Nest into what it became. I know he approved. We were of different generations, but I think Tori and I were closer to his and Rachel's beliefs than they realized. We had never fit in with our privileged lifestyle in the city. I envied them their lives and experiences. It was more than most people ever come close to, yet they never really fit in either. I guess we were all outcasts to an earlier, simpler time. It is something both Tori and I recognize and will spend the rest of our lives trying to communicate to others, Tori through her music, me through my writing. It is a huge challenge, and a large responsibility.

On what turned out to be the last day, Jake and I had a long conversation. We sat on the deck of the lodge, warming ourselves like lizards in the brilliant sunshine. He said we were about the age he and Rachel were when we came into their lives. I told him that was a matter of perspective. They came into our lives and changed ours much more than we changed theirs. Even with all the money Tori and I invested in Ravens Nest, Jake and Rachel never really changed. They kept to a simple philosophy and lifestyle, not adding luxury to their personal lives, only comfort. All our money went to buildings and land. They kept the same old car, shopped at local thrift stores, didn't spend money on travel or trinkets like so many newly wealthy folks do.

Regarding heirs, he said we needed to do what they had done, since, like them, we have no children. I told him Tori and I had been thinking about that. We wanted to see this land in the hands of the people who had tended it for so many millennia. We wanted someone on the Institute Board from the Northern Ute Nation, and had recently initiated contact. Tori had visited the tribal council several times and had two individuals in mind to take on the mantle of guardians of Raven Ridge Institute. The Institute was well set up with conservation easements and property covenants to ensure it would continue as we all wished. I told Jake that Tori and I had plenty of help, unlike he and Rachel when we first came on board. He grinned that wide smile of his, then made a comment he'd made many times: "money does change things, doesn't it?"

Within this past year—a time of reflection and adjustment for both of us—Tori has spent hours sitting on the ridge by Jake and Rachel's house. We have converted it to a library and research center, but Tori still tends it with love and care. A pair of ravens built a nest in a tall cedar near the creek below the house, and they spend a lot of time sitting on the roof, even when Tori is nearby. Scolding her mercilessly, by themselves at first, then recently with their young, they circle overhead as she smiles and talks to them. Tori says with annoying confidence that it is Jake and Rachel, at least in spirit. I don't argue with her on such spiritual matters. It is unusual for ravens to nest near humans, but Tori claims she sees an energy around both birds. When they fly, they circle over the house and original lodge, Jake and Rachel's first love, the homestead ridge I call it. Deer Ridge. They loved planning for all the new property, but as Jake said, Deer Ridge would have been all they had if it weren't for Tori and me. He mumbled something like "you love your first child the best." He wouldn't know, but he loved Tori and me like his own.

I won't go into detail about their ending. That will remain unwritten, mysterious like so much is in nature. There will be no end to the Ravens Nest and Raven Ridge story. We have done our best to ensure the story will evolve and cycle and change, but not end. In nature, life continues on. "Sunsets and sunrises," I can clearly hear Jake say. Native peoples knew the cycle of life. No beginnings, no endings. So, on that thought, I say farewell to two friends, a second father and mother, guides and teachers. The cycle will continue to roll on. The sunsets will fade into sunrises. Each will promise new wonders.

Jake asked me to end this story. I will not end it, but push it forward in its unending cycle by quoting something he wrote years ago:

"The wind will continue to rustle the juniper branches, the lizards will scamper by, pleasantly ignorant of the changing world around them. It will be the same world I was familiar with, but by then, I will be floating the universe seeking new answers. Atoms of oxygen and phosphorous, freed from gravity of this planet, will seek the company of a companion now millions of miles away. A new star will grab onto the quarks that once wondered about time and space. A new earth will coalesce and after time, another being will ponder the meaning of what it saw. And there will probably still be no correct answers to the questions created by space, time and the mystery called life."

CHAPTER 6

Wisdom

Tori SAT COMFORTABLY on a lichen-covered boulder, scanning the distant hillsides, green with spruce forest speckled with golden aspen. She thought of the many times she had sat on a similar hillside and watched the summer fade into autumn. Since she lost Al four years ago, the changing of the seasons was gaining more significance to her. Not sure how many more remained, she thought back to her last days with Jake and Rachel so many years ago. It was hard then for her to understand their readiness to depart this life, but on this golden autumn day, beneath another early October Colorado bluebird-sky, she now understood. She was content, but tired, and life didn't have the same spark it always had for her.

She watched Bernice, doll-like far down the grassy hillside, almost dancing as she ran beside Belle. Tori had wanted to be up here with Bernice to share this day as well as share her thoughts. She had spent the past two summers working with Bernice, who interned at the Institute during

her last years in college. After Bernice's graduation, Tori hired her permanently to help with managing the business. She felt a closeness to Bernice that she had never felt with any of the other young people she had worked with. Just like their mentors Jake and Rachel, Tori and Al did not have children. But unlike them, she and Al never adopted a young couple as did Jake and Rachel. She and Al became part of their family and inherited the Institute and all its property. This was what her adopted parents wished.

Watching a red-tailed hawk soar overhead, Tori regretted she and Al had not done the same. They had planned for the future, with a Board, mostly of Ute elders, now in charge of the future of the Raven Ridge Institute. But there was an ache now for her personal, spiritual future.

That was why she wanted to come up to this spot to talk to Bernice, to pass on her wisdom and her advice as a mother or grandmother. Bernice was orphaned at 18 just as she started college. She had never been close to her parents, but they had provided for her education, after which she would survive or fall on her own. Tori knew that Bernice occasionally dated, but was not close to anyone at the moment.

"Hey Tori," Bernice shouted as she came running up the hill, chased by Belle, barking at whatever dogs insist on barking at when nothing else is visible. "I saw a beaver. Thank goodness Belle didn't see it."

"I didn't see any ponds down there." Tori took out her binoculars and focused on the creek.

"Behind that aspen patch. Can't see it from here," Bernice said as she plopped down next to Tori, panting in rhythm with Belle, as she sprawled on the ground.

Tori opened her pack, reached into a bag of dog cookies, and gave one to the panting, expectant Belle. She fished out a bag of trail mix and handed it to Bernice.

"Thanks," Bernice said, then took a swig from her water bottle, looking at the sky. "I just love the colors. The blue of the sky complements all the reds and golds." She picked a leaf from a current bush, mottled red and gold. She held it up to the sky and smiled. "What a perfect day."

"Don't you know by now, Bernice, that every day is perfect?" Tori said as she grinned and brushed a few strands of white hair from her face.

"Tori, I don't know how you always manage to be so positive."

"'For someone my age', she thinks to herself, but politely leaves unsaid," said Tori with a smile.

"No, Tori, that thought didn't even enter my mind. No matter what age, you always find the good side to everything." Bernice reached over to hold Tori's hand, then let it drop as she eased back on the ground, her feet on a rock.

A painted lady butterfly landed on a still-blooming scarlet gilia about two feet from the now sleeping Belle. Tori reached out, almost touching the butterfly. "I have seen literally thousands of butterflies come past the lodge back at Ravens Nest. Did you know they migrate? Don't remember if it was painted lady or some kind of skipper, but they came flying at eye level, passing for ten minutes. You see something like that, there is no way not to be positive about the world. It is truly a miracle."

Bernice watched the butterfly bounce away, disappearing down the hill. "I didn't know they migrated. I thought they just died with the first freeze."

"There are a lot of things I learned after I moved out here back in..." Tori hesitated, "lord, I forget just when it was we did move out here. That should be etched in my mind. It was so long ago," she looked down as she tried to remember. "Oh well, it was a new life for me. Like being born, or reborn."

"You were a city girl, weren't you?" Bernice asked.

"Yes, and Al, too. City born and raised, but with enough sense to know we were missing something pretty important in our lives. I credit everything after that to Jake and Rachel. They taught us so much."

"Tori, no one who spends any time at Ravens Nest cannot be aware of Jake's and Rachel's presence. I wish I had known them."

Tori smiled as she slipped deeper into her pensive mood. "Yes, I just hope I am passing on some of what they taught me."

"Don't short yourself. You may have learned from them, but you are who you are because of yourself. And you know that."

Tori silently reflected on her life. Yes, she was a city girl, trapped for over twenty five years in a life she didn't belong in. She started over as the "adopted" daughter of Jake and Rachel at Ravens Nest. She didn't think of herself as a famous musician, which she was. She didn't see her accomplishments as the many music awards she received, the world tours, the TV interviews, the scores of two movies. She felt her greatest achievements were as a naturalist, ecologist, farmer. Of course life was easier with the millions she inherited from her real parents, but she rarely used that money and when she did, it was used to buy more land and build the Institute. And the proceeds from all that were used to help the local community and the Institute's education programs.

Even though she had arranged for the entire estate to go to the Ute nation, safeguards were firmly in place to keep the Institute and the property as she, Al, Jake, and Rachel planned many years ago. Now, she saw in Bernice someone she wished to be involved in it—to carry on in Tori's place. She saw Bernice as a young Tori of fifty years ago. But one who came on the scene knowing already things that Tori learned the hard way.

Life had changed almost unrecognizably around her, but one thing Tori felt strongly that wouldn't change, and shouldn't change, were her values and beliefs. She needed to make sure she passed those onto Bernice.

"Bernice, I know you lost a lot when your folks died, but I have wondered, did you ever get a chance to have a good mother-daughter, or even father-daughter, talk? You know, about what they learned in life, what they saw as important."

Bernice grinned at Tori. "You gonna tell me about the birds and bees? Or butterflies?"

Tori burst out laughing. "God no, Bernice. You know more than I probably do about all that. No, I mean the things they wanted you to know about life, what's important, how to survive."

"Like you, I had to figure a lot of things out on my own."

Tori frowned and studied the ground for a few seconds. Reaching over and picking up a dried, brownish-yellow aspen leaf, she said, "I may have learned a lot myself, but I had a lot of help. My dad gave me the talk before I got married, then again as we sat one night in the lodge just after it was built. Mums tried once, but she did a horrible job. I loved her, but she was trapped in the New York society life. Some things I don't think she really understood. I'm not sure she ever really understood my desire to leave her type of life and live a totally different one, completely alien to her."

"Tori, we have had many rambling conversations over the past couple years. I think I know you like a book." Bernice looked a little puzzled.

"I know, but I am thinking of a sort of summary. Kind of like gluing the pieces of a jigsaw puzzle together rather than taking it apart."

Just then they heard an elk bugle and whistle from somewhere close by. They looked around. Belle perked up and cocked her ears. Nothing was to be seen. Tori thought back to the first time she heard an elk bugle. She and Al were hiking near timberline in the San Juan's. There had been a light dusting of snow the night before and they wanted to have one last expedition that year before the hunters took over the hills. As they sat by a copse of stunted bristlecone pine, a huge elk came trotting over the ridge. They then saw about two dozen cow elk coming up the meadow towards them. She and Al didn't move for several minutes, letting the scene become forever etched in her mind. Al wrote an essay and she composed her *Autumn Symphony* based on the scene.

Those were the moments she wanted to make sure Bernice felt as well as saw and heard. "This is what I want you to glue together. The pieces that are colored the blue of the sky, the fading yellow of aspen, the deep green of the spruce, the white puffs of cloud. And the shapes of deer and pika in meadows and rockfalls, eagles in the sky, the sounds of aspen leaves fluttering in the wind and the haunting call of the elk. Ready to pass on life as it has been passed on for thousands of years. Life changes but life stays the same."

"Tori, sometimes I think your previous life was as a Ute or Shoshone or Arapaho sitting on this spot hundreds of years ago. An autumn sky, clear with no jet contrails, snow on the way, stocking up on elk meat and berries for a long winter. Hurrying to head down to the lower country before snowfall. I suppose you have written a song about such a scene already?"

"No, but you know my song writing days are over. Some things do fade away and end. Actually a lot of things do. Well, all things do eventually. That's why I want to make sure they don't end with me, but are transferred to you and others."

"I have a feeling you have taken care of all that. I've seen the covenants and rules for the Institute Trust. You have locked in a lot of things, and I have talked to some of the Board members and they are clones of you. And your music will outlive me and my grandchildren, if I ever have any. What is left?"

"The simple things, Bernice, the simple things that we take for granted. The things so simple and small, we tend to miss them, ignore them, forget them."

"You are starting to get pretty esoteric," Bernice said as she petted Belle, resettled at her feet. "I've heard the speech so many times, I could give it myself." She smiled that enticing way she did, crinkling her eyes, scrunching her nose into what Tori called the elf look.

"You are going to spoil this for me, you know. You think you can give it, huh? And what do you use to back up all that accumulated wisdom? All right. I want you to define the word wisdom for me." Tori looked at Bernice with the penetrating look that she perfected for Rachel and Jake. It drove Al crazy. He kept saying she was looking directly into his soul and he felt naked, and not naked in a pleasant way with her watching.

"Is this the Tori version of wisdom or my own?" Bernice's smile had turned into a serious frown.

"Oh no you don't. I asked for your version. You can't use mine. That is part of wisdom. You put together all your experiences, all your understanding of consequences into your own words. Wisdom is totally yours, maybe based on the work of others, but purified into your own thoughts. Otherwise it is not wisdom, but just part of your education, your gleaning of knowledge of others. You can read Kant or Aristotle and repeat their wisdom, but it won't mean anything." Tori waited, looking into Bernice's eyes, which were unable to hold the stare. Bernice looked down at Belle, then up at the sky. Tori never eased her look, struggling not to burst out laughing. She had practiced this too many times to blow it by making light of it.

Bernice tried to smile again, but it quickly fell off her face as she felt Tori's emotion. "I apologize. Yes, Tori, I would love to hear your thoughts. You know I respect you more than anyone. I feel like I know you very well, but I look forward to getting a summary. I am all ears. I know I don't have a good definition of wisdom."

"Have you ever heard my version of *It's a Wonderful World?*"

"What? Boy was that a sharp right turn." She hesitated as she thought about the question. "I don't know if I have heard them all, but I do have the performance live at Red Rocks."

"I would say they are all the same, but each one is different in some way. That night was special at Red Rocks. It was not long after Jake and Rachel left us. I did that arrangement for them. The song itself is special. So many people have recorded it. I think I first heard it by Louis Armstrong. But the version that means so much to me is by Iz, the Hawaiian. The song itself is so optimistic, but knowledge of his background adds something to it. Iz's story got to me. He died from his obesity and left a wife and children. But his being true Hawaiian and their history, well, that made it special. How a person from a culture that has been all but destroyed can be so hopeful...I wanted to put my story into that song. The words were the same, the tune basically the same. But it was my own."

Bernice continued stroking Belle. "It is one of my favorite songs. The first time I saw the video of that concert, I cried when you did that song. Your introduction set the stage. We all felt your passion. It still brings a lump to my throat."

Tori smiled. That was the reaction she wanted, from

everyone who heard the song. After she first sang her version, on the porch at Ravens Nest, she bawled like a baby. She had dedicated it to her adopted parents. As he often did, Al wrote an essay on the song and its history. Tori's introduction to the song at Red Rocks included a long quote from that essay.

"I mention that song because it was an early attempt to capture what I thought was my wisdom into a song. I look back now and know that I was premature. Wisdom takes time. It usually requires grey or even white hair to mature. You may have knowledge and great perception. But you my wonderful friend are too young to have your own wisdom." Tori chuckled. "But you can understand the wisdom of others."

Tori thought back to the countless conversations she had with Jake. Rachel lived and practiced her philosophy, but Jake loved to talk about it, to challenge the young Tori. They usually sat under an ancient juniper, or along a stream at Ravens Nest, but one instance they were sitting on a ridgetop ledge maybe near here, she couldn't remember exactly. She always learned something from those conversations and felt she knew Jake like a book. But he always surprised her. His wisdom brought together so many disparate webs of knowledge. It did challenge her to connect the dots. Now, she wanted to do the same.

"It is all about people. As much as I love to be out in nature, to understand the great web of life, to sit in places like this and think about what all this means," she slowly moved her hands from horizon to horizon, "it is always pulled back to us. You and I and all the others. We all have to realize this belongs to us and we belong to it."

"Even though most people don't appreciate it," mumbled Bernice. "That is like Iz being so positive when he and his people got screwed."

"Precisely!" exploded Tori. "Yes. The human race is screwing this planet and it will in turn crush us like a bug. But we don't give up! Caring for life is what our core value is about. Or should be. And life includes people, no matter how blind and stupid they may be."

"I guess I have known that your music is both mournful and positive at the same time. That makes it so special to me. I have never figured out how it can be both. But, yes, you have captured that feeling: Bless us, god, as humanity destroys everything you have given us."

Tori reached over and grabbed Bernice's hand. She held it with both hers and gently squeezed. "Yes. You know why? It is the only world we have. And there are some of us who appreciate this very special gift called life. And while we watch as our society collectively has failed, we still hold hope and we do all we can to make it special. Even as it may be slipping away. There is something bigger than us. That is the final message. So we have to hold out hope and be positive. What we see and are part of is only the tip of the iceberg."

Bernice knew when Tori's passion took control of her. She had heard many of what she called sermons from Tori, when it was like some otherworldly spirit took over the body and voice. She could almost see a glow surrounding Tori.

"We need to know the world around us, be open to new ideas, realize our beliefs and opinions should constantly be challenged. But besides knowing what is out there, we need to know who we are and what really is important. We get so inundated with information, we get lost in the confusion. Let the chaff be blown away in the wind, recognize and save the seeds. That isn't easy. And never, never lose sight of this marvel called life, and the fact we aren't on top of the pyramid. We are one in a crowd. Not enough people realize the importance of butterflies and ravens and aspen trees lining a meadow as they burst open with spring green."

She thought back to how she really started learning when she moved out here. She was an adult, with a career, with strong ideas of her own. She had a college degree, had traveled in Europe, mingled with her parents' New York City high society crowd, and thought she was pretty important. Yet, she knew something was missing. When she met Jake and Rachel, they treated her as no one special, like she assumed she was. Jake especially challenged her many opinions and taught her about the natural world, of which she had been completely ignorant. He made her think, which she soon realized no one else, including many college professors, had done before.

Tori continued, "Great sages throughout history have talked about the same thing. Know thyself. How many people have phrased that thought in various ways? Socrates: "an unexamined life is not worth living." Plotinus, or was it Plutarch?: "never cease chiseling your statue." Marcus Aurelius; the Buddha; the Tao te Ching: "he who knows himself is enlightened." Paracelsus: "each man has the essence of god."

Bernice gave Tori a quizzical look. "You have all these things memorized? I've barely heard of some of these. And you can quote them?"

"Part of wisdom, my dear. You glean what has meaning. You piece the puzzle parts together. You read, absorb, discard what has no meaning. Always be open to ideas and opinions. Every opinion stated by others will either be accepted, rejected, or used to modify your own beliefs. But nothing is totally worthless, even if you reject it. The very act of rejection forces you to re-evaluate your own beliefs. Very few thoughts are original. There has been someone somewhere sometime who has thought every single thought you ever have. That's okay. But you and I have an advantage.

We can compile all these thoughts together and weave a tapestry with it."

"Or a song," interrupted Bernice.

"Sure. We think we have original thoughts. And they may be original to us. But we came too late to come up with a brand new thought to place in the world's bin of knowledge. That is no reason to stop thinking, though. It is fun to sort through writings and discover that someone else was thinking just like you. My expertise may have been music, with melodies, harmonies and words, but just like literature, it is putting together previous thoughts. The only problem with my expertise is we rarely have the music itself preserved. I would love to listen to the flute music played by the Ute ancestor ten thousand years ago. Or the harp played by Greeks and Persians. We always overlook the Chinese. I bet they rocked."

"Are we getting distracted? Wisdom, Tori, wisdom. You were saying,"

"No, there is no such thing as distraction. We just take paths that weave back and forth. They all come back to the same trail." She chuckled. "Sometimes the trails do get tangled."

"So wisdom is knowing who you are?" Bernice never got bored with Tori, but sometimes she had to refocus, both herself and Tori. Bernice never met Jake, but from what Tori had described previously, Bernice felt she was seeing Jake's influence rambling in a hundred different directions.

"Yes. We don't come into this life knowing what we want. Oh as a child we may have dreams and fantasies. But with education, learning, knowledge, we grow, our dreams change. That is why a young person can't possibly know what they really want, who they really are. And shouldn't be worried about it when they don't yet know what path to take. You know the old saying about if you aren't learning, you aren't growing and if you aren't growing, you are dying. You are always seeking, discovering, learning. I thought I knew I wanted to play music. I knew that from high school. But I constantly changed, shifted, put new meaning into music. Yet, I felt in my soul that I was not satisfied. Both Al and I were missing something in life. That is why we made such a huge shift. We found ourselves as the old saying goes. We were on the right path, although we still didn't have it all together, even after we met Jake and Rachel. We kept seeking. Only now can I look at myself in the mirror and feel totally comfortable with myself. I know who I am, what I want, what I am still looking for, what I want my legacy to be. That is wisdom. That time when knowledge turns into insight and understanding. I know we are such a small part of what is out there, but we all do fit in like pieces of a very large puzzle."

"Do we spend our entire life spinning in circles, always looking?"

"Some people certainly do. Unfortunately, too many people don't even look. They just let life happen. What a waste. Some people let their god make decisions for them. Some people are afraid to think, to be alone, to even ask the tough questions. Most people are simply afraid. But do we spin in circles? Of course. You know my belief in circles and cycles. All life is a huge circle. "

Belle stood and stretched, circled counter-clockwise and laid back down by Bernice's feet. "You said people are afraid. Afraid of life, of living?"

"Yes, afraid of examining that life, thinking about what is out there."

"But life was so much simpler for Socrates. His life was easier to examine, without all the complicating technology."

"Yes!" Tori exclaimed as her eyes widened. "What was in his head was probably more pure in terms of meaning, purpose, consequences. It wasn't jumbled with all the extraneous irrelevant garbage that we put up with nowadays. All that just complicates what I am getting at. Life itself. Our place in it. Our relationships with earth, animals, nature. And the entire cosmos. And how everything cycles in and out, up and down. Don't let quantum physics, the Big Bang, eternity get in the way. Those are details. How do you fit in? Is there a god, some powerful force we cannot even imagine? What comes next, if anything? You see, I am close enough now to feel that pull. I look forward to opening that next door and looking into the void. It doesn't worry me at all. I see a song out there calling me."

"Wisdom comes in old age and is the questioning of death?" Bernice was starting to get confused with where Tori was going.

"I wouldn't look at it quite that way, but sure. Wisdom is the key to understanding eternity."

"Boy, Tori, you are getting too weird for me. Maybe you are comfortable with this, but it is getting pretty woo-woo for me."

"But I want you to think about it. I know you are too young to understand it all, and you probably shouldn't yet. You are still searching and learning. Someday, when your hair is white, I want you to remember this conversation. I will be long gone, but I want you to carry on what we have put together as our way of saving our knowledge, putting meaning to it."

"But will it matter 500 years from now?"

"How long ago did the Buddha live? Socrates? They made a difference."

"I don't exactly put myself in the same category."

"Why not? No one knows at this point. Just maybe, you might be the person who really does come up with an original thought!" Tori laughed as she picked up a small pebble. "This was once part of a huge solid mountain. Look at it now. Wait a while and it will be nothing but a grain of sand on its way to the ocean."

"Yes, you are contradicting yourself. It is meaningless. It was once solid, then it just disappears into nothingness."

"I wasn't finished. It will become part of solid rock again and rise up into another mountain. Circles, cycles, we repeat until everything blows up as the sun explodes, then we continue on."

"Okay, that's it. You are starting to freak me out."

"Sorry, Jake did that to me. I guess it took hold. Back to words of wisdom. Be yourself, be honest, truthful, respectful, curious, creative. Give yourself time alone to think, but center your life around your goals, how you relate to others. You are a goddess, part of a collective super intelligence. Put yourself first, but do it in a way that helps others. There, are those enough words to live by?"

"Thank you. And thank god I wasn't looking to you for the birds and bees lecture. I can't even imagine where that would have ended up."

Tori smiled, "Some things we just know. No one taught us how to breathe. I would have added common sense to my list, but I don't think there is a good definition of that one."

"That might be a good place to end, but you lost me somewhere. You started out by saying we need to be part of a community. It is all about people. Then you veered off by saying we need to know who we are and what we want. Then you digress into circles and cycles and the eternity of the entire cosmos. You haven't tied it all together. I know I would rather sit up here in the rocks and trees, and I get the feeling you prefer it too. That way you have the solitude to contemplate your navel and what it wants to be when it grows up, but yet we need to be with people. That doesn't compute."

"Okay, it does seem a little disjointed. I probably jumped too far too fast. Maybe age speeds things up. I know the seasons and years seem to be racing by for me. What is left of my mind may have been on super fast-forward."

Belle jumped up and started barking. Bernice quickly grabbed her, then looked in the direction Belle was straining. She stood up as she saw a man walking over the hill towards them. She expected to see a hunter with a rifle and dressed in blaze orange. Instead, she saw a middle-aged man, carrying a walking stick, dressed in camouflage, with long hair, a long beard, and walking erratically.

"I don't like the looks of this," she said as Tori slowly stood up and watched the man.

"Here is a leash for Belle," Tori said as she opened her pack, pulled out a rope, and handed it to Bernice. Bernice clipped it to Belle's collar, but was more interested that Tori pulled out a small object and wrapped her hand around it, hiding it from view.

Tori called to the man. "Hi, fine afternoon isn't it? Are you hunting? We didn't see your vehicle anywhere near here."

The man stumbled as he stopped. He didn't seem to notice them even though he was walking directly towards them. Belle was still barking and pulling on the rope that Bernice was holding onto.

"That dog dangerous? He is scaring me. I don't like dogs." His speech was hard to understand, not with any accent, but slurred and not clear. He held the staff in front of him as if ready to fend off an attacking dog.

"We have her on a leash. She is just barking to warn us

of a stranger. Can we help you?" Tori opened her hand just enough to adjust what she was holding, then closed it again. She said softly to Bernice, "Just stand still and don't let Belle loose. No need to worry."

"Who are you?" the man stammered. He rubbed his nose as he looked around, as if looking for someone else.

"We are enjoying this nice day, but we were getting ready to leave. What are you doing here?"

The man started to come closer, but Tori put up her left hand and said, "That's close enough."

"Where is Benjamin?" The man kept looking around.

"We saw Benjamin back behind you a few minutes ago. He was walking uphill towards that ridge," Tori said as she pointed to the east. They had seen no one, but figured she had better distract this man. "He asked us to tell you to follow him."

The man looked where Tori had pointed. He then looked back at Bernice who had made Belle sit, although still growling.

"You gonna sick that dog on me as I leave aren't you? Maybe I ought to teach that dog not to bark." He started to step closer. So quickly that Bernice hardly saw what happened, Tori stepped towards the man, raised her hand and pointed it in his face. She quickly pushed the spray nozzle and the man leaped back, screaming as he dropped the stick and put his hands to his face. Tori had pepper sprayed him in his eyes.

"Let's get the hell out of here right now." She reached for Bernice and pulled her away from the man, now rolling on the ground screaming and rubbing his face.

"What did you do, Tori?" laughed Bernice as she grabbed her pack, pulled Belle and followed Tori as they ran around the man and trotted past him. They then slowed to a fast walk towards their vehicle, parked about two hundred yards away.

When they got in the truck, they looked back and saw he was still laying on the ground yelling.

"One little fact dealing with wisdom," Tori said as she drove down the rocky road, "when confronted with a potentially life threatening situation, throw caution to the wind and do what you have to do to protect yourself. Act immediately and worry about the consequences later. Now you can use your satellite phone to call 911 and tell the sheriff that a drug-crazed man accosted two women up here and he was pepper sprayed and probably dangerous. And that seems to be without a vehicle and could be in danger himself."

Bernice started laughing as she stared at Tori. "My god, Tori, you surprised the hell out of me. Was he really a threat? Maybe he was just lost."

"Lost my ass. Well, yes he was lost. His mind was somewhere not on this planet. Think about it. Two females alone miles from nowhere, one of them an old lady and this obviously drugged out or drunk man appears out of nowhere, incoherent and not making any sense. Do you think I acted reasonably?"

Bernice kept laughing as she asked what Tori had sprayed in his face. Tori reached into her jacket pocket and lifted out the little spray bottle. She handed it to Bernice. "Be very careful with that, young lady. Good for anything from grizzly bears to rabid wolves to dope heads. No permanent damage but you saw for yourself what effects it has." Finally Tori laughed as she looked at Bernice's face.

"I guess I was scared, but I didn't think about it at the time. You didn't give him much chance did you?" She carefully handed the bottle back to Tori, who just as carefully put it in her pocket.

"I think we will both start shaking in about three minutes. I will get a couple miles down the road, then I think we all three may need to take a potty break."

"Good lord, Tori, how did you keep from peeing your pants," Bernice laughed as she looked in the back seat at Belle, fast asleep. "You did good Belle, but I noticed you did pee before you got in the truck."

"How do you know I didn't already?" Tori looked down in her lap, then looked at Bernice, now laughing so hard, tears were coming down her cheeks. "By the way, make sure the doors are locked."

"Wisdom, my ass, girl. That was pure fear, plain and simple. And tell me where I can buy one of those."

Five minutes later, Tori pulled the truck over as they hit the main road. A hunter camp was set up by the creek, with a hunter tying his horse to a picket line. He waved at them as they drove up. They explained what had just happened. The hunter called his partner over and smiled as he said, "Bob, these ladies just had a run in with the crazy. She pepper sprayed him."

"Great," Bob said as he petted the horse. "We ran into him yesterday way up in the middle of nowhere. I had to point my gun at him, something I have never ever done to anyone. He scared the bejesus out of me. I don't know what he was on, but he was just plain crazy. Did he attack you?"

Bernice said, "No, but we weren't about to take any chances. I think he was ready to go for the dog since she was barking like crazy."

"You got one smart dog. She knew this guy was a danger. And I think he was. I called the sheriff this morning and they said they were looking for him, but couldn't send someone up here until later today. Have you called them?"

"Yeah, we gave them the exact directions, although who knows where the guy will be now."

"You pepper sprayed him in the face? Well he is probably laying in the nearest creek trying to drown himself."

Everyone burst out laughing, even Belle, although her laugh sounded more like a bark.

A few minutes later, the sheriff called back to confirm directions and let them know a patrol car was on the way. The man was an escapee from some institution and was considered dangerous. The State Patrol was on the way, too, as well as a search and rescue group.

When Tori and Bernice got back to Ravens Nest, Tori said, "Let's go into town for a nice Mexican dinner. Don't you think we deserve it?"

"Yes, and I don't know if we ever finished our wisdom discussion. I still have a lot of questions."

"Well, to tell you the truth, I did have one more thing to give you." Tori pulled a couple small notebooks out of her pack. "I wanted to tell you about these. Didn't get a chance up on the mountain."

"Things sort of got a little crazy up there didn't they," Bernice laughed.

"I'm starting to realize more and more how Jake felt towards the end. The world was getting too crazy for him and he felt he had passed his time and didn't belong anymore. There are times I am starting to feel that way myself. This afternoon helped that feeling."

Bernice looked at Tori with a frown. She opened her mouth to speak, but Tori put up her hand to stop any words from coming out.

"No, let me go on."

She opened one of her small notebooks and handed the other to Bernice. "I started scribbling in these decades ago. To be honest, I kept a diary in high school, was more consistent with the scribbling in college, but let it slide when I was in Europe in the early 90's. Back in New York, I started carrying these and would jot down ideas related to my music. That's when I really got serious about music as a career. Up until then, I knew music in general was my calling, but didn't know how it fit in. Like most young people, I couldn't fit the pieces together.

"I was becoming more unhappy. I led a life of privilege, but felt something was missing. I met Al, fell in love, and settled in to something that just didn't feel complete. I had it all, but I didn't have what counted. Even my journal scribbling was forced, not meaningful."

Tori thumbed through the notebook, then went back to the front pages. "Let me read you this:

"I heard thunder reverberate through the mountains for the first time. That was the voice of God I heard. Those were the first real commanding words I ever heard. They called my name. They said, 'Tori, live. Listen. I am talking to you.'" She turned a couple pages, then continued, "the reds and oranges overwhelm my world and my words. The wind. The wind. It whistles and caresses, dives and swirls. Can the wind sing a song? Oh yes. It is a hymn. I can see the wind. It is dancing. It passes the cliffs and paints the reds even brighter. Like cleaning the Sistine Chapel. It washes away the grime and makes the colors fluoresce."

Bernice stared at Tori, feeling that this person she loved was glowing, her white hair as luminescent as her words.

"I came alive when I first visited Colorado and Utah. Jake and Rachel were these strange people who lived on the land and who were part of the land. They belonged. I didn't belong in the city. I knew the first week that I was destined to be here. And the rest, as they say, is history."

Bernice looked through the notebook Tori had given her.

"So these are your thoughts and dreams."

"Oh more than that. I am giving all these journals to you. There are several dozen more. They are my life, my music, my career, my philosophy. Jake never asked about them until his last few days. My writing wasn't secret, but no one asked me what I was writing. A lot of people write diaries or journals, so I thought it wasn't a big deal.

"Some of it became my songs. Al did the same thing with all his books and articles. These were thoughts, words, phrases, tidbits. Here, let me give you a sample. 'Bruce with his curly locks was majestic. His drumbeat across the field was music of epic proportions. His eyes penetrated, his voice carried power and sang the hope of his kind.' That became the basis for my song *Bruce*. Critics and reviewers said my song was about my hero Springsteen. That cracked me up. The song is about Bruce the old bull bison on the ranch. Bruce was king of the herd. No one dared come close to him. But I could. I could walk up to him and stroke his nose. He would threaten to charge anyone else who even looked close at him. I could talk to him. When I wrote it, I was telling the story of Bruce and his kind, almost killed to extinction, but come back, standing in the wings, waiting their time. But somewhere along the line, I did think about Bruce the musician and I put in a couple ambiguous references that could be interpreted about what Bruce was singing about. So people thought the song was really about the musician, but was truly about the bison." Tori smiled that impish smile of hers and took a drink of water.

"But isn't this private? Your inner thoughts? I shouldn't see this."

"I am way past caring about that. I am trying to bare my soul to you, to share my most private inner thoughts. Nothing to hide. Not even my thoughts about Al in those early days when he was having an affair."

Bernice gasped and put her hands to her mouth. "Your husband had an affair? And you didn't leave him?"

Tori put down the notebook she held and took the one Bernice had. "Let's see, these are in order, so somewhere around here," she stopped and quickly thumbed through the book. "Okay, try this on for blind love. Or stupidity. Take your pick." She started reading. "Al left again for France. He is so naïve. He really thinks I am buying that crap about book research. He is screwing his bimbo. Or she him. He comes back. I can't. I won't give him the bed pleasure he thinks he needs, so he goes 5000 miles to get it. He will get my companionship. He is worth that. As long as he comes back. He is a little boy who thinks he has grown up."

Tori stopped, then flipped a few more pages. "Believe it or not, I wrote a song about the affair. He never guessed. I called it a *Taste of Tea*. The tea stood for testosterone: They say tea is a welcome afternoon treat. Tea can satisfy but tea can addict as well. Tea in the afternoon can keep you awake, sate your desire. But tea can be poison if taken undiluted. Tea for you, tea for thee, never never tea for three."

"I never heard that one." Bernice frowned. "How could you put up with that? Tori, I am shocked."

"I had trouble at first. The song was one of my very early ones. Didn't go over well. No one really understood what it meant. In the city, I was wrapped up in my teaching and trying to get into the business. Once we came out here, I think I realized there was a lot more to life than a roll in the hay. After all, Al did know her before he met me. He just couldn't decide. I was prepared to leave him once we moved, but he figured it out. He finally grew up, just as I did, only in a different way. One thing Jake never realized, he helped me understand what genuine love and devotion was. What belonging was. I belong to the land. The land loves me and I love the land. Now that is an affair. Jake gave the fatherly advice I never got from my own father, yet he never even knew it."

"Tori, your handwriting is very hard to read. Strange because I have seen you write other things and you have beautiful penmanship. Artistic."

"I guess you inherit a puzzle then. Yours to have and to read if you can. You will get the hang of it once you read a few. I will read some to you if you need help with translation."

"I don't feel I deserve this. Tori, you are giving me so much." Bernice wiped her eyes as they blurred with tears.

"Life is taking and life is giving. My song *Dao* sums it up. Nothing new there. You don't enjoy the warmth of a fire in the evening unless you just came in from the cold. You don't taste the goodness of your food until you've gone hungry. Plain old yin and yang. I was given a lot, now I give the same to someone else. You take now, you will give later. In the song I called it..."

"Humble pie," blurted out Bernice. She laughed as she leaned over and hugged Tori. They both held each other tightly, neither wanting to let go.

"I've bared my soul today and I hope I haven't confused you too much. After a couple Tecates and a big plate of chili rellenos, I think I can clarify a lot of things. I believe I got a little off track this afternoon and didn't quite get across what I intended."

"No, Tori, I think I fully understand. It all boils down to one thing. Pick a fantastic, street smart, intelligent mentor, latch onto them like glue, learn, observe, and stand back. Life becomes meaningful about that time."

"And once in a while, let your hair down and don't take things too seriously. Life is too short as it is." Tori brushed back her hair and started humming a tune. "I think I have come up with a new song."

CHAPTER SEVEN

LAST SONG

On a sunny day in a mountain meadow
Flowers coloring the world below
Sunset clouds from above.
Tori Reynolds

TORI SAT ALONE in the lodge great room. Although most other people called it that, she thought it sounded too pretentious. She always referred to it as Bruce's room, in honor of the bison bull she befriended years ago. Tori shared the large building with Bernice and several of her young interns, but this afternoon she wanted to be by herself, so had sent them to the Reservation to meet with the Elders, who were now mostly in charge of Raven Ridge Institute.

She thought back to the night years ago when she sat with Jake in this room, when he passed to her his place and his role. Now she was the elder, the ancient and wise one, and she, too, like Jake and Bruce the old bison bull, knew her time was over. The past three weeks her swan song had immersed her completely. It literally was her last song and she wanted it to summarize her entire life. No small chore she thought, as she stared into the hypnotic flames in the fireplace. She frowned as she ran through the words again.

125

The music was easy. She had nailed that a week ago, but she still was not happy with the words.

Tori had pure white hair and the wrinkles of her weathered face showed the time she had spent outside over the years. Battles with melanoma on her face and wrists had left a few scars, but she was content with herself now. Her songs lately, and there were only a few the past several years, reflected her introspection, her philosophy. After she lost Al to multiple melanoma, and after she had settled on her own replacement in Bernice, her role had all but disappeared in management of Ravens Nest and Raven Ridge Institute. This was the way Jake had done it and now it was the way she wanted things to happen. She completely trusted Bernice, almost at middle age, and fully in control of Ravens Nest and Raven Ridge. And even though management was mostly from the Elders, they too, trusted Bernice in day-to-day operations. Tori wanted to quietly fade out.

She sat down at the grand piano that still graced the corner of the great room, her cello on its stand nearby. She played the five-minute song without singing the lyrics. She was satisfied. It had the soulful, reflective, yet optimistic feel that she wanted. When she added lyrics, if she could ever be satisfied with them, it would enhance the hopeful edge. This would be her legacy, not the fifteen albums and countless awards that graced the balcony walls upstairs. Tori had always shunned the fame and publicity her music gave her and her humility had increased the past few years. She never bragged. She still felt Al's presence when it came to that. He had won many awards, including a Pulitzer, and he had set the example for dismissing the need of celebrity.

Returning to sit in front of the fire, she thought more about her song. She wanted one song, one set of lyrics, one melody, to sum up her life. As she ran her hands through her hair, she sensed a vision. She could see, then hear, her father, Jake, and

Al, all laughing at her. They seemed to say, "Tori, one song? You think you can put all your thoughts, ideas, dreams, into one song? Come on girl, you don't need that final song for your legacy. You can sing your goodbye, but that song won't be your legacy. You've left your legacy already."

Her father understood why she left New York and shunned the family business. He could have set her up in his financial world on Wall Street, but he knew she danced to a different rhythm. He was proud of her and she knew that.

Jake transformed her and made her comfortable and owner of her new life and new world. He saw her as his legacy. She still yearned for the wisdom he had. He would tell her she had more wisdom than him.

And then there was Al. Her life partner who knew every thought she ever had. Even though he strayed early on, he came to his senses and she forgave him completely. He was devoted to her and they were perfect complements for each other.

She wished she could talk to any of them right now. Her eyes glistened with sorrow knowing she was alone, but would be joining all them soon. Very soon. That thought brought a smile.

But the last song—to sum it all up in one grand piece of music? Her lyrics, her melodies usually came so easy, and most had deep layers of meanings. But how could several lines of words pull all those years, all her thoughts into focus?

She liked the opening line which also was her tentative title "Don't Say Goodbye"

Don't say goodbye,
We will meet again
You went ahead and I stayed behind
But now we will live as one.

We will learn to fly
Over the rainbow,
Where circles connect but never end.
Eagles soar in unending waves.
Life is a mystery and a sacred trust.

The blue of a Colorado sky
Meets with the white pillows of clouds.
The thunder echoes forever between the mountains.
And the sun sets in the distant seas.

Don't say goodbye,
We will be one again
As we were before
When the world was young.

Passenger pigeons will fill the skies
From horizons east to west.
Bison herds thunder across the plains
Outnumbering the stars in the heavens.
Salmon will fill the rivers with silver and red.

On a sunny day in a mountain meadow
Flowers coloring the world below
Sunset clouds from above.

Don't say goodbye
We will meet again.
Our hearts are one
In a circle of love.
Don't say goodbye.

She knew the critics would jump on the song and find
fault. They would say Tori missed this last song, she tried

too hard, it didn't resonate like her other works. They would see her as too preachy. She shrugged. She always was much harder on herself than others were. Was she reaching too far? Too personal? May be, but this one was for herself and meant to be very personal. Most people would not get it. That was all right. She wouldn't be around to hear their reviews anyway.

She sat with the cello and caressed it. Closing her eyes, she started to play. She thought back to the first song she wrote for the cello. It was a sad song. It always brought tears to Rachel's eyes. She knew it meant different things to different people.

She wanted her music to touch people, to make them think. And when they did that, her music became their music. Personal, but with different meanings for each listener. That was what art should do. Whether paintings, music, literature—it should stimulate. She and Al had this discussion many times. Al wrote mostly non-fiction, but in his later years, he explored creative writing. He wrote about her music, sometimes writing the lyrics. She wrote music to accompany his work.

A late summer thunderstorm came up on the ridge from the south. Lightning filled the large windows on the south side of the building. Thunder bounced from ridge to ridge, across the valley, over the nearby mountains. It echoed forever. "That is what I want to do," she whispered aloud. "I want to echo forever."

She wanted the moment to last forever. It did, for her.

The next morning, Bernice and her students returned from the Reservation. As they entered the lodge, laughing and joking, they stopped suddenly. Bernice screamed as she ran over to the piano. Tori lay on the floor, cello by her side. Bernice stooped down and gently pulled the hair away from Tori's face. Her eyes were closed but a smile was on her lips.

Bernice saw the notebook on the floor nearby, open to a page full of Tori's scribbling. She recognized the words. It was the song she had been working on, words crossed out, written sideways, underlined. At the bottom of a page only half filled, very clearly, were written the words: Don't Say goodbye.

Bernice sat down on the floor with Tori's head cradled in her lap. Rocking back and forth, her tears dropping silently on the tile floor, she gently kissed Tori's weathered forehead and whispered, "This is not goodbye. Just a kiss until we meet again." And Bernice always considered that day as the day she started her own life.

PART II
JAKE'S STORIES

A Season in Paradise

We have to celebrate the good here tonight.
We have met wonderful people and shared a
once-in-a-lifetime experience. No matter what
happens from now on, no one can take
that away from us. We are the future and
that future is so full of hope.
Paradise Lodge employee

THE FIRST TIME I walked into the old lodge at Paradise was to get out of the fog and rain on a Sunday afternoon in July, 1968. As I looked around the cavernous main lobby, my eyes wandered up to the ceiling high above. It towered over massive log pillars and log walls. I eased into an overstuffed leather chair, absorbing the years that these chairs sat here in warm comfort. That was my first summer working in Mt. Rainier National Park. I met Karen, worked at the greatest summer job on earth, and came into my own for the first time in my life. I knew my life was ready to change.

I slumped into that same old chair on a late summer evening a year later. I still marveled at this place, one of the landmark inns in the National Park system: a magnificent log building built in the era of the Civilian Conservation Corps or even earlier, reeking of a time long past, when luxury came in the form of grand log hotels built in the awe-inspiring shadows of our national jewels. In this case, it stands in the shadow of Mt. Rainier, the dormant, glacier-

and rainforest-covered volcano always present, looming above like a sleeping dragon. I knew it well. I was working my second summer on the trail crew at Ohanapecosh, the ranger station far below, along the river of the same name, on the southeast flank of the mountain.

It was August 25, Christmas for the many seasonal employees who would soon be leaving the mountain to return to their lives around the country. During the real Christmas, this lodge is buried under dozens of feet of snow, only the peaks of the highest roofs protruding like ships on a frozen sea. Celebrating Christmas when all the summer employees were still here was the tradition, because working at this Park was a one season job. The deep snow doesn't allow entry to the masses of tourists until mid-June, and snowfall drives them out soon after Labor Day. Since most of the workers were college students, we were gone by then, too, and I fell into that category.

Only I wasn't going back to school. I had graduated from the University of Montana in May and was awaiting a decision on my fate. With my degree, I lost my college deferment and it was now a race between the Army and the Peace Corps to see who would assume control of my body. I hadn't even bothered to look for a permanent job after graduation.

The meaning of this Christmas celebration meant something special for me as it did for many that evening. I had fallen in love with that same Karen I met the year before and spent the summer with her on the mountain. She worked in one of the souvenir shops at Paradise. My summer was as high as the clouds capping the mountain this late August eve. Like many of my co-workers, I lived for the moment and ignored the choices of fate that awaited me. It was truly a summer in paradise, but it was ending. Saying it was a magic summer was another trite cliché, but it applied.

Most of the employees putting on this celebration were the college students who worked at the lodges, gift shops, and restaurants, either in Paradise or nearby Longmire. It was a tight knit group, whose culture differed from mine. I worked for the Park Service. I was one of the elite, even though I was only a seasonal. I came from down below, jargon for anywhere down in the rain forests of the low elevations. Although I didn't wear the uniform with the arrowhead badge, I must have exuded the air of a government employee. My girlfriend worked up here, however, so I was one of those outsiders who was accepted.

I sat deeply embedded in the leather chair, with Karen in my lap. Real Christmas trees were set up, fully decorated with tinsel, popcorn strands, and shiny, colored balls. The large lobby, surrounded with a log-railed balcony, was festooned with wreaths, crepe paper and other Christmas decorations. The massive log pillars of the main room were draped with fir boughs. The managers of the lodge had gone all out to treat us to this celebration. The few tourists still staying here smiled and pointed a lot as they gathered for the announced celebration. Mostly, it was the seasonal employees who gathered around to say goodbye.

Karen and I splurged for an expensive dinner in the dining room. She was leaving in three days for her home in California where she would start her third year of college. I would head back a couple days after that to my home in Iowa to await my fate. My future was not in my control and that was the mood for many of the guys here. After supper, we went up to Charlie's room in the attic. Charlie went to Harvard and he was here with his fiancée, who attended Bryn Mawr. They both worked in the lodge itself, so were able to have drinks delivered to his room. Singapore Slings, if I remember. We sat in Charlie's cramped little room and laughed a lot and toasted the good times. Then we all drifted downstairs. The mood was a strange combination, somber as well as cheerful. A summer in a make-believe world was ending and lives would scatter across continents. Too many lives would go to Viet Nam. The guys knew this and their girls felt it as deeply. We all wanted to hang onto the summer and this night forever. So we forgot about the danger lurking in the outside world and drank and laughed for the moment.

The overhead lights went out and the Christmas lights on trees and along the balcony railings blinked on. The magic started. We sang Christmas carols and raised our glasses to our friends. The guests at the lodge thought it pleasantly amusing and sang along. But they had no idea of the deeper meaning.

One by one, the waiters and maids, busboys and dishwashers took the microphone and said their goodbyes. Some related humorous stories, some broke down crying. The mood changed. No guest could understand what was happening. We were a large family and we were being torn apart, never to come together again. Some would return to school, some would wander on to other temporary jobs. Many summer romances turned into lifetime loves. Some ended that week in tears and realities of life. Nothing in the summer of 1969 was permanent. The times were too turbulent for twenty and twenty-two year olds. The hope of those days was overshadowed by the uncertainty. The guys were lined up like unsuspecting sheep, although they did suspect. I knew two who were headed for Canada the next week.

Randy, a supervisor in the dining room, announced that two days earlier he received his notice of induction into the Army. Amy, his girlfriend cried as she stood by, holding his arm tightly. Other friends in the audience cried out loud, not knowing this news beforehand. He bit his lip as he tried to continue.

"I look out here and see many innocent faces. We cannot

look into the face of Steve Jones since he left three weeks ago. He joined the Marines rather than go in the Army. Bobby Bates left us back in July. He is in boot camp now. Ben wrote me last week from Canada. He loves it there. Some of you here last year knew Ron Dennison. He worked in the bar. We received word from Janey who worked in the Visitor Center gift shop last year that Ron was killed at Kai Son in May. Ron was the master of ceremonies for our Christmas show last year." Randy stopped as he choked up. A cry of surprise tinged with anger ran through the audience. Amy hugged him tighter and squeezed his hand.

"This night means so much to us. We are caught up in times beyond our control. Paradise is a magical place and you are all magical people. I love you all and will probably never see most of you ever again." Tears were running down his face, but he managed to continue with choking voice.

"We have to celebrate the good here tonight. We have met wonderful people and shared a once-in-a-lifetime experience. No matter what happens from now on, no one can take that away from us. We are the future and that future is so full of hope." He stopped and turned his back to us. We could see him shaking and holding his handkerchief to his face. Amy tightened her arms around him.

Karen held my hand tighter. She knew my fate was up in the air as well as many other guys in the room. There were sounds of crying as well as a shout of "come to Canada with me, Randy." That brought on applause and other shouts of "don't go." I cringed when I heard one "fuck the Army." I was afraid we were losing it.

Randy turned around and simply said, "Thank you and god bless everyone here."

We sang another Christmas song and then Ben went up to the microphone. Ben was the clown of Paradise and I had never heard him utter anything serious. He was always joking, but he was serious when he started speaking.

"I wrote a poem for this occasion and hope I can read it. Randy spoke for me as well. I know a lot of guys will be leaving for the Army and you girls can't do anything more about it than we can. So we think of this big mountain up there." He looked above the dining hall on the north side of the building. "We think of the flower meadows and the trips to Camp Muir. We think of the glaciers and the rivers. We celebrate that tonight. We think of the peace of this place."

He held up a piece of paper, with his girlfriend Jill holding a flashlight on it. She had her arm around him as he struggled to read.

> I look up at the peak
> Capped with cloud.
> And try to speak
> Being humble and proud.
>
> Like friends all together
> We spent a summer of love.
> In all forms of weather
> Always looking above.
>
> It has been there forever
> Like we wish we could all be.
> Too many friendships will we sever
> Like this small Christmas tree.
>
> I leave with a tear
> In my eye so sad.
> I long to soon hear
> This world is not mad.
>
> So goodbye dear friends
> Think kindly of me.

As your life forever wends
On safely and happily.

As happened to so many speakers, he choked up and had
to walk off in Jill's arms. I found it interesting few of the girls
spoke. As I looked around in the dim light, most had been
crying. Billy, the master of ceremonies, dressed in a Santa
suit, again took the microphone and said we should sing one
more carol. He said he wanted to end on a happier note, but
thought it appropriate we sing "Silent Night." I thought it too
somber, but that is how the evening turned. We would party
late into the night, but things go one way versus another for
a reason. This moment was bittersweet for many and it was
the end of youth for some of us. Now we entered the crazy
adult world and left Paradise for memories and dreams.

The lights were turned back on and most of the employees
drifted off to their own parties and celebrations, or wakes. I
sat in the comfortable chair as Karen visited with several of
her co-workers, most of whom she would never see again.
I reflected on the events of the night. Thinking about the
significance of this to me and to many of those my age, I
remembered a sheet of paper in my pocket. I pulled it out
and unfolded it.

I had been thinking and writing earlier that day, sitting
on a rock looking down on the lodge while Karen was still
at work in the souvenir shop. The peace of the rocky crag,
blue skies and light breeze made me think of an event that
happened only a year earlier, on election night in California.
It seemed to bring a lot of things together, oddly though,

by pulling them apart. Our world was in fact being pulled apart and had been for several years. As I struggled to put meaning to things, a word kept coming into my thoughts. Earlier that day, I overheard a tourist at the visitor center say the word when he came out of the building and looked at the sky. He said to his wife, "honey, it is very diaphanous." She looked at him, not sure what he meant. He replied, "the sky is diaphanous, the mountain is diaphanous, the whole world right now is." I went back in the building, found a dictionary, and looked up diaphanous. "Yes," I thought, "he's right. The world right here and now can be called diaphanous by some. If you didn't look beyond that big mountain."

Later, when I hiked up on a crag in the Tatoosh Range by myself, I pulled a writing tablet out of my pack. I always carried one for whenever I wanted to capture certain thoughts or experiences. I started writing a poem, crossed out lines, added new words, wrote sideways on the page. It was hard to read, and it wasn't done. None of my poems were ever done by my standards. I read it to myself sitting in that big overstuffed chair.

The Diaphanous Sky

The first time my sky clouded from its diaphanous
    blue,
I sat in a high school cafeteria in stunned silence.
The principal in trembling voice announced, amid
    static over the intercom,
The President had been killed. More static, then a
    click.

Whispers grew into a disbelieving buzz,
Silence was impossible. We all had to know.
Attention for the rest of that black November day
    was lost,

Beliefs never to return in the same way.

It began an era, more importantly ended another.
The sky changed colors, the clouds became opaque.
Young minds that cared, and many did not,
Saw things in that sky not there before.

The second time the sky changed, it thundered
    behind dark clouds.
The effect more sinister, hatred looming closer to
    the surface.
The black minister was dead, the college professor
    announced.
His voice not just shaky, but choking, eyes wet from
    tears.

The times they were a changing rang the song,
So full of hope, trying in that diaphanous tone to
    enlighten us all.
Confusion colored the sky a muddy brown, the sun
    wavered,
It added one more question to the clouds of doubt.

In quick succession, the third quake struck.
A June day, a night of hope. California spoke and it
    said "Bobby,
Lead us out of the wilderness." But the wilderness
    was black as night.
Bobby lay dead, as did hopes, like cluttered rags in
    a closet.

The sky shimmered blue, the clouds streaked with
    a sunset orange.
The trees still lined the horizon wherever I looked.

I had no mirror, I stood on an isolated mountain
   road.
I looked into the sky. Diaphanous no more. Life had
   smeared it grey.

I thought about the Christmas party and the emotions
it wrenched from many of us there. Maybe that tourist
thought the sky and mountain were diaphanous, clear and
transparent, delicate. Not me. Life was getting very cloudy,
very uncertain, very ugly. But then, this mountain and its
sky might just be an island of clarity still left in this crazy
world. That's why this evening was so special. We were all
safe in this paradise of refuge. The summer was over, our
refuge was over. We were going into that cloudy world out
there. A world that recently killed Martin and Bobby and
was daily sending young lives to be destroyed in a faraway
jungle for no sensible reason. Whites and blacks were rioting
and cities were burning. The songs we listened to were full
of love as well as protest. My heroes were not the heroes
of my parents. There was a disconnect from the peace and
friendship and love in a place like this compared to what
was out there in that other world. That world made no sense
to me and many others of my generation.

Karen came back, wiping her eyes. She looked at me, then
reached down and pulled me out of the chair. "I saw Jason up
on the balcony. I think he is stoned, but he wants to take his
raft down to Lake Katherine. He wants us to go with him."
Jason was another Parkie, working at Ohana with me. He
was on the utilities crew, with the unenviable job of cleaning

toilets in the campgrounds. He was from Longmire so he was considered a local. This was unusual for a seasonal employee in the park. But he hung out with the rest of us and rarely even returned to his home on the other side of the mountain. Jason was a lovable character, always joking, and an accomplished rock climber. He spent most of his weekends climbing on the ice and rock of "his" mountain and spent his evenings playing hearts or pinochle with the rest of us in the Ohana apartments. He knew many of the climbing guides at Paradise, so he belonged here much more than me.

"Do you want to go?" I asked Karen. "What are we going to do on the lake? It's not that big. If Jason is stoned, do you trust him?"

"The worst he can do is fall asleep in the raft. I think he just wants something special. He knows this will probably be the last time he will ever see me and maybe you as well. This is his Friday so he will be climbing on the mountain the next two days. You might be gone before he gets back."

"You really like Jason, don't you?" I asked Karen. I looked up and saw him walking towards us with Melinda, a co-worker of Karen's. I thought back two months earlier when the four of us hiked up onto the glacier above the lodge. The girls were wearing bikinis, for which we made fun of them. They paid for it later with sunburns, but at the time, we slid on the snow and threw snowballs. That was the mood of the summer. Play now, worry about it later.

"Hey man, peace." Jason threw his arms around me, then hugged Karen. He was definitely stoned. I had to laugh as he broke into a big smile. "Cool party. Hey dude, I'm floating. Let's all go float on a groovy lake, black as the night. It's a farewell cruise." He reached into his shirt pocket and pulled out a handful of peanuts and tossed them into his mouth.

"You got the raft?" I asked as he leaned against Melinda.

I thought back to a day in early July when Jason and I took his little yellow raft and floated the Tieton River on the east side of White Pass. The river at that point high on the ridge was no more than a raging stream. But he wanted to show me the thrills of white water rafting. We put the raft in and were immediately swept into the current. We had given no thought to where we would go, or as quickly became apparent, how we would even get out of the water. The water wasn't dangerous, but it was one series of spring melt rapids after another. After about half a mile, we decided the prudent thing to do was to stop our adventure before it got really ugly. We tried to paddle to shore but could find no slack water. I finally grabbed onto some willows along an outside curve in the river and got us out of the main current. We were able to tie the raft onto the shore and get out. Jason hitchhiked back to the truck and drove back to get me. We drove down the road another mile and stopped at a turnoff. And as we opened a couple cans of beer to sit and watch the scenery, we heard a muffled roar. We walked out to a small rock outcrop where we could see the river bending away from us. It went out of sight as it dropped off a thirty foot waterfall. We both looked at each other wide-eyed and silently mouthed one word in unison.

Jason now smiled at me, then reached over to hug Karen again. "Yeah, I got the raft. I want you to go on a cruise with me."

Melinda kissed him then said, "Let's go. I'll drive." She looked at Karen and me. "I'm okay. He's been wanting to do this all night. Means a lot to him. Not sure why," she trailed off, raising her eyebrows.

We drove the few miles down to the lake, nestled along the highway. Jason was singing Beatles songs the whole way. Karen and Melinda talked about some of the people they knew at Paradise. There were lots of affairs and plenty of gossip. Most of it was about people I didn't know. Jason was off in his little world so I doubt if he cared about most of it either.

The raft was partially inflated, so we took only a few minutes with the bicycle pump to fully inflate it. Jason was first in the raft, carrying his knapsack with him. Before we were in the raft, he pulled out a bottle of red wine.

"I want to toast my best friends." He took a swig from the bottle, then handed it to me. We all settled in the raft and pushed off shore.

"Jason, we need glasses to properly toast each other. This isn't proper," I said with a laugh.

"Just take a drink," Karen chided me.

"No, my best buddy is right," Jason said as he reached into his pack. He pulled out two paper cups. "Sorry, this is all I have." The cups were bent and crushed, but he pulled them into shape and handed them to Karen and me. "Mel and I can share the bottle."

He poured some wine into each cup, then lifted his bottle for a proper toast. We all touched cups and bottle, with Melinda touching each with her fingers.

"I am going to the top tomorrow, by the west route. Haven't been there this year. It's a tough one. I want you to wish me well. My best buddies. I will stand up there and salute you. This has been a good summer. And now it's over. Karen is a California-dreamin' blond and you, Jody, are the best hearts player in Ohana." I never figured out why he kept calling me that, but from the first week we were working at Ohana, he called me Jody. I think it was a twist on Jude, from the Beatles song, which he knew I loved. I gave in and let him do it.

"The world out there stinks, and I know Jody won't go to Nam. Let's all pray for Jody."

"Jason," Melinda took his bottle from him, "if you are climbing tomorrow you don't need the alcohol messing up the weed. Take it easy."

"She isn't going with me," Jason laughed as he pulled the oars. We were now in the middle of the small lake. The sky was black, with the west horizon still the lighter blue of a determined twilight. Stars were dotting the sky overhead. From the lake, we couldn't see the mountain, but we all felt its presence. You always did. It gave a feeling to all of us of comfort, like an old blanket we could pull over us to protect us from the cold and the bad things out there.

I took a sip of wine and looked at Karen. I could tell she was crying silently. The night had been emotional and we would all remember it. We drifted quietly for several minutes. No one said a word. All of us were deep into our own thoughts as we huddled in the raft. An owl hooted from a tree on the west shore of the lake.

After a while, I spoke. "I'm the only one here who's at risk right now. Jason, you still have a 2A. And you girls don't get drafted. Well, I won't either. I just know that the Peace Corps will get me first. So don't worry about me. If I'm not worried, then you don't be either. Who knows, I might be back here next summer. They are coming up with a lottery in a couple months and I will get the highest number. Just wait and see." I held up the cup for a last toast. I could see Jason starting to fall asleep. I didn't believe what I just said, but I hoped I convinced them of my sincerity.

Two days later, when I drove up to Paradise to pick up Karen to take her to Sea Tac for her flight back to San Francisco, I heard the news. Karen ran out to me before I even parked the truck.

"Jason is hurt. We have to go down to the hospital."

"What happened," I stuttered. "What hospital?"

"They flew him to Enumclaw. He fell yesterday. A whole rock face broke off with him on it. He slid about a thousand feet down the mountain in a rockslide. Took them all day to get him out. Finally got a helicopter to fly him. Several broken bones and I don't know what else. He's pretty busted up." Karen's voice cracked.

"When did you find out?" I asked. I didn't know what else to say. I knew Karen had strong feelings for Jason, but I also knew I didn't need to be jealous. Karen liked people and expressed her feelings. She didn't worry about appearances.

"Only a few hours ago. Melinda came by. She was really torn up. She was on her way to the hospital. She had been waiting for him at Longmire. He was late coming back. She called up here and the climbing shop told her. They made it sound worse than it was. She really thought he was dead."

"Well, let's get going. If we are going to stop by and see him, we need to allow more time to get to the airport on time. Your flight is at 6 o'clock, right?"

"It's actually 5:45, but we should have plenty of time to at least stop in and say hi. That is if they will let us even see him." Karen lowered her eyes as she bit her lower lip.

When we walked into the hospital, we passed Melinda coming out the front door. She hugged Karen, then looked at me and held my hand. "He's okay. Pretty bunged up, but not in too bad spirits considering. Dumb shit fell on that same rock a year ago. Almost broke a leg then. He says he learned his lesson this time." She laughed and shook her head. "He will be glad to see you. I didn't have any lunch. I need to go home and get something to eat. I guess this is goodbye again." She hugged Karen again and held her, then let go and kissed me on the cheek.

We stood there for a minute and watched her drive off.

Then we walked in and asked for Jason's room. The nurse told us we could only spend a few minutes because they just gave him a shot to help him sleep.

Jason looked up as we walked in the door. He smiled, exaggerated now by a missing front tooth. He looked terrible. One leg was held up by a pulley, an arm was in a cast from shoulder to hand, his face was scratched and swollen.

"You look like hell warmed over," I said, as I reached down to touch his good hand.

"Oh, Jason, are you all right?" Karen said as she tried to hold back a laugh. She reached down to tenderly kiss his forehead. "Now maybe you can get a 1-F classification." We all laughed at that.

"If they have a classification for stupidity, maybe I will classify. Guess I kinda screwed myself up pretty bad."

"I'd have stopped to get you something, but we only just found out. No one really knew how bad things were."

Jason smiled as he looked over at his bedside table. "You brought yourself. That's a gift enough for me. I have something for you." He motioned at the table. "I want you to have a little plush bear, Karen."

"One of the nurses gave it to me. I already have a couple more. You need something to remember me by down there in San Francisco." He drawled the word Francisco.

We looked at the chair across the room and saw about a half dozen stuffed bears and rabbits.

"What the ...," I stopped and smiled. "Jason, old buddy, how many girlfriends do you have in this country?"

"I think they just feel sorry for me. Anybody as stupid as me deserves pity."

The nurse came in the door and motioned for us to leave. "He needs to sleep. I think he wore himself out playing with all his new toys. One more minute, then you do need to leave. I'm sorry."

Karen reached down and picked up one of the plush bears, a small black bear with a red collar. She kissed it, then kissed Jason on his right jaw. She turned away and went to the door. "You take care and get well." Then she hurried out into the hall.

Jason hollered after her, "You take care of plush bear. He was my favorite..."

I held his hand. "Gotta get her to the airport. Guess this is goodbye again. I don't need to say it do I?"

"No, you get outta here. Be careful. Thanks you guys. You don't know what this means to me. Take care of my favorite blond. Love you." He coughed as the nurse came to stick a thermometer in his mouth.

I said to the nurse, "keep the girls away from him. And watch your behind." I glanced at the nurse's ample behind, smiled, and waved at Jack as I walked out the door.

It was a difficult parting for Karen at the airport, but she would soon be absorbed in her third year of college, her first at Berkeley. I had two days' work left, then a long drive back east to wait for my fate.

However, that wait didn't last long. The day after Karen left, I walked down to the ranger station from the apartment to get my mail after work. I looked at a large manila envelope addressed to me. It had something knobby in it. Several bumps almost broke through the envelope. It rattled when I shook it. It was return addressed from Washington D.C. The Peace Corps. I held my breath as I opened it. Grains of rice fell out. I pulled out a packet of material. The cover letter began with "Welcome to the Peace Corps."

I let out a scream and started jumping up and down as I walked. I made it! I escaped Viet Nam. I ran back to the apartment, spilling more rice as I ran. What was this thing with rice, I wondered. As I walked into the apartment, the LP was still playing that I had put on when I left to get the mail. The song was "The Way We Live" from the Johnnie Rivers' *Realization* album. I liked the tune, even though it was a little depressing. But then, this was the age of protest and there was a lot of protest music:

> "Just open your eyes and look around and tell me what do you see. Can you understand the things people do and the way they treat each other... And tell me how far has man really come when today he's still killing his brother...If you don't have the answers right now, I'll see you after a while. But if next time I still look this way, you'll know why I don't smile."

The sadness of the song was a slap in the face. I stopped and sat down to read the letter. I was accepted into the Peace Corps. I would be a rice farmer in the Philippines. I had to be in Los Angeles three weeks from that day. There we would immediately fly to Hawaii for a week of shots and language training, then Manila for in-country training. I thought about the song and I thought about my new life. Yes, I would stay out of Viet Nam, although I would be over in that part of the world. It was not something I really preferred, but it was certainly better than the one other alternative. Why did it have to be this way? I just wanted to work in a place like Mt. Rainier. That was what I was trained for.

Why couldn't we all just keep on having a summer of fun in a magical setting like Mt. Rainier? All the good things and good people, being torn apart in this crazy world. I wanted to smile, but I thought of the Christmas party, and Jason lying in his hospital bed, and Karen wiping back tears. I didn't have the answers right now. I might never have. I put the packet of information back in the envelope and picked up a few grains of rice that had fallen on the floor. I sat there and listened to the music. No, I couldn't understand the things people do and the way they treat each other. Would I find out in the Philippines? Would any of us who stood there in the lodge at Paradise on that August Christmas, 1969, ever find out? I thought of the long drive back to Iowa. How and what would I tell Karen? I restarted "The Way We Live," and closed my eyes. Would I smile when I opened them and looked around?

Canyon Engagements

*The thunder rolled off the rim and fell
into the canyon, echoing off the cliffs
and disappearing into the silent river
millions of years below.*
Jonathan

THE FIRST TIME I saw the Grand Canyon my reaction was probably typical of most people. I had driven down from San Francisco, anxious to start a new job at the canyon. I was tired from the nonstop drive, but this promised to be the start of my career. Thus, I was savoring the experience. I drove to the first overlook, trying not to focus on the famous chasm in front of me. I wanted to see it for the first time head on, not as the background while worrying about driving off the edge. It couldn't be done. I tried to avert my gaze, but I knew what was coming as I got out of my blue Volkswagen bug, slammed the door, and looked up. Oh my god!

My first thoughts were not of the view itself, the mind-altering expanse of nothing, the incomprehensible span of time exposed by geologic forces, or of the immense silence as the wind blew off the rim into a sky that went as far down as it went up. Believe it or not, my first thoughts were: "What was the reaction of the first Spanish explorer as he rode his horse up to this point and could go no further?" Of course the Utes or Paiutes or Anasazi had lived here and down there, for millennia. There was no first view for them. It was always here. You have to go back to some lost dude at the end of the ice age, chasing a mastodon or being chased by a saber-tooth cat before you got a real American's first thoughts. I can imagine his reaction as he chased that beast up to the edge and it (or he) kept on going, disappearing in free fall down to some noiseless thud at the base of the cliff far below.

At the time, I didn't reflect on that original scenario. I focused on what that European treasure hunter thought, after wandering through the desert and wasteland for weeks, chasing some elusive idea of golden cities out here in the middle of nowhere. His daydreams were lost in thought of that bonita senorita he left crying at the dock back in Cadiz or Seville as he sailed off months ago, promising to return with bags full of gold and other unknown riches. Now he was thinking he would be lucky to get his ass out of this endless desert, full of scorpions and rattlesnakes, cactus and a searing sun. And he was the one to ride two miles back and tell Coronado and the main party there is this big hole in the ground and there is no way in hell they can ever get around. Yeah, Pedro, go lay in the shade for a while. You're hallucinating.

Actually, I doubt if mine was the typical reaction. "Oh my god, Ralph, come here and look at this!" "Wow!" "What happened down there?" "It's even better than the movie." "Holy mother of saints, Gertrude, this is amazing! Quick, come take my picture." Or something similar.

I got used to the view. I was now employed by the Park Service at the South Rim, in a summer job as foreman of a surveying crew. Me? Leading a survey crew? I have a degree in forestry and had taken one survey class in college, almost flunking it. We met for three hours every Thursday afternoon my junior year and surveyed the campus at Ft. Collins. I could never get a survey to close. Never mind every

Thursday that spring semester, it either rained or snowed and I was miserable, freezing my fingers trying to level the transit.

But I knew what a transit was, and I guess that convinced the personnel clerk in the San Francisco Regional Office of the National Park Service that I was their man. He did say they were desperate and had been trying to fill the job for months. I was desperate for a job. So I said yes, went across the Bay to pack my few earthly possessions into the back seat of my VW and here I was, two days later. They were going to pay me to live and work right here, the very place that lost Spaniard sat on his butt-tired horse four hundred some years ago, mouth gaping open in wonder and dismay.

In the ensuing weeks, there were many nights when I stood somewhere along the Rim (butt-tired myself from working all day trying to get surveys to close), mouth gaping open in wonder, but thankfully not in dismay at that huge hole in the ground. The awe never did stop, but I think that was a good thing. We all need to be amazed, stupefied, lost in wonder at something we just cannot get a handle on. This was it for me.

When you live in a place like the Grand Canyon, you try your best not to become used to a view like that. You fight the urge to become jaded: "Yeah, canyon looked cool this morning with the mist from last night's thunderstorm. Now, what's for supper? Hey, Brad, you done with the newest *Playboy?* Toss it over here."

Dave and Brad, my survey crew as well as my roommates, could go out every night and babe hunt at the shops and lodges along the rim. I couldn't. Well, I shouldn't have, but I did anyway. My deal made weeks earlier back in California was as soon as I got a job, Samantha and I were getting married. I was thinking permanent job, but this might be as close as I could come, so we set a date. I was spoken for, and being a good Midwestern farm boy, I had to obey that deal. But that didn't stop me from looking.

Brad was your typical 60s era college student. Long blond hair, good looking, athletic, he was here for the trip. He still didn't know what his major in college was, but he would figure it out eventually. He would skip a final to go rafting, then come into the professor begging to make it up. He had a little boy charm that never seemed to fail him.

Dave was more serious, a fraternity type at the university in Albuquerque. He was here for the money, the image. He was in accounting for the potential fortune and country club status. He collected friends as a way to gain future favors. This job would look good on his resume, but it was just another job where he could gain what successes he could, hide any failures in this anonymous remoteness.

This was my foot in the door for my career. I took it seriously.

"Hey, Jonathan, big dance at the Roundup in Tusayan tonight. Wanna come?"

"No, I have to try and re-calculate that survey we did of the parking lot. I must have done something wrong with the math. I want to try and close the gap," I answered.

Brad grinned at me as he combed his blond curls with his fingers. "'Fraid you might get laid? Girls are just itchin' for a Park pass. We can get them in. I managed to get a couple of the employee decals. I figure that's good for lots of nookie."

"Good grief, Brad, grow up. Is that all you think of?" I moaned, but knew that boys would be boys. Maybe I was frustrated I couldn't be anymore.

Dave tossed him a couple condom packages. "Damn right that's all he thinks of. Got a better subject?"

"Well, you might think of doing a better job at work. We don't start getting these surveys to close, we all might be in deep nookie if you know what I mean. You're part of the team, you know."

"Guy gets married and all of a sudden he's through having fun. We'll bring you back a phone number. Or not." Brad laughed as he slapped Dave on the shoulder, and grabbed his jacket off the back of a chair as he walked out the door. I watched them get in the car. Beyond them, hugging the horizon, clouds were building in the desert and moving our way. Another storm.

They drove off in Dave's Mustang, spinning gravel as they headed out of the Park Service employees' parking complex. Let them go, I thought. It did beat doing math. I played with numbers for a while, then went for a walk. I ended up at the rim. I usually did. Clouds were building, now pillowing out across the canyon onto the North Rim. I watched the blackening sky as it started shooting fire. The North Rim disappeared as the rain curtain descended. I felt a few sprinkles, but it looked like the action tonight would be over there. And maybe down in Tusayan, but that kind of action is short lived. And judging by the hangovers the next morning, questionable whether it was worth it.

I strolled along the path, watching the reactions of the tourists as much as the scenery. The people that night were mostly older. The college kids were somewhere else, maybe down in Tusayan. The younger couples were waiting in line to get into the Bright Angel Restaurant. Some people were oblivious to the view. Others were filling their listeners' ears with tales of biblical floods, dinosaurs wading through swamps, extra-terrestrial beings. The know-it-alls were usually pot-bellied men in baggy Bermuda shorts, waving either a cigar or cigarette in one hand, a beer in another. The ladies politely listened, then adjusted their pearl necklaces and jeweled earrings. I wondered why these people were here.

I started to walk across the parking lot of the Bright Angel when a car honked at me. I figured it was some lost Californian, but then heard a voice call, "Jonathan, hey Jonathan."

I looked at the car, not recognizing it. A hand waved for me to follow. The car stopped on the edge of the road, Richard got out and walked over to me. He was my boss and had been extra kind and patient with me as he guessed I was struggling in this job, well out of my element. He was in his thirties and had worked at the park for several years. He cut through crap and focused on the details—of work and probably life as well.

"By yourself tonight?" Richard had a way of talking that always put him on my level. Even though he was the boss, he didn't treat me like a subordinate.

"Yeah, the boys went to Tusayan. I wanted to catch up on work."

"Jonathan, don't worry too much about it. It will come. Just give it time. I'm there whenever you need help. You know that."

"Thanks," I said, as I noticed several other folks in his car.

Richard nodded towards the green Ford station wagon. "In-laws just came in from Ohio. We're out for a night at the El Tovar. Saw you and wanted to tell you to come in a little early tomorrow. Got a job I want you to do over by the school. The boys can continue with the parking lot by themselves. Well, gotta run. We have reservations at eight." He winked at me as he turned to go.

"Thanks. Have a good evening," I muttered, mostly to myself as Richard backed the Ford out, past a pickup that had pulled in beside him.

I watched him park at the El Tovar down the road. I thought about this fancy landmark. It was well beyond my means, but not Richard's. I had wandered through the gift shop several times, wondering what I could buy for Sam. Or what I could even afford. We had set a date a month from now for the wedding. I needed to decide where we would have the ceremony. I wanted it outside, on the rim, but away from the crowds. I heard there was a pedestal with a stone cross along the rim just west of the village. My mother would demand a location with religious overtones. I didn't care one way or another.

I also thought about Richard. Why was he being so nice to me? He was the landscape architect in charge of me and my crew, responsible for getting this work done. I wasn't doing a good job, but he was patient with me. He often stopped at our work to give me pointers. He helped me do the paperwork. He never got excited nor did I ever see him in a hurry. I liked him better the more I was around him.

The rain started to fall the same time a bolt of lightning hit about a mile away. I counted to five, then the thunder rolled off the rim and fell into the canyon, echoing off the cliffs and disappearing into the silent river millions of years below. I was a mile away from my apartment, so I quickened my pace. I almost made it. The downpour slammed into me when I was about a block from home. Funny how running doesn't keep you any drier than walking. You are just wet for a shorter period of time.

The next morning, I left the apartment before Brad and Dave were out of bed, still moaning from the night before. They had crashed into the apartment sometime after 2 in the morning, but they left me alone. I had no sympathy for them as one of them spent the next half hour in the bathroom throwing up. I thought back on my college days, only recently over. During my first two summers, I played that game of "let's see how much beer we can drink before we throw it all back up." My college education taught me one thing if nothing else—drinking 'til you passed out was what the economists called a short term gain. The long term was payback called a hangover. Besides, I was an almost married man and at some point, one had to grow up. The boys were still in college and obviously had not learned that lesson yet. The way they smoked pot and guzzled beer, sometimes I wondered if they ever would.

Richard wanted me to monitor the work a D7 Cat was doing in shaping a new road. This was a promotion in terms of my responsibility. But I had no idea what I was supposed to do. The operator knew what he was doing, so I just stood there holding a survey rod to check whether he was getting the proper elevation. He was, without my having to move. Later that day, Richard stopped by and complemented me on the good job I was doing. I wanted to say that I didn't do a thing all day, but maybe my presence brought out the good qualities of the gap-toothed old cat skinner. I doubt it.

When Richard got the wedding announcement a week later, he called me into his office and congratulated me. He asked me where I planned to live. That was one of the small details I had ignored so far. I needed to request an apartment in the married housing complex, but I was putting it off for some reason. Richard picked up the phone and called the maintenance engineer in charge of employee housing. He talked a while, then turned to me and asked if I wanted one or two bedrooms. He smiled as he said it, but explained that he was asked the question and he didn't want to put words in my mouth. I grinned as I said I sure hoped I didn't need more than one.

"You know, the spouses of Park employees have first priority for working at Fred Harvey," Richard said after he hung up the phone. The Fred Harvey Company was the famous concessionaire that ran most of the lodges and souvenir shops at Grand Canyon and other National Parks in the West. "Does Samantha need a job?"

I raised my eyebrows as I thought about the question. It had never occurred to me. "Don't know. Guess I should ask her. She is in college and will be dropping out to get married. Guess she can't continue that here, can she?"

My mind quickly drifted off, heading hundreds of miles north. What did I really know about Sam, and what she wanted. She wanted out of the broken home she still lived in. She liked the outdoors: hiking, skiing, white water rafting. I met her while she was backpacking with friends at a high lake in the Sierra west of Reno. She was shy and quiet, like me, preferring to read a good book rather than go to a party. But what would this isolation do to her plans to get an education, to perfect her design skills as an architect? Was this fair to her? I could see her face, hear her laugh. But did I know her thoughts? I quickly drifted back to the present when Richard handed me a slip of paper with a name and phone number.

"Here is the person you should contact. I know Beverly and I'm sure she can get Sam a good job. Give her a call."

"Another thing." He leaned back in his chair and looked out the window. "You don't want to be a surveyor or engineer do you? I mean career-wise. You have a degree in wildlife?"

"Yeah, specialty in non-game and ecosystem management.

I've always wanted to work for the Park Service. I worked a couple years at Lassen on the trail crew. Nothing permanent seems to be open now. Fish and Wildlife, Forest Service, state wildlife departments, nothing. Guess I have to take what I can get."

Richard pulled the bread-board out on his old wooden desk and looked up another phone number. He dialed and looked at me as he started talking. "Bill, Richard here. I've got a cracker jack seasonal working on my survey crew but he has a degree in wildlife of all things and needs to get beyond packing a transit around. Yeah, wildlife, but he says ecosystem big picture side of things. Getting married in a couple weeks and I'd like for you to meet him. Maybe you can help him out. Even a seasonal ranger job would suit him better than survey crew leader." A long silence. "Yeah, top notch. Sitting here right now."

I was pretending not to be listening. Actually I wasn't listening. I was bothered about my lack of knowledge of Sam and her career. Now I thought about mine. This was what I wanted. I dreamed since high school of becoming a park ranger. My hero was Lassie—I put up with her master being not quite as smart as his dog. I wanted to live out West, roam the mountains, breathe that wild air. I was out of college, free from Viet Nam with a very high lottery number, ready to do something I was trained to do. Was I ready to get married?

Richard broke a pencil point as he started doodling. I knew he had been talking about me. I felt uncomfortable but I hadn't heard what he had been saying. "I know, I've been looking for a long time but I'm sure I could find another. Okay, I'll let him know. Thanks. Oh, we still on for Saturday? Great. See you then."

Richard put down his pen, which had replaced his broken pencil and looked at me. "Go down the hall right now. Third door on your left. Bill Perkins, Chief Ranger. My friend, you may be in luck. He had a last minute cancellation of a long time seasonal ranger. Scheduled to start next week. Needs to find a replacement. He owes me and if he likes you, you might have a new job soon. Only a seasonal, but a foot in the door. Be smart and good luck." He stood up and shook my hand.

"Thanks," I stuttered. This sudden turn of events left me in total surprise. "I hate to leave you in a bind. I know you looked a long time for a crew leader."

"Hey, don't be a martyr. You don't want to be a surveyor. This is a career opportunity. I'd take it in a second myself." Richard pushed up his glasses with a finger. "Don't worry about me. Besides, it's not guaranteed. It's up to you to impress him. He prefers teachers for these jobs. Tell him you wanted to be a teacher. Maybe you will teach wildlife management yet. Be sure to let him know you've worked other Parks. He worked at Lassen years ago. I think he met his wife there. It's special to him."

Later that afternoon, when I walked into the apartment I shared with Brad and Dave, I was in a fog. I had a new apartment in the married housing complex that would be ready next week. I had a new job starting immediately. I was going to be a seasonal Park Ranger. My duties would vary from taking fees at the entrance station, to staffing the visitor center, to doing interpretive walks along the rim talking to visitors. I had a week-long orientation session to attend and I would wear the uniform, including Smokey Bear hat. It was only a four month job, but Bill left the impression it might be continued longer.

How would I tell Brad and Dave? Turns out I didn't need to. When they walked in the door, they grinned at me and threw their hard hats at me. "You lucky asshole," Brad said as he came over and hugged me.

"Good work, Jonathan," Dave said as he flopped down on the couch. "You know who we got for a boss now?" he said sarcastically.

"One of you get it?" I asked.

"Hell no. Richard said he got a special program person off the reservation. I think he wanted to get rid of you. Said he just got a call this morning. BIA had a kid trained in surveying they wanted a job for. We get a 'yetahey' Navajo. Damn."

I picked up his hard hat and tossed it back to him. "Glad you're not prejudiced. I bet he can at least close a survey. More than we can do."

The next weekend, the boys said they wanted to hike across the canyon. I wasn't up for the hike, knowing they would probably be stoned the whole trip. Besides, they would need a ride back from the North Rim. I offered to bring them back. This would give me a chance to explore the North Rim, which I had never seen. The snow was mostly off and the road crew had just opened the road. The North Rim was a totally different experience and seeing it before the hordes of tourists would be a treat. The South Rim was getting more crowded every day.

Brad and Dave left the South Rim for the depths of the canyon right after work Friday. They were setting a rapid pace as I watched them sink lower and lower on the Bright Angel Trail. They planned to camp at Indian Gardens the first night, although knowing them, they might end up going all the way to Phantom Ranch. Depended on how many beers they packed with them and how many were empty by Indian Gardens.

I waited until Saturday morning to drive over to the North Rim, and had this part of the Park almost to myself. There were still pockets of snow at this higher elevation and it was definitely cooler. I wandered through the Grand Canyon North Rim lodge and drove out to Cape Royal. When I got back to the campground, I met Joe and Karie. Like me, they decided to enjoy the cool climate of the North Rim before the tourists descended on it. Karie was a nurse at the South Rim Clinic while Joe, an EMT with the local ambulance, worked as a janitor at the South Rim Grade School. He was probably no more than thirty-five, but his grizzled beard made him look much older. Karie, while not attractive, was one of the most popular locals in South Rim Village. Her hair was already graying, which she didn't try to hide. She also didn't hide her scorn of most Parkies, the permanent employees who worked for the Park Service. I didn't fit into that category. Yet.

"Have you read *Desert Solitaire* by Edward Abbey?" Joe asked as I was smoothing out a spot for my sleeping bag in a site opposite theirs. I didn't own a tent and planned to sleep on the ground.

"Finished it last winter," I said. "Loved it."

"Did you know Abbey worked here as a seasonal early in his career?" Joe was considered an expert on local trivia. Most of his knowledge was interesting, but irrelevant to most everyone else.

"No. I knew he was at Arches."

"Yeah," Karie said. "He was a seasonal ranger right here at the North Rim. Stayed at the old ranger station. Supposedly he built, or maybe just used, a fire lookout on top of a huge old ponderosa right outside the station. We were going to walk over there and try to find it. I'm sure they don't use it anymore, but who knows."

"I'm game," I said.

We found the huge old dead pine about a hundred yards south of the ranger station. There were no signs, no fence around it, nothing to indicate it was anything more than a big dead pine. On the south side of the tree, nailed and attached by bolts and metal strips was a steel ladder. The ladder hugged the trunk, with little room for toe holds. It went straight up for nearly a hundred feet. I looked at Joe, who looked at Karie.

She was the first to speak. "Not me. I want to live long enough to bear offspring. If I somehow didn't die during the climb, I would so traumatize every cell in my body, no egg would ever leave the ovary."

"Hell, my sperm are strong enough to make the climb. I'll go with them." Joe tested the stability of the ladder, then hopped up to the first rung, about four feet above the ground.

I looked at Karie. "If Joe is brave enough, guess I am too." I looked up at Joe, already fifteen feet up the ladder. "Just keep those sperm to yourself for the next ten minutes," I hollered. He rubbed the side of the tree, sending a flurry of small bark pieces down on me.

I waited a minute for Joe to get well above me, not relishing the thought of him falling and taking me with him on his free-fall. He yelled for me to come on, "the ladder is sturdy as a rock and is just one hand over hand, feet following." As long as I didn't look down, I did all right. I was slowly edging up when I heard a voice from far above me. "Come on slowpoke. The view is fantastic."

I looked up. Joe was leaning over the edge of a small board platform on the very top of the tree. The view was becoming better the higher I climbed, but I still tried to look only at the rung above me, one at a time. When I reached the top, I finally became scared. The ladder ended and I had to reach above me to scramble onto the four foot square platform made of old two-by-six boards. The opening was in the middle of the platform, now exposed with the trap door hinged open. Once on top, Joe let the door down so we wouldn't fall through. There was a little railing around the edge, but I certainly wouldn't trust my life to it. I tried to envision Abbey or anyone, sane or otherwise, standing here watching a storm flying by, lightning striking anything over two feet tall, wind swaying the tree back and forth.

I suddenly felt akin to those old sailors who climbed the masts of schooners or caravels, or whatever else bounced along the waves of a surly ocean, to sit in the crow's nest, looking for land, whales, mermaids, or whatever their fear-strained eyes cared to envision. "My god," I thought, "I have lost my mind. This is insane."

Joe was calling to Karie, ant-like down below, another world away. "Hey, it's cool up here. Sure you don't want to come?"

Karie didn't even bother to reply. We couldn't tell if she was waving to us or flipping the bird. She was probably thinking how lonely her eggs would be for the rest of her widowhood.

I put my hand on Joe's wrist as he grabbed onto the railing and spit over the edge. "Might want to be careful with that railing. Don't think I would trust it. I really don't want to lose my balance."

"Don't be a weenie." Joe started to jump up and down, listening to the squeak of the boards. "Did you know John Muir used to climb the tallest pine he could find in Yosemite Valley during a raging winter storm? He would sway back and forth as the winds topped fifty miles an hour, rain coming horizontal. He didn't even have a ladder. What a rush. Wow. Wouldn't you like to be up here during a storm?"

"I assume that is a rhetorical question." I shuddered at the thought. Actually I didn't let myself shudder. I was afraid the slightest vibrations would have knocked me off the edge.

I pictured Abbey, or anyone else for that matter, clambering up here either during or right after a lightning storm to look for new fires. The view was awesome—the canyon digging into the southern expanse, a pine forest disappearing into the northern view. It was quiet, with a light breeze blowing over us. An occasional car engine near the lodge was the only sound other than chirps and burbles of birds below. Far off to the east, the Kaibab plateau curved down into the desert. Green melded into brown. The Reservation. Home of the Navajo Nation. Miles and miles of nothing. Actually, it was miles and miles of nothing in every direction. But what a view of nothing. There was more nothing now than when that Spaniard stood over there on the opposite rim. He was intruding on the land of the Apache and Ute and whoever else lived here then. Every square inch was someone's home. They just took a lot of space to live. Now, after we had kicked most of them onto reservations, we left the space empty. At least we thought it empty. It was full of life if we cared to look. I was looking when I heard Karie yelling at us from down below. I couldn't tell what she said, but Joe yelled back at her that we were on our way down.

"You go down first," Joe finally said. "Bad luck to cross each other. I was first up, I need to be last down."

With that thought of starting my descent, I decided to enjoy the view a few more minutes. If climbing up those last two feet with no handholds was frightening, the thought of dangling my legs off into the ethereal void, groping for a steel rung one inch in diameter, holding onto nothing but the twenty- or forty- or sixty-year-old who knows how rotted-platform, nailed onto a rotting dead top of a dead for-who-knows-how-many-years pine, well it scared me almost more than just staying there for the rest of my short life.

"Need to buck up the courage a few more seconds," I said as I looked at Joe. He was pulling a candy bar out of his shirt pocket. He stuffed it into his mouth and wadded the wrapper into a ball and threw it down at Karie. Then he yelled at the top of his lungs, "Watch me, I'm Superman. I can fly."

This man had no brains, I decided. I hoped his courageous sperm were smarter than him. "Sure you don't want to go down first?" I asked.

"Bad luck, Captain Kirk," Joe said as he patted the top of my head. "Down when you are ready. Elevator is waiting."

I suddenly had the vision of being twenty feet down and Joe unzipping his pants and whizzing off the edge. I wouldn't put it past this moron. Why did I come up here with him? I didn't know him well, other than listening to his jokes in the bar after work. He was crazy and probably contagious as well.

I made it down safely, always looking up at Joe, about five rungs above me. Karie smiled at me as I hopped off the last rung, and said, "Have fun?"

"Listen," I said, "if you ever see Joe packing a parachute, don't let him leave the house. I think he liked it up there."

"Oh, he's like a little kid sometimes. He had a couple beers after we set up camp. He needs to let off steam."

A couple beers? And this guy was above me the whole trip? I decided to go to the lodge to eat supper, never mind the cost might strain my budget. I had to stay away from these two the rest of the night.

When I got back from my late dinner, Joe and Karie were in their tent, their campfire down to glowing embers. I lay my sleeping bag on the ground and was asleep within five minutes. I awoke once during the night as two deer walked by, nearly stepping on my head. I was out of my bag and packing my day pack for my hike out to Widforss Point by the time the first chickadees were scolding the world for waking them up.

It was a five mile hike one way and I had the trail all to myself. As I hiked the long path to the secluded point in the pine and aspen forest, I thought about what I was getting into. This would be my park. My responsibility. I would make up the story I wanted to tell about this place and I would tell it to all kinds of strangers. Was this the career I really wanted? Would it even be a career yet? I loved the land, the natural system. I knew the animals, the flowers, the trees. I understood the geology, the ecology. Did I know the people? Could I deal with the boys of all the different crews of life? Could I make Joe and Karie understand why they should care about this place and other Parks?

Could I deal with what was happening to the South Rim, Yosemite Valley, Estes Park, and all the tourist attractions? I stopped dead in my tracks as soon as I rounded the last bend in the trail and saw the first view of the Canyon, hidden from view for the past several miles. It was the same canyon, but just like the lookout points along the South Rim, every view was totally different. I could barely make out the buildings perched on the South Rim. The breeze was rustling the aspen, which grew right up to the cliffs. The world fell away at my feet, just as it did in all other places along both rims. But it looked different to me. Or was my perception of reality changing with my new circumstances?

I sat down on a limestone ledge and took off my pack. Opening a bottle of orange juice and filling my hand with peanuts, I drew a deep breath. My world had changed dramatically the past few days, yet I'm not sure I understood it. I did not understand the view I was looking at either. It was enormous, breath-taking, mind-altering, and still beyond full comprehension. That probably would never change, even if I sat on this cliff every day the rest of my life. That's why I was here.

Somewhere down there along the North Kaibab Trail hidden in that long gouge below me were the boys. They would still be hiking strongly, although the rubber legs would be kicking in soon, especially as they started the long hike up. I hoped they had eased off the dope. It would make their journey much more enjoyable, although I'm not sure their idea of enjoyment matched mine right now.

Back at the campground, Joe and Karie would be up and probably doing something outrageous, like throwing rocks at chipmunks or maybe letting the air out of my tires. They were little kids just like the boys. Only they could be mature if they tried.

I heard the cry of a hawk above me. He swooped by, then he was below me, catching the thermals of the sun-heated rocks. I watched him as he rose and disappeared beyond the cliffs to the west. There was no mystery for him. He just did the same thing every day, looking for food. My eyes left him and settled on nothing in particular. That was the only way to enjoy this view. Don't try to figure it out. Every movement of the eye brought new wonders, new scenes, new details that changed with every cloud, every shift of the sun.

I thought again of that poor Spanish conquistador who first stood over there, a speck on the south horizon. Then I went beyond him, back to the ancient prophets. They would find an entirely different meaning in this scene. They would attach god-significance to it. I suppose God did do all this. All depended on how you wanted to define God. I'm sure those desert-hardened, parched-lipped old hermits did the same thing I was now doing when they stumbled out of the desert of the Sinai. They asked a lot of questions, none of which could be answered in any satisfactory form. When they got no answers, they went back to their tent, ate a few crumbs of bread and drank some watered-down wine, and made up answers. Answers that still have us scratching our heads to this very day.

I had been studying the geology of the canyon and knew the rock layers: Kaibab Limestone, Toroweap, Coconino. Each layer is distinctive, with its own story. You walk back in time as you walk down in elevation. Ancient oceans, ancient deserts. Some form cliffs, some erode easily. Hermit, Supai, and Redwall, which is actually gray, but is red because the Supai above stains it. And the Inner Gorge, the bowels of the earth, nothing older than that. Millions turned into billions of years. You walk for half an hour down the Bright Angel, or any trail, you travel through eons of history.

I wanted to know the names, but names handcuff one's imagination. I hoped people didn't just learn names and think they knew what was here. You have to walk down into these places, get off the trail, sit in the shade of a cliff and feel the rock. Run your hand across the sand or the fossil shells and shark teeth. You have to watch the lizard scurry across the heat-baked sand along the river. You have to stand on the edge of the water and look up and try to understand the upside down geology from the bottom.

The river drains half a continent—waters from high alpine peaks to sagebrush deserts. It all comes through the little "gap" below, looking like nothing but a trickle from my bird's eye perch. But it's a monster. It took all this rock and flushed it down the river, carrying it past thousands of generations of watchers. It swirled and drifted, thundered, and crashed past rock, through rock, over rock.

Brad and Dave would be climbing up the long Kaibab

Trail by now. They would be tired, sore, achy. I hoped they were stopping to feel the rock, the coolness in the shade, the heat of the sun. This wasn't an endurance trip to express their manhood. It was a pilgrimage, a trip to Mecca and beyond. I had made short trips down the Bright Angel, the Hermit, even a tentative stab at the Hance in the previous weeks. Each time, I saw the tourists clomp down in boots, in sandals, even barefoot. They went around a curve, took a picture, picked up a small pebble, then struggled to get back up the few hundred feet they ventured. They had conquered the Canyon.

As a Ranger, they would be my audience. How could I, how could anyone, deal with it? Was I right for this job? Could I handle it? Maybe the Grand Canyon was not the place to start. Maybe I should wait for something simple like Black Canyon in Colorado, or Craters of the Moon in Idaho. Something low key and less well known.

I would soon assume responsibility for Sam, who was probably packing right then for her trip (and probably thinking she was soon to assume responsibility for me). She had never been here. I would watch carefully her expressions as she saw the canyon. But what if I was disappointed. She probably wouldn't see that Spaniard. What if she didn't feel the sun as it heated the ocean, fueled the winds that would drift the seashore sands? If she didn't, could I teach her to see the dinosaurs, the sharks, the trilobites crawling along the bottom of the once vast sea that was now a sea of limestone? If she didn't have the same feeling as me, could I succeed with thousands of tourists?

A Kaibab squirrel scolded me from the top of a large pine. He jumped from branch to branch, bobbing his fluffy white tail and perking his tremendous ears. He was like the Anasazi. This was home and he didn't see the view. It was always here and it was his world. Maybe life was easier when you didn't have a flat Indiana prairie to compare this to. When you didn't realize a fourth of the entire history of the earth was exposed. Like peeping through a crack in the tent at the county fair carnival, catching a glimpse of the girly show, seeing what may best be left covered.

I looked up at clouds drifting overhead. A jet contrail left its mark as a plane-load of strangers made a journey from LA to New York. Would most of them even look up from their mystery novel to peek out the window at the drama below them? Their loss if they didn't, but maybe their loss if they did as well. We all lost if we looked at this without a tear of awe, of confusion, of total disbelief. Some of the visitors I encountered had this awe, but many just wanted to snap a photo and mark off Grand Canyon on their list of conquests. Could I relate to my audience?

The sun was directly overhead now. I had been sitting on the limestone ledge for hours. But what had I been doing? I didn't go to church anymore, but maybe I had just been attending a church more relevant than anything built by human hands. So I was thinking about those prophets after all. Was I thinking of God?

I realized I needed this view. I needed it like some people need extra vitamins, or medicine. Our bodies, just like those of deer and elk seeking salt licks, know when to take in something missing. We flock to a place like this canyon, if only to drive up, get out, take a picture, wander the gift shops, then drive away. We may not know why, but we need to experience the awe, the power and energy of raw natural beauty. I wondered if I would be asking too much to expect people to understand why they are here. They are drawn here but just as they arrive, ready to absorb the energy this place offers they leave. Unfulfilled. How can I help them? Or was I asking the same question those desert-crazed prophets of old asked but never quite got answered. Without the religion, I want people to see God.

I slowly got up, stared off into the abyss one more time, then shouldered my pack and headed back into the forest. I looked for the big-eared squirrel. It was gone. The hawk was gone. The trees were silent. I had taken in what I needed. Now it was time to go pick up the boys at the trailhead as they stumbled out of their wilderness.

Alpine Thunder

*The sky turned into a strobe light.
Lightning flashed from cloud to cloud as well as
hitting the ground. One bolt hit so
close the thunder was instantaneous with the
flash of light. Jill screamed.*

MIKE AND JILL rode onto the top of the alpine plateau about noon. Jill could tell since she was finally sitting level rather than holding onto the saddle horn to keep from falling backwards off the horse. The fir and spruce of the high plateau forest were shadowy in fog so thick they could hardly see each other only one horse length away. They had ridden into the clouds when they entered the last aspen stand a half mile below. Mike hadn't bothered to check the weather forecast. It was July and each day was the same. Sunny in the morning, clouds rolling in about noon, then thunderstorms and rain. July in the Colorado mountains meant monsoons. Mike was used to this, but Jill was not.

They came prepared, expecting to get wet. There were plenty of nooks and crannies of trees and draws in which to hide if the lightning and rain got too bad. The expanse of this high elevation plateau was vast and lightning could hit only so many spots.

"What are the odds of a lightning bolt finding two people and three horses in thousands of acres of space?" Mike rationalized to Jill. She was not thrilled about coming,

but he asked her to be with him and they were still on their extended honeymoon. He was determined to go on this trip and she didn't want to become a widow this soon after they were married, so she agreed to come.

"Might as well either get lost or be hit by lightning together," she sighed as she packed her gear. Sometimes Mike was like a little boy and Jill felt she was always protecting him from himself.

The trip up the long and little traveled trail was slow as they got used to their horses, Nellibell and Frog, and Queenie the pack horse. Queenie belonged to Franklin, Mike's co-worker, and was rented to the Forest Service for the summer. Mike hadn't asked Franklin if he could use Queenie, but since Ted, Mike's boss, sent the mules out with the trail crew on the other end of the district, Mike didn't have a choice. Ted said Jill could accompany Mike for safety, so Mike took that as indirect permission. Queenie rarely was used and Mike guessed, after putting on the pack saddle and loading it with gear, that she had never been used as a pack horse. Mike rode Frog, leading Queenie with Jill trailing on Nellibell. She wasn't used to riding, and her slow pace set the rhythm of the ride.

The trail was in remarkably good shape, considering the trail crew probably only maintained it once every five years; the public didn't even know it was here since it was not marked on most maps. Used extensively years ago by area sheepherders, it seemed like every other aspen trunk on the four-mile-long trail was carved, decades ago, with initials, women's figures (showing 145 varieties of breast shapes and sizes according to Jill, who didn't find them as interesting as Mike), and dates, as far back as the teens and twenties. The oldest was 1909: a very clear gray scab on still pure white bark, although the tree itself showed only a faint trace of life.

As they emerged from the dark spruce forest and guessed they were in a meadow that indicated the top of the plateau, Jill moaned, "my god, Mike, we can't see anything. The trail disappeared. Where do we go?"

Mike looked around for landmarks, but it was like sticking your head in a dark closet and looking in all directions. Every direction he turned was the same—a mist of fog so thick he could barely see his hand. "I'm sure the trail is here, but it's a little tough to see. I know we need to go west. We'll probably pick it up again when we hit trees." Mike's confidence was shaky in times like this when he was stretching the truth.

"And you know which way is west?" Jill didn't like what she knew was coming.

"Oh this is just a passing cloud. We might just sit here for a few minutes. West is this way," he nodded his head.

"Mike, dear, I can't even see you. And I suppose it's only a quarter mile to the trees. Just like the trail up here was only a mile or so long. A Mike-mile?"

They sat for a few minutes, then Mike got off to check the pack saddle. The diamond hitch was still tight. This was a matter of pride for Mike. A real Forest Service cowboy was judged by how he packed his pack saddle and how he tied it on. A diamond hitch, or better yet a double diamond, was the test of competence. Mike had never even heard of a diamond hitch until a year ago. Now he had tied one all by himself and it was holding quite well. Jill's saddle was slipping, so she got off and tightened it. Mike had made her saddle up by herself that morning, and with only a few words of encouragement she passed muster.

But she now wondered what she had really passed. Some sanity test? What was she doing here? "Mike, we can't see anything," she said again. Sometimes repetition got Mike's attention. "How can we go anywhere? Should we set up camp here?"

"Good grief, no. It's only noon. We can't stop now. I want to get as far as Blue Lake by late afternoon."

"How can we get anywhere but maybe fall off a cliff? I'm hungry. And look, it's starting to rain." A light drizzle was now falling, but at least that was accompanied by a lightening of the fog.

"See," Mike said, as if he were somehow responsible. "The fog is falling away and the rain is clearing things up. Look! I can see trees over there." He pointed into the fog, which still looked the same to Jill, but at least she could now see him point.

"I think the altitude is affecting you. I don't see anything, but now I can't see it while I'm getting wet. Let's eat. It is lunchtime." Jill reached into her saddlebags and pulled out her lunch sack.

"You going to sit here on wet grass?" Mike started to get his lunch out as well.

"Got any better ideas, Fremont? Was one of your long lost ancestors the Great Pathfinder? I hear he got lost somewhere near here. Recognize it?" Jill got off Nellibell and spread her rain gear next to a patch of alpine forget-me-nots. She picked one of the delicate blue flowers and put it in her mouth.

"Haha. Real funny. Well, it is getting lighter. Mark this down, it will be light enough to see before you can finish your lunch."

The two huddled on the ground as the drizzle increased to a light rain. They heard thunder off in the distance. Mike looked up. "That's weird. Don't usually hear thunder in this type of weather. Hmm."

"Why should that or anything surprise me? This whole thing is weird. You are weird to even think this is weird," Jill said in disgust. She continued to eat her lunch.

The horses stood with their heads drooped nearly to the ground. They weren't even trying to eat. Now that they were in the lush grass of the top, they were too tired to eat. They had nipped at every grass stem on the long climb up the hill.

Jill finished her lunch as Mike nibbled at his. His pride was wounded. He wanted to impress his bride, but he wasn't succeeding. She was right, he really had no idea where the hell they were. The trail was not well marked on his topo map.

"We'll have to go west," he said aloud. "But the adjacent Third Meadow in the valley below us curves north as it winds west, so we'll need to veer north a little to avoid the cliffs." Elk Creek was miles away to the north, so they had plenty of plateau to their right before they needed to worry about falling into that canyon.

By the time he finished lunch, Jill had re-adjusted Nellibell's belly strap, and Mike looked at his damp map one more time. He started to show it to Jill, somehow trying to prove he knew where he was, but she climbed into the saddle and said, "Let's go. If you insist on getting us lost, let's get started."

"I'm not lost. I know about where we are."

"Yeah, we are about on planet earth." Jill was not interested in Mike's feeble attempt to justify himself.

The fog lifted slightly, so Jill could see Mike leading Queenie off into the mist. Although much of the trail had been through aspen stands on the way up onto the plateau, there were still some scattered aspen on top, although most of the forest on the plateau was spruce-fir. They entered another aspen stand and Jill heard Mike yell. She couldn't understand him, but when she reached him, with Queenie shifting uneasily as she passed by, she saw what Mike was pointing to: an aspen with the usual naked lady, and the initials GFM, July 17, 1939, carved on the foot wide trunk. The tree next to it was engraved August 4, 1942.

"See, we are on the trail. I knew it was here somewhere."

Jill shook her head in disbelief, and pulled wet strands of red hair out of her eyes. They continued on for an hour, then Jill once again heard Mike shout something. He had managed to get out of her sight, although Nellibell could tell where he was. As she got to him, she drew in her breath in surprise. The fog had completely lifted. They were sitting about 100 feet from the edge of a basalt cliff that fell off into a valley far below. The valley was clear, with a small patch of sunlight shining onto a meadow dotted with beaver ponds. They looked up as the fog magically lifted, replaced by low clouds that showed pale blue between them.

"Now that shouldn't be there," Mike muttered. "Where is that? This doesn't make sense." He had a look of total confusion on his face.

Mike got off Frog and pulled out his map. The corner tore as he tried to unfold the wet paper. "What the hell? This map is wrong."

Jill let out a laugh that was half scream. "The map is wrong? Hey Pathfinder, would there be any possibility you are so lost you don't even know what state you are in?"

Mike just stood staring, first at the canyon, then at his map. He rubbed his chin, then looked up at Jill, still on

Nellibell. Jill laughed again at the clownish look Mike gave her. His mouth was open, but no words were forthcoming.

Jill smiled as she pushed her hair out her eyes again. "This our campsite?"

"This can't be. That's First Meadow. That is right below where we hit the top. We circled around. We are right back where we started. How the hell…"

"Guess you didn't head straight west, did you?" Jill stifled another laugh, then bit her lower lip to keep as straight a face as she could.

"We should be way over there." Mike looked at the solid wall of spruce forest to his right, appearing ghostly in the distant fog. "Way over," he trailed away as he stared straight ahead.

"Okay. You got a little disoriented. Let's go. We've been lost most of today. I want to get camp set up before dark and we get totally lost."

Mike hopped up on Frog and quickened his pace as he headed for the timber. Now that he could see and now that he really knew where he had to go, he was wasting no time making up for their delay. Jill had to kick Nellibell to keep pace with the other two horses, rapidly putting meadow between them and her.

Clouds continued to open up and move northeast, letting the sun warm and dry the soaked riders and horses. Soon they were underneath a nearly clear blue sky. They wound through the trees, weaving in and out of meadows and passing lakes and marshes. The top was nearly flat, with only a few peaks in the distance. Mike recognized Conejos Peak, or what he thought was Conejos Peak, but he didn't say anything to Jill. He knew he made a fool of himself once and figured he probably would again before this trip was over.

They came to a low rise and a rock-studded expanse of

flower-speckled meadows and small ponds that stretched for a mile. From this high point, he could see the low wall off to the west that defined the Continental Divide. It didn't seem much higher than where they sat, but between it and them, there was not a tree over ten feet tall, the alpine forest of stunted trees called krumholz. He looked behind him, from where they had ridden. At the time, it seemed they were on flat ground, but from here, it was obvious they were steadily climbing uphill.

"I think that lake over there is Blue Lake," Mike nodded at a lake several miles south and below them on a lower plateau. "I'd just as soon camp here where we still have a few trees for protection." He looked around him, then rode back to the last stand of spruce, still about thirty feet tall. He got off Frog and walked around. He didn't want Jill to see him hobble as he tried to get life back into his aching legs.

"Here looks good for a honeymoon cabin. Whatcha think?" Mike smiled at Jill.

"One spot looks as good as another. What now?" Jill let the sexual innuendo go unanswered. No need to disappoint Mike this early.

Jill was not an experienced camper, especially on a pack trip like this into a vast wilderness. Neither was Mike, although he had been on several trips in his short Forest Service career. He had never been responsible for tending the horses, setting up these weird tepee tents, or picking a route of travel. Jill was used to the convenience of a real kitchen, with a gas or electric stove, a sink, and other odds and ends such as tables and chairs.

"I'll set up the tent. You get a fire going. Lots of wood laying around. I have to cut a few poles for the tent."

"You have to cut down trees? Why?"

"That's the type of tent this is. Form a tripod from trees. That's what holds up the tent."

"That seems like a waste. Can't you use a standing tree?" Jill was active in Audubon Society and detested all the clear cutting she had seen when she was growing up in Oregon.

"Sure. You find three trees spaced just right, leaning just right, with room between them for a tent and we can leave them standing. It doesn't hurt anything. No one ever gets up here. It's not like cutting trees where people see them. However, if you want to sleep out under the stars, that is your choice. This is the only tent we have and there is only one way to put it up." Mike realized his voice was condescending, but at this point, he didn't care.

"I think you should throw this tent away when you get back and buy something modern. This is the 1970's you know. You are not Gifford Pinchot and can go out and cut trees for boughs to sleep on and all that old pioneer stuff." Jill felt she had the moral and the upper hand in this discussion. Mike said nothing more as he found and cut three small dead trees.

As the sun slipped behind the low ridge of hills, they finished cleaning up their supper dishes and sat down by the campfire to enjoy the purple and orange fringe of clouds brushing the western horizon. The day had started fine, turned sour and wet for a while, but now was ending on another bright note. Until the shooting.

Without warning, a shot blasted out from somewhere nearby.

"What the?" Mike said, as he jumped up, expecting to see a bandito coming at them with a rifle. "Who's shooting?"

"That sounded close," Jill said, as she looked in all

directions like Mike did. She focused on the horses, hobbled and staked near the edge of the trees. They were still munching on the bagful of oats each had been given. Frog was twitching his ears, but Queenie and Nellibell were concentrating on eating.

"Who's there?" Mike yelled as he walked towards where he thought the shot came from. Nothing in reply. "Hey!" Still no answer.

"I think sheep should be somewhere nearby. Probably just the herder shooting at a coyote." Mike returned and sat back down, but Jill was not there.

"Jill?" Mike looked in the tent but she was gone.

"Over here," Jill replied from the nearby trees. "Maybe you just stand there and whiz on a rock. I don't do that. I'm going to bed." She came back to the tent, buckling her belt.

Just then another shot rang out. It sounded like it came from the exact same place. Mike and Jill looked at each other again but didn't say anything.

"This is kinda weird," Mike said. "It's getting too dark to really see well enough to be shooting anything." Queenie snorted and Frog nickered. They were through eating, but were picketed near a small streamlet so they could get water if they wanted it.

After another minute, the shot sounded again.

"They are at regular intervals, it seems," Mike said. He walked a little further away than he did the first time.

Jill disappeared into the tent, ready to ignore whatever idiot was out there. "You need to carry a gun if you do this anymore. For bears or crazy sheepherders."

Mike didn't hear her. He came back a few minutes later laughing. "It's some kind of device that uses a bottle of something to drip into something that makes a bang. Sheep are just beyond those trees and this thing obviously is set to make a bang every minute or so. I guess to scare off coyotes.

Pretty dumb coyote if they think someone is standing in one place shooting every minute. Especially after dark."

Mike came into the tent. Jill was already in her sleeping bag and had her back to the tent door. "Turn off the lantern and go to sleep. Guess we will have to sleep all night with that racket?"

"Guess so. Gonna get cold tonight," Mike mumbled as he climbed into his bag. His voice carried a wishful tone that she would have zipped the bags together but he didn't bother to say anything. This would be no continuation of the honeymoon, he realized.

The next morning, Mike was first out of the tent. Only two horses were standing where they were supposed to be. Frog was not there. There was no frost, but the dew was heavy on the grass.

"Dammit, Frog, where are you?" Mike yelled.

This brought a muffled question from Jill, burrowed deep in her sleeping bag. Mike couldn't understand her question, but he responded despondently, "Don't see Frog. Stupid horse is gone."

He quickly walked around the camp. It was easy to follow Frog's tracks in the dewy grass. Frog had hopped clear across the meadow and was slowly heading towards the sheep camp. He was hobbled, which restricted his movement to hops. His tendency to wander off in hobbles with this frog-hopping gave him his name. Knowing this trait, Mike had picketed him to a tree, but the rope was trailing behind Frog, still tied on the small uprooted tree.

By the time Mike got back to camp leading Frog, he was

soaking wet below the waist. Jill was still nestled in her sleeping bag when Mike opened the flap and said, none too friendly, "Get your ass out of there. The tent is coming down in five minutes." He really didn't mean this, since he didn't want to pack a wet tent and even with the sun now peeking over the trees to the northeast, it would take a good hour or more to dry the canvas. "This is not a good way to start the day," Mike mumbled to himself as he searched for dry wood to start a warming fire.

Two hours later, Mike cinched the double diamond hitch, and climbed into the saddle to head west. His sour mood transferred to Jill. She followed in silence, hardly saying five words since she unhappily crawled out of her warm bag.

They circled south so Mike could check on the sheep, and the herder who had kept him awake half the night with the shooting machine. When he found the herder, they were unable to communicate. Mike knew about ten words of Spanish, and the herder didn't recognize any of these, Basque being totally different than Spanish. After minutes of futilely waving arms and pointing in all directions, Mike waved goodbye to the herder, and made a futile effort to count the sheep, which were scattered over a half mile of rock-dotted meadow.

Jill made friends with one of the sheep dogs while the men tried to talk, and as she and Mike rode off, the dog followed them to the edge of the flock. She was afraid it would keep following, but Mike reassured her the dog was protecting the sheep and making sure they didn't take any mutton with them. When they passed over the small rise where the last sheep were grazing, the dog stopped and pushed the furthest sheep back towards the main flock.

By early afternoon, they were close to the western edge of the plateau. When they reached the Continental Divide Trail, which at this point was only a series of rock cairns—

with no visible trail connecting them—Mike pulled out his camera and started taking pictures. As he positioned Jill on the trail for a picture, she noticed an impressive cloud buildup to the southwest. This had been hidden by a rocky ridge up until that point.

"Mike, those clouds look bad. They are really building fast. Look, you can see them growing now."

"Well, it's about that time. Guess we should start down. We need to go south, but I don't see where the trail goes." He looked at the cairns, which led west and up rather than south. The trail went to the end of the rock breaks, which meant going higher towards the summit, then it wound south and down off the top. He rode to where the rock wall ended and could see Green Lake below them, along with scattered stands of trees. To get there, they had to go uphill, which he didn't like doing with the clouds growing by the minute.

"I think we'd better hurry. It will take us a while to get over there," Mike said, pointing to a high point to their southwest.

Jill took off her floppy hat and brushed back her hair, adjusting the rubber band on her pony tail. "I don't like this. Look, I just saw some lightning. Oh, Mike, this is getting dangerous."

"Let's move fast." He spurred Frog into a fast walk.

They made it almost to the top when the first gust of wind slammed into them. The sun had already disappeared into the blackness of the growing clouds. They entered a stand of krumholz as the first lightning strike flashed overhead.

"Get off the horse, quick," Mike shouted as he hopped off Frog. He quickly tied him to a tree and tied Queenie about ten feet away. He ran to Jill and tied Nellibell, then grabbed Jill and crawled into a thicket of trees about four feet tall. He pushed her to the ground as rain started pelting them.

"What about the horses?" Jill screamed as a lightning flash struck about a mile away.

"They are on their own. It's every man, women, and horse for themselves." Mike lay on top of Jill as the storm hit full force.

The sky turned into a strobe light. Lightning flashed from cloud to cloud as well as hitting the ground. One bolt hit so close the thunder was instantaneous with the flash of light. Jill screamed. She heard the horses whinny, but was afraid to look up. Mike raised his head a few inches but could see only horse legs shifting in place. His rope tying had improved over last night.

The rain turned to hail as the lightning increased even more. Jill was crying by this time. Then as quickly as it started, it was over. The hail decreased and the lightning was fading to the north. The wind died down and the hail stopped, with only a few rain drops falling. Mike lifted his head to see the horses dripping wet, backs and saddles covered with white.

"I've never seen anything more pathetic," Mike laughed as he brushed off his back and got to his knees.

"Is it over? Did we die? Is it safe to get up? Mike, you should stay down."

"You don't think God would put us through that, then let me get hit by lightning when it's all over, do you?"

The sky lightened as they both stood. Rumbles of thunder echoed throughout the canyons to their north.

"I'm freezing. For crying out loud, the ground is covered with hail, I'm soaking wet. We're going to freeze to death. Why did I ever let you talk me into this?" Jill slowly started moving around. She wiped her face with her wet sleeve. Her tears were hidden on her rain-soaked face.

"Well, I could have been up here by myself, you know."

"What a wonderful choice you gave me. Come with you

and be miserable, freezing to death, scared to death, or be at home wondering when I would get word that I was a young widow. They would never have found your body and I would have had to wait ten years before I could get your insurance."

"I think its seven years and you look good in black."

Jill hit Mike on the shoulder. "That's not funny. I want down out of here. I want to go home."

Mike tried to put his arm around her, but she pushed him off. "It's okay. Look, there is blue sky up there. The sun will be out in a few minutes and we can ride down off the top and set up camp. We can get a nice fire going."

"You get anything to burn in this frozen wet hell hole, you will have performed a miracle. Everything is sopping wet. Including me. Us. The horses."

Mike walked over to inspect the horses. They were pawing their feet, with eyes wide open and ears perked up. He untied them and led them over to Jill. He tried to wipe off her saddle, but it was still wet.

"Just get on. I don't think we can get any wetter. The quicker we get down, the quicker we can get warm."

By the time they left the stunted trees, the sun was shining. Water vapor was rising from the ground, the rocks, even the horses. They reached the summit and found where the trail was very defined going down the hill. As they hurried down the steep and muddy trail, their bouncing in the saddle hurt since they were so cold.

About halfway down, Queenie slipped on a muddy side hill section of trail and fell down, rolling onto the pack. The action jerked the lead rope out of Mike's hand, nearly pulling him off Frog. Mike's first thought was a broken leg. Queenie wallowed as she tried to stand, but kept falling on the slick mud. The pack loosened and slid on her side, making her efforts even harder.

Mike dismounted and grabbed Queenie's rope. He helped her shift to a more level spot and pulled to help her up. Mike was shaking, with the cold as well as with fright that he would have a horse with a broken leg miles from nowhere. Now Mike could remove the pack and inspect Queenie's legs. Everything seemed all right. Jill had held onto Frog's reins while Mike helped Queenie—they didn't need him taking advantage and wandering off.

"Can we just camp here?" Jill whined.

"There's nowhere level. We have to get further down. Hold onto Frog while I redo the pack. It will only take me a minute. Don't have to go very far with it."

Within twenty minutes, they stopped next to a dense stand of spruce at the bottom of the hill. They were by a small stream next to a meadow. There was no trace of hail on the ground, but everything was wet. They quickly set the tent up and Mike wandered through the trees, breaking off dry branches. He came back with a huge handful and set them on the ground. He went back into the trees and returned with an armful of dead spruce needles.

"These are actually dry. It is so dense in there, the ground is almost dry in places." Mike laid them next to the pile of branches.

Jill frowned. "You get a fire going. I'll put stuff in the tent. At least it's dry in there. I'm not even hungry. I just want to get on dry clothes and lay in the sleeping bag. I've never been so miserable in my life."

Mike tried to laugh but it sounded more like a cough. "Look at it this way, it's something we can tell our grandkids."

Jill didn't laugh. "It will take sex to have kids. You will be lucky if ever again," she mumbled as she disappeared into the tent.

Mike shrugged his shoulders. So they got a little cold and wet. Hey, this was adventure. So she didn't think so. "No sense of adventure," he mumbled. "Women," then he bit his lower lip.

He took the horses down to the creek, but only Queenie drank. He didn't blame any of them. They weren't interested in grazing, although they did perk up when he gave them their ration of oats. He made sure to tie Frog to a stout tree.

Once the fire was going, the sun was below the trees to the west. Jill did come out to sit by the fire, but she had on almost every shirt and sweatshirt she had with her.

The next morning was cold again, but not a cloud in the sky. Mike managed to get another fire going. Jill was cheerful as she cooked eggs and the last of the bacon. Their food was almost gone, but this was their last day. They took a walk around the meadow as the sun quickly dried the grass. They marveled at the profusion of wildflowers. Just a few hundred feet in elevation made a big difference in the plants in the meadows. As they walked around a small rise, they came upon a large lake.

"See, I'm not lost. Green Lake. Good fishin' here I'm told."

"It is pretty," Jill said as she held Mike by the arm. She reached down and picked up a small rock and threw it in the lake. It skipped twice on the calm water.

"Look, over there." Mike pointed across the lake. A herd of twenty elk were grazing a quarter mile away. "It may have been miserable, but this is the experience of a lifetime."

"Yeah," Jill laughed. "It should only happen once in a lifetime."

A red tailed hawk flew overhead, screaming its lonesome cry.

"Even if it's only once, it's worth it," Mike said as he watched the elk cross the meadow and disappear from view.

Jill looked at Mike, smiled, then shoved him into the shallow water at the edge of the lake. "No sense of adventure? I call this an adventure," she said as Mike fell in slow motion into the ice cold water. "Now I agree with you. It is worth it." She walked back to the horses, laughing the whole way.

MEMORIES OF A WILDERNESS CABIN

*Although its world here hadn't changed much,
the world outside this sheltered mountain valley
had changed beyond recognition. Maybe that
was what I felt—I was in a time warp, where this
cabin reflected a time lost to the rest of us.*
James Osborn, District Ranger

I STOOD AT THE edge of the meadow one September noon and marveled at the peacefulness of the setting. The log cabin was old but dignified, almost hidden in a stand of aspen and spruce near the headwaters of the Chama River. It was obviously man-made but it didn't offend my senses. From the first moment I saw it, I felt it belonged in this secluded place. Snow-capped peaks surrounded the valley in a majestic, protective wall. Small waterfalls lined the gray cliffs; green forests blanketed the mountainsides. Just beyond the trees in front of the cabin, the vast meadow swept across and beyond the river, sloping upward to more trees. This was a wildness that most of us never experienced.

I was alone. Other than the cabin, the only human signs in this sanctuary were the trails—the unmarked foot trail winding from the road three miles distant, and the old sheepherder trails, marked only by the time-blurred carvings on aspen trunks. This was not a painting, I had to remind myself. When I closed my eyes, the symphony of sound overtook my senses. Birds proclaimed their presence by chirps, twitters, and squawks. Amazing, I thought. I had noticed them before, but once I really listened, I heard them emptying their souls of song, saying farewell to summer abundance.

A week before, I had no idea this cabin existed. That is until receiving a phone call from Alex at the Forest Supervisor's Office.

"Jim, you aware of the Armand special use permit?"

"No, never heard of it. But then Frank handles those permits. If it's not a problem, then I may not even know we have it. You know my hands have been kinda full the last year with the timber trespass thing down here."

"Yeah, figured you might not know about it," Alex drawled in his monotone. That voice was usually enough to keep me away from him and his made-up crises. "You need to close the file. We gotta get rid of these isolated cabin permits. Regional Office been on my case. We have five on the Forest. Your permit is in the name of Caroline—he pronounced it car-oh-lean—Armand down in the Chama Basin. She is an old lady, daughter-in-law of the homesteader who built the cabin. It's non-transferable. Once she croaks, the permit is history. You get to have a winter lightning strike."

"Alex, I really love your compassion. What the hell is the rush? Don't you have anything else to do?"

"Rules are rules. Why should some old lady who for sure never goes up there anymore, keep this cabin? It's only a matter of time. I hear she's in a nursing home down in New Mexico and will probably be dead by year's end anyway."

"Then I suggest you sit there and read obituaries and when she dies, you let me know. Okay? I gotta go. A permittee just walked in and he looks like he wants to spit nails in the wall. Later."

After that phone call, which disturbed me the more I thought about it, I realized I should go see the cabin. Frank, who handled special use permits on the district, was off on his annual black powder elk hunt, so I couldn't just ask him about it. Besides, I needed to better explore this corner of my district. I had seen it only once and that was from a small plane looking for a fire.

Standing among the few remaining flowers and the tall grass of the front yard, I felt the spirit of the cabin. A gust of the autumn breeze swirled yellow aspen leaves past my face. I couldn't order the destruction of this piece of someone's life without knowing more about it.

I had run across many old deserted log cabins in the forests I worked on in my career, but this cabin was different. This cabin was not deserted. It was alive, still being used. It had a history. I pulled the file folder out of my pack and glanced through it.

I learned from the file that it was called the Armand Cabin, named after Peter Armand, a sheepherder and homesteader who built it decades ago. It was still owned by his daughter-in-law, but most recent bills had been paid by her son, Jesse Armand, from Arizona. There was not much history in the folder, although correspondence went back decades. There were annual bills for collection, a few plats and drawings, changes of ownership from father to son to wife, a few letters from my predecessors detailing what repair work needed to be done, but not much else. The fact that a recent letter from Jesse included a power of attorney from his mother and a request that all bills be sent to him in Arizona must have been what prompted the phone call to me from Alex. Not a smart move on Jesse's part, I thought. Didn't he know the cabin's days were numbered? He had to. Every year, the Bill for Collection mentioned the permit could not be transferred.

Before I could brace myself to tell Mr. Armand he had to destroy his cabin, and probably a piece of himself as well as his ancestors, I wanted to contact him and at least learn the history of the cabin. It really wasn't something I had to do for my job. It was something I had to do for myself. Already, in the few minutes I had spent in the cool shade of the front yard, the cabin touched me with some mysterious calling. It had seen much history, shared the lives of three generations or more, weathered storms and blizzards, lightning and floods. Although its world here hadn't changed much, the world outside this sheltered mountain valley had changed beyond recognition. Maybe that was what I felt—I was in a time warp, where this cabin reflected a time lost to the rest of us. In a slowly changing ecosystem, in a rapidly changing world, this place kept the past alive.

I walked around the cabin. Large Engelmann and blue spruce bordered what would have been a yard anywhere else, an extension of the aspen grove, the wildflower meadow, and the river a few yards below, meandering through the expansive meadow crossing the valley. Moss-covered flat rocks served as stepping stones down the gentle slope to the riverbank. A few more lined the way to the lichen-covered, wood-slab outhouse. A faded sign inside that door, barely readable—hand painted long ago—told the user in poetic language to leave the door open when in use, close it when not. The view was relaxing, conducive to easy passage. My translation. I smiled as I thought of the philosophical musings of users of the seat over the years. Maybe great books were written (or at least read) or new inventions were made, inspired by this view. I certainly could understand the plea to leave the door open. Very few people on this planet could look out on such a view while doing their daily chores.

As I contemplated the scene, a lone elk whistled in the distance. The haunting sound echoed from the cliffs and bounced off every aspen. One followed another for several minutes. Soon, an elk answered from the western edge of the meadow, a half mile away. They trumpeted in competition for a few minutes, then both stopped. No confrontation, no locking of antlers in fierce battle. That might happen, but not in front of me that day.

This cabin had a long history and my task was to order and write its obituary. I needed to do it respectfully. I circled around it again. There were both a front porch and small back porch. It looked like the back room had been added onto the original cabin and a lean-to extended the back porch. I found one window that wasn't either shuttered or covered from the inside. Peering in, I noticed the cabin had only two rooms, with a partial loft along one end. The inside logs looked as new as the day they were peeled. They had survived much better than the gray, weathered outside walls. There was a large fireplace and a pot-bellied wood stove along the north wall and an antique wood burning kitchen stove in the newer room. It looked like the add-on served as a kitchen, but I couldn't see any more than that. Amazingly, there was no evidence of vandalism, although this place had obviously been unoccupied most of the time for probably decades.

There was a plastic-covered letter tacked on the front door: "Hunters, hikers, or visitors. This is private property, under permit from the US Government. If you find yourself trapped in a storm or in need of shelter, make yourself at home. We only ask you to respect our work and care we have given this, our legacy from our grandparents. Thank you. Jesse and Edna." There were directions on where to find the key, which was well hidden, but with a little map reading skill, one could find it and enter the cabin through the back door. The locks were designed to keep out bears and varmints, but people were trusted to enter if needed. Jesse and Edna trusted people more than I would. Their faith seemed to be well placed though.

A large glass jar sitting against the wall next to the front door was stuffed with wadded notes. Some were on plain sheets of paper, some were on the back of tin can labels, some on torn business cards, one on a weathered dollar bill. All thanked the owners for emergency use of the cabin. I found one quite poignant. It simply stated: "God bless you. Your cabin saved my life. Next trip through, I hope to meet you. You answered my prayers." The writer's name and address were added to the bottom of the note. He was from Houston and the date was 1961. It was written on the ripped out title page of a pocket-sized King James Bible.

As I hiked back to my truck—parked almost three miles away near the end of a new logging road—I wondered what my Forest Service was doing to this area. I kept thinking of the cabin and what it meant. My thoughts shifted to what we were doing in forest management. The world of this cabin was gone, blown by the wind like a fallen aspen leaf. Disintegrating like the wood planks of the weathered gray outhouse. I had to learn more about not only the cabin but also this piece of hidden wilderness. I inherited the plans for massive logging of this valley. Those plans now seemed wrong to me.

The first thing I did when I got back to my office was to compose a letter to Jesse and Edna Armand of Yuma, Arizona. I thought of calling them on the phone, but I wanted to think carefully of what I would say. I had explicit instructions from not only the Forest Service Manual, but from my boss, or at least his staff, and I was expected to follow those instructions. Yet, this cabin might be an integral part of the life of at least two people. What would it do to them to just out of the blue say they had to tear it down? For what reason? Some bureaucratic rule that ignored any common sense? I could follow rules when they made sense to me, but the closer I got to retirement, the less common sense seemed to enter into some management decisions.

Something about that cabin and its location affected me. It "spoke" to me, in the New Age jargon of my niece. Back in the early 70s, New Age was a new term and not in common use. At the time, I didn't understand the changes that were happening and the woo-woo goings on that were starting to be spoken and performed. Chanting, crystals, feelings, emotions. Common stuff nowadays. My niece introduced me to the strangeness. She told me that I had to listen to the trees. I was their guardian and they were speaking to me. I heard something—whatever it was—whispering in that September breeze coming off the high peaks, and it was blowing right onto that cabin and echoing onto me.

Dear Mr. and Mrs Armand,

I visited your cabin along the Chama River yesterday. Everything looked fine and well maintained. You have done a good job in caring for the permit. I am evaluating some of the special use permits on my district and yours is scheduled for review. We are in the process of determining what should be done with some of the special uses like your cabin that don't fit with our existing Multiple Use Plans and the upcoming land management planning process. Since the permit is in your mother's name and is non-transferable, we need to discuss your plans for it.

Before I make any decisions, I would like to discuss with you some of the history of this cabin. How did the cabin fit in with early use of the Chama River Valley? Was it part of grazing management of the early days of the National Forest? How was the cabin and surrounding area used by your grandfather and father? Did early Forest Rangers use the cabin? When did it stop being used for grazing and become a summer home? I want to determine if it has historical significance in early Forest management.

I look forward to visiting with you the next time you are in the area. If that won't be soon, please let me know so I can schedule a phone call with you.

Sincerely,
James D. Osborn
District Ranger

It sounded too bureaucratic. After reading it a couple times, I was not sure what it said. What was my purpose? I was beating around the bush. But I sent it anyway. It was a first step and hopefully did not put fear in poor old Jesse's heart of his having to bulldoze the cabin. There were other old cabins in my career, part of illegal mining claims, that I had no hesitation burning after years of legal wrangling.

They were trespass and we had followed proper procedure to get rid of them. This cabin was different. Yes, it did speak to me. I had to understand what it said.

A week later, I received a letter from Jesse. Edna was in poor health and wouldn't be coming up this way in the near future, but in two weeks, Jesse was driving to Santa Fe to visit his mother in the nursing home. He would stop by and talk to me if I had time to visit. The cabin must have been talking to me because I had a three-day meeting in Santa Fe the same week he would be there. I wrote him back, detailing my schedule. Four days later, he left a phone message: he would meet me at my motel on a Wednesday evening.

I wanted to go back to the cabin for another look around, but the year's first winter storm hit two days later. Two feet of snow stranded hunters everywhere and effectively closed the backcountry until late spring.

We sat in a comfortable corner booth of the motel lounge until 11 p.m. that night talking, mostly about the cabin. It was obvious the cabin was as much a part of Jesse's life as were his wife and children, to whom he was devoted. This discussion made my job more difficult.

Jesse was a likable person, quiet, but knowledgeable on many things. He looked older than his age, solid like the old Marine he was, with close cut white hair. He knew the cabin's days were numbered. He wanted to keep it as long as he could use it. He had high blood pressure and recently was diagnosed with diabetes as well as cataracts. His children rarely visited the cabin and didn't have the connection to it he did.

His grandfather Peter Armand came to the Southwest in the late 1800s from a farm in Wisconsin. Since his ancestors had been sheep herders in the Pyrenees, east of Pamplona, he had sheep in his blood. He settled in Colorado and started taking his sheep into the remote and almost unknown Chama River headwaters. He pioneered the first wagon trail into the valley and the first year built a log lean-to about two miles from where he eventually built the cabin.

He had five children when he settled in the area, three boys and two girls. The first few years, he spent the entire summer in the mountains, leaving the family back at his small ranch near Chama. Peter told them stories about his grandfather, who would spend months on end roaming the Pyrenees with no human contact. The second summer that Peter roamed with the flock in his adopted mountains, his youngest son died of typhoid fever during an epidemic that ran through the area. He didn't know about it until over a week later. His wife was distraught. Andre, Jesse's father, made a trip by himself into the valley to find his father. For a twelve-year old, this was a hair-raising experience. Although the village of Chama was only about ten miles away, it took Andre several days to find his father. Luckily, Andre found the lean-to and a stash of food his father hid nearby. Peter left the sheep to rush back to comfort his wife, returning a week later with the entire family. While he was gone, his dogs did a wonderful job of protecting the sheep, still in the same meadow. The sheep had eaten it down to the dirt, not having enough sense to go down a rocky path to the valley floor. Peter founds signs that a cougar had been stalking the flock, but his dogs had kept it away.

Having the entire family with him, Peter decided he needed to build a suitable dwelling for them to stay during the summer. Maria couldn't bear to remain at the Chama ranch, near the fresh grave of her baby. The whole family spent the rest of the summer cutting trees to build a small cabin. They picked out a spot further up the valley, next to a small spring. After a week, Peter realized this cabin would not do for a permanent structure, so he rushed to finish a temporary cabin, leaving the job of building a permanent cabin for next year. His work with Andre made him realize the young boy was a good worker with natural skills for building.

The next year, he hired two Southern Utes to help construct the new cabin. And with three mules to haul logs, they quickly felled more—and straighter—logs, and dragged them to the new cabin site. They decided to put the new cabin further uphill from the river and on the edge of a small meadow. Jesse remembered Andre telling him the meadow was full of columbines. He couldn't step anywhere without stepping on one of the beautiful blue flowers. Living out of a tent for a month, they disassembled the temporary cabin and used the logs for the new building. Andre hauled mortar mix from Chama, to chink between the logs. Manuel, one of the Utes, was stronger than a mule, according to Andre. Using a makeshift travois, he hauled a wood stove all the way from Chama, then turned around and brought back a bedframe and bedsprings.

Although the floor was level, the cabin itself was tilted slightly on the hill. Peter didn't notice this until the cabin was half done, although young Andre had told him several times it looked crooked. They originally built a sod roof, but after the first winter, realized that was not acceptable. The next year, they hauled in metal sheets for a better roof. About the time of the first light snowfall in early September, Peter said it was done for the year. Maria then came to put finishing touches on the inside, and the cabin was improved and added to over the next twenty years.

The sheep were under the usually conscientious care of a Mexican named Juan Pedro. Peter had worked with him off and on for several years, but entrusted the operation to him that year. Peter only occasionally went up the mountain to check on things. He was enraged to find a whole grove of aspen carved up with quite explicit pornographic carvings. Juan Pedro said he didn't do it, that they were done by Fernando, his cousin who helped him for several weeks in July. Peter said he would not allow that type of art on his range and made Juan Pedro re-carve the drawings to hide what he considered obscenities. Andre hiked up the trail one afternoon to admire the art. He thought it quite good and was sorry to see it defaced and cleaned up. He did blush over a couple of the drawings but would never tell Jesse what they were.

Peter had the whole valley to himself for grazing, but did find competition from sheepmen from the San Luis Valley once he got on top of the 11,000 foot plateau. It was a free-for-all up there, so he didn't spend much time at that high elevation. The range wasn't free of snow until mid- to late-July most years, so there really wasn't much feed. He preferred to graze the small benches and vales on the slopes bordering his valley. A large wildfire had swept up the mountains east of the cabin three years before Peter came to the valley. Even until the current time, many of the slopes were still not forested. Jesse remembered as a young boy those hillsides being covered with wildflowers, much more than they were in the 1970s. Aspen were starting to come back by then, but there was still good sheep feed.

Peter died in 1930 and Maria two years later. One of Jesse's earliest memories was sitting on his grandpa's lap in a rocking chair on the front porch of the cabin. His grandma, her hair pure white and tied in a bun, brought him a fresh rhubarb pie she had just made. He remembered he and his grandpa eating the whole pie in one sitting. Although Jesse and his folks lived only a couple miles from Peter and Maria's home ranch northwest of Chama, Jesse didn't remember too much about that ranch. He did remember a lot of details about the cabin.

Jesse couldn't wait to get out of school each May. They rarely could get to the cabin before June, but as soon as they could, they plowed through snowdrifts to drive the wagon to the cabin. Many years, they could not ford the river, it was so high and fast. The river was always changing course in the huge meadow, with new channels every year. The main road into the basin was washed out several times, although it never crossed the river except just outside Chama. Jesse told of one spring when they couldn't even get the horses up to the cabin and they had to walk in five miles, mostly over snow drifts up to five feet deep. Sitting on the front porch, two hundred yards from the river, they had to shout to hear each other, the sound of the river was so loud.

Jesse grew up at the cabin, spending all or part of every summer there until he was 29 years old. He enlisted before the Second World War started, spent two years in the South Pacific, and when the war was over, returned briefly to the valley. Andre had developed cataracts and couldn't see very well, and because of that, Jesse found the cabin to be in a mess. By then, Caroline, Jesse's mother, did not like going up to the cabin. She was getting arthritis very bad, and what people didn't realize at the time, was showing early signs of Alzheimer's. Jesse spent part of that summer making more improvements to the cabin, bringing his new wife up to his "secret paradise" as he called it.

That brief history brought me up to the present. Before we parted, I had to ask Jesse another question.

"Jesse, you are very close to this cabin, aren't you?"

"Yes sir," he said sternly as he thrust his chin up in true Marine Corps manner. "That cabin is my life. Of course, I don't live there and rarely get up there anymore. But I grew up there. It is my grandparents. My parents. Mom hasn't been there for probably ten years. Maybe more. Afraid she doesn't even remember it. That's the hard part. It meant a lot to her and she doesn't even remember it. That's tough. Not fair. Not fair," he trailed off, his eyes looking down.

"Jesse, you know the cabin cannot be transferred to you. What will happen when we can't keep it in her name anymore?"

Jesse looked down at his empty Corona bottle. He pushed it around, lining it up with the other two on the table. He looked up at me. I couldn't tell if he was ready to laugh or to cry. He rubbed his eyes, then took out his handkerchief and wiped his face. "Damn cataracts. Dad had them too. I have surgery scheduled for next month."

"Mr. Osborn, I'm getting old. Mom won't be with us much longer. She's nearly 95. Edna is not in very good health. When I can't hike up there anymore, then I'm all done and the cabin can be removed. But I can still get up there. All I ask is a few more years. Does that hurt anyone?" He looked at me with watery eyes.

At that point, I had to stall for a minute myself. I looked at Jesse, then thought of Alex's comments to me on the phone that day he called me. "Jesse, I will drag this thing out as long as I can. When the time does come," I didn't know how to phrase it politely so I just blurted it out, "When your mom dies, you don't need to let me know right away. I will have to do something when I find out, but sometimes other work gets in my way and I have to set priorities. I would love to hike into the cabin with you and hear some more of its history."

We didn't have time that night in Santa Fe to get into

more details about the Forest Service part of the story. That was the part I needed to know. To me, Jesse and the cabin were one. I didn't like losing a little of my professionalism as I confided in him, but I liked Jesse and I didn't like what this impersonal bureaucracy wanted to do to him.

I called Jesse a couple times in the next few weeks before I finally connected with him again. I learned in conversations with him and Edna that after the National Forest was created in 1905, Peter applied for a grazing permit for his band of 2000 sheep. He held the permit until the year before he died. Then he transferred it to Andre, but the Forest Service cut the numbers to 1500. That soured Andre on his working with the agency. A few years after that, he let Jesse deal with the Rangers. Usually any mention of the government caused Andre to start cursing. It didn't help that he hated FDR and some of his agricultural policies. Jesse thought the family actually benefited from the New Deal, but he could never talk to either his father or mother about it.

After the war, Jesse decided not to continue with the family sheep business, but instead he went back into the military. His brothers and sisters were in other jobs as well. Although he was stationed in California most of the time, he always found time to come back to the cabin for at least a couple weeks during the summers. Just before Andre died in 1959, he sold his sheep to a neighbor, who got the Forest Service to change the permit to cattle. Sheep never again grazed the valley. Jesse always thought that a shame since he felt the valley's plant communities were better suited for sheep than cattle. The cows tended to hang down in the main meadow and didn't get up very far on the slopes. Jesse felt the meadow deteriorated after that. He never saw dandelions until the early 60s and it was at that time he noticed the aspen starting to increase in what used to be flowered meadows.

Two months after I last talked with Jesse, I learned that his mother died in her Santa Fe nursing home. I didn't want to hear this, but Alex did have his antenna out and he found out from a Forest Service friend in Santa Fe about the death. In the early spring, Jesse left a phone message that Edna, his wife of 40 years had passed away. I had been stalling Alex, claiming I was inundated with other work and would get to the permit soon. I told my boss, the Forest Supervisor, I wanted to wait and visit the cabin one more time in the summer. I needed to decide on how the cabin would be removed since there was not road access to it. Secretly, I was starting to think of a plan to let it stay, at least for the remainder of Jesse's lifetime. That would be tough for me to do since the rules were pretty straightforward. The cabin was in her name, she was dead, the permit could not be transferred. End of discussion.

But I couldn't do it that way. I needed time. Coincidentally, I didn't get more pressure from the Supervisor's Office. Alex had prostate surgery, which gained me the time I wanted.

The historical significance of the cabin became my focus. I wanted to check on its use in the early management of the Forest. Maybe it was used as a Ranger Station at one time. I would have to ask Jesse more specific questions. If I could somehow stall for even a year or two, I might save Jesse from a body blow that he couldn't handle right now. I had seen the tears in his eyes and heard his voice choke when he reminisced about the cabin and the fact its days were numbered. It was part of him, part of his life in a world that was pummeling him with death. He needed the reassurance of the cabin. I wanted to help him go up there and spend all summer in that safe haven.

I made several calls to Jesse during the spring, but was never able to connect. He didn't return any of my calls. I began to get worried. I dug through my notes and found his son's address. He was a lawyer for a lobbying firm in Washington, DC. I called him in early June, but he was on a month's leave visiting his sister in Australia. Her husband was at the U.S. Consulate in Sidney; she had not been back to the States for three years. Honoring her dad's wish, she had not even come back for her mom's cremation. There was no funeral.

I decided to hike into the cabin to see it one more time, but also to see if possibly Jesse was there. I was almost unable to get to where the trail left the road for the cabin. A culvert in the new logging road was plugged with debris and spring runoff had eroded the road for nearly three hundred yards. A ten-foot deep gully now replaced a large section of road. A good advertisement for keeping culverts clear of debris, I thought. The engineers would love hearing about this. This would be an unexpected expense for their budget. As I neared the curve where the trail took off, I had to stop while fifteen bull elk crossed the road. I loved this valley more every time I saw it.

At the wide spot in the road that marked the start of Peter's old wagon track, I saw the truck with Arizona plates. I remembered it from the Santa Fe motel. It was Jesse's truck. There was nothing in the back of the truck nor in the front seat except an envelope on the driver's seat. The door wasn't locked and when I looked at the envelope, I could see it was addressed to me. It wasn't meant to be mailed, but written in ink in large letters were my name and title. Nothing else.

I looked at the envelope and thought the worst. I held it for a several minutes, looking up at the stunning scenery surrounding me, holding back my emotions. I didn't want to open it. I tucked it in my shirt and started walking.

A sense of foreboding kept my pace to the cabin hesitant but steady. As I approached the last meadow before the cabin, I smelled smoke. I ran the last few hundred yards but stopped as I saw the cabin. It was a pile of burned ash and twisted metal roof. There was still smoke rising from the ash, but it had obviously been several days since the fire. Even the outhouse was burned to nothing. Since the vegetation was still wet from the spring melt, the fire had not spread anywhere.

I looked around, wishfully, yet without hope, for any sign of Jesse. Nothing. It was all over. I knew "it" meant Jesse as well. I knew the body would be hidden in the rubble. I sat down, my head in my hands, and cried. It was a natural evolution of things. It was life, and it was death, my fate and ultimately the fate of this valley.

I sat there, looking first at the ruins, then up at the walls of the surrounding mountains, still snow-capped and gleaming white in the bright sun. I wanted to see Jesse walking down out of the forest to the cabin. I pulled the envelope out of my shirt, and slowly opened it. Handwritten in large elegant cursive, the note read:

Dear James,

Well, old friend, it's over. I thank you for all you did for me. You are a friend and I know you have done what you can, but there is only so much you can do. I appreciate your efforts.

You are probably sitting by the cabin now reading this. Don't worry. I'm sure it is a mess, but I left $5000 cash with Mom's lawyer in Santa Fe, Mr. Franklin. It is for cleaning up the site. By cutting only a half dozen trees, I think you could walk a backhoe in to either bury or remove the stuff that didn't burn. This is a beautiful place. It will grow back.

I don't like tombstones. I don't want a tombstone for me or for the cabin. My favorite passage from the Bible is from Ecclesiastes 1:4. "One generation passeth away and another generation cometh: but the earth abideth forever."

I came and now I passeth away. The same for the Armands in this valley and for the cabin. You will remember me as you look at this valley. That is all that will be left.

The sheriff will bring in people to search for me, but you will never find me. You will only find the elk and the eagles. I left word with my children and they will be out soon. They will understand. Their lives are different and their generation passeth away from mine. But this valley abides and they will appreciate that.

It had to be this way. I've lost everything that has ever mattered to me. The cabin was next. I couldn't stand to see it taken from me by strangers. You understand. Thank you and God bless you.

Your friend,
Jesse

I stood up and pulled out my handkerchief. I looked up at the brilliant blue sky. Shielding my eyes from the sun, I scanned the distant cliffs. I wiped my eyes as the tears blurred the magnificent view. I smiled and silently said goodbye to Jesse. I put the note and envelope in my pack, looked around one last time, and started the long walk back to my truck. I never again set foot in that valley. When I got back to the office, I called my boss and requested a transfer. Four months later, I moved a thousand miles away.

Lightning and Fire

*I was not an expert in this by any means, but it
didn't take a genius to deduce a fire started here
and spread uphill, getting hotter as it went.
This was the origin of the fire.*
John

THE SUMMER HAD been dry, with not much monsoonal
rain. Towering, dazzling white cumulus clouds built
up every afternoon like bubbles in a bubble bath, but
produced only dry lightning. Fire danger was high and
the Forest Supervisor was edgy. This national forest was
high elevation and did not usually have big fires. But this
Supervisor was not known for sitting back and taking
things as they came. He wanted his forest known for being
ready to cut timber, graze livestock, and fight fires.

Although I was trained in the basics of fire-fighting, I'd
had very little fire experience in my four years with the
Forest Service. I didn't even know there was a separate
fire-fighting organization among all the land management
agencies. That was something I thought happened only in
fire-prone areas like Idaho or California. I plodded along
in my day-to-day duties—laying out timber sales and
inventorying timber—ignorant of the well-organized fire-
fighting business. That changed on a Monday in August.

Upon returning to the ranger station after a day spent
stumbling through spruce stands along Camp Creek—
trying to find enough timber to put up a three-million board

feet sale—I was met by Steve, my boss, with instructions to get my fire gear. We had a fire to go to. I had been looking forward to a shower and a hearty supper since I dropped my lunch pack into the creek at lunchtime—a great horned owl was disturbed by my presence and as it flew from its perch nearly knocked me into the creek—and now here I was at day's end, ready to quit, but in reality, just beginning.

I ran into the warehouse and grabbed a hard hat and fire shirt. I didn't have a pack of all my gear ready to roll as did fire-hardened folks. Perry had the pickup loaded with shovels, Pulaskis, extra water, and two sleeping bags. Steve hopped in, with me between him and Perry. We were off to the north part of the district, the only ones available since the other crews hadn't returned from the field yet.

We drove for two hours, up Bear Creek, then across Pool Table Park, turning onto an old logging road that faded into narrow skid trails. When these petered out, we picked our way through openings in the forest until we came to the slash of an old timber sale. Perry finally stopped as the sun was falling behind a bank of clouds.

"I talked to air recon and got a good idea of where the fire is. Couple trees, with fire on the ground around them. Kinda open, but with grass and downed crap all around. I think I can visualize where it is," Perry said as we got out and loaded our packs. Mine was still damp from the creek seven hours before.

"Is this the old Deer Creek sale?" asked Steve.

"Yeah, I administered the sale. Closed it three years ago," Perry answered. "Sounds like the fire is on the ridge that was the west boundary of the sale."

"Rocky ridge with mostly scraggly spruce with a few foxtail pine? I think I was out there once. We had some blowdown from an old sale just north of there if it's where I think."

Perry rubbed his face, a habit that he had when talking while he was excited about something. "Best I can tell. Said the ridge fell off steep to the west, to a creek with a series of small waterfalls at the bottom. That sounds like Cat Creek and this is the only rocky ridge that fits that description."

"Damn," Steve muttered. "That's still about a mile walk, isn't it?"

"Oh, I don't think it's that far. We came quite a way after the last skid trail. They accessed the west block of the sale from another road, but that is totally blocked off." He was taking tools out of the pickup and laying them on the ground. "I had the cat operator put some big boulders in the road just past where we turned off back there. Should have put up a gate."

"Rocks are the only way to go. Damn hunters tear up the gates around here," Steve said as he grabbed rations from the supply box and stuffed them in his pack, then handing me the box. I put some in my pack and set the empty box back in the pickup. Steve handed me a headlamp with extra batteries. I hadn't even thought of bringing any form of light. I didn't know this part of the district. I didn't know fire. I had nothing to say.

I was already tired as I brought up the rear of our trio heading to a fire in the increasing darkness. I carried a shovel and Pulaski. Perry perched the chain saw on his shoulder and picked up the gas can, while Steve carried a piss pump and two Pulaskis. Perry was whistling as he led the way. He knew this area and he loved fires. No matter when or where there was a fire on the district, Perry was always the first on the scene. I think he could smell smoke from ten miles away.

Walking became easier when we left the harvest area, which was still covered with slash from the logging. The spruce was dry site, common on the north end of the district, with not much vegetation on the ground between trees. After a while, I could smell smoke. The wind was coming directly at us. Except for the yellow glow of the fire, the sky was totally dark by the time we reached the burning tree. Perry set his saw on the ground and all of us laid down our tools. We needed to assess the situation, he said. A large forked Engelmann spruce was on fire all the way to both tops. Fire had fallen into the duff around the base of the trunk and had spread over about a tenth of an acre. Two old, dead trees lying on the ground were also burning. The ground was rocky, with the old needles and twigs of the duff at least six inches deep.

Looking at the fire, I remembered my first fire years ago when I was a college student working at a state park for the summer. I saw flames like this and ran up to them, thinking I had to start beating the flames down. Everyone laughed as they watched a greenhorn meet his first wildfire. I knew better by now. There was no hurry since this fire wasn't going anywhere. We had plenty of time to leisurely put a line around it, fall the tree, then mop up. It sounded easy, but would involve a lot of hard work.

Steve sat down and pulled out a canteen of water. "Well, boys, let's plan our attack." He looked at me as he took a swig and wiped his mouth with his sleeve.

"Don't look at me. I'm the greenhorn here. We put a line around it. Then what?"

Perry rubbed his chin and laughed. "Drink a lot of water, then piss on it all night. I think we should stay here till dawn. I sure don't want to walk out in the dark. Hard enough walking in here. Besides, that will be good overtime."

Steve tossed the canteen to Perry. "Shit, Perry, that the

only thing you think about? A little overtime?"

"No, I think about a lot of overtime." Perry chuckled as he took a long drink and tossed the canteen to me. It was empty.

"Well, there's no hurry," Steve said. "Let's rest up a little. Fire ain't goin' nowhere. Might as well lighten our load and eat a few rats."

I must have had a really confused look on my face as Steve explained, "C rations, John. C rats. Mighty nutritious and fun stuff to eat. Not fit for real rats. They wouldn't eat it if you sat it in front of them."

"We don't want to dig a line around it first?" I thought this was a pretty casual approach to fighting a fire.

Steve started opening his box of rats. "You want some exercise, go ahead. See those rocks?" He pointed to the top of the rocky ridge. "Not goin' past those. And this duff burns real slow. We'll be here all night. Will only take an hour to get it lined. Save your strength for the mop up. That's the fun part."

"Yeah, that will be about the time I need to go back to the truck to radio in," said Perry.

"Think again," said Steve. "I brought a pack set radio. Since I carried this heavy monster, I get to rest while you mop up."

"No, I think John needs the training. We will evaluate him as he does all the work." Perry grabbed my shoulder as he got up. He picked a couple boxes of rations from the pack, handed me one, then sat down and started opening his. "Time to eat."

After we finished off the meals, which tasted pretty good to me since I was hungry enough to eat the box, we stood and picked up our tools. The fire in the forked spruce was almost out. Perry kicked and pounded on it with his shovel to test the stability of the upper branches. They looked solid. He fired up the chain saw and quickly cut the tree down. Steve held onto Perry's belt as he watched the upper part of the tree from behind Perry. If a limb started to fall, he would yank on the belt, Perry would drop the saw and both would run away in the direction of Steve's hand on Perry's shoulder. None fell during his cutting, but the limbs shattered as the tree hit the ground. There was still fire in the tree, and as it fell, the impact loosened charcoal and exposed burning wood to the air, igniting two more spots in the duff.

"Lucked out on that one," Steve said as he picked up burning chunks of limbs and threw them back towards the trunk.

"Easy," Perry grinned as he started sawing the tree tops into smaller chunks. "John, roll the clean pieces out of the fire. The burned ones, put them over here and just let them burn. We'll need a warming fire in a few hours."

We continued to dig a line around the fire, exposing mineral soil. Luckily, there wasn't much rock, although the duff was deep in places, occasionally up to 10 inches thick. Fire had burned down into it around the trunk and other scattered areas. Within an hour, we were able to sit down and inspect our work. There were no flames, except in two chunks we had piled in the middle of the fire area. We dug down to mineral soil around these so we had a nice place to sit and to lie down. Since it had smoldering duff on top of it, the now exposed soil was warm and felt good to sit on. Duff and smaller branches still smoldered and smoked in a few places, but other than mop up, we were done.

Once it was quiet and most of the light from flames was gone, we were able to notice the storm off to our east.

"Geez, look over there," Perry said as he stood up. "I never noticed that before. Guess we were too busy here. Looks like the Sangre's are gettin' hammered," referring to the Sangre de Cristo mountains.

"I didn't notice any cloud buildup earlier. Must have come from the south or southeast." Steve dug out another box of rations. "Better keep our strength up. We may have some more fire from that. Man, that's quite a light show."

I walked over to the small rock outcrop at the top of the ridge and got a clearer view. Lightning was almost a steady glow of flashes, cloud-to-cloud and cloud-to-ground. Most of it was too far away for the sound of thunder to reach us, but an occasional rumble echoed in the distance.

Now that we had stopped digging and sweating, I noticed the cool air. I didn't bring a sweatshirt, but Perry walked back to the truck and returned later with the two sleeping bags. They were dirty and well worn, but we only needed them to lay on or to drape over us. Steve told Perry and me to lie down and get some sleep. He would take first watch, then wake one of us in a couple hours. As I settled down, I could see Steve stirring up the burning logs and even throwing on small limbs. "Funny", I thought, "we try to put out the fire, yet keep enough going to keep us warm." I fell asleep right away.

I woke several hours later to hear Steve and Perry laughing. They were swapping stories about other fire experiences and various work stories. They had worked together for at least five years. Seeing that I was stirring, they tossed a shovel my way and said it was time to go to work again.

I grumbled in half sleep, "Wait a minute. I thought we were going to finish this at daylight."

Perry stood and picked up the backpack pump. "It may be daylight before we get this out cold. Steve is worried we had a bunch of new starts from that storm. He wants to get out of here as soon as possible. I'm going down to the creek and get water to put on these logs. Better move your ass or it may get squirted instead."

I fought to get out of the sleeping bag. Whenever I slept in a bag, I usually contorted myself like a pretzel. Steve watched me unfurl. "Time to mop 'er up, John. Find every hot spot and stir it 'til it's cold. No fun but gotta do. We can't leave until it's as cold as Liz's ass."

"You know for a fact Liz's ass is cold?" I didn't realize what I said until it came out my mouth. Rumor around the office for a year was Steve was having an affair with Liz, the office's lead secretary.

Steve laughed. "Don't know about her, but I know mine is getting pretty damn cold. I need to go to work to warm up."

We spent the next two hours on our hands and knees as we crawled around the burned area putting out every little ember. The tree was the hard part, with fire eating halfway through the trunk in places. That meant chopping out the fire with an axe, then dousing it in dirt and finally a squirt of water on the tougher chunks. Perry made three trips down to the creek and back before he said enough was enough. He had fallen four times the last trip down the rocky slope.

Just as the unseen sun turned the eastern clouds salmon pink, Steve announced, "Okay men, I think I can declare this honker officially out. Dead as my brain about now. Let's go home and get some sleep before they call us out again."

We picked up all the gear and stumbled down the hill the way we came hours earlier. We reached the truck as the sun peeked over the horizon.

I didn't even stop in the office when I got back. Since I only lived a few blocks from the work center, I walked home from there. I took a shower and crawled into bed. My wife offered to make me a big breakfast, but I was asleep before I could decline.

I awoke at two in the afternoon, still tired. I called the office, but Liz seemed to be the only one there. She told me not to come in the office that day since I already had my 8 hours of work and if I worked anymore, the overtime would have to be paid by my regular work. And there was no money in the budget for that. I argued that the fire should be overtime. I knew better than to apply any logic to budget matters. Liz laughed at me and told me to enjoy the day off. I asked if anything was happening. She said something about some new fires, then said she had another phone call.

I puttered around in the garden the rest of the afternoon, then watched TV all evening. The next morning, finally feeling rested, I went to work at the usual time. I found the office deserted. The door was still locked, which was unusual since several people usually came to work an hour earlier than that. When I went to my desk, there was a note from Liz.

"John, Frank wants you to take a load of plywood and 2 by 4s to the big fire. He is Fire Boss, the big cheese. Martinson has assembled a forest team with Steve as a Division Boss and Fire Boss Trainee, Perry the Helibase Manager as well as several other things, and I am head Time Keeper. Big training fire. Stop by the lumber yard in Monte Vista and buy eight sheets plus twenty eight-foot boards. Here is a map on how to get to the fire. Everyone, including me is already at the fire. Liz." It was signed at 5 AM.

Well that pissed me off. What big fire? Why wasn't I called earlier? How come everyone else was there and no one called me? I just came off a fire with Steve and Perry. If they were called, why wasn't I?

The reason became obvious as I thought more about it.

I was nothing but a grunt firefighter. I assumed other folks on the district were qualified for other fire or camp jobs. I had never been on a fire bigger than the one I just came off. My timber crew was young enough and worked every day doing something akin to manual labor. I'm sure they were called as part of a twenty-man crew. Since I sat behind a desk half the time and almost fell in creeks when I did get in the field, I quickly gave up thinking and complaining about not being called.

I gassed up the stock truck, drove quickly to the Monte Vista lumber yard, loaded the lumber and headed east toward Alamosa. Feeling important, I raced along at 70 mph. My headiness took a quick nose dive when I saw in the rear-view mirror all the lumber fly out the back of the truck and splinter as it crashed into fence posts along the road's edge.

"Holy shit," I muttered. I slammed on the brakes and pulled off the highway. Luckily there were no cars coming from either direction. I backed up and got out of the truck. "Damn, why didn't I tie this stuff in?"

I hurried to throw the broken wood in the truck before anyone else came along. Only about five boards were not broken. I didn't dare show up with all this broken wood, so I stopped at the lumber yard in Alamosa, bought wood to replace the broken stuff and left the pieces with them to dispose of. They didn't like that, but I said I was in a hurry to the fire, which was very visible from town.

Smoke curled into the sky, blotting out Mt. Blanca almost twenty miles away. The plume rose from halfway up the western flank and I could see flames midway up the ridge. I didn't need the map Liz had drawn. From the highway ten miles away, the vehicles and activity at fire camp were visible. Signs and long streamers of red flagging were posted at every possible intersection. The closer I got, the more government vehicles of all kinds passed me heading the opposite way. I wondered if camp were being moved or evacuated.

As I came through the last small stand of juniper trees, I had to stop for a crew of firefighters marching across the road. They had just come off a bus and were walking single file, yellow-shirted and carrying shovels and Pulaskis. I had no idea what to do next. I pulled off the road near a dozen green Forest Service trucks parked in a line. There must have been a hundred people, all in yellow shirts milling around. Large wall tents were either standing or being erected in two lines, creating a village street. Several small travel trailers were parked in these lines, with signs out front telling what they were: Resources, Time, Check-in, Supplies, etc.

I found the red and white sign with Fire Boss printed on it. That tent was where I needed to go I figured. I walked over to it and as I turned the corner, I almost ran into Frank. He was wearing a red vest with Fire Boss printed on it as well. I think Frank wanted it known to all mankind he was the Fire Boss. When he saw me, he smiled and said, "Welcome to Camp, John. Got the lumber?"

"Yeah, it's in the truck over there," I said pointing somewhere behind me. I was turned around by that time. "I had no idea where to go with it."

Frank turned and yelled to someone in the next tent. "Tom, come over here and follow John. He has your boards." He smiled at me and said to show Tom where it was. They would take care of it from there. That was the last I talked to Frank for three days. He disappeared into his tent, holding a map and talking to another red-vested person.

The camp crew took the lumber and disappeared. I stood by the truck watching the frantic activity all around me. I had never lived in a hive of bees, but this had to be what it was like. Buzzing was replaced by laughing, yelling, a chatter of all tones and intensities. Flying was replaced by feet trampling the ground in small steps, running in varied paces and strides, and standing in place, shuffling feet while talking either frantically or jokingly. I saw mass confusion ranging from frenzy to boredom. Either someone was in a hurry to get somewhere else, or they were slow to go nowhere with plenty of time to discuss some situation. I had nowhere to go, no one to talk to and nothing to discuss since I had no idea what to do.

Finally, after wandering around a while, I saw Liz sitting at a table in front of the "time" tent. She was shuffling papers and talking to different people who came to her deferentially as if she were the queen bee. She looked up and smiled when she saw me standing there. "Well hi, John. Welcome to camp. Checked in yet?"

"I'm here but I guess I haven't done anything official," I replied.

Liz laughed. "You look like a lost little boy." She took a drink from a cup of coffee and looked up at me as she rested her fingers over her mouth. I had never thought of her as attractive, but her pose was just then quite seductive. "First time?" she asked as she brushed her hair out of her eyes.

That phrase sounded strange in this situation. It immediately took me back to a foggy night in the back of a '58 Ford Fairlane in a lonely country road. That was what my date said to me, laughing as she said it. I quickly shook off that thought. I suddenly thought of Liz in that car.

My confused look made Liz laugh again as she signed a form set in front of her by a woman in a red vest. "In a fire camp, silly. Your first time in camp? You look totally lost and confused. You need to go next door and check in. Then come over here and I will get your time sheet started."

I walked over and checked in. The woman asked what crew I was on. I shook my head and said weakly that I didn't know, I'd brought supplies here for the Fire Boss and now I was here and not on any crew. She sorted through several files, then said she would put me down as camp crew.

I suddenly felt out of place more than ever. I was more important than a camp crew. I knew that had to mean something about as lowly as a gopher. I walked back to where Liz was sitting. She motioned for me to sit down.

"Don't feel bad. This is about as confusing as I've ever seen a fire camp. Martinson wants people on the forest to sharpen their fire skills. Many people here are trainees. A lot of folks aren't sure what is going on. Why don't you go over to Transportation and see if they need drivers. It's a couple miles to the fire and it's a real rough road. I heard they were looking for someone to drive crews. It will keep you off the mountain wielding a shovel. This is a real rough fire. I don't know why they are even bothering to fight it."

She filled out the heading of my time sheet, and said I needed to give her my time slips daily so she could put the time on the official time sheet. Then she said, "If you don't have a sleeping bag, you might want to go to supply. I heard they were down to paper bags. Do you have a tent?"

I shook my head no.

"You should find a tent to sleep in if there are any. Otherwise use the back of your truck. This ground is full of cactus. Oh by the way, don't give the keys to your truck to anyone, no matter what they say. You may need it."

I slowly found my way around, discovering a few people I knew from other parts of the forest. Wayne, the Forest Engineer, was chief of the transportation section. He was glad to see me and said he could sure use me. They were short of drivers and needed someone to drive the six-passenger pickups to the drop points, delivering crews and bringing back returning crews to camp. I glommed onto this job and did it for three days. The road was nothing but a track across sand and between rocks. It took over an hour to get to the destination. I met interesting people but the returning crews were generally too tired to say much. They complained about having to hike straight up the mountain to line a fire that was going nowhere but to more rocks. I was glad I escaped that duty.

During the few hours in the middle of the day when I wasn't driving, I found very interesting places to explore. This camp was only a few miles south of Great Sand Dunes National Monument and at the base of the Sangre de Cristo Range. There were sand dunes mixed with rock outcrops and small streams that came off the mountain. I found several arrowheads as I wandered my new-found wilderness.

On the second day, while I was waiting for the night crew to come off the hill, I explored the area where we parked. There were four other vehicles besides mine. I found a campfire ring that looked like it had recently been used. There were burned pieces of wood in the ring, but also scattered off to the edge of it. It looked like the area next to the rocks lining the fire circle had been raked. Above that, there was burned grass. Large boulders formed a boundary above the ring. Almost. There was a small gap between them that was now covered with burned grass and brush. The burn wasn't very hot since part of the twigs were still intact. Above this rock gap, the area opened up and burned material was thick. The further uphill it went, the more ash and less unburned vegetation was present. I was not an expert in this by any means, but it didn't take a genius to deduce a fire started here and spread uphill, getting hotter as it went. This was the origin of the fire. I thought it had been lightning started. I think everyone else figured it was as well. After my quick exploration, I walked back the fifty yards to the truck. The other four drivers were sitting there watching me come back.

"Hey John, feel better now?" Andy asked, thinking I had gone up there to take a leak.

"Andy, do you know how this fire started?"

He looked at me, then at the others. "Lightning as far as I know. They had a really fierce bust the other night. I watched it from Alamosa. Never seen such lightning. Constant for about an hour."

Ben stood up and started to walk to his truck. "I heard one of the crew say they came across a tree just up from here that had been hit by lightning. It exploded. Bark and pieces of wood scattered for yards around this big ponderosa pine. They had their investigator look around. They are sure it started somewhere in this area. Went uphill from around here somewhere. That was pretty obvious."

I looked uphill from where we sat. "Did they finish their investigation?"

Ben looked at Andy. Andy looked at Pete. Jerry looked at each of us in turn. All raised their eyebrows and turned up the corners of their mouths. No one knew.

"What you getting at John?" Andy asked, reaching down to pick up a piece of flint.

I wasn't sure whether to share my discovery. I thought for a few seconds. Then I stood up and motioned for them to follow me.

Ben was the first to get up. "Crying out loud, John, you act like you found a body or something."

I showed them the fire ring, then pointed uphill. At first no one saw anything. You had to look between and uphill of the large boulders. Then it was obvious. The burned area went uphill in a spreading V pattern. About one hundred yards above that, the big pine tree stood, its trunk split by a huge, fresh lightning scar.

"So what is it, John? The lightning tree or this campfire? Did they both start the fire?"

"Let's go look," I said as I clambered up the slope. The rest followed.

When we got to the tree, we walked around. None of the bark showed any sign of fire. It had obviously been hit by lightning, but we didn't see evidence it started a fire. None of the scattered bark and pieces of wood were burned. Yet the grass they lay on was burned.

"I'll be damned," Peter said and he picked up some bark strips. "Who investigated this? I don't know beans about fire, but I can tell this stuff didn't burn."

Ben took off his hat and ran his fingers through his hair. He looked at Andy. "Hey, remember day before yesterday, when we first drove in here? There were those three boys walking down the road. I wondered what they were doing here that early in the morning."

Andy said, "One of the guys on the crew I was hauling made a comment. Something like, 'hey, aren't those the scouts that were camped up there at the end of the road?' That crew was one of the first on the fire. He said there were about five or six scouts camped up here when they first got to the fire. He thought it was strange there were no vehicles. Just the kids and four little tents. They were all gone when the crew came down in the evening."

"Isn't this all very interesting?" I said as we got back to the trucks. The first crew was walking down the trail towards us just as we got there.

"Hey guys, rough day?" I asked the crew leader.

"Goddamn steep sonnabitch. Christ, I don't know why they don't take us up in choppers. They took some up there today. Landed above us. Fairy bastards get a free ride up there but we have to walk up that wall of rock." He threw down his gear and pulled a canteen out of his pack. He drained the last of it, then threw his gear into the back of my truck.

"Don't know," I replied. "How long you been here?"

"First night. We got here about midnight."

"You know what started this?" I asked, setting his Pulaski in the truck.

"Everybody says lightning. Ask me, it started right over there behind those rocks. I know this hill got creamed by lightning. We came across about three trees up there that look like they got hit." He motioned up the mountain. "But go look behind those rocks. Fire doesn't burn downhill in an inverted V shape. Bunch of scout assholes camped here that first night. They ran off when we first drove up here. Scattered like a bunch of quail. I think their campfire got away from them and they tried to put the fire out but couldn't. You can see where they tried to hide it."

Another one of the crew was listening to this discussion. "Yeah, some dumbass BLM guy investigates and says it was that tree up the hill got hit by lightning. It got hit all right but that's not what started the fire."

"Did you talk to the investigator?" I asked.

"He didn't talk to any of the crew. He just walked up there, said 'yep, there's the start' and left. Didn't talk to anyone. Guess they all bought the lightning story. It does make sense. Lightning may have also started it. There was enough lightning the other night to burn down the whole mountain range. So who knows. Does it matter now?"

One of the crew hopped in the back of the truck and said, "Hey driver, we're all here. Let's get back. My ass is so tired, I think it will just shit out any food that gets down there."

Another of the crew piped up, "Yeah Carlos, your brains

are shit anyway. I notice you look really dumb after you wipe your ass."

The conversation was quickly deteriorating, so I got the guys in and we drove off. I figured I had done my duty today. I would mention my fire origin theory to Frank or whoever would listen to me.

When I got back to camp, I tried to find Frank. He wasn't in his tent. I did run into Steve, who was studying a map with someone I didn't know.

"Hey John, keeping busy? You don't look very dirty." Steve was covered with dirt and soot.

"What the hell you been doing? Rolling in the ash?" I replied.

Steve's friend slapped Steve on his shoulder and said, "damn right on. Old sure footed Steve tripped and fell. He grabbed a burned tree and then continued to fall, sliding on it. I think he must figure it attracts girls." He spit out a laugh as Steve frowned at him.

"Laugh it up Tinkerbell," Steve growled. He looked at me. "Yeah, I fell, after he pushed me. Tinkerbell is the one who was trying to tap dance on a rock and fell off and pushed me into this tree."

"Whatever." I figured I better stay out of this little discussion. "Steve, I'm looking for Frank. I want to talk to someone about how this fire started. I think I found the origin."

"Yeah, the scout campfire? We know about it. We caught the kids. They are scared to death. I think they are out of the woods, though. There were probably several origins. Too much lightning to blame it entirely on the scouts. But we will follow up. There was a campfire ban here, so they shouldn't have had a fire to begin with. Scouts," he muttered.

"Oh by the way, John, got another job for you." Steve got up and led me outside the tent. "You do a lot of work with Digger at the *Prospector*," he said, referring to the editor of our local weekly newspaper. "They've done some good stories about us. Digger was up here a few minutes ago. He wanted to talk to someone about the fire and what this camp is all about. How about you talk to him and give him a story. We don't have anyone up here to handle the media and we are getting a lot of attention. Put your talents to work."

Steve looked down the row of tents and saw Digger wandering towards him. "Hey Old Digger, come here. You talk to John. He will fill you in and give you a guided tour of camp."

I went off with Digger. Good thing I wandered the camp myself earlier, doing a lot of listening and asking a few questions. A week ago, I didn't know anything about a fire camp, but now I could talk to a newspaper reporter and act like I was an old pro at this. Digger got some good pictures and did a reasonably good story, quoting me about every other paragraph. I also talked to several other newspapers and did a recorded radio interview. The Supervisor sent me a letter after the fire was over, commending me on a good job with the Fire Information.

I was getting comfortable in my new life in the fire world when I woke up Sunday morning to a fog that hid the entire camp in a damp cloud. When I went to the vehicle area, Wayne told me there were no crews to take to the mountain. I would drive and pick up the night crew but all crews were coming off the mountain. The fire had reached the rocks lining the upper half of the mountain and had basically gone out on its own. It was raining, mixed with snow up there, and the forecast was for more of the same.

Wayne captured the situation. "Can't see squat, but nothing to see since there ain't no more fire anyway. Rock don't burn very well. Martinson got his training fire. Time to go home and back to work. Thanks, John." Wayne ran off waving at a vehicle that was pulling out.

That was it. I drove out and picked up the last crews stumbling down the mountain, wet and cold. When I got back to camp, I wandered around for a while longer and watched the camp break down. Liz gave me my time sheet and said to give it back to her at the office Monday morning.

I was walking back to my truck when I heard someone shout my name. I turned and saw Perry walking toward me.

"Hey stud, whatcha doin?" He grinned at me and tossed me an apple. "Better go to the dining area. They're giving away lots of food."

"I haven't seen you around. Where were you?" I asked as I rubbed the apple on my sleeve, then bit into it.

"Helibase manager. Known you were here, I could've given you a ride. Whatcha been doing?"

"Oh, nothing exciting. Just driving troops back and forth."

Perry laughed. "Helluva lot better than scrambling up that sonofabitch mountain. God, I can't believe they made people hike up there and try and scratch line. Chopper pilots didn't like flying up there. Wind currents were hell. Don't matter, it's over now."

"I was wondering why they did all this," I said. "Seems a waste of time."

"Big waste of time and money, you ask me. Martinson saw a chance to play with fire and he grabbed it. Training fire, he says. I took him up in a helicopter two days ago and he was like a little kid. I wanted to shove him out the door and tell him to grab a shovel and try and scratch a line down there." Perry rubbed his chin, now with a week's growth of stubble.

"Guess we go home now and try and return to normal,"

I said. I threw my apple core at a rock.

"Normal?" Perry slapped me on the back. "You figure out what that is and let me know. See you back at the office." He turned and walked slowly back to the unfolding camp and disappeared into the remaining chaos.

REDFERN VALLEY RECOLLECTIONS

From across the valley, I could see the crater left
by the explosion. We wanted potholes for ducks.
I think we had a pothole that would hide a T-Rex.
Tom

THE EXPLOSION SENT chunks of sod and mud flying a quarter mile across the valley. I quickly threw myself behind my truck, amazed at the force of the blast. The sound came about the time the debris flew over me—a deafening thump, quickly echoing throughout the valley. I was thankful I thought ahead to put a barricade on the road where it entered the valley. Few people came up here, but I would have been hard pressed to deal with an accident to innocent tourists caused by a blast from a ton of dynamite.

As I straightened up after the blast, I watched the cloud of dirt and pulverized meadow slowly fall back to the ground. After a while, when some visibility returned, I stood there with my mouth hanging open. From across the valley, I could see the crater left by the explosion. We wanted potholes for ducks. I think we had a pothole that would hide a T-Rex. I started the long walk across the meadow. I got to the hole about the same time as Captain Peterson. He was laughing as he came up to the crater. I was still too stunned to say anything.

"Well sir, we got rid of the dynamite." He took off his helmet and leaned over to look down into the crater. Dirt and clumps of sod were still slithering down the nearly vertical sides. It was at least twenty feet deep, and thirty or forty feet in diameter.

"Not exactly what I wanted, but, hey, we take what we get." I tried to smile.

"Well, sir, you didn't want any powder left. We couldn't take it and you said you couldn't leave it here. We gotta get going now. This was the best we could do."

"I know. I thank you for what you guys did. Too bad you had to spend all that time pulling your trucks out of the mud. But, I appreciate that you did what you could. I hope you got some good training out of this."

"Yes sir, I think we picked up a few good pointers from all this." He smiled as he pinched a wad of tobacco in his lips. "We gotta go, sir. We cleaned up the camp and smoothed over the ruts the best we could. Too wet to do any more." He looked back at the creek crossing where half of his fleet of deuce and a half dump trucks had been thoroughly mired for much of the weekend.

I shook his hand and said, "Thanks again. We appreciate your assistance." I lied. I regretted involving them. It had been important to me, but it was just a weekend of exercises to them. They got to drive their big toys and play with matches, so to speak.

I watched the last of the by-now-familiar olive camouflage trucks drive down the dusty road out of the valley. I went over and stared at the mess at the creek crossing. I shook my head in disbelief. Then I slowly walked across the valley. They did actually blow several good potholes that were just the right size. Not the 40 or 50 I had hoped for, but maybe 5 or 6. Then the crater. My god, I said to myself. I sure hope the Regional Manager or the Forest Service Ranger doesn't come out here. At least until these things fill in with water. Some of the smaller ones already had a few inches of water in them. In a couple days, they should be filling quite nicely.

I looked around at the rest of the work. The long dike was built across the end of the meadow. It didn't look too bad, I mumbled to myself. It should serve as a dam all right. The small rock dams in the creek looked good as well. Maybe things weren't the disaster I feared. It just was a comedy of errors getting to this point. The sun was sinking behind Redfern Peak to the west as I started walking back to my mud and sod splattered truck. Clumps of sod littered the road.

I paused and looked around me. Redfern Valley was a beautiful setting if you didn't look at the creek through its center. A one-hundred-year-old ponderosa pine forest covered the hillsides, with a few clumps of aspen dotting the eastern slopes. The broad meadow was grass-covered. Foot tall sedges and other meadow grasses waved in the cool breeze. A few red flowers were sprinkled among the yellow dandelions. I hoped that would change. Dandelions shouldn't be here, but then we were lucky to have any green in this valley. The creek was a gully twenty feet deep with bare dirt banks, continually caving in as spring snowmelt or winter rains deepened the erosion. That's why we were working to heal the damage.

A hundred years before, the forest ringing the valley was clear-cut. Railroads came through this and adjacent valleys, harvesting the trees like fields of corn, stripped to the bare ground, filling the air with the smoke and dust of locomotives. No one seemed to care about conservation in those days. Then the railroads were abandoned. Settlers entered the valleys and brought their cattle and sheep.

When grasses and flowers started sprouting after the trees were removed, then the livestock chewed the vegetation down to bare ground. Nature was not given a chance to heal itself. The rains came and the soil started to flow down the denuded hillsides and on down the creeks. Then the creeks couldn't hold the heavy runoff and they deepened. Soon nothing remained but bare eroded ground, filled with gullies and mudflats. The more it rained, the deeper the gullies eroded.

Over time, some healing did take place: the hillsides reforested themselves and now the pine was thick. The pre-railroad forest was naturally open and park-like. This forest, trying to return to its natural inclination, was interfered with once again by humans—we put out fires, not understanding that fires were as natural as rain and snow. But we did too good a job and now we faced a forest that was almost as unnatural as a hillside of stumps.

The meadows, drier than their original counterparts, filled with grasses and flowers nourished by snow and rain, but the scar down the middle was like a scab that wouldn't heal. It flushed water completely out of the valley. Historically, during heavy storms and spring runoff, water overflowed the banks of shallow streams and spilled across the meadows, like spilled milk soaks a tablecloth. Not so now. What should have been wet, spongy meadows became dried and cracked in the intense summers.

So we came to the rescue, hoping to do it right this time. I was in charge of the watershed and waterfowl restoration project since most of the valley was a state wildlife area. The upper end of the meadow and much of the hillsides were part of the national forest. So I worked with the Forest Service and its local district representative, Ken. He and I had collaborated a few years earlier on a small watershed project in Redfern, which hinted at what could be done. This much larger project was for a complete job which would cost a lot of money. We were dealing with budget cuts that would continue for the foreseeable future. Ken and I sat down one day in Redfern Valley and considered the matter.

"This looks good but it's only a drop in the bucket," I said to Ken.

Ken, trained as a musician in the 60s, but working for the past twenty years as a forester, and now a wildlife biologist, answered, "You have to start somewhere, Tom. I grew up poor in Philadelphia. A big day for me was to get an ice cream cone. Guess we are looking at an ice cream cone out there."

"Well…" I paused as I dismembered a dandelion, "I want the whole carton of ice cream. Hell, I want to own the ice cream factory. We need to do more, or this little bit won't work. I see it as our duty, what we are being paid to do."

"Eric started with nothing." Ken was referring to the hydrologist who played up the erosion still going on in the valley and got funding to put those few rock check dams in the upper creek. One dam, made of wire baskets filled with softball-sized rock, had already slumped out of kilter in the previous winter's rain-on-snow event. Rain-on-snow, not uncommon at this elevation, put a lot of water on the ground in a very short amount of time. Most people called such a thing by its more common name—a flood.

"Eric did a good job and he took a lot of credit and publicity. That's all right. But it's not nearly enough. We need to do more. You got ideas on what needs done?" I had recently transferred to the area and was not familiar with a lot of the history yet. I looked at Ken, then scanned the nearby horizon.

"Sure. I had experts from the Regional Office out last year and they wrote up a three-page list of projects. More dams in the creek. You got to stop the velocity of the water.

Slow it down. That's where we are getting our damage. Fast water, with no time to spill over the creek banks, keeps cutting down and lowering the water table. We have to raise the water table. Can also do it by a long dam over there." Ken waved in the direction of a side drainage coming into the main valley near its mouth.

"Then dig or blow a bunch of potholes. Allow that water table to fill some potholes for ducks. This used to be a great waterfowl area. At least, that's what some folks think. Old timers used to come out here and blast ducks and geese to no end. That was before the logging." Ken raised his eyebrows, a bushy black growth that almost hung over his dark brown eyes.

"Not something we can bring out a bunch of Boy Scouts to do in a weekend or two." I liked the potential of the project but immediately was seeing the impossibility of the cost of it.

"We need bulldozers, backhoes, dump trucks, dynamite. More important, we need a source of rock. When Eric did these cages, he had to pay big bucks to haul in river rock."

I interrupted. "We don't have rock out here? We are in the mountains."

Ken shook his head and shot back quickly. "Look around, Tom. See any river rock anywhere? We need loose rock we can pick up and move. There aren't even any outcrops around here. Know how much it costs to haul in dump trucks of rock?"

I sighed. I looked around and he was right. I didn't see anything that looked even half promising. "You and I can both think of a hundred places loose rock is just sitting there in the way."

"Yeah and it's all miles from here. Doesn't matter whether it's two miles or twenty miles away. Wherever it is, it ain't right here. And that's where our costs go through the roof."

"So how can we get it here? In a way we can afford." I looked at Ken and he looked at me. "You got connections with the good angel Gabriel?"

Ken laughed. "Tom, remember, I was a poor black kid growing up in Philadelphia. I stole enough things that no matter what else I do in life, I'm going straight to Hell when I die."

"You'll be splittin' those rocks we need up here." I stood up. "At least you won't be lonely down there. I'm sure we all will have lots of help."

"Yeah, and no one up here to send those rocks to." We both laughed as we walked back to the truck.

Ken started to unlock the door when he erupted with an "Oh shit. Dammit, Tom."

I watched him as he fumbled in his day pack and pulled out a knife. I started to say, "what the hell?" but stopped myself as I looked in and saw the keys still in the ignition. We were locked out.

"Ken, I thought your boss made a policy that you keep a spare key hidden on the vehicle. I talked to him a while back after he lost a key. You didn't hide one did you?"

"Screw you. I haven't had time to make an extra yet. Don't worry. Remember I grew up in Philly. Turn your head. I don't want to give away my hard-earned secrets. This is one of my tickets to Hell." He laughed a rather sinister laugh and had the door open before I even knew how he did it.

"How…" I didn't bother to finish my thought. I got in just shaking my head.

We both hit up everyone we could think of for funding

but got nowhere. Of course our own budgets were tight. Ken couldn't stick his knife between the numbers. I contacted Ducks Unlimited, the Sierra Club, our own state contacts, every group I could think of. Nothing. Several people knew about Redfern Valley and several sympathized with me and wished me luck, but no one had cash.

We both worked the numbers and came up with projects running into the hundreds of thousands of dollars. Cost-benefit was a big part of any analysis and the benefits were the type that are difficult to tag numbers on. Costs were much easier.

One weekend in August, while driving up to Independence Canyon to hike, I encountered a National Guard convoy enroute to field exercises. I watched in amazement as truck after olive green truck plodded by at twenty miles an hour. Dumps, dozers, backhoes, big toys. I started to grumble about them when the thought hit me. "Use them. They want to practice with their dozers and dump trucks, let them do it in Redfern Valley."

Over the next few weeks I learned that we could forget about using regular military, although there were several bases within a couple hours drive. The local National Guard contact laughed, telling me what I wanted was an engineering battalion and they were not that, but there was an Army Reserve engineering unit about a hundred miles north.

Ken and I made an appointment one September day and drove up to talk to Captain Benson. His eyes lit up when we said the word explosives.

"You got work for explosives? My boys are always looking for those opportunities. Need some rock moved? You came to the right place."

I looked at Ken and he looked at me. We both smiled.

"Sir, we've got a deal, and if you have a few weekends next year, we can put you to work." We told him what our ideas were. He smiled as he took notes.

"Ken can work out details with you." We shook hands and left.

Those were heady days, that fall, as Ken and I planned and completed piles of paperwork, looking forward to doing great things for Redfern Valley. We even had some rock sites planned, including one spot along the highway about ten miles away that needed rock removed to expand a parking area for fishermen. They could blast away without endangering passing cars, with paved highway most of the distance to Redfern.

I liked working with Ken and admired his knowledge of both the land and the people. He was very astute about what needed done for the resource as well as about the politics of his own organization. For me, it was easy. There were not many potential projects like this that could do fantastic things for wildlife, especially non-game, which was my specialty.

In this case, the public as well as our bosses would probably support whatever we wanted to do, as long as we could get the budget. Both our agencies had been proposing this for several years and it looked like we had finally gotten some money, although not nearly enough. That's where this free labor came in.

Ken had his own engineers go to Redfern and survey and flag the dam and dike sites. He even calculated how many truckloads it would take. It was a lot, but we were planning for the best case. Silly us. The one thing we didn't do was talk to other people who had used or tried to use the military to get work done. But that is getting ahead of the story.

Ken and I were anxiously awaiting the second weekend in May as the boys in khaki were to arrive Friday night and spend Saturday and Sunday morning blasting rock and hauling it to the dam sites. They were also scheduled to blade back a huge eroded slope and push dirt into the creek so it would wash down and silt in behind the new dams. It all seemed so easy.

They came in as scheduled Friday night and set up a sprawling camp well hidden in the trees. I was scheduled to work with them on Saturday, with Ken taking over on Sunday. Friday night, Ken lined out Lt. Williams, so he knew where to go and what to do early Saturday.

When I arrived at 9:00 a.m., I was hoping to see trucks already hauling rock. What I saw was a bunch of guys in camouflage sitting around a jack-knifed water-tender drinking coffee.

"How you guys doing this morning?" I asked, struggling to be polite.

"Fine, sir. Just waiting. Can't do anything without our coffee first."

"Something wrong with the truck?" I really didn't want an answer. I was getting an uneasy feeling about the work ethic I was seeing. Or not seeing.

"Don't know, sir. Haven't seen the sarge for a while. Nobody tells us anything. I think most of the brass are up the highway at the blast site. We don't have water yet. They needed the haul truck and we don't have anything here to pull the tender with. Tried to pull it with the cat and see where we got. Think we may have tweaked the hitch. Shit man, nobody knows what's goin' on." He got up from the log he was sitting on and went behind a tree to take a leak. He finished, came back, pulled out a pack of cigarettes, lit up and sat back down.

I looked around, not sure what to do. No one was

working, guys were sprawled like a bunch of rags, looking totally bored. I drove back to the rock site to see if the blasting was progressing any better.

It wasn't. Trucks were parked right where the rock was supposed to be blasted. Five soldiers were standing by one pickup talking. I walked up and was greeted by the customary "sir." I was starting to get tired of this military formality. They may not have been trained to get work done, but they were polite to authority.

"How's the powder work going?" I asked, again, not sure I wanted an answer.

"Looks like we forgot the blasting caps. Or wire, or something. Can't shoot. Got the powder here but can't use it. Lieutenant is off somewhere trying to figure out what's going on." He spit and lit up a cigarette.

"So you haven't got any rock?" I asked a rather obvious question.

"No, sir. Don't look like we will have any. Think they are rerouting the deuces to someplace back up by Honey Lake. Some stuff up there we can haul."

My fuse was burning. Maybe I could somehow use that to blow something up. I felt like it. "Where is Lt. Williams? I need to talk to him."

The tall one who had been silent up until then answered. He threw a rock at the hill then looked at me. "Don't know. Haven't seen him for two hours. He told us to wait till he got back. So we're waiting."

"Do you have radio contact with him?"

"No sir. All we can do is wait. Damn, we don't even have any coffee."

My hopes of getting anything at all done that weekend faded to almost zero. I thanked the soldiers, hopped in my pickup and raced back towards Redfern Valley. I passed two deuces coming out of the valley. I blinked my lights to stop them, but they continued down the road, then turned north towards Honey Lake.

I drove on up the valley to the big eroded hillside. Finally, there was something happening. A D-8 was slicing down the steep cut bank to something manageable. He was moving downhill from the top of the cut, widening it and easing the slope. It looked good to me. He had a way to go, but this was more like it. I watched him for a while. He worked that cat like a violin string. It was smooth and easy going. If we didn't get anything else, having this big cut laid back would be progress. The tread cleats made excellent small check dams all up and down the raw dirt slope. A little grass seed thrown on that would catch easily.

It turned out that was all the progress we had. I finally caught up with Lt. Williams about 3 o'clock that afternoon. He apologized for the snafu but said they would get some blasting done Sunday before they left at noon. I told him thanks, but silently told myself I'd believe it when I saw it. I never saw it. Ken worked on Sunday and his tale of woe when I saw him Monday was almost as pathetic as my experience.

The D-8 had finished the slope, but absolutely nothing else was done. Turns out they forgot the dynamite on Sunday. They took it back to their bunker overnight and had a mix-up who was supposed to bring it Sunday. Since they quit at noon, there wasn't time to do anything. The big excitement Sunday was a backhoe used to fill in their slit-trench latrine had fallen in. Ken's description of that episode had me laughing. Laughing was much better than crying.

They were scheduled to return in two weeks, but before the Sergeant left Sunday, he informed Ken that something else had come up and they wouldn't be back. The rest of the summer was booked. Ken told him "next year," thanked them and sent them a letter with an official U.S. Forest

Service Certificate of Appreciation, as well as a State Division of Wildlife Thank You. They in turn, sent a letter and their own special certificate of thanks for cooperating with the U.S. Army. I told Ken he could hang that one on his wall. He not so politely declined.

When I drove up valley to throw grass seed on the freshly exposed cut bank and inspect the dozer work, I noticed a low rise that was covered with broken rock and different vegetation. Since it was a former sheep bed-ground, it was covered with well-matured fertilizer that over the many decades had compensated for the fact it was trampled and compacted by thousands of sheep hooves. It was covered by a different kind of grass and had no dandelions in it.

Both Ken and I had driven by this dozens of times and never even noticed it. It was only about half an acre and didn't seem like much, but the thought occurred to me that this might be a site to get rock. I paid a local backhoe operator to go out there and dig around. We found broken and fractured rock as deep as he could dig. He knew this type of thing better than I did and his estimate was that this was a unique geologic formation that would give us as much rock as we wanted to dig. And no dynamite needed. Our rock problems were solved.

We did more checking that winter and found a National Guard unit not too far away, an engineering battalion, that would love to come up and use their dumps and dozers to help us out. This was their big yearly exercise and they could be here for a long weekend, starting Wednesday night. They had another project over by Beaver Creek that they would spend a week on, then come on over to us. I had a much better feeling talking to Captain Carson than Lt. Williams the previous year. This guy seemed much more professional. I didn't know if these guys were a better unit, but something told me I could get better than the Keystone Cops of the year before. Time would tell.

Now that we didn't need the powder to blast rock to haul, we would use some to create additional potholes. This time, we had to figure what we would need to blow holes in the ground and we bought it ourselves. This opened up a whole new can of worms neither Ken or I had ever dealt with. If nothing else, we were learning a lot. Whether it would ever be useful again, that was another thing.

We had to special order the dynamite. Of course my department didn't have any expertise, but I knew the Forest Service would. There was only one person on the Forest Service qualified as a blaster and he had to order it, pick it up, and deliver it himself. It could only be stored in the bunker the Forest Service had at their local work center. Ken had to jump through a dozen hoops to get it and use it. When he said the Army was lighting it off, a few eyebrows were raised. But we had two tons of dynamite purchased and stored, ready for use.

When May rolled around again, Ken and I were ready to see Redfern Valley restored properly. We awaited the arrival Wednesday night of the US Army. True to form, we got a call from Lt. Tomson Wednesday noon, saying they were taking a day longer in Beaver Creek and would roll in about noon Thursday. About 4 pm Thursday, the olive camouflage

dumps started arriving in Redfern Valley. There must have been close to a hundred vehicles in all, mostly pickups and troop carriers, but still a slew of deuces and lowboys with cats, backhoes, and other equipment I didn't have a clue what they were. These guys came prepared for war.

Our first snag came when they wouldn't camp where we planned for them. They insisted on going on the other side of the creek. Ken was in charge that first night and he failed to impose the authority of the Department of Agriculture over the Department of Defense. They camped across the creek. But since there was not a creek crossing there, they made their own. When I got to the site Friday morning, I couldn't believe what I saw. The first crossing went all right, when they crossed the creek to their camp. But when they tried to drive all those big vehicles back across the meadow, the churning up of the soil that first night resulted in a form of bottomless mud. Vehicles were buried past their axles. It was like a scene out of a war movie, where the whole regiment was mired in mud. Good thing our valley was eroded away to start with; they caused more damage than they repaired. Half their fleet was stranded on the wrong side of the creek. The other half was either sitting parked on this side, covered with mud, or still mired in mud, with cats and backhoes pulling them out, then slowly trying to repair the mess they made.

I worked with two sergeants to identify a crossing they could use about a quarter mile up the creek. It was dry there, although they had to remove a dozen trees to make a temporary road to reach it. I say remove, since they didn't have chain saws, they uprooted the trees with their D-8 cats. I was praying no public would come up there and see what we were doing. It certainly was not what we approved in our Environmental Assessment for the project.

Once the equipment was on the right side of the creek,

they finally went to work. The backhoes and dozers were scraping the hill and rock was plentiful. It was just the right size and the haul was only a couple miles. I left Friday, feeling good about things. Finally. They only got a few hours work in, but these guys were good. I looked forward to coming back Sunday and seeing the whole thing almost done.

When Ken called me Saturday night, he said things went really slow with the potholes. The cats had almost completed the long dike across the meadow and most of the dams were finished. Jack, our Forest Service blaster, got the dynamite delivered. It took him two trips and he wasn't comfortable leaving it piled next to their camp—they had to ferry the cases by hand across the bog hole of that first creek crossing. He refused to drive his truck along the makeshift road they constructed on the other side of the creek. Ken asked him how much safer could it be with the powder being guarded by a couple hundred National Guardsmen. They had MPs and they had big guns and they were on duty 24-hours a day watching over that powder. We had planned to blow most of it Saturday, but they blasted only a half dozen of our planned six dozen holes.

That was what greeted me Sunday morning. Somehow, and I never did figure this out, more of their vehicles bogged down Saturday evening: they were trying to ferry the cases of powder over to the meadow for the potholes and those trucks got stuck in a different place. When I drove into the valley, I saw trucks where they shouldn't have been. The Sergeant tried to explain why they were there, but the only thing I heard was they still had a ton of dynamite unused and they were getting ready to close things down since they had to leave by noon.

"Wait a minute," I asked. "What are you going to do with the powder? Can you take it with you?"

"Oh no, sir, absolutely not. We cannot transport it. No

way, sir. It's yours."

This scene was so ridiculous, I had to laugh. "Time out, here, Sergeant. It has to be used. We can't take it back. I don't have anyone to haul it and we have no place to put it. You have to blow it up."

"We are closing camp down. Two hours from now we are outta here, sir." I wanted to tell him to quit calling me sir. I know it is ingrained in them but it was getting on my nerves. And this whole project was getting on my nerves as well. What the hell was I going to do with a ton of dynamite sitting in the middle of a meadow, surrounded by mud holes where two-and-a-half-ton dump trucks had churned things up getting stuck and unstuck?

"You have to blow it up. Now."

"Well, sir, the best we can do is scrape out a little trench right next to where it sits, push it all in there, and spark it."

Sir. Weren't you going to add another sir, I thought to myself. He only called me sir once. "Do it. Can you push it in safely? That okay to do?"

"Oh yes, sir. You can throw that stuff around no problem. Just don't put a cap on it. Has to have a cap or that stuff is harmless."

I doubted that, but as long as they were the ones doing it and I was standing a half mile away, then let them play dodge ball with it for all I cared.

When I asked him what a whole ton of dynamite in a small depression would do, he just smiled at me, adjusted the toothpick in his mouth, and said, "You just watch, sir."

About that time, Captain Peterson drove up in his mud spattered pickup. He jumped out and came over to me. "What do you think, sir? To your satisfaction? We got a little bogged down in places, but got most of your stuff done. What you going to do with the stack of powder?"

"Well, your Sergeant and I have a plan and you better stand back."

The sergeant grinned and said, "Captain, sir, we will touch off the whole pile. Going to dig a scoop out, then push the stack in and set it off." The Sergeant smiled and spit out the toothpick, replacing it with another from his shirt pocket.

The Captain looked at him, then at me. He started to say something, then stopped. He looked over at the dynamite, stacked neatly in a pile about five feet deep. His surprised look told the whole story. "All right Sergeant, you are the powder monkey. You say it's safe, let's do it. We have a long drive to get home."

I drove the mile back to the highway, posted a road closed sign, which I luckily had in the back of my pickup, then I drove back to the edge of the meadow to watch. Most of the military vehicles were either leaving or were already on the road home. I watched with interest as the cat finished scraping the hole, pushed in the cases of dynamite, covered them with a foot or two of earth, then crawled back across the meadow and drove onto the lowboy. It soon rumbled past me, the guys waving and laughing. There were only two vehicles left by now. A solitary figure was moving quickly around the earth-covered dynamite. And after a few minutes of standing there writing in a notebook, he walked around the mound one last time, then walked quickly back to his truck. He had already laid the wire. He looked around one last time, hollered to me to take cover. I walked behind my truck, although I was sure I was safe enough. I heard that familiar "Fire in the Hole" yelled at the top of his voice. Then he pushed down on his detonator. What I heard and saw will remain with me for the rest of my life.

Ken and I drove out to Redfern Valley two months later, taking the Forest Supervisor for a tour. He was impressed with all we had accomplished. The potholes were full of water and a small pond was backing up behind the long dike. The mud hole had grassed over and the humpy ground looked natural if one hadn't seen it when it was dotted with Army green trucks half covered in mud. Both Ken and I received cash awards for the work and we were written up in the Regional newsletter.

At my going away party a year later, when I transferred to the other side of the state, I unwrapped a big package. It was unsigned, but I suspected Ken, the way he smirked when I picked it up in front of the crowd. I opened it and unwrapped an old dented yellow hard hat with big red letters "Master Blaster," signed: Captain Peterson, US Army.

ON THE TOP

On the top—sky islands they call them in the Southwest—the world is sub-arctic, not too different from Alaskan tundra. The lakes and potholes are countless, merging with grassy meadows and fingers of forest that intertwine like a maze until the whole thing falls off the cliffs.

GENE STOOD ON the edge of the rim, or as he thought to himself, literally on top of the world. He gazed down the cliffs as they fell off below him, sloping through forests of pine and aspen into the slickrock canyons to the east. Beyond, the vastness of Utah washed into an endless panorama of red and orange. He had to get off Buck and walk for a while, stretching his knees. Buck kept pushing him as if to say "Get out of my way. You don't want to sit on my back, then walk faster, tenderfoot." Gene did not consider himself an experienced horseman, although he did a good job of pretending to be in this corner of the cowboy West. He had a limit of a couple of hours of riding after which he had to get off and walk in order to keep some life in his aching knees. He never understood how the old cowboys could ride all day and half the night. Maybe that's why they walked like they had full diapers.

He pulled out a new roll of plastic flagging, this one orange and black candy-striped, to continue marking the route for the new trail. He wanted it to follow the rim for a

"

ways, wind into the trees, then back to the view, creating a peek-a-view experience. Too much of the rim's edge and a hiker would grow numb to the view. And the view was what it was all about.

Basalt cliffs line the top of this mountain plateau, the long-ago product of fiery lava flows that cover what is now called Rocky Top. Where the lava stopped, the world now falls away for several thousand vertical feet, finally exposing the sandstone bedrock that makes southern Utah what it is today. Slickrock, they call it, and that's what it is. Whites, reds, pinks, oranges—the rock eroded fast enough to keep vegetation off most of its slopes, yet was hard enough to form cliffs and domes and stair-step formations that never fail to fascinate.

On the top—sky islands they call them in the Southwest—the world is sub-arctic, not too different from Alaskan tundra. Although it is still below timberline, there is not a bump or hill on this level expanse of meadows, lakes, and forests poking high enough above the surface to indicate where timberline might be. Gene loved to wander this high elevation plateau during the short snow-free season. The lakes and potholes are countless, merging with grassy meadows and fingers of forest that intertwine like a maze until the whole thing falls off the cliffs. And he loved to look off the edge of this world into the desert world stretching to the horizon far below. "Combine the two," he was fond of saying, "and you have a world class experience." He was now combining the two by means of a trail that would wind for miles along the rim.

Ever since he transferred to this district three years before, he had heard about the unfulfilled dreams of former forest rangers: "We need to build a Rim Trail." He heard it so often, he couldn't believe nothing had been done, and had found no evidence of anything ever being started.

He was going to do it. In his lengthening career with the Service, his patience had grown short with the incessant planning. "Paralysis analysis" was the not-so-jokingly stated phenomenon he and his peers encountered.

"No one does anything anymore," he complained, "all they do is plan. We study, and analyze, and plan. We evaluate something to death until finally everyone gives up and we don't do anything. We are so afraid to do anything because someone out there won't like what we do. And boy, we sure don't want to offend anyone do we?" He looked at Buck, as if he expected Buck to answer. Buck pricked his ears, rolled his big eyes towards Gene, then just stared, nostrils slowly flaring in and out. His was a world of smells, not words.

Gene talked to himself, more so nowadays it seemed. He told his wife Jennie that no one else listened, so he had to talk to the most intelligent person around. She got so tired of hearing him say that, she didn't even listen, not even to the good ideas he did have. So Gene got out of the office, came to places like Rocky Top, talked to his horse, his truck, the trees—they seemed to listen. At least they didn't argue against him. When he tired of talking to himself, he had to act or else he would have been talking about himself as well as the others who didn't do anything.

Buck shifted as he reached down to delicately nip the top of a thistle flower.

"How the hell do you do that, big fella? I try to do that and I'd be at the dentist office getting spines pulled out of my gums." He shivered at the thought of that.

Buck pointed his ears again, then nudged Gene, knocking him backwards.

"Okay, okay. Let's go." Gene shifted the reins in his hand, then swung up onto Buck and started down the trail. He veered further into the trees, leaving the cliffs behind for the moment.

After hearing so much about this potential trail, and after discovering the beauty of Rocky Top, Gene had reached his saturation point of non-action. A year ago he decided to build the trail. He rode back and forth along the rim for several days and decided the trail could be easily built. He did a quick one page Environmental Assessment to cover the project, even though he didn't need one for a small project like a trail. Then he went to work figuring out how to build the trail without the funds to do it.

With a quick phone call, Gene secured the state prison's hotshot fire crew, the Firebirds, to start construction. All he needed was something very similar to a fire line scratched in the ground and a few trail blazes and rock cairns to mark the trail. This was to be a foot trail only and should be non-controversial. Matter of fact, Gene thought, it should be welcome by all.

As he rode Buck down to the south end, where the Firebirds would start the next day, he felt on top of the world. Finally, he would get this mythical trail started.

The next day, Gene got a phone call that the Firebirds would be a day late since they were dispatched to a small fire. Then another day delay. Gene was sidelined by a two-day meeting in Cedarville and by then, almost forgot about the trail. That is until 9 o'clock that evening as he was getting ready to go to bed.

"Gene, Walt Dickerson here. Got a big problem with what you are doing up on the Top."

Walt was branded as an enemy by Howard, the Forest Supervisor, but Gene got along well with him. Walt was hired specifically by the Slickrock Wilderness Alliance to ride herd on what the federal agencies were doing in this part of the state. Walt was straightforward and confident and Gene liked that. He said he was paid to pay attention to Gene and Howard and all the other feds who were screwing around with this natural wonderland; and he made no bones that he thought the whole state south of I-70 should be made not only a huge national park, but wilderness as well. Gene didn't like that extreme an attitude, but he silently agreed with some of Walt's ideas.

"You got a crew from the state pen building on that trail up there, don't you?"

"Yeah. Remember I told you what we were going to do. The Rim Trail. You said it was a great idea. Well, I'm a gettin' it done. As we speak. Well, as soon as I can get the crew up there."

"They are there. That's why I'm calling. You broke the agreement we had. You assured me it was going to be non-motorized. Foot only." Gene didn't like the tone of Walt's voice.

"I didn't break anything. It is non-motorized. Foot and horse only. That's what we planned all along. What makes you think otherwise?"

"You been up there since yesterday morning?"

"No. The crew kept getting waylaid. I didn't know they had even been up there yet. Just got a call this afternoon that they were called to Idaho on a fire." Gene was telling the truth on this. He got the call right before he came home and it really ticked him off. He had planned on getting the trail started and now his main source of labor was really letting him down.

"They, or somebody, were up there. They started building the trail yesterday afternoon. I saw what they did. They are building a goddamn road, Gene. It's wide enough to drive a tank down."

"You're shittin' me, Walt. They didn't tell me that. They were supposed to let me know when they started. I needed to line them out. I was out of town the last two days, but nobody said nothin'."

"Go up there tomorrow, friend. If you wanted a foot trail, that sure the hell ain't what you got. I'm in town right now. I can go with you."

Gene thought a second, then said, "No. I better go myself. Sounds like we had a little snafu. I never made it on the ground to line them out. They kept canceling on me. I didn't know they were there. Honest. That's a foot trail and if they got started wrong, they screwed me over. We'll get it straightened out. Not to worry. I don't want ATVs or 4-wheelers on it any more than you do. You know that."

"Better be that way. We are supporting you on this one but your bosses don't like anything I like and I think Howard would stymie the whole thing just because he hates my guts. I'm with you on this, but I have to stay low key. I'll fight him tooth and claw on the timber sale, though, and you know that too." Walt sounded too threatening for Gene's taste on this.

"Walt, pull your claws back in on this one. I'll straighten it out. And between you and me, I agree with you on the timber thing, but I've got internal problems on that and you know it."

"Just be careful. You are the only ally I have and I don't want you compromised. Take care and let me know. I have to go back home Tuesday so if you don't reach me here, try the city. Ciao."

Gene hung up the phone and just stared at it. He was walking a thin line on this. He had to be very cautious with Walt. Right now, the agency, in the form of Howard Thomas, Forest Supervisor, was neutral on any new trail, but adamant the next ten years of timber sales on the Mountain Lake District would come from Rocky Top. Way up there at almost 11,000 feet elevation, the island in the sky paradise was for the most part undisturbed, and logging would be an offense to Gene and everyone else he knew. Except Howard. Somehow, this thing had become a challenge to Howard's authority or his manhood or something dealing with his massive ego. Gene was indeed on thin ice.

The next day, Gene hiked up the Lookout Point Trail to the very southern junction with his new trail. When he broke out on top, he was shocked. Sure enough, the crew had been there. They had found his flagging, which picked up the trail as it came up through the basalt cliff and out on top—where Gene had instructed Kim Johnson, the Firebirds' supervisor, to build a "lightly scratched trail." It was a road. They had leveled a nice wide trail, free of rocks, tree roots, anything that might interfere with an ant strolling down the boulevard.

"My god, what a mess," Gene exclaimed to the trees. "This isn't what I told them." He looked around to see if anyone was there. He was by himself. "You stupid assholes!" he screamed as he threw his pack down on the ground and started waving his arms in frustration. "Damn it all to holy hell!" He walked down the trail, then turned and stomped back up it.

He would have to call Walt and really apologize. But it wasn't Walt who concerned him. He had screwed up, but he didn't know what he did wrong. It wasn't his fault. Well, it was his fault he relied on someone he didn't personally know and had never met. Kim was a state employee and offered free labor. The Firebirds had a good reputation for getting work done. It was a case of miscommunication about standards and he had to get it corrected immediately.

Walking along the "boulevard" he was relieved to find

that the crew had only done about two hundred yards of trail. "They must have only begun when they quit and left. Good thing they were called away. This is not accessible by vehicle, nor by horseback. There is no way on earth an ATV can even get to this section. Not from below. Not the way I hiked up. It was tough even walking through the narrow ledge in the cliff."

Gene kept talking to the trees and views—whoever was listening—as he assessed the situation. "On top, the trail is between the cliff and a rock field of boulders that will prevent access by bicycle, ATV or motorcycle. No damage done except to my reputation with Walt."

He sat down on the edge of the cliff and stared at the view for ten minutes. Listening to the wind in the trees and the chickadees scolding him settled him down. "I'll get my own trail crew to come up here tomorrow and narrow the trail by throwing rocks, limbs, even some grass seed on the edges of the new trail. It will be all right. Walt overreacted and I did, too."

Gene gave up on the idea of having the Firebird crew construct the trail. He called and left a message for Kim to cancel the work. He never heard from Kim, although he knew the crew was gone on fires for the next six weeks. He sent his own trail crew up and they scratched out a usable trail over a mile long. He hadn't planned on their working on this and it meant they didn't do maintenance on about twenty miles of other trails that summer. Some of the trails were in such bad shape, this lack of maintenance wasn't noticed. He did have Ralph, his crew supervisor, make a quick horseback recon of the trails and cut out the large trees that had fallen across the trails over the winter. It was all about priorities, Gene told his boss. And priorities change all the time for all kinds of reasons. Max, the Ranger, smiled when Gene explained the situation. As long as Gene dealt with it, Max was satisfied. Max didn't get excited about a lot of things.

Nothing else happened on the trail the rest of that year. Gene fussed about how to complete it. He was basically alone with the project. It was his baby and he had little support or funding from the Supervisor's Office and the Regional Office, and Walt wouldn't help with private funds since this was small potatoes on SWA's priority list.

On a cold and snowy day in February, when the trail lay under a few feet of snow, Gene sat with Max in their warm office shooting the breeze. Max said he'd had a call from Carter, a hunting buddy. He was a District Ranger in Arizona and took off a few weeks each summer to race horses on endurance races across the West. He had four horses he trained for this and that was his passion. His Forest Service career was essentially a hobby, with his horses as his main interest.

"Carter wants to do a race here, across Rocky Top. Start here in town, go up the North Slope, over the top, down into Cedar Mesa. Something like 75 or 80 miles. They have a rule that the horses and riders have to have so much elevation gain and so much level and so long, and access for vets to check the horses after so many miles. I don't understand it all; Carter's the expert. He thinks we have the perfect course. That give you any ideas?"

"Yeah. I gotta do a special use permit for the damn thing. When's he want to do it? Kinda short notice, isn't it?" Gene sat back in his chair and looked at Max, then out the window. Snow was swirling so thick, he couldn't see the horse barn across the parking lot.

"Damn," Gene muttered as he stared out the window. "Andrew is off today and he usually feeds the horses. I bet they didn't get fed. I better go out there and chunk 'em a bale. Else they'll start eating the fence again."

"Think about that race. That may be an answer to your trail," Max said as Gene hurried out of the room.

Gene pulled his collar up as the wind and snow hit him. Leaning into the wind as he struggled out to the barn, he wondered how that race might help build the trail. Make the participants stop and build trail as they raced across? "What does Max know I don't?" he asked Buck and Fox as he broke the twine and scattered a bale of hay. These were the only two horses left on the District. Blackie had been a troublemaker, so they had transferred him to the San Juan Forest two months earlier, and would get a new trotter next spring. Howard was into horses and he said he would drive back to Missouri and pick out a good trotter. Gene thought there should be higher priorities for the Forest Supervisor, but these old cowboys liked their foxtrotters. The ranchers did well and good with local plugs, but the Forest Service had to travel halfway across the country to get a horse that wasn't any better than the cow ponies bred and raised in the mountains. The old-boy network still ran the outfit, and these old boys were right out of the Pinchot days and the old timers who lived on their horses.

Gene was grumbling about that quirk of the Forest Service, when he stopped mid-throw of hay and said, "Yeah, they will build trail." He finished feeding the boys, as he called them, then hurried back into the office.

Max was still sitting there, reading his mail and sipping his soda when Gene stuck his snow-covered head in and smiled.

"You look like you swallowed a horse apple, Gene."

"You knew how to do it, didn't you?" Gene took off his

coat and shook the snow off.

"Figure it out?" Max smiled and put his feet on his desk.

"Their route across the top is my trail location, isn't it? They don't really need a well-defined trail. They prefer to just race cross country, don't they? I simply flag the route and tell them to stay on that and with a couple hundred or so flying hooves, they pound out a trail and I have a really cheap labor force."

"Better than a wayward prison crew?" Max snorted a laugh and set down his can of soda. "May not give you a final trail, but it's a pretty good start don't you think?"

"The trail location is already flagged. They pound out the tread a little, we can go in and put in a few rock cairns, a blaze or two, we got us a trail. Thanks for the idea."

"Your idea. I never told you a thing. Hey, go hang up your coat and come back in here. I just got a call from the boss. Need to talk to you about it."

Gene didn't like the sound of that. He didn't really know how he stood with Howard. Sometimes Howard treated him like part of his favored elite, part of the time he almost shunned him. He tried to think what he may have done to irritate Howard, shrugged as he threw his coat on his desk and grabbed a handful of cookies from his lunch sack. He went into Max's office and closed the door after Max motioned him to shut it.

Max leaned forward and cleared his throat. "You're not hot on the big timber sale Howard wants up there are you?" He looked out the window towards Rocky Top, but swirling snow obscured the view.

"You know we shouldn't be doing that scale of logging up there. We can pick and pluck a few like we been doing for 50 years, but not ten million feet. That's not what that country is about."

Max replied in his slow drawl, "Yeah. We're about done

with the mom-and-pop deadwood thing that's kept this county out of subsistence ranching. Everyone and his dog has had a small deadwood sale up there for about three generations. That's not the way to manage that. But I agree, I really don't want a ten-million foot sale up there either. But the boss says it's all we got left. I think he is right about that."

Gene wiped his hands on his pant legs as he finished his third cookie. He leaned back in his chair, propping it up against the wall. "Max, we don't have to cut every last stick of timber on this mountain. If we're out of trees, then we're out of trees. Someone has to have the balls to tell somebody up the line that we simply can't produce ten million feet. Not here. Not anymore. We're done. Finito."

"How would you like to be the one to tell that someone?" Max looked at Gene with the strange quizzical look that always puzzled Gene.

"What do you mean?"

Max laughed. "Settle down. You look like a deer caught in the headlights. Howard said that Bob just wasn't cutting it as team leader on the Environmental Assessment. He wants that EA done and signed before September. He asked if you would take over as team leader. He respects your planning and writing ability. He says you did a great job with the grazing problems and thinks you are the one to get this done." Max raised his eyebrows and scratched his chin with his left hand. Gene noticed that Max hadn't shaved and his hand made a rasping sound as it swept over his face.

Gene started to speak a couple times but only made a strange grunt both times. He squinted his eyes and finally spoke. "Hell, Max, I'm not the timber staff. Bob is in charge of timber. I can't take over his job. I got enough to do with the West Slope Grazing EA. We're still overstocked up there and Andrew and I are up to alligators with those boys and their trespass cows. What the hell does Howard think I can do, fly?"

"I have a feeling he knows you are against any sales up there and this is a way to shut you up. Pretty big trust in you if he thinks you would not use this opportunity to sabotage the whole thing. Sort of prove up or shut up. Guess he thinks you can do both the timber and grazing jobs. Might take a few weekends work, but I think you can do it. Give Andrew a little more responsibility on the range stuff. I think you've had him on a short leash. Give him a little more rope."

"Geez, Max, I don't know. I've been crossways with Bob lately anyway. Something's bothering him." Now it was Gene's turn to rub his face. He took off his glasses and looked at them.

"Keep a secret? I mean really keep it?" Max questioned Gene with his eyes.

"Yeah. You having an affair?" Gene kept a straight face but Max burst out laughing.

"Shit, Gene, get real. Who'd play around with this old fart? Is that what you gentiles think a Bishop does in this little Mormon town? Seriously, Bob is on his way out. Howard is fed up and didn't even ask me. He told me he is working to transfer Bob. I'm not sure what Bob did, but you know Howard. Cross him and you are fish bait. Sounds like he will detail Tim out of the SO over here next summer. But he isn't familiar with the Top like you are and you work well with the ID team out of Cedar. I don't think the word "no" is acceptable here. You don't want to cross Howard."

"I get the feeling I am already on his list. I can't figure him out half the time. I thought he was still pissed at me over the cuts we made, or didn't make, in his opinion, on the drought last year."

"That may be, but you're his boy on this one. Have some compassion for me. I'm the one that has to break the news to Bob when he gets back from his vacation."

Gene got up, still surprised at the turn of events. "As the saying goes, that's why you get…"

"I know, the big bucks," interrupted Max. He tossed his empty can into the trash, then reached in and pulled it back out. "Oops—forgot, you will report me to the recycle cops." He handed it to Gene before he walked out the door and disappeared into the rest room.

Gene stared at the closing door, then wandered back to his desk and slumped into his chair. He stared out the window as the snow fell even heavier. He wrote on his desk top calendar, "Horse race permit, reflag trail, Rocky Top EA, set ID team meetings, sleep in spare time. Eating optional."

One of Gene's concerns was resolved a week later. When Bob returned from his vacation, Max immediately pulled him into his office and gave him the news not of Gene taking over his EA duties on the Rocky Timber Sale, but of his transfer to the Lost Creek District on the adjacent forest. He said since Bob would be gone, he was assigning Gene the job of the EA. That last piece of news was insignificant compared to the rapid transfer, which took effect in 30 days. Bob stomped out of the office and immediately took another couple days off. Gene hardly saw him again, much less talk to him.

Gene started holding regular meetings with the ID team members. He went to Cedar for the first meeting, but decided it made more sense to have them here on the district rather than in the SO, even though that meant 4 people driving two hours versus one person driving. All the members, including the forest silviculturist agreed that not only was a large timber sale not appropriate, the timber wasn't there in the first place. No one trusted Bob's inventory calculations. Pockets of trees were mixed with rock fields, lakes, all kinds of hindrance to building roads or skid trails. Even if the trees were there, they were young, slow growing and hard to access. For years, local ranchers had driven their stock trucks up there with small backhoes and even horses and pulled out dead trees from the bug epidemics of the 1930s. That kind of logging was feasible. Modern industrial logging would be nearly impossible.

Walt was busy in his Salt Lake City office all winter. Evidently their budget was almost drained and he had to spend time helping raise more money. Although he played up the devastating effects of the potential timber sales promoted by the Forest Supervisor on Rocky Top, he also played up the so-called efforts to allow more motorized use, including the construction of an ATV trail along the Rim. Walt knew better. After Gene learned about Walt's newest ad (dirty little trick he called it), he spent a day fuming before he picked up the phone and called Walt.

"Walt, Gene here. I just saw your latest fund raising ad. What the hell you talking about us wanting to build an ATV trail along the top. You know that's not true!"

"Settle down, Gene. I know it and you know it. We're playing hard ball here. It helps get money."

"You are distorting the facts. You wonder why Howard hates you and your organization? This is why."

"Hey Gene, speaking of Howard, you know what he tried to do last month? He cornered me in a meeting up here and said he would support our non-motorized trail if we would back off a little on our fight with the timber sales. That dumb butt really thought he could horse trade on that. I told him his stupid trail was already non-motorized. I said you assured me of that and I had your letter to prove it. Remember that memo you sent me after your prison crew screwed up? He looked at the letter and sputtered, then stomped off. I can't believe he honestly thought those were equal bargaining chips."

"You showed him that? That wasn't an official letter. That was just a note from me. Oh shit, he will somehow throw that back in my face."

"Hey, I didn't mean to get you in trouble. He was just so greasy and I think he honestly thought I would support that timber sale. What a toad. He wouldn't press you to make that trail motorized would he?" Walt really sounded surprised.

"Hell no. Our own plans say non-motorized up there. We have closed old logging trails and hunter trails, but haven't exactly enforced them."

"You got that right. All the times I've been up there, I've never seen a green rig. You ever written a ticket to anyone on a closed road up there?"

"No, but I've never caught anyone. Have you?" Gene thought he had him on that one.

"Actually, I did run across a couple boys on motorcycles last summer. They were racing across a meadow and when they saw me, they tried to do a quick turn around and they ran into each other and tumbled the bikes. It was great. One of them bent a wheel or something and he had to push the bike to the road, over rocks, across a marsh, with the wheel catawampus the whole way. They were still struggling to get to the road when I stopped laughing and just drove away. I think they expected me to help them. They could rot out there for all I cared."

"Walt, your compassion is showing. What a good Samaritan. I suppose you'd leave a little old lady up there if she had a flat tire."

"Only if she was on an illegal road," Walt laughed. "Hey,

I'm sorry about the trail ad. But you gotta do what you gotta do. I know you're helping us. How you gonna build the trail this year? More of the prison crew?"

"You don't wanna know. I've got other fish to fry this summer. You hear about my new assignment?"

"Oh no, you moving?' Walt's voice flashed panic.

"No, no, nothing like that. I've been assigned, by Howard no less, to be the lead on the ID team for the Rocky Top timber sales." As soon as he said that, he wondered if he should have.

Walt laughed. "I guess I did hear that. Howard told me before he made an ass of himself with his Middle East type diplomacy. I didn't have a chance to ask him more about it. We should be home free now."

"That puts me in a tough position, you know. I have to be fair and objective. We have to honestly look at the options." Gene felt a thin layer of ice come between them.

"You haven't turned into the enemy now, have you? Listen buddy, you're on our side."

Gene was starting to get a little irritated with Walt by now. "It's not about being on sides. I got a job to do and I'm doing it. We should both be after the same thing."

"Yeah. Hey, I'll be down there next week. Wanna go up on top with me?"

Gene wanted to end the conversation. "Give me a call. See what we can do. Listen, I have to go now. Just had a permittee walk in here. Good talking to you. Later."

Walt was playing games. Howard was playing games. Gene just wanted to do his job, call a spade a spade, and all that simple stuff. He didn't want to be a politician. Just the simple range con and wildlife biologist who got out on the ground and knew what needed to be done for the land. Not for scheming politicians who didn't mind screwing people around to get their ego massaged. Maybe he needed to go saddle up Buck and head for some wild country. Max would be up for that. Unless of course, Max was off playing politics of his own somewhere.

A few days later, Gene was in the office doing overdue paperwork. Darlene, the office manager, was up front. No one else was in the office. Gene heard the back door open and he felt this presence enter his room. He looked up and Howard was standing there. His face was red underneath his big Stetson. He didn't even say hi to Gene, but motioned for him to come with him. He walked into Max's empty office, with Gene close behind, and shut the door. He didn't ease into any small talk, but thundered in his booming voice, "Gene, you been talking with Walt Dickerson?"

Gene looked Howard in the eyes and said, "yes sir. I talk with him often. His job entails..."

Howard cut him off and boomed again, "Fuck that son of a bitch. He is using you and trying to screw me. That bastard is trying to make me look bad and he's using you. You tell that son of a bitch that the new rim trail is non-motorized?" Howard was mad and his voice was echoing throughout the room and probably the building as well.

Gene sat down and crossed his legs. Howard had just pissed him off and he was not going to be intimidated. No more from this big egomaniac. Gene continued calmly, "the new rim trail is non-motorized. Has always been. Was never intended for anything but non-motorized. It's been that way for years, even when Jerome first dreamed of a trail up there."

"I was going to use that trail as a bargaining chip with those SWA sons of bitches. You just screwed me from doing that." Howard was still standing, which made Gene uncomfortable. He knew the game of communication and one person standing over a person sitting was the ultimate in power control. He stood up.

"I'm not playing games with that trail. We always intended that as a foot and horse trail and we'd violate the Forest Plan if we planned any differently. I'm just trying to get it built, which is a hell of a lot more than anyone else has ever done. No help from your office so I'm doing what I can. Besides, this is one thing they agree with us on. We can't fight them about every single thing we do." Gene was keeping his cool and it surprised him. Howard was at his peak in intimidation.

"I want those timber sales up there. You are my man for getting that approved and doing the EA. I could have gotten their support by trading them a non-motorized trail for the timber. You screwed me over on that." Howard was almost yelling now. Not that his voice was far from that anytime.

"Howard," Gene sat back down. He would take these postures the way they fell. He was low man on this totem pole any day of the week so he might as well be comfortable while getting reamed out by the big boss. "Walt and his group would never under any circumstances ever in a million years, support any level of timber sales up there any more than the little firewood sales we do now. I know Walt. Even if you threw in a dozen Playboy Playmates and a villa in Tahiti, you would never get them to bargain. Never. They know the trail is non-motorized and they know the timber sales are going to be a tough sell. I'm—,"

Howard cut him off again. Gene thought for a second Howard was going to hit him. "Don't tell me what I can do. I could have gotten something from them. They know I can do what I want and they have to play ball with me."

This guy is off his rocker, thought Gene. He started to

get worried then. He wondered about opening the door so Darlene could see the crime when Howard smacked him around the room.

"You better play straight with this EA. And I want to see it on my desk by September. You understand that? This is our timber for the next decade and I'm not going to miss our targets. You do whatever PR you want and play your naïve choir boy part, but we need that timber. Screw Walt and his group. All they want is to bring in donations. They don't give a rat's ass about the resources. You understand?"

"I understand what my job entails. The ID team is working on this and we are all going up there again on Thursday. Wanna come with us?"

"Hell, I gotta be in Washington tomorrow. I know what's up there. You guys just look at the data. The timber is up there and we have to go log it. You just do your job."

Howard turned and walked out the back door. Not a goodbye. Just a slamming door. He slammed the door of his car as well and spun gravel as he sped out the parking lot. Gene watched him leave, knowing he had just been reamed out by the best. All he could do was say very slowly, "that son of a bitch."

He looked up and saw Darlene standing there. She was almost trembling. Her face was flushed. "Gene, are you all right? I was scared. I could hear him screaming at you. What happened?" She walked over and put her hand on his shoulder. She said quietly, "I'm still shaking." She was.

"Us cowboys are tough. He was kinda ticked off wasn't he?" Gene laughed nervously, then realized he was a little shaky himself. Darlene sat down next to him, pulling her chair up close.

She said very quietly, "I've never seen or heard anything like that. What happened?" Darlene needed some kind of explanation, so Gene told her the whole story. He talked for a solid ten minutes. Both of them were startled as Beverly walked in the back door and poked her head in the office. Beverly was Darlene's assistant and had stepped out to run an errand to Beaver's Store just down the road. "You two having fun back here? Want me to close the door?" She grinned and winked at Darlene.

Darlene started to tell Beverly about the episode but decided against it. At least right then. She would tell her later, as well as everybody else when they got back in the office. "Just a little budget crisis. Nothing that would interest you. Go mind the front desk." She almost glared at Beverly.

"Well you're kinda sour. Okay, you don't want me here." Beverly pouted all the way up to the front desk.

Later, when Gene filled Max in on the episode, Max grimaced. He told Gene to keep doing what he was doing. He would talk to Howard. He said he had gotten some rough talk from Howard as well and there were rumors about Howard's wife leaving or Howard having cancer or about a half dozen other terrible things. This had not been a good week for Howard and the whole forest was on alert to try and avoid him. Max reassured Gene and apologized for the way he was treated.

The trail took back seat to other things that summer. The endurance race happened in July, but it didn't have nearly the effect Gene wanted. They pounded out a trail in places, but in most areas, the ground was either so rocky or so marshy, it didn't do much except stir up dust or mud. It was back to plodding along with his trail crew. Walt promised some volunteers to help on weekends, but produced nothing.

The ID team had several meetings, cementing their consensus that the timber was not there and what was there, should not be cut. It wasn't the time or the place to have large timber sales. Road access was terrible, and improving the one poor road up to the top would have significant effects, none desirable. The Top, a maze of meadows, lakes, swamps, and timbered fingers that meandered for miles, was too valuable for recreation and scientific study. Not for sawlogs.

September passed and Gene was struggling to finish the EA. They had several alternatives, only one of which proposed harvesting more than a couple million feet of timber. A new timber staff joined the district in late August, and he made several trips to Rocky Top, each time with Gene. He asked Gene whose idea it was to harvest this area. He said it was insane. Maybe the word was asinine, but either way, he didn't want to be involved in it. This country was too high in elevation, the soils were too sensitive, growing season too short, other values too high to put a road system through this alpine rockpile. Gene loved the support, which confirmed what almost everyone else knew. Except Howard.

Howard was called to the Washington Office in early August for a three-month detail. Rumors were he wouldn't return. Seems he had one of his outbursts with the Regional Forester's staff and that sealed his fate. He never returned to the forest and he passed away in December. He was diagnosed with an inoperable brain tumor and died within two weeks of the diagnosis.

In October, Gene rode Buck along the Rocky Top rim, anticipating the snows to come. His beloved trail was two miles long, with about five more to go. Buck was adorned with long orange flagging, normal procedure in hunting season. Gene didn't trust hunters not to mistake a horse for a deer; stranger things happened every fall as hunters from the city swarmed the area. Gene dismounted, and Buck nudged him as he stood on a section of trail. Then he pawed a front hoof, reached his shaggy head down, and yanked up a clump of bunchgrass growing in the middle of a rock pile.

"Buck, old boy, you got a pretty good life, don't you? You stand around eating this fresh grass or hay and once in a while you put up with us dudes climbing on your back and coming up a rocky trail. I kind of think that ain't a bad way to live." Gene adjusted his chaps and shook off his Stetson. He climbed on Buck and looked off the edge of the world, to the slickrock far below.

The gold of the aspen was gone and the naked white trunks stood on the slopes far below like skeletons scattered among the green pines. White rock outcrops, sprinkled with black boulders, stretched below the hidden highway halfway down the mountain. Pink and orange cliffs outlined the canyons further down. Gene heard an elk bugle, whistling to his harem somewhere in the vastness below. The wind picked up, waving the now dried grass on the edge of the cliffs. Gene caught his hat before it could sail off. Dark clouds were gathering to the south.

"Let it snow," he said to Buck. "I need a break. Gene zipped up his vest, orange side out. Buck picked his way down the narrow rocky trail that disappeared below the edge. Gene whistled a tune he couldn't get out of his head. The only words he could remember were "a long and winding road."

ELK PEAK PASSAGE

*This could be the highlight of Amy's life
as well as Elizabeth's. No matter what happened
from now on, nothing could top this moment.
A wrinkled but steady white-haired old lady had
achieved something probably none of the
other 185 had done tonight or possibly
had ever done before.*

AMY REMEMBERED HOW the idea first came to her. Her co-workers in the District office had laughed when she suggested a bonfire to burn the piles of old scrap wood at the Work Center during the November full moon. "We can have a weenie roast and marshmallow party, watch the flames, drink a little hot cider (and maybe other things as well), and howl at the moon." A few folks said she had gone off the deep end.

Maybe the wolf howling went too far, she thought. But overall, people needed to lighten up. She knew she did. The big grazing permit crisis had wound a lot of people up tight. "No sense of humor left around here anymore," she said to herself. This job should be fun, she kept saying, but people didn't seem to believe it.

The bonfire idea fell flat, but the idea of doing something during a full moon flickered on and off over the winter. Something involving the public that was non-controversial. The concept turned into sponsoring a public hike under a full moon somewhere out in the forest. The more she thought about it, the more it appealed to her. Who could possibly object to that?

Now in the latter portion of her career, she felt everything she did caused grief to some interest group. If she wasn't offending the cattlemen, it was the loggers. If not the four wheelers, then the Sierra Clubbers. There was no safe haven to turn to anymore. This wasn't the same Forest Service she started with decades ago. As a pioneering woman in the agency, she fought prejudice for years, and she had to fight the attempts to use her to meet quotas and fill positions she didn't want or didn't feel qualified for. Amy was tired, disillusioned, and less and less satisfied with her job and her career in general. Maybe her superiors had lost the ability to make decisions. She hadn't.

So Amy finally decided one April day to just do it. She always bounced her crazy ideas off her partner. When they were really stupid, Dee would let her know.

"Deeby, I am going to do a bunch of moonlight hikes. Moonwalks. Not a Michael Jackson thing. A real hike under a full moon."

"You crazy? Greg gonna let you do this?" Dee heard Amy's tirades about her boss too often. But Amy was also doing things lately that surprised Dee. "You didn't even ask him, did you?" Dee knew Amy very well.

"Not even asking permission. He is an idiot. He'll find some reason for me not doing it. The Bozo doesn't have a clue what's happening on the district anyway. Take him until next year to make a decision. Screw him. I'll be retired by then anyway." Amy smiled broadly at that thought.

Dee looked at Amy, thinking about her past and her career. "You know, you deserve something good. You have been the most under-appreciated employee this outfit has seen in a long time. You just sit back and take all this crap. I don't know how you do it. You are right. You go do it. I think it will be great. What a hoot. I'm glad you turned down those Ranger assignments. You would have sunk into a pit of frustration. You've enjoyed this interpretive stuff all along. Like you always say, just do it. Don't worry about what anyone thinks. People will love it." Dee hugged Amy and held her tight.

Amy's idea was not unique. She had read that an agency or community in Minnesota—or Wisconsin—had done this and it was very popular. Even somebody else in the Forest Service was doing it out of Laramie. So what if it wasn't her idea. No one here ever thought of doing it, so if it worked, she would be satisfied. If it didn't, well, you didn't get anywhere by not trying. In this outfit, you didn't get anywhere now days anyway, so... She paused with that thought. "I need to quit being so negative," she told herself as she drove to Elk Peak to scout out a possible location for a moon hike.

Elk Peak would be a tough place to initiate a new program like this: a three-mile long trail, with an elevation gain of two thousand feet. The thought that maybe she should start someplace easier was foremost in her mind. "Maybe I should have the first moon hike at an easier location."

She stopped at the trailhead, figuring how many cars could park there. "Maybe 50 people might show up, so that means probably at least 25 parking places. No problem, since the parking area has a very wide spot on the road on a wide curve, making it seem even larger." She had hiked the trail many times and knew it was a good trail, with only several rocky, steep spots. The top of the Peak was wide open, with scattered rocks and fantastic views. "This would work, but it really should be the second hike. An easy trail needs to be the premier moon hike. Where could it be?"

On the return drive to town, she detoured several miles in order not to get back to the office early. She didn't want to see Greg. She had been so frustrated with him the day before when he flip-flopped on a decision about the Canyon

Byway parking lot location. The Byway project had begun a few years before her transfer to the District, and she worked on it for two more years. The project had gone through planning, Environmental Assessment, public involvement, and the final decision—the whole works. Greg's predecessor submitted a grant proposal to the state and now the grant was to expire next year and only half the project had been done. This was the year to finish it. But just a few weeks ago, Greg caved in to two local fishermen who objected to a parking lot next to their favorite stretch of the creek. Now he said Amy had to find a new location.

She drove by the creek and grimaced as she thought of all the work that he had thrown out by his flip-flop decision. "In today's climate, you cannot do anything without offending someone," she muttered to herself. "The decision had been properly made years ago, including the consideration of these few fishermen, and tough cookies to them that their favorite all-to-themselves spot might be discovered by others. It really is the perfect location to put an interpretive sign and parking area," she grumbled to herself.

"Could I do the first moon hike here? Maybe build public support for the parking area. Sabotage the Bozo's change of decision? His action was probably illegal," she mumbled. "He subverted the whole friggin' process. No, just let it go. Fight this one and you lose."

She had witnessed other careers go down the toilet by challenging the boss. All bosses stick together and if she fought her boss, then his boss would come to his aid. "You lose either way, Amy girl," she sighed as she pulled back on the highway. "Can't do it here."

Two miles down the highway, Amy pulled into the parking lot at the new Canyon Lodge. The parking area, along with a new trail to Wagon Wheel Falls, had just been finished. The engineers administered the contract, leaving her out of the loop. On Greg's orders, of course. She was in charge of trail management, but here was a new trail that she had no say in. Of course, she would be in charge of maintenance now that it was on the system, so she did have an interest in the finished project. It was another grant that built the trail in cooperation with the non-profit Limestone Canyon Association. Good public relations, she had to admit, but it still riled her that the engineers got their grubby little fingers into the thing. They were just trying to keep themselves employed since timber road funding was in a nose-dive nowadays. This was another last-minute decision by Greg a couple years ago.

She parked at the far end of the huge gravel parking area. The original plans called for paving it, but since the trail cost so much to build, they had to do a change order in the contract, substituting gravel for asphalt. She locked the truck and started hiking up the trail. Nice, she thought, although wide enough to drive an ATV on. It had to meet ADA standards. Anything nowadays was required to accommodate a wheelchair. She frowned as she thought about implications of that. "I can't begrudge someone in a wheelchair, but dammit, there are some places that will always be foot travel only. To the top of Elk Peak, for one."

As she walked the gently sloping trail, passing through stands of paper birch and aspen, she listened to the creek just below her. Willows hid the water here, but she could see the creek up ahead as the trail curved uphill to avoid big boulders lining the water. It was a soothing sound, especially with the birds twittering. There were a few spots of snow in the shadows under the cliffs on the north slope high above her, but the compacted pea gravel trail was dry and solid. Gravel was another change. The original plan was to pave it. "Too extravagant," she thought, glad to see it was not asphalt. "That may be fine in a city park. Not out here. We need to save some wild things." She felt society was becoming too tame, too civilized and losing touch with anything wild.

She kicked the gravel to see how deep it was. Not very; the gravel will be gone within a year, she complained to herself. "Engineers have no concept of what happens to a road or a trail after they build it."

Because the new trail was not very long, she reached the falls in about fifteen minutes. It wasn't far, and walking on this trail really was easy. Of course, she wouldn't admit that to an engineer. "No bias in my bones," she laughed. She stopped to admire the falls. Not a big deal as waterfalls went, but it was scenic. Then the thought hit her. "This will be a perfect place for a moon hike. Easy walk, lots of parking, close to town, recognizable, a few open spots, although a lot of tree canopy to hide the sky. The cliffs of the canyon would look great under the shadows of a full moon."

She made the decision. The first hike would occur here, in two months. "Things to do," she outlined to herself. "Talk to the Lodge about using the parking lot, write a press release, get on local radio and TV, arrange for a speaker. Then do the same for Elk Peak a month later. An easy hike to start, then a hard one. Catering to all audiences. And non-controversial. What a deal." She jauntily walked the quarter mile back to the truck, humming the Beatles' "Yeah Yeah Yeah..." the whole way.

The next week, setting the press release in front of him for his signature, Amy casually informed Greg that she was going to lead an interpretive walk on the new trail. This would be a couple weeks after the formal ribbon cutting for the trail, an event she learned about just like the rest of the public—in a press release made out of the Supervisor's Office. She was left out of the loop again. She didn't care on that one. Her event would eclipse the dry speeches and ceremonial cutting of a piece of white satin ribbon.

The only hitch came when she was called to a fire in Montana a week before the scheduled hike. She forgot to make herself unavailable ahead of time and when Dispatch called her at 4 am Sunday morning, she didn't dare turn it down. Besides, she was lobbying to get on the Regional Type I Fire Team, and they were the team on this fire. She made some quick phone calls to Dave and Sam in the Supervisor's Office to take her place on the hike. She had consulted them about the hikes and they helped her with the press release. Sam actually had led one of the moon hikes out of Laramie a year before and loved the idea when she first mentioned doing it on this forest.

In mid-June, standing on the edge of fire camp, away from the noise of the electric generators, Amy was entranced by the full moon hovering over the Big Hole Valley in Montana. She savored the sight of the night sky, thinking maybe a cozy group of 50 people, 100 if things went extremely well, were just then strolling along on her moon hike a few hundred miles away. It was her own moonwalk that she was missing! She had planned it, organized it and now she started to feel embarrassed that she couldn't even be there for the first hike. But she soon became lost in the silence of the moment, trying to find the eagle in the full moon (something she never could visualize).

Of course, she had no idea that right at that very moment a huge crowd was overflowing the parking area and overwhelming the restaurant and gift store after finishing a successful hike. Just over 275 people crowded the Wagon

Wheel trail, following Dave and Sam as they tried to lead a huge and unruly crowd. Dave compared it later to trying to lead a pack of puppy dogs, all going different directions at once. "Herding cats," was the way Sam described it.

When she returned a few days after the hike, Greg asked her into his office. He congratulated her on a great turnout, but she could tell he was still pissed.

"Amy, this was after dark. You didn't tell me that."

"It was in the press release you signed. "Hike Under a Full Moon" was the title. How can we have a moonwalk in the daytime?"

"That is a safety issue. Did you think of safety? We could be sued if someone got hurt."

Amy glared at Greg. She started to make a snippy remark, but bit her tongue. Finally, she said, "Yes. I always think of safety. You know that. I am head of the District Safety Committee."

"Talking about safety doesn't keep people safe in the dark hiking down a trail."

"The guys gave a five-minute spiel on safety before they started walking. We all agreed on that. The moon was bright. It's not really that dark. You can see very well. I know it was a clear night. We asked that people bring flashlights. It's dangerous for people to hike on trails in the daylight, too. They can fall, stub toes, get attacked by mountain lions."

Now it was Greg's turn to glare at Amy. His glare rarely involved direct eye contact, though. He always seemed to look behind the person. Or through them.

He suddenly changed the subject and said the Forest Supervisor congratulated him on a great hike. "Barb likes getting good PR and she already got calls from people saying the moonwalk thing was a good experience. But she was concerned about safety. Like me." He did look Amy in the eye on that remark. Amy felt the daggers.

"She asked if you were planning on doing another one."

"Well, yes," she replied. She planned on one every month, the next one to the top of Elk Peak. "Since the first one seemed to be so popular, we thought...," Amy realized bringing Dave and Sam into the picture would make it sound better. Greg didn't trust anyone, but if the SO was involved, he for some reason seemed to accept things better. "Dave, Sam and I thought doing another few would be good PR."

Greg seemed to lose interest now that he had expressed his displeasure at being bypassed. Amy looked out the window and thought ahead. Moonwalks under clear sky or clouds, summer or winter. Weekday or weekend. From what Dave told her, the actual night of the full moon was not the best idea since the moon came up too late. People didn't want to be out that late, especially 30 miles or more out in the Forest. So she would schedule them for two days prior to the official full moon. The moon looked full for several nights prior to the official full moon, but it came up a couple hours earlier and would be overhead at a decent hour, not midnight.

She was still thinking about future hikes when Greg brought her back to earth and stunned her by announcing that Elk Peak would be too dangerous in the dark.

"I guess since you started this, we should continue."

We? Now Greg was part of this? Of course. Something went wrong, Greg had no part in it or didn't know anything about it. Things went right, then he was part of the team. Amy was getting tired of this game-playing.

"But for safety reasons, we should do it in the daylight."

Amy wanted to jump up and hit him. "How do we do a moonwalk in the daylight?" she sputtered. "The whole purpose is to do this under a full moon. After sundown." She hesitated, realizing Greg was not budging. "Kinda defeats the whole purpose." She looked at him. He still had that blank look that drove Amy crazy. She couldn't figure out what he was thinking. If anything.

"I will give the hikers a safety talk," Amy replied. Thoughts were racing through her mind as she struggled to find a compromise that could save the essence of her idea. "I already ask them to bring flashlights. How about we start at something like 5 pm? That way we walk up in the daylight and get down before it is fully dark. They will have hiked up being able to see the trail. The only rocky spots are near the top. They can be on those areas when it's still light."

He bought it. She doubted if he had ever hiked the trail. He rarely went anywhere on the District, so he wouldn't know these details. She thought, "It's a two-hour hike at best. If we watch the sun set up on top, listen to a lecture and eat, it will be totally dark before we even get halfway down. What he doesn't know...."

She walked out of Greg's office and plopped into her chair at her desk, only twenty feet down the hall. She sat back, rubbing her hands through her short brown hair. She was thinking of the streaks of grey showing in her bangs. Dee kept telling her she should dye her hair white. That was a badge of experience and wisdom. No, let nature takes its course. She had earned every gray hair, she thought. If she wouldn't accept promotions she didn't think she earned but was offered only because she was meeting some gender target, then she wouldn't cheat on her hair either. Honesty applied everywhere. As befit her ability to continually shift her focus, her mind jumped back to the hike.

If almost 300 people came for an easy hike the first time, then it was still reasonable to expect not much more than 50 or 75 for a really hard hike, especially on a Saturday evening. After the first hike, Dave strongly recommended to have three or more people helping if needed. So she asked Tim and Fran from her office to help out. She didn't want to be solely responsible for babysitting that many people stretched out on a three-mile long trail. They agreed, although she didn't tell them she wanted them to be her cat herders. She also enlisted Dr. Rawlins, a professor from the local college to talk about the history of Elk Peak and how it got its name from a Lakota-Crow battle over two hundred years ago and which remains sacred to both tribes.

Amy remembered to make herself unavailable for fire assignments two weeks ahead of time. She appeared on a noon news show on the local TV station to plug her moon hikes. The host was a new young anchor, quite handsome and sexy. She had a hard time looking at him during the interview. She was afraid she would catch herself staring at him. Instead, she swiveled back and forth in the chair, almost making herself dizzy. She left the station totally flustered, thinking she did a horrible job, although three people who saw it said she did great. Her comment at the end of the interview—"Well, Stan, we hope to have you join us and do a full moon"—went unnoticed. Either that, or people were polite and didn't want to embarrass her any more than she already was.

Saturday arrived with a few clouds, but mild temperatures for mid-July. Calling Tim in the morning, she found to her dismay that he had forgotten about the hike and was committed to something else. About noon, she finally reached Fran, only to learn a similar story. Fran didn't realize it was a firm commitment and was leaving with her fiancée in a few minutes to drive to Denver for a shopping spree. Dee was unable to assist, having driven to Ft. Collins to visit an aunt in a nursing home. Amy was by herself for the hike. She edged close to a feeling of despair, then backed off. This is not such a big deal, she thought, adjusting her badge and nameplate on her uniform as she dressed for the hike.

Amy worried about minor details, those little things most people would not even notice. She worried that her hair would be mussed, although it was so short, it wasn't long enough to muss. She worried she was getting fat, but she still fit in the same pants she had worn for twenty five years. She fretted over sounding boring, although her voice still had that husky, sexy sound that unknown to her, had prompted folks on the old Bear Creek District years ago to refer to her as Tokyo Rose. She worried about not ever being prepared, but she could go on stage in front of a hundred people and improvise about any subject thrown at her. Amy was cool under pressure and well respected, but rarely was she given the compliments that could cut through her insecurity. Amy drove out of town worrying that no one would show up for her hike.

Arriving at the Elk Peak parking lot a full hour early, Amy was startled to see a half dozen vehicles already there. Fifteen people already, an hour ahead of time! Maybe there was a mix-up on the time. Even before she could get out of the truck, a young boy came up to her and asked if she was the moon lady. Amy chuckled. Yeah, I've been called a lot worse, she thought. Turned out the kid had been pestering his dad so much all day, they came out early in order to run a little energy off the boy.

During the next hour, Amy visited folks as they arrived, having to help people park as the lot soon filled to capacity. Cars and trucks were overflowing onto the roadside. "Oh, man, I am going to kill both Tim and Fran. I need somebody to help."

Answering her silent plea, Bob, an engineer from the office walked up to her right at that moment. She quickly pulled him aside and asked if he could help. All she needed him to do was bring up the rear and make sure people were all right and not get left behind.

When the magic hour of 5 PM arrived, Amy counted noses. There were 185 hikers, all in various stages of excitement, amusement, anticipation. She started out with a quick introduction, then the stern safety lecture.

"What we plan to do," continued Amy, "is to hike to the top before the sun goes down. We want you to experience the trail while you can see it in the daylight. You may not have as good a view of it in the dark on the way down. Just think about hiking back down when you can't see things very well."

"Why are we hiking if we can't see?" asked a girl not much more than five years old.

"You can see. You will just be seeing by moonlight and not sunlight. Just like owls or raccoons." Amy smiled at the girl. The girl giggled and pulled on her mother's arm.

"Will we see any raccoons? We had one get in our garbage can one night. He made a mess!"

"We might. I want you to look and listen for all kinds of things. You can write a story about all the things you see."

The girl giggled again and hid behind her mom's leg. Amy smiled again. Whenever she worked with children, she felt there was hope for the future. She didn't have that same sense when she dealt with adults and the frustration of trying to manage the resources for their children's futures.

Amy explained how everyone would go up in the daylight, rendezvous on the top, eat a picnic of whatever they brought, listen to Dr. Rawlins tell them something educational and enlightening, watch the sun sink below the horizon, then come down in the dark. The trail mostly went through a pine forest, and even with a full moon, it would be dark in some places.

"I asked all of you to bring flashlights but I will also ask you to not use them if you don't really need them. There is enough light to hike by, but your eyes adjust to a different kind of light. Once you adjust, you can see surprisingly well. Someone shines a bright light in your eyes, then they are out of whack again for almost fifteen minutes. If you feel you have to use the flashlight, then please shine it directly on the ground and not up in the air where it can blind someone."

Just at that moment, someone shone a flashlight right in Amy's face. She groaned as she forced a smile. "Thank you. Get it out of your system now, please." Two more beams of light shone on her, but since she had turned facing west, the bright sunlight made them invisible.

It was as simple as that. The objective was to have fun. Do something one might not ordinarily do. Honestly, how many people have climbed a mountain at night under a full moon?

Amy had a mental bagful of environmental education activities she wanted to do on the way up, but as soon as she said, "Let's go!" people started hiking at almost 185 different speeds. There was no pace. Some went fast, some went slow. After the first five minutes, people were stretched out along a quarter mile of trail. Bob was somewhere right in the middle. "So much for well laid plans. But, he is an engineer," she thought.

"Well, I did say the purpose of this was to have fun," said Amy to the man hurrying past her in a wide spot on the trail, trying to catch his small twin boys who were chasing butterflies up ahead. She tried going back and forth so she could mingle and mix. Dropping back to visit with the slower walkers was easy. She soon realized it didn't work too well to zoom forward to catch the leaders. Some of the leaders were halfway to the top while the laggers were still in sight of the trailhead.

The walk itself was peaceful. They went through patches

of aspen and birch, that were swaying and waving in the cooling evening breeze. A few openings in the forest were painted with wildflowers, yellows and whites, a few blues and reds. On this occasion, who really cared what their names were? The point was to see them, smell them, paint them in your memory. It was a memory in the making. She wanted to shout to everyone: "You will forever remember this. Drink it all in. Listen, smell, see, touch, feel!"

Everyone was laughing, talking, joking as they strolled, walked, struggled up the steep pitches. This was indeed like a herd of cats scattered along a trail in the forest. Amy's new memory might be different from the other 185, but she realized the point was not to etch the same memory, but to create a memory. Any memory. Period. At one point when she stopped along with twenty others to rest in a stand of old yellow bark pines, Bob passed her and winked. Did he know something she didn't? Yes, he knew all along this was no organized march, but a fun-filled frolic in the forest. By a bunch of cats. She was surprised he didn't go "meow" at her.

While she had her small captive audience in that pine grove, she tried one of her activities. She turned her group into tree huggers. She had them literally hug the huge old pines—up close and personal, where they could smell the vanilla odor of the bark, see the millions of flakes of bark that were like a three-dimensional jigsaw puzzle.

One lady had an ant crawl onto her nose. Another sneezed and knocked her head on the tree trunk. The whole thing turned into a laughing spell as people realized how ridiculous they looked. Amy smiled. She had gotten them to open their senses and experience something many of them had never done. They became part of magnificent old trees, if only for a minute or two.

By now, Amy had lost track of most of the group. They were stretched along the trail for more than a mile. But from the contacts she was able to make, they were all having fun. No complaints, but a lot of tired looks as they neared the peak. She stopped at the last bend before breaking out on top. Watching for stragglers below her, she could see almost a quarter mile down the trail to where it crossed a talus slope. No one in sight. No sounds either, although she could hear voices and laughter above her. Most of the group was on top. As she rounded the bend, she stopped to take a picture. People were sprawled everywhere. Bodies were on rocks, lying on blankets ("they carried a blanket all the way up here?"), standing in groups, taking pictures, looking in all four directions. They reminded her of a herd of bison, not cats anymore.

She quickly went to the center of the group and explained that people were on their own for twenty minutes to eat their supper. Then Dr. Rawlins would give a twenty-minute talk. In the meantime, people could watch the sun as it disappeared into a cloud bank hugging the northwestern horizon. The colors were already brightening into fiery pink rays reaching to the heavens. The endless plains stretched to two horizons, green and undulating. The town was far below and several miles to the east. The world on the Peak was different, but more amazing since part of her world below was on the mountain top with her.

She marveled at the variety of foods displayed before her. Some people were eating plain sandwiches and bags of chips. There were a few bottles of wine being uncorked, with loaves of sourdough bread, dishes of pasta, and other gourmet delicacies. A large bag of freshly baked peanut butter cookies was making the rounds, disappearing quickly. People were indeed making memories. She laughed as one white-haired man in leather shorts and a red and black checkered flannel shirt pulled out a huge slab of cherry pie, nodding to her as she smiled at him. He told her it tasted better than the pine bark.

A few people started back down the trail before Rawlins even started talking. Amy yelled at them to be careful on the way down. They waved at her, then disappeared into the darkening forest. Just before the professor started his lecture, two ravens appeared, rising up and hovering over the eastern edge of the summit. They rose up silently, swirled in widening circles in the thermals, and cawed their raucous calls as they cavorted on the wind. As quickly as they appeared, they floated down the western side, fading as distant black specks into the now orange and lavender sky.

When the professor finished his informative talk on the local history, Amy jumped up and gave another safety caution. People could start heading down, but they needed to be safe. She knew she had no way of monitoring the gaggle of hikers. Some were anxious to head down, some lingered on top. A few young couples were picking secluded spots to make a different form of memory. She waited about fifteen minutes until the vast majority of folks were headed down. Those left on top planned to stay there for a while. Amy decided it was okay for her to head down. She hadn't seen Bob since she spotted him eating a pizza a half hour before.

Before she left the top, she walked over to the eastern edge and sat on a limestone boulder. The lights of the town and surrounding countryside were outlining civilization. She preferred this much more civilized mountaintop. She was not alone, yet she felt at one with the trees and the rocks. Greg didn't exist. He was just an irritation. The clouds far to the east, towering over the endless plains, were tipped with a purplish pink as the sun bounced off their misty ice particles. This was the type of work she had wanted to do ever since she struggled in college to be part of a man's profession. It had been a challenge and she had chosen to earn her way and not take advantage of what was now being gratuitously offered to her. She was proud of the way she did it. She was ready to pass the torch to the next generation. Like the commercial said, she did it the old-fashioned way. She earned it by herself. She touched 185 people tonight and some of them would remember her. She hoped. She slowly got up, looked around her one last time, said goodbye to the top, and headed down the trail.

Just as she hollered goodbye to the small group still on the summit, she saw an old lady coming into view as the trail broke out of the forest below. As she went up to talk to her, two teenage girls came up to the lady crying "Granner, you made it." Amy had a swirl of emotions ranging from pride to fear. She asked how the lady was doing. She had to be at least 85 years old if a day. She was smiling as she steadily plodded the last few feet to the top.

Looking at Amy and reading her nametag on her uniform, she smiled and said "Hello Amy. Sorry I'm a little late. But I made it!"

Amy couldn't help but reach out and hold her hand. The hand was warm, wrinkled, and amazingly strong as she gripped Amy's in return. She introduced herself as Elizabeth. She had pure white hair, falling out from under a large floppy white cotton hat. She was dressed in white tennis shoes, large denim pants rolled up at least six inches at the cuff, a red flannel long sleeve shirt, and wore a pink flowered day pack. In her hand was a walking stick of paper birch, with strips of bark curled up along it like a papyrus scroll.

"You are not late. You are here and that's what counts. Thank you for coming." Amy, still in surprise and amazement, wanted to hug her.

"My daughter told me I was crazy, but my grandkids said I could do it. I knew I could do it and by God, I wanted to come up here. I grew up down there," she motioned to the lights of the countryside now twinkling far below. "I never made it up here but all my life I would look up to this mountain and wonder what things looked like from here. I would never have done this without your hike."

She wiped her forehead with a large red bandanna she wore around her neck. "I don't have a lot of years left and by God," she laughed, "I'm not getting any younger. Opportunities like this are gettin' few and far between."

She pursed her lips and wiped her deep-set eyes, then looked up at the moonlit sky, now starting to sparkle with emerging stars. Amy thought the old lady was going to start crying. "Lost my husband a few years ago. Married 61 years. We used to sit in the back yard and talk about the way things used to be. Don't matter now. I made it up here. Frank never did. I'll have to do some lookin' for him, I guess." She closed her eyes, then looked at Amy with a smile. Amy could tell her thoughts were far away and long ago.

Her granddaughters came up to her and each grabbed an arm. "Come on Granner, we have supper for you."

Elizabeth smiled again at Amy and said, "Guess my family wants me up there. Think I can make it okay now. Thanks again for what you did."

"I thank you for what you did," Amy replied as she hugged her, fighting back tears of her own. "You have a wonderful evening. Be careful on the way down. And think how much Frank would be proud of you." The lump in her throat made her voice crack at the mention of Frank's name.

Amy turned and quickly walked down the dark trail so no one could see her tears. Once she was in the trees and by herself, she broke down and cried in sheer admiration and pride. This could be the highlight of Amy's life as well as Elizabeth's. No matter what happened from now on, nothing could top this moment. A wrinkled but steady white-haired old lady had achieved something probably none of the other 185 had done tonight or possibly had ever done before. All on account of Amy, she had conquered a mountain and who knows what fears that may have hidden that mountain for nearly a century.

"It really is all downhill from here," thought Amy as she composed herself for the long trip down. She realized her memory had been remade in the past few minutes. It would remain and grow with her. She would never forget Elizabeth and what the old lady not only did for herself, but what she opened up in Amy. Amy was making a difference and she was touching people in ways she didn't realize. She had been her whole career. In her heart she knew it, even if few others did. What she didn't realize was many others knew it. They just never let Amy know.

It was nearly dark, with the almost full moon hanging brilliantly in the sky. Even the moon seemed to be celebrating the event. Amy quickened her pace to try and catch up with the main group. She caught up to a small group of ladies. As they passed from the open talus slope into the trees, the darkness engulfed them. Amy was starting a conversation when one of the women stumbled on a rock and hit the ground with a thump. She quickly came up laughing, wiping her sleeves and brushing dirt off her face. She laughed it off before Amy could say anything. No one could see faces so Amy had no idea who she was talking to. But it was a stimulating conversation. They asked about the old lady who they passed near the top. Amy explained and they all expressed admiration, doubting they could do such a thing in another thirty or forty years.

Amy asked where they were from. They, and about ten

of their neighbors, all women, had driven fifty miles to get here. Their husbands wouldn't come; they were too busy watching a ball game or sitting around drinking beer or whatever guys do. They said they would never have thought to do such a thing, but with safety in numbers, what the hell? They were scared to walk through the city park at night, but hike three miles up a mountain? They knew if the Forest Service was in charge, it would be okay. Amy started to say something when she walked right into a tree. She bounced off laughing. The other lady asked if she smelled vanilla. They all burst out laughing. After a few moments of walking with these ladies, she pressed on ahead to visit with a new group.

The trip down was all she had hoped for. The moon peeked through clouds, bounced off treetops, shone off the cliffs of the Peak far above. Amy thought occasionally of Elizabeth, but she knew she would get down fine. Maybe in time for sunrise, but she would get down.

Nearing the bottom, Amy heard voices coming her way. As she stepped off the trail to let the group pass, one of the guys said "Are you Amy? We recognized the uniform. The moonlight was highlighting your badge." They had read about the hike and knew what was going on.

Amy introduced herself and discovered this group couldn't make it earlier since a couple of them had to work late, but they were starting up the trail at 10 o'clock at night. All because Amy had inspired them. She told them to watch for the old lady and her entourage. And to be sure and enjoy the top. As the girls with the guys giggled, Amy smiled. She wouldn't mind being their age again and doing something like this. Did they at least have blankets?

All too soon, she reached the trailhead. There were only six vehicles remaining. The bright moonlight reflected like sunbeams off the windshield of her truck. She climbed in and collapsed on the front seat. She was emotionally drained, as well as physically exhausted. She took a deep breath and thought of Elizabeth. She took a drink of water and said out loud, "where to next month?"

FINDING JANET

*Firefighting was still a man's job, or
at least had that reputation. Any woman
who had mastered any part of it was
fighting an uphill battle to be accepted.
I was seeing more women, especially on
fire crews, and they probably equaled
men in information jobs. Usually the
women were more talented than the guys.*
Doug Holmes

THIS FIRE CAMP was off the beaten path, in a rancher's pasture, several miles from Challis, Idaho, and not many media were interested. I drove into camp, flashed my press card to the entrance officer, and said I needed to talk with Fire Information. Half of Idaho had burned the past couple months and the press had become ho-hum about the whole thing. Put this fire near Denver and the world would know about it. Up here, it was not important. Folks around here had lived with fire and smoke all summer and this new fire hardly caused comments in Ruby's Café on the outskirts of town. Ruby's was where I stopped for directions to camp. They also served a good Navajo taco.

I knew this fire team. Before the season took off in May, I had twice interviewed Incident Commander Pete Bloomberg. I also had a long history with Todd Richards, the Operations Chief, so I was well known with this group. Well liked, too, as far as I could tell. This team was full of cool heads and professional fire dogs.

I was doing a book on firefighting, focusing mostly on the people involved. Enough had been written about fire policy and the ecological consequences the past few years. I wanted to focus on the young men and women on the lines doing the work. I spent several years on a Type 2 fire crew in college and knew first-hand the work that went into firefighting. Although I never advanced to a Type 1 crew, also known as Hot Shots, I knew the type of people on them. They were the elites. They were good, they were cocky, and they were crazy. They were the ones I would call on any emergency, fire or non-fire. They risked lives to save trees and chipmunks. They loved excitement and challenge. This fire, called the Horse Creek Fire, was a challenge.

I wanted to get up on the line to talk to the crews. I needed to talk to Pete and Todd as well, but while the flames were still jumping from tree top to tree top and sounding like a roaring Apollo rocket, I wanted to be near the crews. I was qualified and red carded as a fire fighter and had all my required gear, including fire shelter, which I'd actually had to use three years ago when researching my first book on fires. I hoped to never have to use it again.

Spotting the Fire Information trailer was easy—with its red and white banner. I stepped up into the trailer and introduced myself to the yellow-shirted officer manning the phone and drawing on a map. He looked up and asked if he could help me. I was accustomed to explaining my project to strangers in similar situations. As a published author known to key people, I had permission from the Forest Service Washington Office to be on the line with fire fighters. However, Fire Information Officer Joe Brooks was not impressed that I was red carded, knew Pete and Todd, needed an update on this fire, and an escort to the line.

Joe Brooks seemed perturbed by my request and muttered I would have to wait for Janet. She was the lead person here and they were short-handed. No kidding. After the length and severity of the past three months, I was amazed anyone was still fighting these fires. I thanked Joe and wandered over to the mess tent. This time of day, overhead—the management personnel who were in charge of the different departments and functions of any fire— seemed to hang out here, nursing coffee or energy drinks.

Pete recognized me and jumped up to shake my hand. I'd said laudatory things about Pete and his staff in my last article for the *Seattle Post Intelligencer* and he appreciated it. I don't say things I don't mean and he knew it.

"A genuine fire hound," he said as he introduced me to the folks around him. "This is Doug Holmes, freelance reporter. Doing a book about us so watch what you say."

I did the round of hand shaking and learned new names, mostly Section Heads, but no one from Ops.

"Where are Todd and his folks?" I asked.

"Flying right now. I circled the fire this morning and they had a flare up over on the west side couple hours ago so went up to take a look. Mostly an air show. The west side of the fire is slopping over into the wilderness, the rest has one old mule trail for access and that's about it. Tough one to get to."

"How's it looking?" I asked, knowing the answer by the worried look on his face.

"Ugly right now. Helluva lightning show two nights ago and we are still picking up new starts. Main fire has collected smaller ones as it marches north. There've been a lot of spots. Been spotting over one half mile ahead. This one has pretty good potential, but this late in the season, we should get a break from the weather. It's a horse race who wins out."

"Weather always does," I replied.

"Yeah, but how many acres does it gobble up before the rain? We're okay here, but go five miles north, you start hitting ranches. Up on Cat Creek there is a subdivision going in with trophy homes snugged up right against the Granite Creek Wilderness. One of them supposed to belong to either a movie star or rock singer. Don't know who."

"Hell, Pete, I'd live up here. Damn beautiful country." I meant it. I had lived in cities long enough to appreciate this type country. It didn't bother me if one had to drive for five hours to get to the nearest big box store. I had been searching in all my travels to find property somewhere in a place like this where I could become one of these urban refugees the locals were learning to dislike. I hadn't found the right combination yet, but I was zeroing in on a couple spots.

"You'd know how to build up here," Pete said as he shifted in his chair. "The new folks are coming from Chicago or Memphis or some asshole place they don't know what fire is. You know the drill."

"Devoted three chapters to it on the last book. You read it?"

"You bet. The autographed copy you sent me is well thumbed. Hit the nail right on the head."

"What's the name of the book?" asked Rita, head of Finance. She was the only one who seemed to be following our conversation. Two others had drifted off after I arrived and one older guy was reading a newspaper.

"Smoke Over Montana," I replied.

Pete interrupted. "Damn good read, Rita. I've got the book in my tent. I keep referring to it. Very insightful perspective on the fatalities at Six Mile. Some things seem so obvious they are oblivious to us. Often takes an outsider to make us see. Not sure I'd call Doug an outsider, though." He looked at me and grinned. "I'll loan it to you if you promise to stay up tonight and read it."

"Like hell," Rita snorted. "I'm only getting about four hours sleep a night anyway. I'm shorthanded just like everyone right now. Have three trainees taking all my time." She looked at me and winked. "You can't begin to imagine what a slave driver this guy is." She got up and apologized for leaving, but said she had work to do.

I looked at Pete. "Looks like the end of season blues is catching up with you."

"Lord, Doug, we can't get people. Folks are so burned out from the long season. Team started in May in Arizona and we've been almost solid since then. I'm ready to collapse myself. Worst year I have ever seen and you know how many years I've been doing this. Have to keep extending crew times and canceling off days. No way to run an outfit."

I pulled out my pad and jotted down a few notes. "Any chance I can get up on the line? I'd really like to talk to some Shots about the year and how they are dealing with one more big one. Or is this a big one?"

"Any other year and this would be number one in the nation. California fires are getting the attention now. We could only get one tanker. Need a dozen. Guess fifty or one hundred thousand acres up here isn't important now. That kind of sums it up ... oh shit, here comes trouble." Pete nodded at a red-vested person heading towards him. He got up and started to leave. "Hey, I gotta go. Check with Janet in Info. She is short-handed too, but knowing her, she will take you personally up there." He nodded west, where the afternoon smoke column turned the sky dark gray with yellow orange tinting the bottoms of the clouds.

Pete headed into a small white wall tent. Before he entered, he spoke with someone and pointed at me. This red-vest turned and walked towards me. I pretended not to see her coming. I changed chairs but found the second one just as tilted as the one I had been sitting in. There must be a government standard that all folding chairs in mess tents be broken or lean backwards. Maybe then, you won't be tempted to stay too long.

I started to read the newspaper sprawled over the table, held from blowing away in the breeze by ketchup bottles. I looked up as she came up to me.

"Hi, Pete says you need to get up on the line. I'm Janet, Fire Information." She smiled as I jumped up to shake her hand, tipping over my chair.

"Doug Holmes," I stuttered, not expecting what I saw. Janet was what I always refer to as a bombshell. Very attractive, short and petite, but what I noticed was her smile. It was genuine. Her blond hair was streaked with gray or a lighter shade of blond It was hard to tell. It was windblown and tousled, giving her a just-got-out-of-bed look, which I knew was not the case. The way she talked, with a slight lisp and hint of an accent, reminded me of a bottle of soda fizzing after being shaken before opening. I knew I had my mouth open, with nothing coming out of it.

Janet smiled again as she sat down. "Looks like I caught you off guard. Long day of reporting on raging wildfires?" She moved her clipboard in front of her, pulling out a blank page to cover a sheet with scribbles all over it.

"Well, kind of. Just drove over from the Sheepeater Fire near Bozeman. Had bad directions to camp here. I was looking north of town instead of south. Found helibase and got sidetracked talking to them for an hour or two." I looked out from under the mess tent to where we could see the smoke column building. "Just in time for the daily blowup it seems."

Janet didn't turn her head to look. She was staring at me. "Oh, yeah," she caught herself, then looked out at the horizon. "Kickin' up good today. Was supposed to hit a ridge full of blowdown and beetle kill. Looks like it did."

"Any chance you can get me up on the line?"

Janet laughed. "Line? You think we are getting any line on that puppy? Mom Nature is playing with us on that dragon mouth."

"Well you got some Shots on it. You haven't pulled them off."

"You're right. We have some crews flanking it and a couple crews about a mile in front of it, up by Eagle Creek. Scoping out a big backfire. You will be bored on the first. You don't want to go on the second."

"Of course, I do. That's my job. I want you to take me up there."

Janet shifted in her leaning chair. She cocked her head and pushed a flop of hair out of her eyes. "Do I look crazy? No, don't answer. Lots of people think I am. I may look a little tired and overworked, but don't mistake that for suicidal."

It was my turn to smile. "Want something to drink? Coffee, juice?"

"Water would be nice. I try and drink lots of water, nothing else. Don't need sugar or caffeine." She looked over towards the Info tent. I quickly walked over to pull a couple of bottles of water out of a stock tank filled with iced drinks. I needed to be quick with her. She was too busy to sit and talk with a stranger whom she already thought crazy. Besides, she seemed distracted by something.

She took the water I handed to her, still keeping her eyes on the Info tent. "Sorry," she said as she looked up at me. "I'm expecting one or two more folks any time. I ordered them as soon as I got here two days ago and dispatch said they were due in at noon today. I'm surprised I'm actually getting help."

She took a drink, looked at me, looked out at the smoke column, then picked up her clipboard and jotted something down. I was trying to figure out how to convince her to let me accompany her out to the fire. I felt like she could read my mind.

"Tell you what. Pete highly recommends you. He said help you if I could. If my new folks come in and they are worth anything, maybe I can get us up there. No media out here, but we really need to run some traplines in the local community and start talking to ranchers up north."

Trapline is the in-house term for taking daily updates and information to local businesses such as gas stations, restaurants, and local officials. Locals liked the information and it was a way for the Information folks to get a read on local opinion and issues. I had helped with some of these on previous fires and found them a good way to establish positive rapport with both locals and tourists. I found myself thinking of one bombshell waitress at a restaurant I had stopped at while helping with a trapline outside McCall several years ago. Janet reminded me of her.

Janet regained my attention as she quickly changed the subject. She started talking about the smoke and how it was changing micro climates in the West. That morphed into global climate change, which then changed to how we would fight fires when we were out of gasoline, which she felt was coming much quicker than people wanted to admit. She was on a roll. I knew why she didn't want or need caffeine. This gal was wound up already. Any further stimulant and she would pop.

I was staring at her. She was magnetic and I loved the way she talked. Not the words she said, but just the way she had of letting them bounce out of her mouth. Her eyes were in constant motion. When they looked at me, I felt as if she were seeing right through me. I couldn't remember the last time I felt someone reading my mind during a conversation.

"Hey, those might be my people now," Janet said as she started to get up.

I saw Joe Brooks walking towards us with two other men. One was wearing a Forest Service uniform and the other had on that familiar yellow Nomex shirt.

"Gotta attend to business. Where you hangin' out? We won't go anywhere today, but maybe tomorrow. Would that work for you?"

"Sure. I'll be here I guess. I won't be hard to find." Before I could say anymore, Janet was greeting her two new helpers and walking with them back to the Info tent. She looked over her shoulder at me and smiled.

Usually my questions and rapid fire manner unsettled people I interviewed. The tables had turned on me. Janet had me rattled. I hardly got any questions in at all. I didn't know anything about this lady. What was her normal job, where was she from, what was her fire experience? She had an air of confidence, yet a self-demeaning manner that hinted at some uncertainty. Firefighting was still a man's job, or at least had that reputation. Any woman who had mastered any part of it was fighting an uphill battle to be accepted. I was seeing more women, especially on fire crews, and they probably equaled men in information jobs. Usually the women were more talented than the guys, at least in my experience, but I had to be careful who I admitted that to.

I wandered around camp for a while, talking to as many folks as I could. Some crews had just arrived and were setting up their tents on the north edge of the pasture. There was already a sea of colored dome tents and a few larger tents with sleeping bags laying in a pile outside. I saw Joe Brooks showing the two new information guys where to set up their tents in the overhead area.

The overhead always set up in a different place than the

crews. Crews wanted to stay together and overhead didn't want to disturb sleeping night crews during the day. I knew it was a class thing. The overhead couldn't mingle with the grunts. The same in any organization—the leadership was elite. They were paid more, but of course they made the tough decisions. The crews did the work, rolled around in the dirt and smoke, risked their lives, and got little attention or credit. That was one thing I wanted my book to point out. Just like soldiers, the crews spilled blood while the generals got their pictures on the news. Been going on since Adam first saw Eve naked. Probably would never change, but I felt I owed it to these firefighters to tell their side of the story.

I went back to my RV and stretched out on the bed for a while. I was dog tired, but I was also on edge with the thought of getting up on this fire that was billowing smoke into the Idaho skies. I loved this work and had roughed out the story line to this non-fiction literary masterpiece. I was toying with making the book a work of fiction, too. My lead character would be a Hot Shot from some California crew. He would save his crew from a burnover, find a stranded hiker and save her from the fire, and... I had so many ideas, I couldn't sort them out. Meeting Janet had given me a new idea for the leading lady. My thoughts drifted to Janet. I had only talked to her for a few minutes, but she had that bubbling enthusiasm which grabbed my attention. Besides that, she was one of the most attractive women I had run across in a long time. Not beautiful, but grab your eyes sensuous.

I awoke an hour later as the sun sank behind the smoke column. It was an eerie red, turning the ground and everything else red in its glow. It broke through an opening and shone like an orange spotlight on camp. I grabbed my camera and took some pictures. The colors were indescribable. It would be several more minutes before the sun set, so I drove outside camp and onto a dirt road that wound up a hill east of the highway. I was looking down on camp, but had a view of the whole valley, now bathed in yellow orange light. Flames were visible from the fire on a ridgetop and the sun behind them highlighted them like something out of Dante's Inferno. I quickly rifled through my kit in the front seat and grabbed a CD of Puccini. "Nessun Dorma" from his opera *Turandot* was my idea of how to complement this scene. It was dramatic to the point of heart stopping. The aria was short, but it climaxed right when the sun set behind the ridge and just on the edge of the smoke column. I was almost trembling from excitement as I started the short drive back to camp. There was no way to capture that scene in words, but I would spend hours rewriting it, never to my satisfaction.

I missed the six o'clock briefing since I had to go into town to get a birthday card for my mother. I had forgotten to do this earlier and didn't know when I would have a chance if I spent the next day or two on the line like I hoped. It was dark by the time I returned to the mess tent.

Most people had already eaten, but as I spotted Pete by himself he got up and threw away his paper plate, still containing half a steak. When he saw me, he motioned for me to come over and sit with him.

"I'd weigh three hundred pounds if I ate everything they put on the plate. I keep telling them only give me half a portion, but it's too much trouble for them. I hate to throw food away, but... Sit down, Doug. You are undemanding company."

"You know me—I'm demanding information every time I see you," I said, pulling out a chair and sitting down. As usual, the chair tilted backward. I got up, kicked the bark mulch around the back legs and pushed the front legs into the ground. That almost made the chair level.

"Yeah, but I can ignore you and nothing goes to hell on me the next instant," Pete answered with a grin.

"Unusual to see you by yourself. You are surrounded by sycophants more than any politician I've ever seen," I said.

"Sycophants my ass, friend. I've got the best staff around and you of all people know it. One more comment like that and you will be sitting here by yourself."

"Sorry, bad joke," I said as I laid my notebook on the table.

"I'm on edge a little. Tough year. Now Janet tells me about an hour ago she got a phone call and they offered her the District Ranger job over on the Nez Perce. Hate to lose her. I count on her a lot."

"Not surprised. I've only talked to her a few minutes, but I am very attracted to her." I thought a second about what I said, then added, "that is professionally. Well," I hesitated, "physically too. Good looking lady."

Pete leaned over and said softly, "If I wasn't married, I'd go after her in a second." Then he sat back and said, "But if I did, she would probably whip my ass. Classy lady. Especially after all she has been through."

I gave Pete a puzzled look. "Like?"

"You've never run into her before?"

"No, this is the first time I've met her or even heard of her."

"I'm really surprised," Pete said, as he leaned back in his chair. He pulled a toothpick out of his pocket and started playing with his teeth. "She has been on my team for two years. I think she missed the last fire you were on with me."

"Last time you had Bobby Bates as FIO. I got along good with him. Funny guy. Guess I wasn't on any fires with you the last couple years."

"Janet was a basket case a few years ago. Her husband died in a horrible car crash. He went off a cliff and the truck burst into flame at the bottom. Took a full day for search and rescue to recover the body. Rumor was it was suicide. Janet hinted that he had health problems, but has never really talked about it. I didn't know her then. She was a technician on a district in Montana somewhere. She relied on him for everything. College dropout. Not much of a go getter and pretty quiet and low key. After he died, she went berserk. Suicidal. Got counseling and turned around. Took time off and went back to school. Degree in journalism or communications. Something like that. Reinstated as PIO on a forest in New Mexico. Did a complete turn-around. Sort of a metamorphosis. Like a butterfly."

"She obviously works somewhere up here now?" I asked.

"Yeah. PIO on the Bitterroot. Damn good one. I rely on her for a lot more than just handling media. She really is my right hand on fires. She is confident herself, but also brings out confidence in others. You should feature her in whatever you are writing."

"Did she remarry?" I knew that sounded a little self-serving, but I was curious about her now more than ever.

"Hell no. I think she is too independent for any guy. I don't think her first marriage was all that great. Realizes now she was walked all over. Not just from her husband, but everyone. I've never seen such a change in confidence or personality. I think a lot of us have it in us, just need that nudge or motivation to turn it around."

Pete groaned as he saw two red-vests approaching. "Trouble, no doubt." He got up, and met them at the end of the table. He talked quietly for a while, then turned to me. "Yep, gotta go. Truck wrecked bringing in a crew. No one hurt, but truck blew a tire and ran off the road into a tree." Pete walked away, shaking his head.

I picked up my notebook and scribbled a few notes, then found myself writing the name Janet several times. Absent mindedly, I found myself doodling. Hearts and flames embellishing Janet's name.

Janet found me scraping the last of the scrambled eggs and hash browns into my mouth at breakfast. She sat down next to me. "I didn't see you at the briefing this morning. What happened to you?"

I looked up at her sheepishly. "Overslept," I answered. I didn't tell her I was feeling pretty sleepy after reading an entire Clive Cussler thriller last night.

"To be honest, you look like hell warmed over," she said as she opened her small cup of yogurt, which apparently was her only breakfast. "If you are up to it, we will go out to the helibase at 0900 and they will ferry us to the Big Creek Hot Shot crew up north. They are preparing to light a big back fire tonight if conditions are right. Todd Richards will go with us. Stay all day if it's safe."

"Oh great," I said, not really feeling that awake. I wasn't fooling Janet.

"We can put it off. You need to be in top shape. We might do a lot of walking and it's pretty rugged country up there. Will miss the action, but on this thing, who knows what may happen. I think Todd is really debating this tactic. Kind of chancy, but they don't have many options. They are really counting on a weather change. Small front coming through this afternoon, which might help push the fire back on itself. Might be their best chance. Fire behavior analyst and the weather guy really can't figure out the predictions."

"Not a morning person, but give me another cup of coffee and I'll be fine."

"You sure? I had to talk Todd into it. Anyone else but you and he wouldn't allow it."

I looked at Janet as she finished her yogurt. "Didn't think you wanted to go yourself."

"Let's just say I'd like to see my name in your next book." She smiled as she got up. "And I think I can walk your ass off up there. Be in the Info office at 0830. Full gear. You have everything? Shelter?"

"Full gear. I'm fully red carded. I'll grab some lunches."

"No need for that. We are ferrying up extra lunches for the spike camp. Plenty to eat. We'll even take extra sleeping bags in case we get stuck up there."

"Okay. You're in charge. Pete said you think of everything."

"Pete is very smart," she said as she walked away, tossing her empty yogurt cup into the trash.

The Bell 205 lifted up out of the inversion, through the thin layer of smoke blanketing the valley. Any thicker and we would have had to wait, but light winds were already kicking up out of the north. The pilot was taking the three of us, then had to return and take supplies to the spike camp by Eagle Creek. Todd asked if after he delivered the supplies, could he pick us up and fly over the west flank. The pilot said he could do whatever we wanted. He had to come back to pick up garbage from the spike camp so this would be a good way to kill a half hour. Seemed a little contorted to me. I figured it would have made more sense to do the supply flight first, then do us, but for some reason unknown or not understandable to me, that was the schedule.

I was feeling good, although the flight was a little rougher than I liked. The fire had really done a job further south, but the burn was spottier on the west and north sides. I could see a lot of spot fires out front. The smoke was drifting in a different direction on each small fire. The main front was smoldering now, although there were still plenty of trees torching. Todd said this was the calmest he had seen the fire. It was laying down good. He said he wished he could figure out the weather. "Winds were damn squirrely" were his exact words.

We circled back north and landed at the spike camp helispot. Janet, Todd and I got out and the pilot took off with his load of garbage hanging below. We took off our jump suits and laid our gear at the edge of the helispot. We would need it later. If I got the information I wanted, we could fly back later that day. Todd scheduled his return flight at 2 pm. He needed to be back to brief Pete.

I found the shot crew leader who was in charge of the backfire. Frank was his name but everyone called him Bob. Something to do with the two large wilderness areas: the Frank Church and Bob Marshall. He had been on big fires in both and made some bet with his crew about which was toughest. He said he voted for the Frank since that was his name. His crew agreed the Bob was far tougher, mainly because they came face to face with three grizzlies with no serious repercussions.

Frank, or Bob, was finishing a cup of coffee and rearranging his red pack. He laughed as I asked him about the backfire.

"Doug, I heard about you from Todd. He didn't want to let you come up here. I read your book and figured you had a pretty good head on your shoulders. Todd is real nervous about us torching this off. I talked him into it, but I still think he has doubts. Shit, man, I got doubts, too. But we don't have many choices."

He pulled out a topo map to point out the area between us and the fire. "Look at this. The country between here and here." He pointed to the ridges and canyons. "Here is where we are. And look what is north of us. The fire is going north."

I could see what he was getting at. There was no way to stop the fire without something like this backfire.

"We don't do this, then we might as well go off the mountain and play cards back in camp. I know there is a front coming in. Look at the winds right now. Going ever which direction." Bob picked up a handful of dust and tossed it in the air.

"Yeah, but you can't predict the wind any better than the weather guys. And I talked to them back in camp. I got the feeling they might as well pull out the Ouija board to predict this one." I looked up at the sky and shook my head.

"Doug, I know this country. I've been on many fires up here. I can read the weather. I don't need a weather man. This is September. This fire will be covered with snow within two weeks. I watch the animals. I can almost guarantee you by mid-afternoon, the winds will settle on a north direction. I don't light a fusee or drip torch unless that happens. It will kick up and mosey off and blow right down that draw and up the hill over there." He pointed to the ridge south of us. "Then it will go up and kiss the area already burned."

"If the wind is going to change, why not just let it stop the fire on its own?" I asked. "Why screw around with a backfire?" I already knew Bob's answer.

"Insurance. Winds may not be strong enough to stop it. Or it may just stall and continue north when the wind changes back to south tomorrow. This is our best shot." Bob grinned and stood up. "We got some more line to build. I don't like to take chances." He walked off to join his crew, starting to pick up chain saws. Their tents were down and there was no longer any sign of a spike camp.

I looked at Janet, who sat quietly the whole time Bob was talking. "What do you think? Is he right?"

"These guys are almost always right. Cocky little bastard, but he knows more about fire than you or I ever will."

Janet stood up, wiped the pine needles off her pants and stood there staring at me. She had a weird smile as her eyes bored into mine. I wondered if I had something embarrassing on my face or in my teeth.

Finally she said, "I thought you wanted to come up here to talk at length with Bob and his crew. Well, Charlie Brown, there they go like the Seven Dwarfs and you sit here like one of the Three Stooges."

"Oh," I said as I broke out of my self-induced stupor. "Yeah." I stood up and yelled at Bob. "Hey Bob, wait for me. I'd like to work with you if I could." I picked up my gear and looked at Janet as I started to hurry after the crew, walking swiftly in their single file march. She shook her head as she picked up her pack and followed.

We spent the rest of the day working with the crew as they cut and widened the line where they would start the backfire. I occasionally grabbed a shovel and scraped line while Janet helped pull brush out of the line. They wanted a really wide, clean line, more than I thought necessary. Todd spent a long time huddled with Bob and several of the crew. I wanted to sit in with them but Janet told me not to join them unless I was invited. I wasn't. He left after lunch when the helicopter came to pick him up.

Most of the time, I talked and listened while the crew worked. This was a good, close knit bunch of 14 guys and 6 women. They had been out together almost continuously on fires since May. It had been a relentless summer. This was their seventeenth fire together, a record for this crew. Although rules require a certain amount of time off after so many days of work, they had been given several exceptions due to the lack of available crews this hectic season. Bob argued against several, but was overruled, much to his surprise. Safety rules were rarely broken. Bob said this was the sign of things to come.

The season was taking a toll on morale. I could tell this after talking to the first two crew members. This was still a good team, but I noticed several remarks that wouldn't be made on a sharp crew. Small things were blown out of proportion. I didn't blame the crew; I blamed whoever was pushing these people. They were tired, but the makeup of a firefighter usually didn't allow the fatigue to show. The tiredness was leading to bad decisions. Bob even admitted this when I noticed he yelled at one of the gals for some little thing she didn't do. I wouldn't have done it either since safety was her reason. Janet went over and talked to her and came back to me shaking her head.

"Doug, I know this crew. I have worked with them before. They're the best, but they need a break. This is a dangerous operation. They're going to torch this off in about an hour. I worry about them. I'm not sure they're ready. I walked down to where they tied this into a cliff. It's not a secure tie. I mentioned it to Bob and he shrugged and said it would be okay."

"I saw the same thing on a Type 2 crew over in Montana. Ended up a guy almost chopped his toe off with an ax. Everyone is tired. Somebody is letting people get pushed too hard. The IC on the Brush Ridge fire said he heard politics was getting involved. This shouldn't be happening. This isn't the Forest Service and BLM that I know. People are edgy and in some cases demoralized. It is starting to worry me."

Janet nodded her head, motioning me over to a rock outcrop out of hearing of the crew working near us. We walked over and sat down. She pulled some raisins out of her pack and popped a handful into her mouth. She started talking while she was still chewing.

"Doug, this is strictly off the record. I trust you. I'm going to tell you some things you may already know, but I'm part of the management of this outfit. I don't like what I am being asked to do. Damn right politics is rearing its ugly head. I'm seeing almost everyone over fifty taking early outs, medicals, or just plain quitting. Something is wrong.

Terribly wrong. I was just offered a Ranger job. I accepted, but if I find the situation on the new unit like I had to put up with on the old, I'm out of here. I had an offer to go to work for a major news network and I had to think long and hard which one to accept. This agency is in my blood and it used to be good to me. It's changing. I've seen it from both sides. I was a common seasonal for years. No one respected me or asked my opinion. Guess that was all right since my opinions weren't that great. I didn't take myself seriously. Well now I see it differently. I am different." She paused as if reflecting on that statement.

She opened a bottle of water and washed down her raisins. She looked at me as if for some kind of confirmation.

I nodded yes. "I have a few years on you. I think. I never ask ages." I waited for some reply but got none. Janet smiled.

"I've been around agency folks for twenty years. I've seen them crumble. Talk to old timers, and by that I mean someone who has been working since at least 1980, before Reagan started badmouthing feds, and you see a sadness, a longing for something that has totally disappeared. Hell, look at the ages of feds right now. Not a new generation. Those who are here now don't have that dedication. Things change. No offense, but you are old for a first-time ranger."

"Yeah, and the change is not always for the better," Janet said as she looked at the crew working its final touches on the line. She brushed off my age comment. "These grey hairs," she said as she held out a strand of her hair, "can tell a long story. But for now, that story is still unpublished."

I could have talked a long time with Janet, but for now, I wanted to finish getting all I could out of the crew. A crew like this depended on each other and by this time of the season, they knew each other's strengths and weaknesses. I wasn't seeing that here. Minor squabbles might go unnoticed by some, but Bob was seeing it and so were Janet and I. I certainly hoped Bob was right and the season was almost over. This was the recipe for disaster.

A sudden gust of wind whipped dust and pine needles into my face. I stood up and looked around for the crew. They were gathering by a large rock outcrop about 100 yards away. Bob called to me, motioning for us to come to him. I couldn't hear what he was saying, but he seemed in a hurry. We gathered our gear and walked quickly towards him.

"We're going to set this off," he said as we got there. "Need to be quick. We want to get this going before the winds really pick up. Usually damn squirrely as the front hits."

I gave Janet a look of confusion as I whispered to her, "does that sound right to you? I mean if he expects worse winds, why light it now?"

"Bob," Janet asked him as if to translate my concern to her, "why light it now? Why not wait until the winds are over? This is a pretty risky thing, isn't it?"

"I'll be second guessed no matter what. There actually is a method to my madness," he smiled as he winked at me. "My experience is that the next two hours can be strange with the winds. If I wait until it seems to be steady from the north, then light it, we might get a sudden reverse shift that could push the fire back on us. Light it now, let it run a few hundred yards, then we have a good black line. Wait longer, I think we lose our advantage, plus it will get dark and I don't trust doing this in the dark. I want to see in case we need to run."

I looked at Janet once again. She was frowning, but didn't say anything. We heard the helicopter coming towards us from the southeast. It circled a while, then flew north. Bob was talking in his radio the whole time.

He looked up at the crew who were listening on the radios. I didn't think to turn mine on until the conversation was half over. Todd was on the other end, circling above us. He was in a serious discussion with Bob. The weather forecaster and fire behavior analyst came on during the discussion. I was surprised the chopper didn't set down so the folks could have a good discussion. After a few minutes, Bob clipped his radio microphone back onto his shirt and told the crew, "It's a go. Get your gear together. Know the escape routes. They are the same as we talked about a while ago. Doug and Janet, I'll review that with you when we are done here."

I needed to talk to Bob about the decision and what factors went into it. I didn't understand, but then I wasn't privy to some of the background. I had the feeling something factored into this that I wasn't aware of. I trusted Todd and Bob. You had to, to survive in this business. None of the crew objected. As a matter of fact I heard a few comments such as "let's light this baby. Now."

Bob explained to Janet and me about the safety aspects. He didn't like us being there, but he was now responsible for us. He wanted us well north of the burn in the safety area they already identified. It was a rock outcrop, with nothing burnable for a hundred yards around it.

We went there and watched several of the crew walk along the edge of their wide line dripping fire. Flames started marching south immediately as a light breeze picked up strength. Once they finished, the crew came back to where we were. The fire seemed to be doing exactly what they wanted. It was making a very good black line, with little unburned material left on the ground. It had gone about a tenth of a mile while I visited with several members of the crew. I got some great material about their thoughts on this fire and on the season. The decision to light the fire then became clearer. There indeed was more to this than I first understood. Part of it had to do with the strange wind patterns on this ridge. You had to have local connections

and a local history of this area to know this. Bob did and Todd didn't. One of the crew was also familiar with it and she said the decision was the right one.

Suddenly a dust devil came at us from the west, then veered north. It knocked hard hats off several of us, almost blowing Janet over. Before we could say anything, the wind shifted to the south. The fire stopped almost in its tracks. It couldn't burn back towards us, but it sent flaming brands high into the air. Several landed near us and started several small spot fires.

"Randy, Steve, hit em hard, now!" Bob yelled, but he didn't need to say anything. The entire crew was already running to put out the fires. Smoke filled the air and the winds whirled in every direction. I noticed smoke coming at us from downhill to the east. I couldn't tell if it was smoke from the main fire or a spot downhill. Moira headed downhill to check it out. She disappeared into the smoke. I had a chill go down my spine as I had to pull up my bandana to cover my nose. Smoke was so thick now, I couldn't even see past the rock outcrop.

Janet yelled at me, "Something is wrong. I don't like this." I could barely hear her over the roar. The smoke shifted again, as the wind returned to its northerly direction. There was smoke coming from behind us. Bob was yelling to his crew, which was now scattered in several directions. I turned up the volume on my radio. Janet had disappeared. I heard Moira's voice come over the air, "Bob, I need help. I'm trapped. Quick, straight downhill from you. I..." The transmission ended. I looked around. I couldn't see Bob or any of the crew.

Janet appeared from the edge of the rock outcrop. She heard the call. She had groped her way to the trees where Moira had disappeared earlier. "I heard Moira call from down there," she said. "She needs help. I don't see Bob or anyone else. We need to go down there."

"Yeah, and fast. I don't understand where everyone went. This is the safety zone. Why are they out there?"

"I don't think she can be very far," Janet said as we gripped hands and picked our way toward Moira's voice. We left the shelter of the rocks and headed downhill. We heard her yelling but still couldn't see anything in the smoke. Suddenly we saw flames below us. Then we saw Moira. She was pinned under a large limb of a huge pine that had just fallen. Several other trees were uprooted.

"Looks like a tornado came through here," I yelled at Janet as I ran to Moira. She had almost escaped the falling tree, but several feet away from the trunk, a large limb had clipped her, falling on her leg. I had the Pulaski, which would work much better than Janet's shovel. I started chopping the limb, while Janet pulled at Moira's leg. Her shovel came in handy after all as she shoveled the dirt from under Moira's leg. Lucky for Moira, she wasn't pinned tightly. About the time I chopped through the limb, Moira pulled the leg free. She felt it carefully wincing in pain.

"I don't think it's broken, but I'm sure going to have a great looking bruise," Moira said as she tried to stand up. She fell back down.

"Don't look now, but we're cut off," Janet said as she pulled my shoulder. I looked up and saw flames above us.

"How the hell," I started to say, but Janet pulled up Moira and motioned downhill.

"That's our escape, down there," Janet started to go around the uprooted pine. There was fire to the south and above us to the west.

Moira called Bob on the radio but only got static. I tried my radio. I got through to Bob but he was hard to hear. I told him we had Moira but were cut off from the safety zone. All I could understand was the word downhill. I took that as confirmation of Janet's directions. I tried to smile at Janet, but a gust of wind brought smoke as thick as ever.

"Take my Pulaski and I will help Moira," I said as Janet was already leading the way downhill. The fire seemed to be coming from the south, heading uphill and north. It looked like if we got past the small front of flames, we would be below it. I was trying to support Moira without actually carrying her. As I hurried to run through the flames, which were in the duff and litter and not any trees or brush, I slipped, with Moira falling on top of me. We both rolled through the fire. I burned my left hand as I grabbed for a handhold. Janet, already through the fire, clambered back uphill to pull us both down. We slid down the steep hillside, knocking Janet down as we went past her. All three of us tumbled down about fifty feet before we stopped against a large fir trunk.

All this had happened within just a few seconds, but it seemed like the world had gone into slow motion for me. Now I tried to stand up, but had a badly twisted ankle. I fell on the ground, falling on Moira's bruised leg. We both yelled from the pain. My hand hurt like hell, but the burn didn't look serious.

The wind was now from the north again and the smoke cleared. Fire was racing uphill above us, seemingly unconcerned with whichever way the wind was blowing. Up there, it looked like it was circling in all directions.

"I don't think any helicopter is going to find us in here," Janet said as she helped us both up. "And I don't think we can get you or Moira uphill through that. We go down. Safety is down here. And don't count on me carrying both of you."

We limped down through the steepest part of the hill, coming to a small meadow in a level opening. Janet told us to sit there while she tried to figure out where we were. Moira and I sat there chatting, both of us somewhere between laughing and crying. She wanted to see the bruise on her leg, so she told me to turn away while she dropped her pants. I was joking about this when Janet came huffing back uphill.

"Good grief, Doug, I leave you for a minute and you undress poor Moira," Janet laughed. "I'm glad I have someone else here to protect me. I'm the only one really able to defend myself."

I didn't even bother to explain. "Whatever you want to think, I don't even care at this point. Where are we?"

"We are just above a long grassy slope that goes all the way down to the valley. Camp is about two miles south. I already called for the helo. They will pick us up at the top of the slope. It's not very level so you may have to climb up into the ship. I doubt if they can land level there. Everything else is fine up top. The burn is under control and doing just what they want. Got a little confusing there for a few moments." Janet pulled us both up. "Time to hobble down just a little further. I'll find the way."

I smiled as Janet gripped my right hand. She didn't let go once I was up. I was glad she would find the way. I was thinking that I had found something very valuable in Janet. I sensed how this formerly insecure seasonal worker was now leading more than Moira and me to safety. I found Janet, but more importantly, she had found herself.

PART III

JAKE'S REFLECTIONS

Soledad's Journeys
Part I: The Voices

The past can occur in the future and the future
can determine the past. If we knew how,
we could travel back and forth between the
past, present, and future.

Before soledad stayed in the old hotel, Stefan told her to listen for the ghosts. She laughed and said sure, she would roam the halls and talk to the spirits. She would soon learn about the hotel's reputation.

As she parked her rental car and entered the grand old building, Soledad was amazed at the time-washed grandeur of the place. It had a stately dignity. The doors were tall, the ceilings lost in the firmament high above. Old-fashioned radiators lined the hallways, the windows were multi-paned, tall, and actually opened. Black and white photographs, framed in simple black, lined the corridors, captioned to impress the viewer with the historical array of famous guests, including presidents and movie stars of the century past. There were also views of the grand new building arising from a freshly landscaped young setting. Living history, with a reputation of spirits reliving it regularly.

She walked into the main lobby, a massive room filled with comfortable old chairs and couches, bound on two sides by stone fireplaces large enough to stand in. It would be easy to fade into a time long reduced to dust. Listen to the ghosts? Yes, she was in the midst of them as she looked around her. The fact that the hotel was festooned in Christmas decorations made the scene almost surreal to Soledad. Pure white teddy bears, nativity scenes, trees decorated with small lights, fake snow and Santa boots and hats. This was the eloquence and grandeur of a more innocent time. Did it have to be gone forever?

After checking in and unpacking, Soledad returned to the lobby and eased comfortably into the deep plushness of a high-backed sofa in front of the massive fireplace. She watched the dancing flames, then noticed the small gas line feeding fake logs. Oh well, some things do have to change, she realized. Small detail. As she looked at the walls and ceiling, Soledad thought there was something missing, small details that diminished the original elegance. It didn't seem important, yet it was somehow significant. Later she would discover why.

The music playing softly from hidden speakers in the grand lobby was not traditional Christmas carols, but she recognized Enya's calming voice, her favorite. So peaceful, she thought. She closed her eyes and listened, feeling the soothing heat radiating from the fake wood fire. Her cat nap took her far away in time.

The Grand Hotel, built over one hundred years earlier, was the symbol of elegance in a frontier town. It towered above not only the town itself, but also the hot springs pool, spread out below. People came to bask in the waters by day, to relax in the carpeted reception halls and suites at night.

Rooms were named Roosevelt and Taft, honoring former guests. Before the turn of the century, it was the first hotel between the Mississippi and the western coast to be wired for electricity. This was to be the future of the expanding country. The elegant hotel exemplified that glorious dream.

Soledad awoke a few minutes after closing her eyes. She had heard the singing of carols and ringing of bells. The bells, however, were not in the hands of carolers, but around the necks of horses. Horses attached to sleighs that were pulling up in front of the hotel. The clinking of glasses in the restaurant next to the lounge was overridden by the laughter and din of conversation as well as song.

She was alone in the lobby; the music had returned to instrumental easy listening. It obviously was a dream. She hadn't visualized anything, but the sounds had been so clear. She could still hear the neighing of two horses and the clopping of their hooves. Her dreams had never before produced such reality of sound. She slowly eased out of her sofa cocoon, watched the fire a few more minutes, then walked back to her room. Listen to the ghosts, Stefan said. Soledad had heard them.

Before she crawled into bed after the long and tiring day, Soledad turned off the lights and opened the drapes. She liked to awaken in the morning to sunlight streaming onto her face. There were no street sounds outside, no sirens, not even far-off traffic on the Interstate next to the river. The old-fashioned radiator was hissing and gurgling in the dark room. This was a sound she had not heard in years. It was relaxing for some reason she didn't understand. She would normally find this irritating. As she closed her eyes, she heard voices. At first she thought they were coming from next door, but they seemed much closer, as if someone were in the room. She leaned over to the small radio on the bed stand, but it was silent. Someone was whispering almost in her ear.

"We have to abandon the project. Technology to get the oil out of the shale is not in the future. Even if gasoline goes to $10 a gallon, we cannot make it pay. It is a losing proposition. Cut our losses and leave. Right now." This was an older man with no patience in his voice.

"But we have a corporate responsibility," said the higher pitched voice of a younger man. "The towns have built up based on our presence. I don't disagree that we must leave, but we have some responsibility to these communities."

"And what line item in our balance sheet involves throwing away money to make someone happy when there is no way we can make them happy. Our bottom line is to the shareholder. We tried something and it isn't working. We can't be Santa Claus to a disillusioned bunch of county commissioners who staked their future on a prayer."

"Our employees are part of these communities. We advertise our goodwill, our being good neighbors. It will make us look bad."

"Yeah, well life is tough. Those employees did their jobs. Now those jobs are done. You tell me how we pay for good intentions. With a future bankruptcy?"

Soledad perked up. This conversation struck a nerve for her. She was a vice president of an international energy company pouring millions into oil and natural gas development. The local communities were struggling to build schools and infrastructure to support the people her company was bringing in. Just like forty years ago. Although Internationale Energia del Sol, IES, was not involved in the frantic oil shale exploration in this area in the 1970s, it was guilty by association today, with environmental groups hounding IES and the energy giants. The boom and bust cycle left towns reeling from uncertainty over thirty years ago.

Soledad was pondering the conversation she was hearing when her attention shifted to the sound of fireworks going off outside. Either that or rifle and shotgun blasts. No, it was fireworks. She could hear the whistling, then the burst high overhead. Then the oohs and aahs of a crowd of people. Applause, then cheers, followed by another whistling.

Soledad got up out of bed, looked out the window. There was nothing outside. She walked to the door, slowly unlocked and opened it, very carefully peeked out into the corridor. Nothing.

She listened. Silence surrounded her. Whose voices had she been hearing?

The voices had disappeared, the fireworks had ended. She walked back to the window and looked out. The sky showed only the brilliance of the Milky Way and a setting quarter moon.

Goosebumps crawled over her arms. She was hearing things, but seeing nothing. Maybe ghosts were heard and not seen. Either way, this was spooky. She dug into her suitcase and pulled out her long robe. Pulling it on and slipping her room card key into the pocket, she opened the door and stepped out into the corridor. Looking for an area hidden and quiet, she walked down the corridor and eased onto the floor next to a pair of white teddy bears as large as she was. Needing sleep but afraid to close her eyes, she sat for a while looking and listening. Yawning, she finally put her arm around one of the bears and closed her eyes.

Silence enveloped her for several minutes. She made an effort to open her eyes and stay awake; it could be embarrassing to have a night watchman find a stone sober guest sleeping with a bear in the corridor. Her eyes closed again. She heard the gurgling of the radiator, the quiet music of the toy merry-go-round on a table by a large window. Those were real sounds. They would only be ghosts to some visitor fifty years from now. That was an interesting thought. If she spoke, would that be heard by her great, great, grand-daughter?

Very quietly at first, then gradually increasing in volume, she heard the murmur of a crowd of people. They were outside. Or was she? Multiple voices blended into white noise, incomprehensible.

A man's voice, close to her said with obvious awe, "It's the President. I told you he was going to give a speech. He can't avoid it. Put him in front of two or more people and he automatically gives a speech."

"There he is, up on the balcony. They say that is his room. It takes up half the second floor. Listen, he is raising his right hand. He is ready to speak."

"Good afternoon ladies and gentlemen. What a bully day, with this bully blue sky. I wish I could move the White House out here. You people are so lucky to be here, in this time and place."

Soledad felt as well as heard the applause and yells of the crowd. She knew that TR stayed here, at least once. The suite at the head of the grand stairs was now named the Roosevelt Room. There was a photo of him addressing a crowd of people from the second-floor balcony. What was the occasion? Could she find a copy of his speech that day? Is that what she was hearing? She had to be imagining all this. She didn't consider herself psychic and had never believed in séances or ghosts or any other type of supernatural powers. She was an important businesswoman, soon to be the regional vice president of a large multi-national energy company. It would be embarrassing to be seen, or god forbid, photographed sitting in her bathrobe on the floor of an historic hotel at midnight. But the voices were so real. The voice from the balcony faded into silence, as did the murmur of the crowd. She opened her eyes to silence. The merry-go-round music box had stopped, the radiator was quiet.

The voices and sounds were disturbing to say the least. But the odd thing was the time periods had been bouncing around between decades. The time periods had jumped from the early 1900s to the 1970s, then back. Why was she hearing this? Why was she hearing the voices of ghosts?

Her scheduled stay in town was for two days. The next day she couldn't keep her mind on her work. She was meeting her new staff at the IES office, discussing her priorities and planning for her new job. More than once, she seemed to lose concentration only to come back to the discussion as one of her employees was looking at her expecting a reply to whatever it was they just said, or asked. She apologized that she had a headache, was adjusting to the altitude, was tired from her trip from Venezuela the day before. She couldn't explain to them that she was reliving her visit with ghosts last night. How could she explain she heard President Roosevelt, in his high-pitched voice, addressing a crowd of people who had been dead for decades? Or that she was overhearing her industry predecessors deciding to close their operations in towns that had invested in schools and roads and subdivisions based on promises that were to be broken.

She asked one of her soon-to-be assistants to research the local newspaper to find the text of a Roosevelt speech delivered in Glenwood back in '05. She said she wanted some ideas of what to say in a speech she had to give in Denver next month. Sounded like a good reason, she thought. That was certainly better than saying she wanted to compare what she heard last night, sitting on the floor of the hotel at midnight. From a ghost.

She made it through the day going from one meeting to

another. She couldn't dismiss the memories of the previous night. She also couldn't get her mind around the conclusion she kept coming to. She was hearing actual voices from the past. If this was true, then she felt she would have no choice but to go into the depths of the vapor caves next to the hotel, curl up in a ball, and wait for the steam to dissolve her into a pile of carbon atoms.

There were a dozen diners in the hotel restaurant that evening. The room was relatively quiet, with only the sound of clinking silverware, crystal glasses, and waiters speaking softly. Until she closed her eyes. Then, the din came on so suddenly, it surprised her. No waiting this time for something to appear. It was like turning on a radio. The voices were coming from dozens of people. There were violinists playing in the corner where a large Christmas tree now stood. Laughter came from another corner of the spacious room. Waiters were shouting in the adjacent kitchen, the sounds of plates being stacked, wine or champaign corks popping—all these were deafening. She opened her eyes as her waiter asked if she would like dessert. The noise stopped; she could hear a pin drop in the restaurant. She looked around and realized she was one of only eight people sitting in the room. She could hear Christmas music drifting from the main lobby.

She signed her bill, stood, and walked into the deserted lobby. She remembered there was a small meeting room at the end of the hall named the Taft Room. It was empty, but the lights were on. A meeting had obviously been held there earlier in the evening, but everyone had gone. Napkins were scattered on the table along with several empty water glasses. A dry-erase board still stood in the corner, with numbers written on it. They meant nothing to her, but she stood looking at them. As she was standing there, a hotel employee walked in. He apologized to her and said he thought the meeting was over. Soledad said she was just walking by and stopped in to see what the room looked like. He said that was fine, he just wanted to make sure she hadn't left something behind. He told her to enjoy the photos on the walls and to take her time exploring the hotel. He actually said the words "don't let the ghosts bother you."

Soledad asked if he often heard the ghosts. He laughed and said he never heard any, but he was new to town. Some people swore they saw wispy visions wandering the corridors late at night. People were always hearing voices in the basement. Strange things happened, such as plates moving around, light switches going on and off, the smell of perfume or of cigar smoke appearing and then disappearing. The hotel even sponsored ghost tours. He laughed and said the spirits probably smelled of brandy. Then he rolled his eyes and left the room, humming the *Twilight Zone* theme.

The frustration of her experiences was distressing Soledad. She knew she was being allowed to experience a secret of the universe. Either that or she was going crazy. Sinking into a chair, she put her head in her hands, elbows on the table, and started crying softly. Almost immediately, she heard a man's voice very gently say, "Governor, you know we have already lost the votes in Denver. We have to focus on the Western Slope. We have to get all the votes we can over here. Even the votes of the ghosts of all the dead miners in Aspen. You know what I mean?"

A woman's voice rose. "Donald, the Governor can't listen to that kind of talk. He has to stay out of the dirt. Every woman in this state now has the vote. Many ladies in this area didn't vote in the last election. We have to change that. If we have to pay them, then you tap your rich mining friends and we buy their votes."

A raspy voice started to speak, then started coughing. When he stopped, he said, "If you are going to talk like that, I will have to leave. After the speech today, my voice is almost gone anyway. I need to go upstairs and go to bed. You boys," at this he laughed, which provoked another fit of coughing, "and girl, deal with this. I can't be privy to it. You know what needs to be done."

"No! I can't hear this!" Soledad almost screamed as she jumped up from her chair. The room hadn't changed. The numbers on the board still watched over the empty water glasses. She reached down and picked up a paper clip from the floor. How had the room changed since the voices had spoken? Surely the wallpaper was different as was the carpet. Probably the table and chairs. The chandelier might be the same, but the bulbs were new. The window glass? Maybe that glass reflected the images of the people she was hearing. She looked at it, but saw her own puzzled reflection bouncing back at her. The thought struck her that this room was actually rather drab. The ceiling did not have fancy molding she had seen in the photos of the hotel after it was first built. The door knobs were plain, not the fancy handles she would expect from a hotel claiming to be the best money could buy. Now that she thought of it, a lot of these little things were missing. Why?

And why were sound waves still bouncing off the walls, but visual images were not? She couldn't be going back in time or else she would see people. Whenever she opened her eyes, the voices stopped. What trick of physics was happening to her? She couldn't control this phenomenon. She knew she would not be able to sleep. Whenever she closed her eyes, voices came. She couldn't sleep with her eyes open.

Soledad struggled the next day to stay awake. Her schedule included a meeting with both a U.S. Senator as well as the Governor. They happened to be traveling through the area and the Rocky Mountain Regional vice president arranged a meeting for her with them. Before the dignitaries arrived, Stefan pulled her aside and told her she looked terrible. He had known her since their college days and admired her business-like behavior. She told her new boss that she had trouble sleeping in a different bed. She laughed when she said the hissing radiator kept her awake. She got through the meeting with the politicians, but fell asleep during the meeting with geologists.

Thankful that she had already signed the new contract, she knew Stefan well enough for him to get a kick out of her situation, but if he knew what she was actually experiencing, he might have second thoughts about bringing her on board. At least this night was to be her last at the Hotel. She was driving to Denver first thing in the morning to catch a plane to Caracas. For sure when she returned in a few weeks, she was not staying at this hotel while she waited for the closing on her new house.

She thought about checking out and staying in a regular motel, but she knew if she put her mind to it, she could get through the night. She was expecting a phone call from Stefan that evening and didn't want to explain why she wasn't there. Besides, she figured, this was too strange to keep happening to her. Her biggest problem was she didn't dare talk to anyone about it. She did ask the desk clerk if anyone ever complained about hearing strange voices. She got the standard laugh and answer that some guests thought they saw or heard ghosts, but no one ever got a picture or a recording. The hotel was actually famous for its ghosts. No help there.

Soledad walked across the street for a pizza and a beer. That usually worked in helping her sleep soundly. Back in the hotel, she hesitated before returning to her room. The basement stairs were at the head of the corridor. In slow motion, she was drawn down the stairs, stopping for a few seconds on each step. She recalled from the hotel literature a photo of a grand saloon in the basement—either the men's bar or the ladies' parlor, and wondered where it had been. Nothing very elegant down here now.

Starting to go back up the stairs and with one foot on the bottom step, she distinctly heard a voice call her name. She looked around. There was no one in sight. She walked down the corridor, past the commercial shops that were now closed. At the end of the corridor was a door. It looked like a closet or storage room, with no room number or any indication of what it was. She walked over and pushed it open slowly. The door creaked.

The room was dark and forbidding. Although she knew she should close the door and go back upstairs, she was drawn into the room. She felt for a light switch on the wall. It was an old-fashioned round dial switch. How odd, she thought. She clicked it and a very dim, bare bulb lit the far end of a large room filled with chairs, empty boxes, and old wooden tables. The boxes had probably held all the Christmas decorations. The room was huge. She carefully walked to the far wall. There were more doors—she tried them all, but each was locked. Filing cabinets lined one wall. As she stood with a hand on a folding chair, she felt faint. Was it the beer? No, it was something about this room. She closed her eyes.

Almost immediately, she heard voices. One was louder than the others.

"Listen sailor, don't ask questions. Just do what you are told. Come over here. Martinez, that your name, sailor?"

"Yes Sir," the young voice answered. Miguel Martinez."

"Where you from Miguel Martinez?"

"My unit, Sir?"

"No, where is your home? You have an accent. You a Mescan?"

"No, Sir. My family is from New Mexico. Outside Santa Fe. We've lived there for generations, before the United States was even created."

"Oh, my God," thought Soledad.

Her grandfather's name was Miguel Martinez. Her family was from Santa Fe for about ten generations. She didn't know much about abuelo Miguel. He had been in the US Navy in World War II. Wounded in the Pacific early in the war, he was sent back to the States to a naval hospital on the West Coast. He recovered from his war wounds but was sent to an inland hospital where he worked as an orderly. Soledad's grandmother Maria received only one letter from him, and the Navy sent word to his widow that Ensign 1st Class Miguel Martinez died from an unnamed, extremely contagious disease, was cremated for security reasons, and his ashes buried at sea. He left a small daughter and an infant son. Grandmother Maria tried for years to learn more about what happened, but the Navy would give no more information.

"Ensign Martinez, you are to completely strip the rooms. It is for sanitation. This is a hospital and no longer a fancy ballroom. All these fancy drapes and woodwork and stone fixtures harbor germs. You guys are bringing these nasty bugs back from the tropics with you and if they catch hold and spread, this whole country is in trouble. We should probably burn this whole place down."

"Yes Sir, I just thought it was a shame to haul all these things to the dump and burn them. This is the fanciest building I have ever seen. The drapes would make good material, that's all I was thinking."

"Ensign Martinez, we are not paying you to think. This is our hotel now and we decorate it how we want. Orders. We don't argue with orders, do we?"

"No, Sir."

Soledad opened her eyes and the voices stopped. She had goosebumps again, was trembling, and starting to feel nauseous, so she quickly left the room, without turning off the light. She walked upstairs to the corridor by her room and stood there for several minutes. Instead of going in, Soledad returned to the lobby. Standing by the front desk was the employee she talked to earlier about the hotel history. Now, he was quizzed by a determined Soledad about the hotel during the war.

"There isn't much information about the hotel during that time," he said. "The Navy basically confiscated the hotel and used it for a hospital. They also took over the hot springs and pool, closing it to the public. A lot of records were destroyed, so no one knows much about the time during their stay." He shook his head and went on to say, "the Navy did gut the inside of the hotel. They tore out the carved woodwork, bathroom fixtures, and drapes. They said it was for sanitary reasons. Some of the sailors brought back strange and very infectious diseases, so a lot of things were ripped out, destroyed, even rooms were closed off and sealed. Reportedly, the main operating room and adjacent morgue in the basement were even filled with dirt and rocks and sealed with concrete. A lot of the hotel history, and dignity, were destroyed. It must have been a sad time.

Excuse me please, I need to answer the phone," he said as he turned to the counter

Soledad stood there for a few moments, not sure what to do. As she started to go back to her room, the employee came to her side. He had noticed her confused look and realized she was the latest to experience the spirits of the hotel. "Ms. Gonzales, after I started working here and learned the hotel's history I've been reading science and fiction dealing with quantum physics and time travel. And what I found could easily explain the visions some hotel guests have of people from the past doing things in this hotel."

He went on to tell her that time is not what we think it is. The past can occur in the future and the future can determine the past. If we knew how, we could travel back and forth between the past, present, and future. It was possible to have some sort of wormhole or something to the past. As he glanced back to the lobby desk to see no other guests, he continued, "the Utes considered the hot springs and surrounding area a sacred place because it allowed this form of time travel. The hotel happened to be built here and whatever this strange wormhole was, it allows people from the past to appear today. By the same token, people from today may very well be showing up to scare the people from one hundred years ago." He laughed as he said he wished he could experience that. When he finished with his time travel explanation, Soledad walked down the long corridor to her room, more confused than ever. Was he pulling her leg? Or maybe he was one of the ghosts.

The phone was ringing as she opened the door to her

room. It was Stefan. He didn't have time to talk to her, he said, so he would just wait until he saw her for breakfast the next morning. She said she had been having trouble sleeping and wanted to talk to him about it. She hung up and sat down on the floor next to the radiator by her bed. Something clicked in her mind. There was a simple reason she, and no one else, was hearing the ghosts. Others may have heard sounds or seen the so-called ghosts, but only she was being given intimate glimpses of the past. Because one of the ghosts was her grandfather? Because he was one of the Navy people who helped destroy the hotel? And now the spirits of the past were roaming the hotel, haunting the granddaughter of a person who helped gut the grandeur of the past? That is why the hotel was haunted. These poor spirits had nowhere else to go. Their elegant hotel had been taken from them. And Soledad was being given the view, or sounds, of a past that had a significant piece of it taken away. Because of her grandfather, who was forced to do something he knew was not right. Is that what killed him? Why did they cremate him without asking permission from his family? And not give the ashes a proper burial. Her family never knew what happened to him. Now maybe she did.

She turned on her TV and lay down. Sleep took her in minutes. She awoke to unusual sounds that she hoped were just a dream, but was afraid they weren't. The moans, whispers, and mattress squeaks she heard so clearly were unmistakable. Lying in the same bed as a young couple on their honeymoon she became much more intimate with Bobsy and Babes than she ever wanted. And at one point, she heard a train go by across the river—a steam locomotive, placing the event decades before her time. Bobsy and Babes would most likely not now be able to do what she was hearing them do in their youth, even if still alive.

Soledad had to leave this room and the haunted bed.

She grabbed a pillow and blanket and went downstairs to the lobby and looked around before she opened the front door and walked into the courtyard. She sat down on a bench and looked up at the towers of the hotel. The fountain was still lit up and floodlights focused on the flags far above. Surely she could escape the voices outside the hotel. None of this was her fault. Why was she being tormented because of who she was? The wormhole explanation just didn't fit since not everyone experienced the ghosts. Yes, she thought, it had to be the connection with her grandfather.

It was cool outside, so she wrapped the blanket snugly around herself, shut her eyes and prayed she would hear only silence. She did, until the cheering got too loud. She heard shouts for President Taft. She tried to open her eyes, but they wouldn't open. It was like someone was holding something over her face. There was a huge crowd, just like the one she heard when Roosevelt gave his speech from the balcony.

She heard someone say, "I don't know who she is, but she is sure dressed funny. Look how she keeps her eyes shut. Careful, don't hurt her."

Faintly, a different voice said, "Quick, call 911. I think she is a guest. Looks like she is breathing, but it doesn't look right."

"I'm afraid she will get stepped on. Let's try and get her out of the courtyard and into the hotel. Quickly, because I want to see the President. He is not hard to miss."

She heard the ambulance sirens far off, heading closer to the hotel. She could feel someone massaging her arms. "I recognize her. I think she is in Room 106. I saw her at dinner last night. I hope the ambulance gets here quick!"

The voices in the crowd became louder and clearer. "Quiet, the President is going to speak."

Soledad opened her eyes, finally. She was in bright sunlight, wearing a long dress and blue shawl around her shoulders. There must have been several hundred people on the expanse of lawn. She was clearly in the courtyard of the hotel, but it looked much newer than the hotel she walked into three days ago. People were waving handkerchiefs and homemade signs saying Welcome President Taft. A band was playing by the pool.

That vision faded in a mist as the daylight turned to night time. Three people in windbreakers embroidered with Glenwood Ambulance were lifting her onto a stretcher. She was breathing with difficulty. One of the EMTs placed an oxygen mask over her face. She couldn't hear them, but could clearly see their lips moving. That image faded in a mist as the crowd appeared again. She faintly heard a voice say, "Were losing her. Her heart stopped."

The shouts rang out louder than ever. "Quiet, the President is speaking."

"Fair ladies and good gentlemen, I am proud to be here today in this wonderful town in a wonderful state. Isn't this the best time to be alive?"

The roar of the crowd was deafening. Soledad found herself standing up and joining in the applause.

Soledad's Journeys

Part Two: The Spirit

*I can send you back as you, Soledad, with all you
know, all you learned from being Soledad. And a
lot of what I know. But you won't be Soledad in
your new life. You will be a new person,
but a person with the powers of a shaman,
a holy person, a curandera.*

I OPENED MY EYES as if waking from a deep, complex dream,
and confused whether I was awake or still dreaming. I had
no idea where I was, when it was, or even who I was. I
think if I had looked in a mirror right then, I would have
been surprised who was looking back at me. Blinking and
rubbing the sleep from my eyes didn't help. I couldn't see
anything. Apparently, I was outdoors, but in a fog or heavy
mist. There were no details.

I heard a very faint call that seemed to say the word
Soledad. It wasn't coming from anywhere in particular.
From inside my head? No, it was coming from in front of
me. The voice seemed to be a young girl, calling gently for
Soledad.

Wait a second, I thought. Soledad was my name. Yes, it was
coming to me. I was Soledad, a successful businesswoman,
in my early fifties. I had been having trouble sleeping the
past few nights. Maybe I took sleeping pills. No, I had never
done that in my life. I sometimes had really weird dreams
that flopped back and forth and all over the place. But that
didn't seem right in this situation. Something strange had

happened to me. But what?

A strong breeze blew the mist away and stung my face. Swirling in patterns of light and dark, it slowly lifted and passed to my left. The sun broke through the clouds and birds started singing. There were trees behind me, a forest of pine and aspen. Snowcapped mountains towered above a green valley in front of me. Now I could see the little girl coming towards me. I didn't recognize her at first. Who was she and how did she know my name?

My memory was returning. I had been in Colorado, visiting my new office. I was starting a different job, but hadn't moved there yet. I stayed at the Grand Hotel, a famous landmark. Now it was coming back. I had been haunted by ghosts in the hotel. They kept me awake by talking to me. Or something like that. But I wasn't in the hotel now. I was outside, but not in a place I recognized. What was going on? I must be still asleep. I rubbed my eyes again, but nothing changed.

"Oh my god," I said out loud as the girl came up to me and grabbed my hand. The girl was me. A young me. At least she certainly looked like me. Or me of over forty years ago. I must still be dreaming.

The girl spoke in a voice I had not heard in years, "No, Soledad, it is no dream. You have come home. I was sent to welcome you. The others will be by soon." She giggled as she tugged at my hand.

I remembered the laugh. I hadn't laughed that way in years. How could I describe it? A laugh of innocence? A laugh free from the constraints of maturity? She knew me. Of course, she was me. What a dream!

"What others?" I asked as she swung our joined hands back and forth. She really was me. Her right hand had the little scar from when I accidentally stabbed myself with a pencil in third grade. The time Juan tried to put a frog in my book sack and I swung my hand at him, hitting a pencil he pointed at me.

"Mama, Papa, Tio Benito, Abuelo Martinez. And the big you." She smiled and turned to lead me towards the stream down in the valley.

"Wait a minute. Where are we?" I was starting to get a little worried. Why wasn't I waking up? Then I remembered. The ambulance, the people talking, the way they were dressed. I had gone outside the hotel, but the people gathered in the courtyard were from another time. I was going back and forth from now to then, whenever that was. Someone put me on a stretcher, but I wasn't really on it. I was back in time watching someone speak from the balcony. I was dressed funny. It was like fireworks going off inside my brain. I had stood up, applauded at the President along with the crowd, then I must have fainted. That's all I remembered. Then I woke up here. But it didn't seem like a dream.

I looked around as we walked downhill. It wasn't Glenwood Springs. I'm not even sure it was Colorado, or anywhere I had ever been. Certainly not Santa Fe where I grew up. Not Venezuela where I most recently worked.

I stopped. Little Soledad kept pulling on me to go forward.

"No, I have to figure out what is going on. I don't understand..."

She giggled again. "I'm not even going to try to explain it to you. The big you has to do that."

"What do you mean the big you? You said that before."

"Your soul, Soledad. You are dead. This is where we go home to." She let go of my hand and ran ahead, then disappeared.

I stopped. "Okay," I told myself, "it really is time to wake up. Was the ambulance and all that commotion part of this dream? But wait, I hadn't been able to sleep for two nights. When I closed my eyes, the voices started. The voices from the past. Not my past, but the past of history. There are no voices now. Except for the little girl. Me.

"What does she mean I am dead? I was taught that when we died, we went to a heaven in which we would see angels and all our old friends. The streets would be made of gold and people would be wearing white robes. Well, it didn't take me long to dismiss all that once I started living and thinking on my own. I quit going to mass and gave up most of those innocent beliefs. But I never replaced them with another dogma. I read the popular books about souls and gods and seagulls, but I never processed my own theories. Why should I? My older friends occasionally think about their own deaths, but to me it is a needless worry. I don't even have a will. My only son is dead, my divorced husband lives a life without me, my parents are dead. What do I care what happens when I leave this Earth?"

I sat down on the grass and looked at the distant mountains. There was a large cloud forming over the double peak to the right. It started coming towards me, faster than I had ever seen a cloud move before. A bald eagle flew overhead and circled above me. The cloud and eagle stopped over me. Lightning struck the ground in front of me. The cloud disappeared. When I opened my eyes after the flash, there stood Mama.

"Deo y Jesu," I said as I jumped up. It was Mama, not in her old age, but as the mother I remembered when I was a young girl.

"Welcome, Soledad, my sweet little niña. It is so nice to see you. Don't say a word. This was confusing to me when I got here. I won't explain, other than to say we are sorry you came here so early in your life, but we are so glad to have you here."

We hugged. I felt her touch. She was crying. I realized I was also.

"Mama, I don't understand. I..."

"Soledad, dear, you had a tough time there at the hotel. It is over now. You are home, and we can spend as much time together as you wish. I understand you met my papa, your abuelo. Or at least you heard him. He is here as well, as is your papa. And Danny. We will all get together after you meet yourself." She laughed. "That sounds so strange, but you will understand."

She hugged me again, then stepped back and disappeared. The eagle flew low above me, circled high, disappeared in the distance. I felt the presence of something behind me, so I slowly turned to face a light so bright, I had to shut my eyes.

The formless, shimmering mass of light slowly faded to a pleasant glow.

"I really am dead. You are God," I said, stepping away from the light.

"No Soledad, I am not God," the voice said gently. It was not a man or a woman. I couldn't recognize it. It seemed to be more in my head than a person's voice.

"Then who or what are you? This has to be a dream." I was scared and started to cry. If I wasn't dead, then this fright would certainly kill me.

"Soledad, you are me. I am you. To simplify it, I am your soul. You were me incarnated on Earth. I was with you every step of the way." The voice laughed softly, then enveloped me with warmth. "I believe you once called me the big you. Remember?"

"Oh my God," I whispered again. I couldn't say anything else.

"No I am not God, and you have to quit saying that. There is no God. We are all god. I can see this will take a while to get across to you. We have all the time you want. I am in no hurry to return in our new form. You can help me decide later who I return as next."

I looked around again, seeing the same valley, the same mountains ahead of me. "Please let me wake up. This is a dream."

"No Soledad, this is not a dream. You are not of the Earth any longer. Your work is done. You are home. We will spend a lot of time discussing what happened. It usually takes a while. You are confused because there was no obvious end for you. You got caught in a strange time distortion. I could say it really wasn't time yet, but these things are not planned. There is no grand vision and no one had you programmed for living a year or one hundred years. It happened in a strange way and you were not prepared. It has happened to me before."

The light was vibrating in intensity, dimmed a little, and a human form appeared ever so slightly. "What do I have to do or show you to prove this is not a dream, Soledad? We need to cover a lot of ground and I want you to understand things."

"If I am dead, how and when did I die? The last thing I remember was at the hotel, with the strange voices."

"Oh, that was a little strange, wasn't it? Several things came together and, well, let me try to piece it together. As I said, no one plans these things. We are not pre-programmed. Some angel does not have a clipboard that says Soledad is scheduled to die on April 13 at 9 pm. Besides, there are no angels."

I squinted at the form of light and asked, "Then what are you?"

"Certainly not an angel. I am you. Or more correctly, you are an extension of me. Some people have called us souls. I am not alone. There are many of us." The being shot light out as if waving an arm.

"Are you a person? A human? From Earth?"

"Now you are getting into the tricky stuff. Not really. And this is not Earth. But," the light quickly interjected anticipating Soledad's next question, "it may appear like Earth to you because all of this is from your own imagination. Your own experiences based on your life. From now on, it is all in your head."

"You are telling me I am imagining all this? Then I am dreaming!" Soledad almost shouted. She looked around and the mountains disappeared and she was surrounded by water.

"You are in control, but I can play a few tricks with you. Let me continue. There is a lot of ground to cover, so to speak." A field of flowers replaced the water.

"Okay. I am dead, you are my soul, and I am now in heaven." This thing that had the audacity to call itself my soul was jerking me around.

"Not heaven. There really is no such place. Nor a hell. Let's call it another dimension."

That reminded me of something. If I was being jerked around, I would play along. I replied quickly, "Like a 'brane?'" I remember reading about those recently. It's like another universe. A parallel universe?"

"Something like that. But let's go back and ease into this. I am your soul. I am not human and I am not on Earth. Actually some of us have people on other planets, but I don't want to confuse things right now. I, or actually you, go to Earth to help me get my merit badge, so to speak." The being laughed heartily. "I just now made that one up. Sorry. We live on a certain plane, depending on our progress in achieving perfection. Get so many points, and I move on. But in the meantime, I take the form of, well, you in this case. I have done this many times. On Earth, I or you achieve certain things, or live certain lifestyles to give me the experience I need to become more perfect. You realize this is

simplifying things."

"So, you are my guardian angel. So to speak." I smiled at that comment.

"Only to a point. Well, not even to a point. I have no control over you. I know what you are doing, in a general way. It's not like I am with you every second. I don't watch you in bed with your husband for example. Or anyone else," it added with a certain edge to its voice.

"Well, it's nice to know I have a little privacy."

"I show up in those little moments when you hear that little voice you call intuition. Remember when you just know something is right or wrong? That is me trying to give you a hint. If I recall you didn't always follow this instinct."

"Like the time I had that affair? I suppose you knew about that."

"Yes, and you knew it was wrong and would hurt others. You did it anyway and always regretted it. There are limitations to what I can do. But I learn from it. That is what is important. Maybe that is why you existed."

"You are saying I was born and lived just so you could experience the guilt of an affair?"

"I don't know that. Maybe, but I learned a lot more than that. Things aren't usually that simple. Maybe I needed experience in running a business. Or losing a son."

"I always felt guilt that Danny died because I was unfaithful and caused his father to leave me. Is that true?" How did this thing know so much about me?

"Don't make heavy assumptions like that. Neither you nor I will ever know. It happened, you learned something from it. Maybe I did too. I never experienced losing a child before."

"You said you do this often. I am not your first human?"

"Soledad, you ask so many questions. Let's walk a ways and let me explain. We will never get you convinced about what is happening until I get a chance to explain."

"Okay. You lead the way. I obviously don't know where we are."

"You want familiarity? Here it is." The scene quickly changed to the Sangre de Cristo Mountains outside Santa Fe.

I gasped as I recognized the trailhead of one of my favorite childhood trails. "Oh, I know this place. I haven't been here for years."

"I am your soul. You are an extension of me. I only have one person at a time. Or, let's call it a student. You go to Earth to live a normal life. This is not a straight line thing for me. My next person could occur a thousand years ago or a thousand years hence. When we finish discussing your life, you will help me decide who is next. Your life is over. You don't go on to something else. You only existed to help me."

"What happens to me, then?" I was becoming more exasperated.

"Nothing. You don't exist anymore. It's all over. However, you can come back to greet a loved one just as your mother came to you. It's all due to the brain waves of the person coming back. For example, you can't go meet a stranger or someone who never knew you. But when someone dies who you knew or loved, they can bring you back in their minds. They see you and you come speak to them, but that's it."

"So, there is no heaven where I live forever in ultimate happiness?"

"Sorry. I have to move on and your part of me is done. There is no infinity for you. Now me, that is another story."

"That's not fair," I said in a rather whiney voice. I felt like a kid being sent to her room when the adults started talking serious stuff.

"I don't make the rules. But continuing on—I may go back in a human form to do good, maybe evil, or anything in between. You were an invention of me and a tool for me to use. I set up the circumstances of your existence. Once you appeared on Earth, you took over and led a life that I observed without interference. Or at least much covert interference. I thank you for that. You are here now as a courtesy, for me to let you know what happened and what I learned. I will get into that later. Think of it as a debriefing." The form laughed again.

It continued, "you can meet whomever you wish, as long as you knew them. You met your mother. You can visit as long as you want with anyone else who has died before you. You will even get to meet your grandfather, even though you never actually knew him. Because of the unusual circumstances at the hotel, you did get to meet him in a way. Thus, you can visit him here if you wish."

Looking around at the familiar view from an open hillside, I paused and said, "I miss Canosita, the little white dog I had as a girl. We walked up here a lot." I stopped walking as if to test the big me.

"I know that. Say hi to Canosita." All of a sudden, a little white dog bounded past, stopped to look back, then returned and jumped on me. I burst into tears, laughing and crying as I hugged my closest friend from childhood. Here I was back in my childhood, walking with my beloved Whitey as if forty-five years hadn't happened.

"It's you, not me. Your thoughts are very powerful. You need to be careful in using this new power."

We proceeded to hike to the top of the ridge, with my soul explaining things all the way. In spite of his or her pleas to quit asking questions, I could not stop. Canosita ran all the way with us, chasing rabbits and barking at a doe and fawn. It was a perfect summer day and I didn't tire at all. That in itself was enough to prove to me that I was not dreaming. I had been slowing down in recent years and couldn't even finish a game of tennis anymore without collapsing from exhaustion. I didn't need a drink nor did I get hungry. And the strange thing was the sun never moved in the sky. Time ceased to exist.

I figured I had to give this thing a name, rather than referring to it as *it* or the *big me,* so I started calling it Anna, short for *animus* and *soul.* It didn't seem to care, just laughing that infectious laugh of hers. Or his. I will use the feminine from now on. Anna had been involved most recently in the American Revolution, the Civil War, the Russian Revolution, and the Norman invasion of Britain. She had spent time as both man and woman, white, black and all other colors, rich, poor, sick, healthy, just about everything imaginable.

We spent a lot of time reviewing my life and what I thought I had learned. I was amazed and a little embarrassed that Anna knew so much of what I did. I guess it makes sense. How else could she learn from my life? In a strange way, though, it made me feel quite important, knowing I was her representative. Of course, every person has this soul shadow, so I was nothing unusual. I asked Anna, "does every single person have a soul? Are there new souls being created to account for the increase in population?" She said there were a few who occasionally slipped in, and those were usually hard core criminals who seemed to have no respect for life, the serial murderers, etc. Even some animals had souls, but that seemed a little fuzzy even for Anna. I guess there are some things even the higher ups don't understand.

"If I am your representative, why can't I remember your other incarnations?" She responded that when I (Soledad) came to Earth, I was a new being.

"That isn't fair. You benefit from my being, but I don't benefit from all the work I've done. Why can't I remember the past lives?"

Anna was clearly exasperated with my questioning, but simply asked me why I thought I was on Earth. What had I learned? That really stumped me. I sat down on a rock outcrop near the ridge top while I reviewed my life. "I never really thought about it. I lost my religion in my early twenties, even though I was raised a strict and traditional Catholic. I got caught up in my career and got lost in the material things. When Danny was killed by a shark while swimming off the coast of Australia, I lost a lot of my direction. That's when I put full time into my work, had another affair, then lost my husband soon after to a divorce. I've been drifting through the years ever since."

Then Anna really blindsided me with the next question. "Why did you come to Glenwood Springs and specifically the Grand Hotel where you eventually died?" I had to admit I had no idea whatsoever. With this, her light brightened, then faded. She was silent for several minutes. I wondered if she had fallen asleep or if I irritated her beyond exasperation. Finally, with a loud sigh, she said, "it was to help your grandfather."

She went on to explain, "Your grandfather did not return to his soul when he died. He became trapped in a time warp and stayed on Earth. He and several others in the hotel were frozen in time and couldn't return."

Evidently that exact spot, the piece of ground on the hillside above the hot springs which was sacred to the Ute and others before them for thousands of years, is where there is a thin spot in space-time. This allows shamans and others to visit with their holy people. Maybe their souls.

The hotel, built unknowingly on that sacred spot, got the reputation for ghosts because some guests and workers were caught in the time warp and are calling for help to get out. Anna reasoned that I came back to release Grandfather. By hearing his voice and making that connection with him, he was somehow able to return to his soul. That helped him, but more importantly helped his soul to move on. But it did something to me, causing me to get stretched in time. I was in both the present and the past, part of both worlds. In the present, I had a heart attack. Although my body was there, being carried away by ambulance, part of me was also taken back in time. For a few seconds I appeared a hundred years ago as part of that world, but I soon collapsed there as well. When I fell over, I faded away and just disappeared from that world. People talked about it, but any news of it got lost in the excitement of the President's speech that night.

I asked Anna, again, who she reported to, and whether she had to impress God in order to move on. Her response was the same, "There is no God, we are all god, collectively." Then she went on to ask me another strange question, "Do you know about the seagull from a book published in the 70s?"

"Of course," I said. "It was popular for a while, then faded from celebrity." Anna went on to explain that the book's philosophical concept was essentially what we were talking about. "Humans tend to get lost in the flock of mediocrity. They need to break free and strive for perfection. When they reach it, they move on."

I asked if Anna were human once and then moved on to being the soul. She only said, "what do you think?" I didn't know what to think.

When we reached the top of the mountain, we sat for a while, mesmerized by the view. The Rio Grande Valley stretched far below us, with mountain peaks and alpine meadows surrounding us. A pika chipped at us from the rocks below. Anna surprised me by asking a question in a very quiet voice. "Are you satisfied with your life?" I couldn't believe she asked that, and replied that I sure wasn't satisfied with the way it ended. "Other than that," she said.

"I cannot answer that without thinking about it for a few days. Or weeks. Or whatever passes for time here. It seems like I have been here for days, but I haven't seen a sunset yet."

"You won't unless you wish to. Remember, I told you that you will experience whatever you wish."

With that, the sun jumped to a spot hovering on the western horizon. The clouds turned red and salmon, then purple. Alpenglow turned Anna's light an orange pink.

"I guess I shouldn't have done that. Now we have to walk down in the dark."

Anna laughed. "You really aren't paying attention are you? Is that what you wish?"

The mountains disappeared and we were standing on a wave-washed shore, a blue ocean spreading beyond the horizon.

"Oh no, I shouldn't have done this. It makes me think of Danny."

As I said that, Danny appeared riding a wave on a surfboard. He came ashore at our feet. He was young and handsome, tanned, with sun-bleached hair. He grinned as he came up to hug me. His "welcome, Mom" had me hugging him so tightly, he begged for me to ease up. I couldn't even see him through my tears. I started to introduce him to Anna, but then I noticed Anna had moved a couple hundred yards back from the shore. Danny knew what happened to me, so we spent seemingly hours talking about our own deaths. He shrugged when he said he was "kinda stupid" to be swimming by himself like that so far from shore. I was pleased that he said he didn't feel any pain when the shark hit him. It happened so quickly. He felt badly when I recounted the days of pain I felt afterwards.

When Anna returned, she greeted Danny, then asked me if there were any others I wanted to meet. I said sure, but wasn't there all the time I wanted for that? Anna said yes, but she wanted to spend some time talking about her next life. This seemed so strange to me, I couldn't believe I would have any say in that.

"You need to meet your grandfather and mother now." This was unusual since I had no memories of my grandfather. In that moment he was standing with us, a young man in a crisp Navy uniform.

"Bella nieta, I want to thank you for my life. You released me from a living hell. And my own flesh and blood. I cry that I never had a chance to know you. Or my own daughter. But I want you to tell me all about yourself and your growing up. I just met your mama for the first time and we have spent a wonderful time together."

"Well abuelo, I also want to know about you. This seems so strange to me that you are a young man, my grandfather, talking to me like a grandfather would talk to a young child. I am much older than you."

He shook his head. "I don't understand. When I look at you just now, I see a young girl of maybe 15 or so. And I see my own hands as shriveled and old. My voice is old." Miguel held out his hands for me to see. They were the hands of a twenty-five year old working man.

I looked at Anna with a very confused expression. "Anna, what do you see?"

"This is interesting. It is different because of the unusual situation. Usually you will see what you want to see. You will appear to others as you want them to see you. Remember when you first arrived, you saw yourself as you imagined yourself. Miguel never lived to be an old man, but somehow, he aged in his spiritual confinement. He is seeing you as he wishes he could. You see him as he would have been if you had known him. I find this all very fascinating. Time is playing tricks on us."

Miguel continued to thank me for releasing him from his prison—in the hotel as a hospital—a situation he didn't understand and couldn't describe other than being caught in darkness of time, only able to call out, or relive his days in the hotel. He was able to hear the voices from long ago of others who had lived there when the hillside was a grassy meadow above the magical hot springs. He instinctively knew a descendant of his was staying in the hotel, but he couldn't reach me. He had asked me to help him, but he was sure I hadn't heard him. Finally one night, he was freed. When he met his soul, it was explained to him that my death had finally freed him. He apologized to me but thanked me again. I was so surprised, I couldn't say anything other than I was glad I could help him. I wanted to be a little mad, but I couldn't be. He was so happy. He was just like me, as he was discovering what this was all about. We talked about that for a while, but I pressed him on what his life was about and what he remembered of my grandmother. He knew my mother as a baby, but he was sent overseas before he had much time to spend with her. He never saw her again, until he got to spend time with her here in what I still wanted to call heaven.

Both of us must have thought of Mama because she appeared when we started talking about her. All three of us spent what I felt were hours if not days talking and hugging and just enjoying each other's company. Soon Papa joined us, and Danny re-appeared, as well as Grandmother, too. It was a once in a lifetime, or death-time, family reunion. If what Anna was saying was true, we would not get this chance again, so we made the most of it.

Too soon, Anna came to take me away for our conference on what she was to do next. We appeared on top of the mountain in the Sangre de Cristo Mountains where we had hiked earlier. Sitting on a large boulder next to a field filled with columbines and bluebells, Anna started the discussion.

"Soledad, if you could go back and do something you felt like you didn't get to experience during your life, who would you pick to go back as?"

"That's a strange question since you already said I don't get to go back. Right?"

"That is what I said. I just wanted to get a feel for something you feel you missed out on. If you missed it, then I missed it as well. I want your perspective. It helps me choose my next life."

I felt an irritation starting to rise. "You know what you need to get your ticket punched. Remember, I don't get to participate in your other lives. It shouldn't matter what I think."

Anna knew I was not happy with the arrangement. "Soledad, I don't make the rules. Well," she hesitated before continuing, "actually, there aren't any rules. Maybe I should say tradition."

"Of all people and situations where tradition should be forbidden, this is one." I knew my face was turning red. "I think the tradition stinks. I do all the hard work, make all the decisions, suffer the tragedies and heartaches, get through the tough times, sweat, bear children, change diapers, work my butt off to make ends meet. You sit up here on your throne and gain all the knowledge I give you, then when I die, you debrief me, glean all my hard-won wisdom, and then say bye-bye, you're finished. Now you get to enjoy a new life. That stinks."

I knew I had blown it. I remember Papa once commenting to me after I insulted his father, it was like I just spit on the Pope. Well, I felt like I had just spit on God, even though I knew Anna was not God. At this point, was there any real difference?

Anna didn't respond. She sat there, her light flickering brighter, then dimmer. At one point, it faded almost out. I started to say I was sorry, but the light flashed brilliant, then moved to envelop me.

"You have strong feelings, don't you Soledad? I admire that. You care. Not very many do. Please, let me tell you what I can do. It is unusual, but we can make it work. I need to explain something first. Have you ever met anyone who has a special power? Someone who can see or feel other people's energy? Someone who can talk to dead people? Someone called a witch or shaman or prophet?"

I knew exactly who she was talking about. "Yes. A curandera in Santa Fe when I was a young girl. I called her a witch. Now I know better. She could heal people by just touching them. She said she visited spirits. We accused her of drinking spirits. Papa spanked me one time because I threw a tantrum about not wanting to see that witch again. Later, I met a shaman in South America, a traditional Incan shaman who saw people's energy. He was magical. I learned a lot from him."

Anna said, "There are people with very strong powers, but modern civilization isn't very compatible with this. A lot of people used to have these powers, but nowadays, there are very few. Do you know what gives them their powers?"

"They just have them. I don't know why."

"They are chosen. By us. I can send you back as you, Soledad, with all you know, all you learned from being Soledad. And a lot of what I know. But you won't be Soledad in your new life. You will be a new person, but a person with the powers of a shaman, a holy person, a curandera. You will see energy, talk to people from the past, heal by touching people, remember the wisdom you have gained in another life. That is what those people are. They had strong feelings such as you just expressed; they were sent back and not just tossed aside as you feared you would be. When you die after that, you have been prepared to become just like me. A soul. One who has moved on to the next level. Like the seagull. This is the next stepping stone in life. Does that interest you?"

I couldn't believe what I just heard. "Why didn't you tell me this to begin with?" I asked in an embarrassed but hurt tone of voice.

"Most people don't show an interest. Remember what I said about being in the flock of mediocrity? To get out of the flock and strive for perfection, you ask the questions you just asked. You want to learn what I learn. It is relatively easy to get from you to me. For me to move on, now that is much more difficult. Much more." Anna laughed her deep laugh.

"Yes, yes, Anna, I would love to do that. What do I need to do?" I was excited at the thought.

"You don't do anything. But I need to make sure you understand. You won't remember your life as Soledad. You will know the lessons learned. You will remember the wisdom I share with you. But you cannot go back in a time or place where you will know anyone from your life as Soledad. And you won't know events, such as who won the

World Series, or when the stock market nose-dived." Anna laughed heartily at her last comment.

That is how I was allowed to write these words. I told Anna I wanted to record all my thoughts and experiences. She said that was okay, but they would never go anywhere. I told her fine, it would help me remember better. And who knows, someday maybe someone would read them.

Anna and I spent hours, if there were such a thing in this heavenly place, talking and choosing my next life. And her next life. My guess was it would be her last since I felt she was probably ready to move on, and I envied her.

The Obituary

We were as unlike as the birds feeding near us. The pigeons were like Frank, predictable, not complicated, eager to grab what was easy. The blue jays were like me, always complaining, noisy, probing, often irritating.
Carl

His LAUGH STARTED as a low rumble. It was not his "that is really funny" laugh, but a cynical disbelief of what he just heard from me. Soon, it turned to his higher pitched belly laugh indicating he really did see the humor.

I squinted at him. "Well, Frank, I take it you finally think my comment funny."

He brushed his white hair back into place since his laughing had ruffled its usually meticulous placement. "I do have to admit, Carl, you fooled me at first. I thought you were serious, but then I realized you were being funny. Or trying to be." Frank looked at me, then smiled quietly, his laughter exhausted.

"I was serious, Frank old buddy. You want to have a good obituary, you write your own. You tell me a better way to leave your legacy. Don't expect me or anyone else to write what you want. I wouldn't let you write mine. You don't know what I found important in life and I certainly don't know what you felt the best about." I looked up in the huge sycamore spreading high above us as a squirrel started scolding the world below him.

"Carl, I told you a long time ago I would be pleased if my obituary said just four words. 'He made a difference.'"

"And what the hell does that mean? Genghis Khan made a difference. Adolph Hitler made a difference. Joe Stalin did too. Does that mean you would like to be placed in their category?" I was still distracted by the squirrel, now joined by a friend in the next tree.

"Damn it, Carl, you know what I mean. I helped people. I made a difference to them."

"Let's dissect what you just said," I replied. I started to continue, but he interrupted me.

"Dissect your own ass. You have to think through everything." Frank exhaled his sigh of total frustration as he slapped his thigh.

"No, Frank, you are not being concise. I am just trying to make sense of what you said. I am not being unclear. You are. You are as vague as that damn squirrel."

Frank and I were sitting on the park bench, like we usually did in late morning. We were two old men, friends since childhood, alternately close, then apart for years at a time, deserted by the death of most of our old friends, looking for whatever adventure was left to us. We both enjoyed watching children play, reliving memories of way too many years. We were as unlike as the birds feeding near us. The pigeons were like Frank, predictable, not complicated, eager to grab what was easy. The blue jays were like me, always complaining, noisy, probing, often irritating. I guess that diversity was what held us together on these daily journeys.

Frank called me a curmudgeon. I called him gullible. We were both right. By this point in our conversation, we both had forgotten how we got to this latest argument. It didn't matter. I enjoyed the verbal battle. I think it irritated him.

Frank investigated the daily obituaries first thing each morning. On this Saturday, he found a long-lost member of our high school class. Neither of us had seen or even heard of him for decades. I didn't have particularly fond memories of him, but I was still interested in how his life had turned out. Frank read the short obit aloud, then lashed out at how crappy it was. He said whoever wrote it was incompetent. Frank looked at me and said that he wanted me to make sure his obit was complete.

That was when I had said quite seriously he should write his own.

"Carl, how can I write my own death notice after I die? I will be dead. Unless I take a .45 and look at the clock, write down the details, then put the barrel in my mouth, I don't know when I will die."

"I know that, dingleberry. You write all but the first sentence. The undertaker can write those details. You write the other ten paragraphs. You put in your history, what you did, who you left behind, what you were proudest of. You can write the entire obit right this moment, leaving only the first sentence blank. What is wrong with that?"

"It's morbid, that's what." Frank started to dig into his pockets for his candy bar of the day.

"What, you think you aren't going to die? Good grief, man, we all die. Every living thing since that first protozoan to squiggle through the sea 4 billion years ago has died. I will die, you will die. If morbid means death, which I think it does, then yes, your life will end in death. Nothing to be ashamed of. Or afraid of. Life happens. Death happens."

"Well, it's still sick."

"Lighten up old man. You are the one searching the obituaries every day. That's sick."

"Well how else do we know who is no longer with us?"

"What does it matter? If you know the person, you will learn they died. If it is someone you knew sixty years ago and haven't seen in over half a century, then it doesn't matter. Does it?" I looked at Frank as he tore off the wrapper of his candy bar and stuffed one end of the bar in his mouth. "You not even going to offer me half of it today?"

"No, butt head. You are pissing me off today. Besides you would just give it to the squirrels. You did the other day."

"Fine, rot your remaining teeth. Ain't good for you anyway. Not good for the squirrels either. And I didn't give it to them the other day. I dropped it and that wily sonofabitch scampered down and grabbed it. I hope it rots his teeth." I smiled as I pulled out a small yogurt container from my pack. I slowly pulled off the foil top and poised the spoon above the pink glob in the cup. "Want some of this. It's better for you."

"Doesn't matter. My obit is already written: Frank made a difference. He made a lot of people feel better. He helped them. Period. You want me to say what was important? There. That is what my life was all about."

"Pretty boring. Would you be satisfied if old Phil had outlived you and read that? Don't you think he would be curious?"

"Don't care." Frank shoved the last piece into his mouth, stuffing the empty wrapper back in his coat pocket.

"The hell you don't. You do care. You should care. And you should ask for more. Most people make a difference. I imagine you made your wife feel better. Your kids needed you. If you would have had grandkids, they would have felt better by your presence. You need more than that. You want to make a difference long after you are gone."

"And you think you have?"

"I am not talking about me. This discussion is about you. You are the one complaining about poor obits. I am just trying to clarify what you want." I finished my yogurt and got up and put the empty cup in the trash bin nearby.

"What, no recycling? I thought you were the perfect environmentalist." Frank grinned at his successful poke at me.

"Touché. Okay, I was lazy. You can put that in my obit. I was a hypocrite at times. Once I even failed to recycle a yogurt container number 1 plastic. So my life is now a pile of rubble."

"Do you have your obit already written?" Frank pulled out his binoculars to stare at two young women entering the park.

"I would leave out the part about making young females feel better by your admiration of them."

"Bite me."

"No thanks, I have better things to eat. And no, I have not written my obit. No one cares. But I have written it before. Several training sessions I was at in my career, we did this as an exercise. And yes, we thought it morbid and gross. But most of us were in our thirties and at that time, it was much too early to write it. But as our instructors always told us, it was a good exercise to make us think about what was important."

I thought back to those times I was asked to write my obituary. I didn't know what to say. At the time, I was still trying to figure out life. Even though I was nearly 40 years old then, I still didn't know what I wanted to be when I grew up. Actually, I never really wanted to grow up. Growing up takes all the fun out of things and most grownups I ever knew were way too serious. Take Frank, for example. He took everything too seriously. On the other hand, most of the adult males I knew only thought they had grown up. Around the office, yes, they were serious, usually with little sense of humor. But get them in a hunting camp or fishing trip, chugging beer or sipping bourbon, they were little boys, totally immature. Even when they tried to act grown up at work, they usually thought themselves much more important than they were.

For a while in my life, the people close to me courted death every day. Piloting a fighter jet screaming low over the Viet Nam jungles brought one too close to death to think seriously about it. Death was a game and few of us thought long and hard about obituaries. We had our wills prepared and we discussed arrangements like that, but did we really think about what we accomplished in our lives up to that point? We lived for the moment, day to day. In war, you sometime lose track of the big picture.

Yeah, life was a game. That should be the lead sentence in my obit, which I wasn't going to write anyway since there would be no one to read it that I cared about. There were no set rules, but we all played the game, by our own rules which we continually rewrote and amended. "Carl played the game of life for eighty-five years, then cashed in his chips and sailed off to the magical sand castle in the sky. There, he continued to be a kid forever."

"Hey Carl," Frank pushed on my leg. "Earth to Carl. You kind of drifted off there buddy. Anything to share?"

I looked at Frank as if he were a stranger. He was. I was having fun in my thoughts and he brought me back to some subject I was batting around. What was it? Oh yeah, death. Now that was an upper. "I was thinking about a training session I attended back in northern California. There were about 15 of us. Some special deal of selected folks from around the region, sent to a state university and tutored on how to be leaders. A big waste of money, but if they wanted to pay me to attend, then fine. It was an honor, but it didn't turn me into a leader. You either are one or you are not. I was too independent for most of my superiors."

"What's that got to do with your obit and what was important in your life?"

"Who said it did?"

"Damn it all Carl, are you off in Alzheimer land? What were we talking about? Why should I waste my breath talking to you if you drift off in some incoherent irrelevant land that has nothing to do with the sentence you just uttered ten seconds before?" Frank was getting irritated. I liked doing that to him.

"Well give me time to develop my case. You always hurry me. I was building up to the subject. Now you interrupted me and I have to go start over again." I grinned at him.

Frank focused his binoculars on a new girl riding by on a bicycle. She had on a low-cut tank top and with her leaning over the handlebars, Frank was zeroing in on a hefty set of knockers.

"What good does that do you, old man?" I reached for the binoculars but he held on as the redhead slowed as she rode by. She waved at us and smiled. She did a little dipsy doo to give him a better view before she went by. I laughed.

"Damn, what would I give to be fifty years younger." Frank slowly put his binoculars back in his knapsack.

"Dorinda wouldn't have let you look now nor did she then, so it wouldn't matter."

"How come girls in our high school didn't have boobs like that?"

"Good grief, what made you think back that far? It's called

evolution. You would have died of a hundred heart attacks if they had. Young men nowadays must have tougher hearts. We are just destined to suffer, I guess. Anyway, you wanted to know what I was talking about. In that training session, one of our assignments was to write our own obituary. The oldest one of us was maybe 45. No one was comfortable in writing anything. It made me frustrated because I was still searching for something to be proud of. I was looking for my legacy. I think we all were. I guess it was a good exercise, but really futile. I don't think it helped any of us. It was premature then but now it is not. I have my legacy. You do too. It is probably too late to create any significant new legacy. Don't you think?"

"I keep telling you what mine is. I made a difference to people. I was kind, helpful, leaving good feelings in people I dealt with."

"But did you have fun?"

"Life is more than having fun." Frank gave me a frowny look.

"Maybe life is more than just making a difference. There are a million variations of what constitutes a difference. How big a difference? To how many people? For how long?"

"Geez, Carl, nothing is simple to you is it?" Frank was looking around for more young ladies, but at this moment, the park was empty. He looked up in the sycamore but the squirrel had stopped scolding and wasn't even visible.

"Of course not. Nothing is simple. Life is complicated. Nature is complicated. It's called the web of life for a purpose. Everything is connected to everything else by a hundred different threads. Okay here goes. My legacy, my obituary will say that I tried to make people think. To understand the complexity of everything. When someone thought life was simple and answers to the difficult questions were simple, I tried to throw a monkey wrench into their thinking. I tried to make them think. Yes, that's it. That is the quality of a leader. I didn't claim to have answers, but I had lots of questions. I irritated people by making them realize they didn't have answers either."

"That is your answer to what was important to you?" Frank asked. He often had trouble figuring out what I was really getting at. I liked Frank, but I enjoyed yanking his chain. He kept trying to simplify life and I just wouldn't let him.

It was interesting neither of us thought the importance of our lives was determined by material accomplishment. I didn't pay much attention to obituaries, but I remembered that most included family—children, grandchildren—career, and hobbies. Throw in awards, offices held (Good ole Tom was deacon in his church, president of Rotary). Those were ego trips as if they determined success. How many times do you read that Tom prided himself on reading 5000 books, or wrote 100 poems or loved to debate the meaning of Socrates or Nietzsche?

Frank prided himself on making a difference. I prided myself on asking questions. Neither of us felt anything else mattered. If people wrote their own obituaries, would this thinking predominate? Maybe because grieving widows or widowers or children wrote the obits, they had to embellish the meaning of their loved one's life by stroking their own egos to make the newly dead person important. How would Tom's widow feel if all he said in the obit that all his friends would peruse was he read a lot of books? It made me think of the narrative in the high school yearbook for each graduating senior. Whose narrative was the longest? The most popular boy or girl of course. Pity the poor geek who only listed being a student for 4 years and no clubs, sports, or awards. I wondered if some of the most satisfied (I won't say successful since that is such an ambiguous word) were those whose narrative was the shortest.

Frank and I sat in silence enjoying the cloudless blue sky. The birds were active, pigeons included. Of course, I ignored the pigeons. They were the attention hogs. I paid attention to the secretive bunting hopping in the sycamore tree. And the nuthatch beeping his way down the pine looking for whatever he could find in the bark. No one wrote an obituary when the merlin came screaming off the top of the power pole and grabbed a finch. We lived life the best we could, then we died. What was the purpose of an obituary, anyway?

I wanted to ask Frank that question, but about that time, he stretched his legs, let out a loud belch and said it was time for him to go to the store. He wanted to rent a movie for that night. Our visits were limited to these morning forays into the park and seldom extended to each other's house or remainder of the day. It was almost as if the rest of life was some secret, not to be discussed at these seminars we held with ourselves.

Maybe that was the fate of old geezers like us. We could only stand each other for so long, although that short time was important to each of us. He thought he was making a difference in my life; I thought I was forcing him to think beyond the box. We didn't obsess with death, but as we were getting closer to that inevitable end, we did pay more attention to it. I likened it to a young man never thinking about marriage, but once he bit the apple and marriage came closer and closer, he probably thought a lot about it. The same with just about anything. You don't pay attention to it until it looms in your future.

"Do you think you can survive until tomorrow with that last peek of boobies?"

"You find something wrong with that?" Frank groused as he stood up.

"Not if one of your life goals is to have fun. Maybe you made a difference in the life of that girl. Ever think of that? It elevated her ego that some old geezer copped a peak of her private assets."

"See, you have to dissect everything. What guy doesn't look at the chest of young women?"

"But you are so obvious about it. You think life is simple. Sex or a well-formed body. I think life is much more complicated. I sneak a peek if it is given, but then I ask why are we attracted to a gland meant for life-giving nourishment. Look at all the drawings of people from millennia ago. Or of native jungle tribes in the tropics. Women go topless all the time. It was natural and men didn't go ape over that."

"That's it. I give up. I'm out of here. Don't get lost going home. Adios." With that final humph in his voice, he walked away, ignoring me as I waved to him and shouted, "I'd like to see that obit tomorrow. But I suggest leaving out the part about ogling young women. Hasta mañana!"

I started to get up to leave, but decided to sit a little longer. Maybe I should write an obituary, I thought, as I watched Frank disappear down the street. Not that I cared to share it, but I was always ready to fine tune my life's purpose. I still had time to achieve a few more things, if only I could figure out what they were. I thought about what we choose to reflect on as we got older. Decades ago, I would have focused on where I would go on my next vacation. I might think about my job and what project I was working on, or who I was influencing, but that was work and when I reflected on things, I didn't want to think about my job. Then, I needed to dream, playing out my fantasies. Now, I needed to reflect on my lifetime of fantasies and whether I met any of them. Time was running short, especially since it was getting tougher and tougher to do the things I used to do physically.

I was lost again in my philosophical debate with myself. I came back to the present when a yellow dog went running by, barking furiously, followed by a young lady in pink shorts and blue running shoes. What a combination, I thought. Color blind people missed the best part of life. I laughed as she lunged for the dog, missing it and bouncing off the grass. She looked around as she got up, grinning a sheepish smile as she saw me.

"Hurt yourself?" I asked her in a very serious tone. By that time, the dog came over to me, his tail wagging his whole body. She walked over and grabbed the dragging leash.

"Sorry about that," she said as she wiped the grass off her pink shorts. She had a green knee from the grass stains, but no visible blood. "No, I only hurt my pride."

"Lucky you landed where you did. Two feet further on, you would have skidded in that pile of dog doo."

"Ooh, yuck," she said as she looked near where she hit the grass. "I thought I smelled something. Not cool. Babsy, leave the man alone." The dog was jumping up on me, trying to lick my face.

"He's all right. Probably smells the yogurt I spilled on my fingers. Babsy? Strange name for a boy."

"Oh, his real name is Babbitt. That is a strange name. Named after my father. He didn't go by it either. He was known as BB. I didn't want to name my dog BB. Might get my father to come when I called him." She giggled as she pulled Babsy closer to her.

I wasn't sure where I wanted this strange conversation to go, but it wasn't going anywhere I wanted it to. I was glad Frank had left. He would be panting as he stared at her breasts, half hanging out the low-cut tank top, although restrained by a neon green sports bra, as well as her butt, squeezed into the pink shorts.

"I am being impolite. Hi, my name is Brenda Thomas." She reached out her hand to shake mine. I smiled at her as I responded in kind. She almost bubbled as she said, "I haven't seen you here before, although I usually come by in the afternoons. Do you come here often?"

I didn't say anything when she said it, but the name Babbitt caught my attention. Was she who I thought she was? "Hi yourself. I'm Carl. I do come here most every day, but it is usually in the morning. An old buddy of mine, Frank, meets me here and we sit like a couple old geezers and ogle the young women, not that it makes much difference anymore." I smiled that impish grin of mine that means I am pulling someone's leg. I didn't know if Brenda would get the sarcasm or not. She did.

"Well, you know us young ladies. We thrive on ogles from geezers we don't need to worry about." She giggled again as she reached over and touched my arm. For some reason, that gesture didn't bother me like it normally would. Brenda exuded innocence as she then reached down to fluff Bab's fur.

"Well Brenda, your name rings a bell but I can't place it. Excuse my mild dementia but you may have to help me place who you are." I found this simple method of prying to usually work.

"Yeah, you are as demented as I am. I don't like to announce myself for obvious reasons. I will start out by saying I have been absent from Canyon Creek for a few years, attending Stanford and now UC Berkeley Law. I graduated from Canyon High with honors and all that fluff six years ago." She lowered her eyes, almost like she was embarrassed.

She should have been. She was the daughter of Brendan Babbitt Thomas, Attorney General of the state and local scion of the Thomas and Ellsworth families who own half the county. Brenda garnered more accolades and honors than probably anyone in history in this part of the state. Her picture seemed to make front pages every week several years ago, either in academic, volunteerism, or sports, but I hadn't heard anything of her since she went away to college.

"Berkeley Law, huh? And why are you running half naked through the park on a day like this? Is this some new type of apprenticeship for Berkeley Law students? Trying to entrap old geezers, then defend us in court?"

"Stop it Carl. This is my home town. Seems like I am a stranger here anymore. I want to be a commoner like anyone else. Hard to do with a name like mine in this town." She pulled her water bottle off her waist pack and took a long drink, then gave a cupped handful to Babs.

"Well I will have to change the time of my park visits if you will come running by in the afternoons." I looked up as my old squirrel friend started harassing Babs, with a barking response by the lunging dog trying to climb the tree.

"Babs, stop it. Sit." She patted the dog, then looked up at me. "You miss out Carl. I have to go back to Berkeley in a couple weeks. Seems third year Law is a killer, not that the past few years haven't nearly done me in already. Summer went by much too fast. I was doing an internship for Judge Williams in San Francisco on the 9th Circuit until two weeks ago."

Brenda and I sat talking for the next half hour. I found her fascinating, mature, intelligent, curious, and all the other traits I admired in anyone, especially anyone under 25 years old. Over the past dozen years, I had lost touch with the younger generation and from what I knew second hand, I was not impressed. My faith was now restored, at least from this one example, although I had a feeling she was a special case. I was relieved to learn she normally didn't dress like she did that day. She apologized for wearing such skimpy shorts but she had packed everything else and had to wear old high school clothes she found in her dresser in her bedroom at home. She kept asking me questions about my life and beliefs, but I wanted to know more about this young lady. She learned enough about me to satisfy her, but our conversation bounced back and forth in a contest to learn as much about each other as we could. I liked Brenda immensely after this short visit.

We agreed we wanted to take advantage of her short vacation and try and pass on to each other our take on the important things in this crazy world. Maybe we knew one of us or maybe both would be short on time so we decided when to meet each other for the next few days. I—for obvious reasons—wanted to avoid meeting her in front of Frank, although I felt somewhat guilty for not involving him. I was afraid he would focus on her abundant physical assets, preventing me from probing into her mind and thoughts.

Several days after our first meeting, I asked her about the topic Frank and I had been discussing that morning I met her for the first time. She responded the way I expected her to. She had never given any thought of death, or at least her own. She had lost grandparents, aunts and uncles, but never thought about her own death. I expected as much, but she was concerned that I was even thinking about my own obituary. I told her that sixty years from now, she might give it serious consideration, but in the meantime, a thought or two could prove useful. She understood the point that Frank didn't. Writing an obituary once every five or ten years might heighten her awareness of how she was evolving her life and whether she was meeting her goals and expectations. But only as an exercise to do that and nothing morbid or depressing. She liked the idea of setting life goals and checking periodically on how you were meeting or not meeting them, and whether they needed to be changed or altered. She said she had never expected to go to law school, although her father had felt it would happen, especially the way he quietly steered her in that direction.

On our last meeting before she headed back to Berkeley, we hugged tightly. I had a feeling I might never see her again. That thought was depressing to me since we had grown quite close, in a grandfatherly-daughterly way. I had no grandchildren and she had barely known her grandfather Thomas. Grandfather Ellsworth had died when she was an infant. I knew there was a reason for the saying that elderly people should surround themselves with youth and not with people their own age. With the latter, discussions always focused on the ailments and medical conditions that could easily become quite depressing. The future was indeed with the young. Brenda kept saying that we use the past to help us navigate the future. The present is only a brief way-station to the future. The past involved lessons learned and was lost in the mists, where it rightly belonged. For years, I had lived in the past. My discussions with Brenda opened the future for me.

News Item from the Canyon Zephyr, *September 16:*

Former naval aviator, Vietnam War hero, instructor at the U.S. Naval Academy and one time Naval Attaché to the German Embassy, Carl Graham Owens, 85, was found dead in his bed by his housekeeper, Wednesday, September 14. Owens owned and operated the Canyon View Animal Sanctuary for the past ten years. He retired from his government career twenty years ago and spent five years with the Humane Society of California before buying the former Randolph Ranch west of Canyon Creek. He was preceded in death by his beloved Emily, wife of fifty years, and his parents. He had no children. He apparently had a massive heart attack in his sleep. On his desk was an obituary which he had been working on. It was up to date except for time and place of his passing. There was no evidence the obituary was related to his death that night. At his request, only a brief memorial service will be held. His obituary (on page D6) specified his entire estate to go to the Humane Society for use as a county-wide no-kill animal shelter. The obituary was unusual in that it detailed his philosophy of life, with only minimal account of his life's activities.

On the day after the memorial service, Frank reluctantly went to the park as was his habit for years. He took Carl's death especially hard. Ties to his youth were being cut one by one, with few left. As he approached the park bench where he and Carl spent so many hours together, he noticed a young lady who had been at the service. She had departed before he had a chance to talk to her. He thought she looked familiar but wasn't sure of her name. She taped something to the bench back, stood silently, then held her hands to her face as she wept. Then she dabbed her eyes and quietly walked away, leading a yellow dog.

As Frank watched her cross the street and get in a red convertible, he cautiously approached the bench. Taped on it was a laminated copy of Carl's obituary. Pinned on that was one long-stemmed white rose, attached to a card with a short phrase written in beautiful calligraphy:

For Carl,

Hasta mañana dear soul.

'Til we meet again.

Blue Gentians and Columbines

*These waters and vapors cured me from
consumption years ago. Use them faithfully
and you will be cured as well.*
Milly

MILLY STEPPED OFF the train in Glenwood as dark clouds opened up and swirled snow across the tracks, nearly obliterating the station. To avoid an episode out here in this spring blizzard, she quickly drew a handkerchief from her sleeve and covered her mouth. It was April and she had spent the last four months in Colorado Springs with her aunt Della. Her tuberculosis had improved some since she came to the fabled high country of the Rockies, but she suffered a relapse in March. Della's friend Mabel told her about friends who moved to the new town of Glenwood Springs along the Grand River. They had made a full recovery, spending nearly every afternoon in the hot springs or vapor caves, and were now hiking in the mountains, breathing clear and free.

The station waiting room was empty by the time Milly entered with her two cloth valises. She set them down, then eased onto one of the wooden benches that lined the wall under the windows. "Now what?" she whispered to herself. She didn't know anyone here, even though Mabel had given her the name and address of her friends. Not knowing Mabel well, she would not impose on unknown friends of an acquaintance. But she had heard stories about Yampah Hot Springs, with its new sandstone bathing house and the Natatorium, the large swimming pool filled with the mineral rich water from the adjacent hot springs. She was starting a new life, or trying to save her old life. Either way, she had made up her mind to live one day at a time. She would not miss her old life in Baltimore. She had been so sick, she figured she had nothing to lose.

The snow let up as quickly as it began. Milly now sat in the bright light of the late afternoon sun, and she could see a bustling little town along the river, at the west edge of a steep-walled canyon. Even though she had been living in Colorado for four months, this was her first experience in the Rockies. She would have been elated except for the bloody coughing fits that convulsed her several times during the trip over the mountains. If she could only share this view with her mother. She knew she would never go back to visit her parents' graves; her tearful goodbye at their granite tombstone in Baltimore was the last she would give.

The gold coins sewn into the deep pockets of her long waistcoat would last a few weeks, maybe two months if she was frugal. Milly would have to find some way to make a living, but first, she needed to find a place to stay. She walked over to the ticket counter and waited for the bald-headed agent to look up; his name plate read "Mr. Thompson." She prayed she could get through the conversation without having an episode. The agent looked up with a frown, but her smile brought one to his face.

"Yes, miss, can I help you?"

Milly took a breath, cleared her throat and said, "I am new in town and need a place to stay. Can you recommend a good boarding house that I would find safe?"

The agent looked over the top of his wire-rimmed spectacles and fingered his gray mustache. "Well, there are several in town and all have different forms of safety." He smiled. "Some I wouldn't say are very safe from fire and there are a couple that may not be safe for a pretty young lady who is new in town. Old Mrs. Winkler is rumored to run a sinful house, with goings-on up on the third floor that Reverend Bender surely would not say was safe for a proper lady like you look to be."

The agent adjusted his green banker's eye shade and laid his pen on his desk blotter. "It just so happens that the Missus and I have a large house and we do rent out rooms, but we don't rent to just anyone. I don't suppose you have any references." He tilted his head again and looked at her over his spectacles.

Milly started to say no, but suddenly remembered Mabel's friends. She pulled out the slip of paper with their names and address, written in Mabel's beautiful penmanship. She showed the paper to the agent and said, "I'm afraid I don't really know them, but a friend suggested I contact them. You see, I came out to recover from a health problem and I was told they recovered completely."

The agent reached through the ticket grill, took the paper and studied it for several seconds. "Consumption, huh? What a shame for such a young girl. You are by yourself? No family? Usually they come with a parent or friend." He handed the paper back to Milly as she slowly shook her head no to his questions.

"I'm all by myself. My parents both died in the past year. I was staying with my aunt in Colorado Springs, but people told me I would do better over here." She put the paper back in her crocheted handbag, careful to keep the bloody handkerchief hidden.

"How old are you, Miss...?" He waited for her name. She looked at him puzzled for a second, then realized what he was asking.

"Oh, I'm sorry," she smiled. "Milly. Mildred Gordon. From Baltimore." She figured her age was none of his business.

"Well, young Miss Milly Gordon, can you cook or sew, or do other useful things?"

"Yes, certainly, but I am trained as a teacher." She looked down at the floor and struggled to not choke up as she spoke. "I guess I may not have much choice."

The agent smiled again and wrote directions on a piece of paper and handed it to Milly. "I have to stay here until the 7:45 comes through. It will be dark by then. My house is on Blake Avenue, within walking distance. Well for me at least. Maybe not for you carrying your belongings like that. How about you walk there now and I will bring your valises when I come home. Just give this paper to Edna, my Missus, and tell her I sent you." He wrote another, longer note, folded it and handed it to Milly, too. "Tell her this will explain it until I get home."

And so began Milly's life in Glenwood. She went down to the hot springs pool almost every day, and the Thompsons came to value her housekeeping, cooking and sewing skills. Edna taught occasionally at the grammar school, and helped Milly get a part time teaching position at the high school.

The Yampah Hot Springs was developed by British investors, under the direction of a dapper mining engineer named Walter Devereux. The imposing sandstone building was completed in 1890, just months before Milly arrived, and he had recently started construction of a luxurious hotel a few yards uphill from the springs, which he envisioned as the envy of the West. Devereux had made a fortune from the Aspen mines, and was sparing no expense for this huge structure, including hiring the contractor who recently built the immigration complex in New York called Ellis Island.

Glenwood City, with help from Mr. Devereux, was nearing completion of a cantilevered iron bridge over the Grand River to connect his new Spa of the Rockies to the town and the railroad. The Denver and Rio Grande, built like everything else only a few years before, was bringing the rich and celebrated to this increasingly famous health spa. Milly was busy teaching the day President Harrison visited the resort, and didn't know about it until several days later, even though it was the talk of the town.

Her health slowly improved, although on snowy or rainy days, she often had relapses, but each one seemed milder than the previous. Within a year, she was almost clear of the deadly disease. She was enjoying her work, teaching full time by the end of the 1892 spring term. Glenwood was still a rough town, being the commerce and distribution hub for the mining activities near Aspen and Leadville. Settlers were pouring into Western Colorado now that the Utes had been removed to reservations. Milly detested that word. She thought it terrible the native people had been kicked off the land they had lived on for centuries, but as Mr. Thompson kept saying, "It was inevitable. Progress means change and there are winners and losers." She argued with him about it occasionally and always ended up so upset she was almost in tears.

She was pleasant to look at but not out of the ordinary. Her long blond hair always caught the attention of both men and women. She attended the Presbyterian Church every Sunday, singing alto in the choir. Several young men at the church tried to court her, but she diplomatically turned them down. She was not quite ready to be with men, something that confused Edna Thompson. Edna told her she was a very desirable young lady and there were lots of eligible young men falling all over themselves because of her. Milly would laugh and say there were so many more men than ladies in this town that was understandable. She was waiting for the right gentleman, not one of the rough miners or cowboys who were so crude and unrefined.

Milly still enjoyed what she referred to as the proper life she grew up with in Baltimore. She had several books that she constantly referred to on the evenings she spent in the Thompson parlor. One of course was the Bible, the family copy that had belonged to her grandmother. She also read the English poets—Byron, Browning, Wordsworth, and Shelley. She often said these poets were her one link to the genteel life of civilization, as compared to the rough life of the frontier she now lived in. Her role, she kept telling Edna Thompson, was to bring some of that gentle life to these raw mountains. Burleigh Thompson, although he enjoyed the company of what he called an innocent and quite naïve young woman, always harrumphed when she stated her opinions.

About a year after her arrival, she came home from school one afternoon to find a young man sitting in her favorite chair in the parlor. He was leafing through her favorite book of Byron's poetry, which she usually left on the table next to the fireplace. It was a blustery March afternoon and she was fighting a cold, feeling none too friendly. She had looked forward all afternoon to collapsing into her chair, with a cup of tea, and memorizing a new poem. The evening before, she had read a Byron poem that attracted her, *To a Lady:* "These locks, which fondly thus entwine, In firmer chains our hearts confine, Than all th' unmeaning protestations Which swell with nonsense love orations." That brought back memories of her earlier life and another young man who sailed east from Baltimore and never returned.

The young schoolteacher paused in the parlor doorway, wondering who this stranger was, when Edna walked into the room and quickly introduced Milly to Drew Simmons. He jumped up, surprised to see this young woman staring at him. The book fell from his hands and Milly gasped as it landed face down and open on the carpet. She grabbed for it at the same time Drew tried to intercept its fall, and they bumped heads. His apology was unheard by Milly as she jumped back in embarrassment.

Edna calmly soothed the situation by explaining that Drew was going to stay at the house for several weeks. He was new to the area, coming from Alaska, looking for a place to settle down.

"I'm sorry if I surprised you," Drew said as he motioned for Milly to sit in the chair he had been in. "I am guessing this is your chair and your book." He handed the book to Milly. "I was wondering who was such a reader of great literature."

Quickly recovering her dignity, Milly smiled and put her hand to her nose. "I must apologize. I fear I am coming down with something and my mind was on my health. I was not paying attention. Welcome to our town Mr. Simmons. You will find that Edna and Burleigh keep a fine, and quite peaceful house. She will add a little fat to your bones."

Turning to Edna, Milly said, "Edna, I was thinking all day of relaxing by the fire, with Byron and a cup of tea. May I go in and make us some?"

"You sit down young lady and put a blanket around yourself. I have a pot of water on the stove and it should be ready now. You and Mr. Simmons can discuss Byron since he has been sitting there for the last hour reading your book." She smiled as she stuffed her hands into her apron pockets and strode back to the kitchen.

"Please, it's Drew, not Mr. Simmons. That sounds so formal," Drew said as he handed Milly the wool blanket that had been folded over the back of the horsehair settee.

Thus began a relationship that surprised them both. As much as Milly tried to learn more about Drew and his life before that night, she gleaned only hints of adventurous and mysterious times in Alaska, Oregon, and California. Drew seemed quite knowledgeable about life and survival, but Milly thought him seriously uneducated in book learning. After a tentative courtship of a month, Milly began the task of grooming him for what she wanted in a man. Drew resisted valiantly, but slowly began to fall to her efforts of domestication.

Escaping as he was from a past with unsavory qualities, Drew managed to keep his history to himself. He was turning a new page and found a chance to start without the darkness of his past. Milly was what he needed. And if she tamed him, then that was the price he had to pay. He found her innocence and naivety a pleasant change from the rugged and often violent life he led in the Northwest.

Milly had him attending church his third Sunday in Glenwood, and by the end of the month he was singing in the choir, but paying more attention to Milly than his hymnal. Drew found employment in the local lumber yard and soon was working with the local mills buying lumber and even shipping it to Grand Junction and as far west as Utah.

Milly was so different from the ladies he had known in the gold camps and fishing villages. In his knock-about life in the wilds, he rarely came across someone well educated and he certainly didn't talk poetry to the dance hall ladies or saloon gamblers. Drew had a minimum level of education, but at least he had heard of some of the poets of the nineteenth century. He listened attentively as she read her favorite poems to him. Her voice had a passion and rhythm to it; he felt she was making up the poem just for him. He was surprised and amazed by this young woman who could not only read the poems with such emotion, but she had many of them memorized. As she spoke, she stared right into his eyes, sending the words directly to his soul.

Soon, he was reading to her, too. One Saturday afternoon, while they were sitting along the creek outside of town, he was reading from her favorite Byron. Standing up to emphasize one passage, he stepped in a gopher hole, lost his balance, and both he and the book ended in the creek. He failed to see the humor of the situation after he slipped trying to get up and landed heavily on his rear end on a large rock. He mumbled that he busted his butt, but Milly was trying so hard to hide her laughing, she didn't hear him; he had to sit on a pillow for several days.

When Drew returned one evening from his next business trip in Denver, he found Milly in her usual place in the Thompson parlor. She was grading her private students' papers, but her poetry books were on the table nearby. She often wrote a quote from one of her "boys"— the British poets—as an appropriate comment to a student essay. Drew sheepishly handed her a package tied with a wide red bow. He sat down in anticipation as she looked at him with surprise. Quickly tearing off the fancy wrapping, she let it fall to the floor as she held up a brand-new book— *Byron's Poems* was embossed on the brown cloth binding. The edges of the pages were gilded, making the book look very expensive. In fact it was. Drew had looked all over Denver to find a copy that he thought worthy of Milly. She laid the book in her lap and stared at Drew. Tears welled in her eyes as she fumbled to say thank you.

Drew said quietly, "Open it."

Milly thumbed through the pages, eyes opening wide at the very small print and thin paper. "Oh my, it reminds me of a bible."

"Inside the front cover, fly leaf."

Milly closed the book, caressed the embossed title,

opened the cover, and read the inscription. Her lips moved silently as she read:

Glenwood, Colorado, August 9, '93

I would here pen a poem but it would be too easily compared with the powerful products of
the gifted author of this volume. It would be as the firefly in the brilliant sunlight.

Remember me as one who possesses the will, the depths of emotion, the sympathy and
love of romance and the beautiful, but who lacks the power to express.

A Friend.

"Oh, Drew, dear, my dear." Milly got up, setting the book on the table. Tears were running down her cheeks as she sat down next to Drew, hugging him tightly. "You are so wonderfully sweet."

She picked up the book and reread his inscription. "Drew, you do not lack the power to express. You are more elegant than anything Byron wrote. Please, read me a poem."

The summer faded into fall as Milly and Drew read together, and rode together, spending all their time with each other, oblivious to the rest of Glenwood and Colorado. The Leadville and Aspen mines flourished, bringing business and culture, and by late 1893, nearly 16,000 people lived in Aspen alone. And many came to the hot springs, suffering from the ravages of consumption. Milly would occasionally go down to the train station and watch the newcomers come off the train. She could tell them at a glance. They would hide their cough with a bloody handkerchief as she had done a few years before. They looked thin and drawn out, often sweating, even on cool days. Milly knew the pain they felt and the hope in their eyes.

Glenwood had gained renown in '87 when Doc Holliday came to town to battle his consumption. He was less successful in this battle than others he had fought. Only six months after he arrived, he died in the Hotel Glenwood, and was buried in a temporary grave on a cold and snowy afternoon with almost no one in attendance. The main cemetery was on top of the hill above Blake Avenue, and any poor soul dying during the winter was put in a temporary grave at the bottom of the hill, and transferred to more permanent digs, so to speak, when the ground thawed. A spring flood the following year washed out several graves, Holliday's one of them. From then on, it was anyone's guess which grave was his. Milly, though not a fan of his infamy and notoriety, was sympathetic to his disease, and several times a year visited the grave thought to be his, placing a bouquet on it of wildflowers then in bloom.

Milly and Drew spent the Fourth of July, 1894, riding the Colorado Midland Railroad to Aspen, winding along the Roaring Fork valley. The repeal of the Sherman Act the year before caused a panic to the silver mines, many of which shut down. Aspen had gone into a depression, with miners and speculators moving on to other places. The two lovers were able to rent horses to ride further into the high country. They spent the long afternoon on the edge of an idyllic mountain meadow, dotted with gentians and columbines. Open next to their blanket was a wicker basket full of Milly's fried chicken and potato salad. They tossed pebbles into the creek and described whatever they thought the puffy cumulus clouds drifting overhead reminded them of. Drew read from Wordsworth and Byron while Milly made bouquets with monkey flowers from the stream and columbines from the meadow.

Milly would forever remember this day as the most perfect of her life. Thinking she had found the perfect place to be and the perfect person to be with, she kissed Drew passionately after he put a garland of sky blue gentian blossoms in her hair. He had been patient with this shy young lady, but their inhibitions flew into the mountains on the tails of the bluebirds on that memorable day. Without thinking, Milly pressed one of the blossoms within *Byron's Poems.*

Seven days later Milly was sitting in the Glenwood train station, waiting for Drew to return from Leadville, when she heard the sheriff tell Burleigh about a train wreck near Tennessee Pass. Six passengers were killed as the car they were riding in plunged into the creek far below.

At the time, no one knew the names of those killed, but Milly had been reading a passage from Bryon's *Corsair* and she immediately knew that Drew was among the dead. She placed the pressed blue gentian as a bookmark where she stopped reading, and closed the book, never to read from it again. She never knew that the gentian's slow fading of color to a transparent skeleton over subsequent decades stained page 425:

> *But bound and fixed in fettered solitude,*
> *To pine, the prey of every changing mood,*
> *To gaze on thine own heart, and meditate*
> *Irrevocable faults, and coming fate—*
> *Too late the last to shun—the first to mend—*
> *To count the hours that struggle to thine end,*
> *With not a friend to animate, and tell*
> *To other ears that death became them well.*

Milly never again left Glenwood Springs. She didn't travel to the high country outside Aspen, nor did she go to the site of the train wreck. She didn't visit her dying aunt Della in Colorado Springs, nor did she travel down the Grand River to the growing city of Grand Junction. She became a full-time school teacher, a surrogate mother to hundreds of schoolchildren in the growing town of Glenwood. She never married and never smiled at another man looking for her favor. She asked one of her older students, whose family ran sheep in the high country, to bring her mature gentian seeds. On July 4, 1895, she planted them on Drew's grave on the hill above Glenwood, then sat down by the grave, pulled *Byron's Poems* from her basket, opened it to the back flyleaf, and wrote the following in pencil, afraid her tears would cause the ink to run.

> *Today, my love flies low over the earth,*
> *like a swallow before rain,*
> *and touching the tops of the flowers*
> *has culled you these.*
> *Kiss them until they open,*
> *they are full of my thoughts*
> *As the world, to me, is full of you.*

The gentian seeds sprouted, but didn't flower that first summer. The next year, she came to the grave every week, waiting for the blooms. Two of the plants bloomed, but not vigorously like their high meadow cousins. She watered them every week, but in the summer of '98, the last one died, and Milly never returned to the grave.

Although she stayed with the Thompson's, cooking and housekeeping, Milly's health deteriorated along with her spirit. Edna had taken ill the spring of '97, dying at the end of July. Burleigh said he couldn't stay in the house where he and Edna lived for the last twelve years of their forty-year marriage. He retired from the railroad and moved to Denver, leaving the house to Milly. She continued to rent rooms to boarders, but allowed only women.

In the spring of '98, Milly helped organize the first Glenwood Strawberry Day, celebrating the gardens and locally grown fruit. Although the day was a success, Milly only went through the motions, allowing others to be gay and happy. Although her students liked her, they recognized the depth of unhappiness. She stayed active in the church, but turned inward when anyone tried to befriend her. People in town knew her as the lady dressed in black, her blond hair always tied in a bun, showing streaks of gray. Milly was friendly, but never let anyone close to her or even know much about her. Minister Bates of the First Presbyterian Church, who knew her as well as anyone, told others that Milly was just passing time on this earth; her heart was already in heaven.

She led the fundraising committee formed to convert the Yampah Hotel into a tuberculosis sanatorium. She could be found most days visiting the patients who came to find a miracle cure as she had done. Like a mother hen, she would take them across the river to visit the Spa of the Rockies. Some days she would accompany new patients to the vapor caves next to the hot springs, giving a spiel as if she were a tour guide. The caves were dark, lit only by candles or kerosene lanterns, and as the Utes had done before them, they laid down in hollows in the floor lined with pine boughs.

During Milly's time there, the management installed

benches and hollowed out alcoves to allow some degree of privacy. People sitting in the damp darkness knew it was Milly walking by with newcomers to the caves as they heard the familiar lecture: "The Ute Indians, before they were ruthlessly pushed off their land and out of their healing waters, used this cave for hundreds if not thousands of years. The water that runs across the floor is 125° and air temperature is 110°. Humidity of course is 100%. You should stay in the heat only 15 minutes before going upstairs to cool off in the cooler waters of the natatorium or in the breathing rooms. These waters and vapors cured me from consumption years ago. Use them faithfully and you will be cured as well." She watched some recover and some die. By this point, she really didn't care, yet she felt it her duty to give people hope where they had none before.

Milly's spirit and health were failing in '05 when the town celebrated Teddy Roosevelt's visit. He stayed at the Hotel Colorado, flirting with the many lady employees of the spa, and he returned empty handed from a bear hunt in the nearby Flattops. Milly had spent many afternoons at this luxurious hotel, finished in '93, just before Drew's death, and was known as the TB lady since she ministered to the sick who came to the pool and hotel. She was determined that TR not leave town empty-handed; it would be a bad image for Glenwood. So she gathered cloth scraps, stitched them in the form of a bear, and sewed on button eyes and nose. At home, tucked in the back of a vanity drawer, she found a large red bow for her teddy bear's necktie. One of the hotel maids gave this creation to the President as he left town the next day. Teddy laughed heartily, looking at his toy cloth bear as he boarded the train. When the train pulled out, the grinning man leaned out the window waving his bundle of rags, shouting "bully to you all. I'll be back again to get a real bear."

Exhausted from her last creative effort, the broken and tired Milly returned home and lay down on the settee by the fireplace where she had spent so many evenings reading her boys' poems. Luanne, her remaining boarder, found Milly's body late that evening when she came home from work. Seventy years later, before the vacant, dilapidated house was torn down, *Byron's Poems*—its cover stained and fragile with age, its pages moldy—was found on top of a trunk in the attic thick with dust, along with volumes by Shelley, Wordsworth and Browning.

Dedicating Daddy's Lake

*Daddy and Momma were a handsome couple.
"The ideal family," stated one magazine article
about her dad. Flora felt close to her
mother, confiding all the girl stuff about
growing up, but she felt a special,
different bond with her father.*

Flora STUMBLED ALONG the trail as it came out of the dark forest into the flower-filled meadow. She was exhausted and her pack was getting heavier by the step, but she was almost to the end of her journey. The trail itself did not have an end, but spread in a spider web of paths leading to lakeside campsites. The growing shadows cast by the nearby wall of mountains overpowered the slanting rays of the setting sun. As one ray of fading sunlight spotlighted Flora, she squinted, held her hand over her eyes to get her bearings, and headed straight for the lake, knowing exactly where Jack would be. She had experienced this scene dozens of times. It was like coming home to an inspiring and refreshing ending. She hoped that inspiration would translate into courage this time.

The gray mountain peak, still striped with snowfields, reflected in the intense blue of the lake. One snowfield stretched all the way down the mountain into the water at the far end. Its reflection almost hid Jack where he sat on the large granite boulder at the water's edge, near the stream that emptied from the lake. It was her favorite sit-

and-think rock, as it had been with her father. Symbolic, she thought; Jack was the rock of strength left in her life now. She breathed a sigh of relief that she had finally made it, although she didn't look forward to telling Jack about her adventure. Her forehead was wet with perspiration mixed with a few drops of dried blood.

Jack was meditating on a dipper darting in and out of the stream, its sooty gray plumage flashing in the light. Hearing Flora approach, he turned to her and said, "Good, you're here. Ready for the ceremony? The sun is almost down." Although Jack was looking at her, he didn't seem to be focused on her yet.

"Yes," she said hesitantly. Then very softly, she added, "No." She slowly took off her pack. She set it on the lichen-speckled boulder and started to unzip the cover.

When she reached to set down the pack, Jack looked at the scratches and bruises on her hands but said nothing. Her slow, almost robotic, movement was accompanied by silence. She was always tired by the time she arrived, taking longer than he did to get to the lake. She appreciated that he hiked ahead to have the tent up and ready for her to collapse in when she finally stumbled into camp.

After a few seconds of awkward silence, Jack started to speak, but stopped when her eyes looked up. They moved past his. They were blurred by tears. Her gaze settled on the highest peak standing sentinel on the horizon. The snow on the high ledges and gullies was turning from orange to gray with the advancing twilight.

This peak and the lake were special to Flora. She called them *Daddy's Mountain* and *Daddy's Lake*. Although both had proper names on maps, all Flora knew them by were these names she had given them when she was four years old. By then she had been visiting them for over two years.

Jack finally broke the silence. "You okay? Is ..." he paused before he said the word as he looked first at the pack, then at her, "it okay?"

"No," she said as she brushed loose strands of blonde hair from her eyes. Tears started to well up once again.

Jack put his hands on her shoulders. "Flora, what's wrong? What happened?" She pushed his hands off and stepped back, tears now slowly crawling down her cheeks.

As she wiped her face with the back of her hand, he stared at her forehead. What looked like a smudge of dirt was smeared blood. He looked again at the scratches on her arms. And there was dried blood on her throat. He fought past her outstretched arm and pulled back her collar. A five-inch long gash spread from her neck down to her shoulder. Her tank top, hidden by her denim vest, was caked with dried blood.

"Flora, what in the world? What happened? Are you all right?" The questions welled up in his throat like the tears now welling in her eyes. Jack held her hands and looked into her eyes; tears flowed down her face; her head fell onto his shoulder. She sobbed loudly.

Jack waited until she composed herself, enough for her to sit down on the lush carpet of meadow grass away from the boulder. Flora had had an emotionally difficult past few months. Her father's recent illness and death, on top of her miscarriage, had taken a toll on her.

Sitting down next to her, he slowly pulled over her dark blue pack. As he unzipped the flap, he saw the brass urn, wrapped with the packing material. The white foam wrapper was dirty. Not dirty, he thought, but gritty. He frowned as he started to pull it out of the pack.

Flora put her hand on his to stop his motion. She looked in his eyes and said slowly, "don't bother, it's empty." She dug into her pocket to retrieve a handkerchief, wiped her cheeks and blew her nose. She slowly put the hankie in her pocket and looked back up to the high peak, now fluorescent with alpenglow. "He didn't get what he wanted."

"Flora, what do you mean?" Jack asked. "He's here. His lake, his mountain."

Flora said nothing. She reached over and pulled the metal urn out of the pack. As she unwrapped the foam, Jack could now see it had been unwrapped and loosely rewrapped. And that the gritty dirt outside was the ash that had been inside. Taking off the lid, she showed him the inside of the urn. "It's empty. He's gone. We ..." she stopped, "he didn't make it here." She made a strange sound as she swallowed another sob.

"How?" Jack stopped short. The immensity of the unfolding trauma suddenly struck him. And either she would blurt out the whole story in a pouring forth of emotion or she would tell him at her own measured pace.

Her thoughts followed her eyes. She looked up at the darkening sky, down to the lake, over to their tent, pitched in the usual place beneath the broken-top Engelmann spruce. She looked past Jack to where the trail left the now dark forest and entered the meadow. In her mind's eye, she saw the trail entering the forest on the other side where the rocky path wound along the rock slope of the canyon wall. It followed the rushing creek, past the pounding waterfall, crossed boulder-covered meadows, and continued through the aspen stand where Jack earlier left her.

After five long miles of trail, she had been slowing down, as usually happened at that point. The "aspen rock grove," she called it. On the edge of a stand of large, straight aspen trees, there was a boulder field. Fallen from the cliffs above the trail, the VW-sized rocks were jumbled across the valley floor. Jack had left her sitting on the large flat-topped boulder she had climbed as a little girl to scramble onto her father's back. Nested on top of his old Army rucksack, her daddy had enjoyed carrying his little flower the last mile up to the lake. As she got older, he never rejected her whimper for a free ride, but he obviously had a harder time with her increasing weight. When she was five, he said "no more." She was too heavy. The amount of gear he had to carry for camping was getting heavier every year. Her mother still came camping with them, but her health prevented her from carrying much more than her sleeping bag.

After Jack hiked on ahead, Flora reflected on their hike. She knew Jack would be up at the lake in just a few minutes. Just like Daddy always did. He would leave Flora and her mother at the flat-top rock to rest while he went on ahead. He would set up the tent and gather firewood before they appeared, tired and glad to have the tent up so they could lay down in it before supper. Usually it was late in the afternoon, about the time the sun started its descent over the wall of granite to the west. Flora could hike up there in her sleep, she had been there so many times. Starting at age three, she came to the lake at least half a dozen times a year. Her father had been coming there since he was ten.

It was a family secret, this beautiful mountain paradise, miles from civilization. In the late 60s it was designated a wilderness area by Congress. She remembered the autographed photo of President Nixon signing the bill designating it Wilderness, along with two other areas in Montana—with her daddy in the background. He had worked with the state's congressional delegation and the Wilderness Society to achieve the designation.

He hadn't wanted to include his family's special

paradise, for fear of drawing attention to it, but with new Forest Service roads and clear-cuts edging closer and closer, he knew it had to be done. It was his last success in this area of the Rockies.

Since to Flora it was Daddy's Lake and Daddy's Mountain, she never mentioned it to anyone outside the family. When she would go camping, she told her friends she was going to "the mountains." As late as her college years, she never went to Daddy's Lake with anyone but her parents.

Flora shifted on the flat rock. Her gaze followed the view from the high peaks to her west, down the ridge across from her and along the valley. Spruce forests mixed with aspen stands, open meadows and rock fields. She had painted this scene several times. It seemed eternal to her, not changing in her twenty-some years of sitting on the rock. She could still hear Daddy explaining the view to her. He was so enthusiastic about his love for the land. He taught her all the names of the flowers and trees. He pointed out which ones she could find on the alpine tundra, which ones along creeks, which ones in the meadows. She knew the geology of the mountains, why they were shaped as they were, their long and turbulent history. Daddy pointed out the glacial polish on the bedrock around the lake and told her stories of the advance of the glaciers, the way they carved the symmetrical valleys and created the mountain tarns or lakes. So vivid, she could hear the glacier grinding down this valley, smoothing the sides, and shaping the landscape for miles beyond. He imitated bird sounds and taught her the difference between marmot whistles and pika chips. She and Daddy picked their favorite animals from each hike and told stories and drew pictures. She could return the call of the bull elk as they bugled and whistled to their harems in the frosty autumn mornings. His love of nature and life in general was so strong. He instilled it in her along with his positive and peaceful nature.

Momma was a talented artist, selling her watercolors, pen and ink, and charcoal drawings in Denver and Seattle galleries. She illustrated all of Daddy's books, and she was very patient in transferring her love of art to her only daughter. Flora's drawings and paintings of the lake from dozens of views in dozens of moods covered the walls of their house. Flora majored in art in college, and helped organize mother-daughter exhibits; she knew how proud her parents were of her own accomplishments. Daddy and Momma were a handsome couple. "The ideal family," stated one magazine article about her dad. Flora felt close to her mother, confiding all the girl stuff about growing up, but she felt a special, different bond with her father. Even though Momma was a strong influence in her life, somehow it was her father who imprinted most on her. The family was a very close three-person team.

Flora was enjoying her rest on the flat rock, reflecting on why she loved this place. She thought of Jack walking rapidly ahead so he could be ready for her arrival. The first time Jack made this trip with her, when she stopped to rest here at the rock grove, he decided to hike on up to the lake by himself and set up camp. Flora's pace was down to super granny, as he called it. He thought he was being gallant. He didn't realize this was traditional and her father had done the same thing for years. Flora was strong in some ways, but her stamina seemed to falter at this specific location. It would take her another hour to reach the meadow and lake. Both Daddy and Jack could make that last section of trail quickly, even packing a big tent and food. Besides, she knew Jack loved fast-paced hiking. The sun was warm. Aspen leaves fluttered in the breeze. A Clark's nutcracker, hopeful of a handout, landed next to her on the rock. She felt she knew him, or his parents and grandparents who had shared their lives here for years. He was family, she thought. Now her only real family was Jack. She smiled, and thought about how Jack came into her life.

At a campus rally, he tripped and fell, spilling beer over both of them. After he apologized profusely, she knew intuitively, in spite of the not-so-elegant beginning, that Jack shared many of her loves.

As Flora did with anything she set her mind to achieving, she did research on Jack the next day. She adored his looks, but she was way beyond judging any guy by that alone. The boys in high school could be lined up like rag dolls she had tossed aside when they failed to meet her standards for intelligence, passion, idealism. You didn't just date Flora, you stood for inspection, then entered a probationary period, if you were lucky enough to get that far. No one to that point in Flora's life had gone beyond the first stages of probation.

Flora was intelligent and self-confident. When she stood, hands on hips, legs apart, her stare could mesmerize a person. Her goals were to continue the passion of both her parents, living a life they would be proud of. Most people mistook this as snobbishness and arrogance, with naïveté thrown in for good measure. Like her mother, she simply cut out the small talk and petty gossip, focusing on more important things. Her sense of humor, potentially outrageous, was often hidden by her serious concentration of whatever she was engaged in. She was certainly not naïve, as Jack first teased her. She loved and adored her parents, who led a life she felt was perfect. Jack called it an idealistic prison, which he was happy to aspire to.

Now studying for his Master's degree in ecological niches, he had spent his senior year researching Andean cloud forests. Both his parents had been killed in an automobile crash his college freshman year, leaving him technically under the guardianship of his uncle, but in reality, a very independent person. His hastened maturity was one quality that drew Flora to him.

They started dating immediately, and Jack received straight A's in Flora's special grading scale for the probationary period of the relationship. Most importantly, Daddy had all but adopted Jack, spending almost as much time with him as Flora did. When Jack would bring Flora home from a date, he and Daddy stayed up late discussing natural resources, often causing Flora to drift off neglected, going to bed while the two men in her life debated their theories of nature. Jack added his youthful enthusiasm and the point of view of his environmental generation to Daddy's perspective.

It was not long before Flora told Jack about her family's secret hideaway in the mountains. As soon as the spring snowmelt allowed them to hike, they started coming up to the lake. He fell in love with the setting almost as much as he fell in love with her. It was their secret place and its importance in her life was strengthened now by Jack's presence as well as that of her father and mother. Jack began to compete, in a friendly way, with Daddy for her attention.

Jack was soon made a part of the family and welcomed into their treks as well as their lives. They would often explore other areas of the mountain range, but their base was always Daddy's Lake. Flora's mother would stay around camp, cooking and painting, always being there to warmly greet them as they returned exhausted from their explorations.

Daddy was a model of the healthy outdoorsman, but Momma's health was always fragile. She never talked about the pain, but one summer trip she told Flora she didn't think she could make the hike up to the lake. By the end of the summer in which Flora proudly announced her engagement to Jack, Momma didn't wake up one sunny September morning.

Daddy told Flora that her mother's wishes were to be cremated and her ashes spread around the lake. They made one last family outing on a sparkling October day. A fresh snowfall blanketed the high peaks, elk were filling the valleys with their trumpeting, aspen were dropping their last few golden leaves. "The end of another summer, the end of a beautiful life," Flora thought. When their quiet ceremony ended, they all hiked down the long trail one last time. Daddy never said a word, being the rock of strength Flora always knew. Jack held Flora's hand as she stumbled, her eyes full of tears, the last half mile of the trail.

Flora opened her eyes from her daydream. She could see Daddy walking back down the trail that day after Momma's memorial. When he passed this rock, he stopped. He leaned over and kissed the rock. What memories did he have of it besides using it to hoist Flora onto his back? Had he first kissed Momma here? Did Momma stop here and rest like Flora did on those long hikes up to the lake? Flora opened her pack and pulled out a granola bar. She nibbled on it, but it was mostly for the camp robber and chipmunks who had gathered while she day-dreamed, now scolding her for not feeding them. Did they remember her as the one who always fed them, despite Daddy's admonitions not to? Her wedding the spring after Momma died was quiet and simple. The official ceremony was along the river in a park outside town. The water flowing by in the river originated in Daddy's Lake. Flora said a silent thank you to her mother as a small part of her floated past. But Flora and Jack had their real ceremony at the lake, with just them and Daddy present, the only place something could happen that meant anything. Daddy said Momma would have been proud, then he left Flora and Jack, walking silently back down the long trail by himself.

Even though Daddy and Jack and Flora still hiked up to the lake after that, things were never the same. Daddy was not cheered up by the lake. He would sit for hours, staring up at the snowcapped summit. One day Flora sat down next to him, placing her hand on his knee. "Daddy, when did you first come up here?"

"Flower, I don't remember." He looked at Flora for several seconds. Then he smiled. "You know the first time Momma and I climbed the mountain?"

Flora moved her hand from his knee to hold his hand. "No, tell me."

"On our honeymoon. How is that for a wedding night?" He cleared his throat. "We never hiked to the summit again after that."

"Never?" asked Flora, surprised.

"You only reach the pinnacle once. Good lesson in life! We climbed the mountain many times after that, but never went those last few hundred feet. You save the glory for one last time. We never..." He stopped and squeezed Flora's hand.

Flora and Jack repeated the family tradition. After their first summit climb, they hiked to the ledge a hundred feet below the summit many times over the years, but had never again gone the last few feet to the top.

Daddy started slowing down several years later. Flora knew he had been seeing numerous doctors, even disguising book signing trips to Seattle and Denver with visits to medical specialists. That last summer, he told her he sprained his left knee and didn't think he could make it up to the lake. He limped when he was around her, but she noticed when he thought he was by himself, he walked just fine.

Finally, he started losing weight and couldn't go to the office many days, and some days, he stayed in bed until noon. She walked in on him a couple times and found he had been crying. She noticed the vials of pills he didn't try to hide anymore.

One day in February, she proudly announced he would be a granddaddy in the fall. He said they could all start going up to the lake and he would be glad to carry the baby. Flora knew in her heart this would never happen, but she played along with him. A month later, without warning symptoms, she miscarried. Even in her own anguish Flora could see her father lose strength, and her own depression often kept her in bed until noon, too. Jack was a tower of strength for them both.

May 3, Flora's birthday, her father went into a coma. Flora and Jack took turns spending twenty-four hours a day by his bedside in the hospice facility. On May 6, while Flora sat by him, holding his hand and looking at the photograph of her and her parents one 4th of July at the lake, he opened his eyes. He smiled at her, squeezed her hand and very weakly said, "Little flower, keep up our tradition. Love the mountain and all it stands for. I'll always be with you. You and Jack..." He smiled at her, then closed his eyes forever.

Both she and Jack knew there was only one thing to do. They would spread his ashes over the lake at sunset. Then the sunrise would accompany his spirit as it brought new life each day. His obituary appeared in newspapers across the country. He was acclaimed one of the founders of the wilderness movement. His books expressed his eloquent appreciation and love of nature. Rather than denounce the wasteful path society had taken, he championed the good we could still do. His was a positive voice. "We are a part of nature, not alone from it," he always said.

Flora knew that she and Jack would continue his crusade. His presence would live through them. None of that would replace him, but it brought a feeling of peace to Flora.

So much had happened those past few months, Flora realized. A great horned owl hooted from the broken-top Engelmann spruce bringing her back to the early evening. She was smiling now. Jack was talking to her.

"What happened?" Jack asked as he held her hand.

"Oh, Jack, I so wanted him here."

"Flora, he is. You know that. He always will be. With your mom. With us."

"It happened so quick. I fell. It spilled. There was a cat."

"Go more slowly. I left you at the rock. What happened?"

Flora leaned over and picked up a small rock, stood, and threw it into the lake. She looked at Jack and smiled. "For luck. You don't know about that tradition."

Flora continued, "I just sat on the rock after you left." Jack rose and led Flora by her hand the few dozen yards to their campsite. They stood by the campfire, and both stared down into the flames.

"I sat on my flat rock for, I don't know how long. It was so peaceful. I thought about Daddy. I could see and hear him. He was laughing. I took out the urn and unwrapped it. I was going to put a little pinch on the rock."

Jack waited. Flora was stronger than he sometimes thought.

"I heard the cry of a golden eagle. I knew it was Daddy. And another golden came from up here, just soaring. It met the first eagle and they both circled over me, and called together. It was Momma meeting Daddy. I know."

Now it was Jack who turned away and bit his lip.

"I was watching them when I heard a strange noise behind me. It was a calf elk running from the trees. A mountain lion was chasing it. The elk ran right by me. The lion didn't even see me. It was coming right at me. I screamed and fell off the rock. The urn fell out of my hands. It spilled and fell down the slope. I tried to catch it. That's when I fell down the rocks, too. Guess I kinda cut myself up." She tried to laugh but it sounded more like a sob. "Oh, Jack, I spilled Daddy."

Jack couldn't suppress a smile. "You know, Flora, I don't think it's that bad. What would your Daddy think right now? What would he say?"

Flora laughed, for real now. She wiped her eyes. "My god, he would look at me and say, 'At least the lion didn't go for you. He sure the hell couldn't get me!' "

Jack chuckled. "The most important thing is you are all right. Does it really matter whether the ashes are there or here?" He looked up at the sky as the half-moon hung above the mountain. "It's all the same. Isn't it?"

"Yeah, I guess. He will always be with Momma right here." She put her arms to her chest. Jack hugged her tightly, held her for a few moments, then backed away.

"Tomorrow I will go back down and maybe find a few ashes," Jack said. "We will still have the ceremony. There is a little left in the urn. Then we will take it up there." He looked up at the top of the mountain, now a shadowy mass intruding into the moonlit sky. "I know a little crevasse it can go where no one will ever see it. Won't that be nice? He is part of the mountain, now. He will be forever."

Jack threw another stick on the campfire and sat down, putting his arms tightly around Flora. They sat silently, huddled together, small figures surrounded by the mountain wilderness. The lake and the valley were peaceful in the cool night air. The moon's reflection in Daddy's Lake rippled as a trout surfaced. The flames of the campfire danced as they reached for the star-speckled sky.

DRIFTING

"Be careful what you hold onto. Sometimes you need to throw something away if it cannot help you." I thought about Sarah. I was still holding onto her, but I couldn't let her go yet. Maybe never. She was my lifesaver many times.

Bert

THE FIRE IN the wood stove had burned down to glowing embers. I eased out of the rocking chair and carefully stepped over Valeri, napping on the bison robe on the floor. I gently opened the stove door and added another chunk of juniper. Its fragrant smell reminded me of past adventures—camping in the desert, contemplating the Milky Way, sipping wine, listening to yipping coyotes. I sat back down and continued rocking. My slow pace matched the tune playing on Enya's newest CD. The music also made me think of the quiet nights and dark skies of desert mesas. The flowing rhythm brought back memories of rafting rivers in northern Idaho during my college days. Those memories were fading into misty shadows, as were the distant mountains across the valley. I stared out the picture window at the snow falling thickly in the darkening twilight. The trees across the draw were turning ghostly gray. A blanket of snow would soften the night and greet the sun tomorrow. I was lost in my past when Valeri awoke and asked what that music was. She liked it, called it sweet. So much time separated her from me, yet were things really that different between us? My only grandchild was 16 years old, and visiting for Christmas. Her folks had driven down to the village for a romantic dinner at the only decent restaurant in Beaver Falls. And here I was babysitting, as much as a grandfather can, a teen-age girl.

Adolescent boy hormones I could relate to. A girl, well, I just wouldn't know about that. She seemed to be on an even keel, but I only saw her occasionally since Alex and Vanessa moved to California two years earlier. I wondered what that weird place would do to a country girl like Val, but she seemed to be adjusting without going off the deep end. No drugs or alcohol and no purple hair or pierced eyelids. Alex and Vanessa were good parents, even if they did move voluntarily to California.

"Grandpa, I need some advice," Valeri cooed in a way-too-sexy voice. She put her arms around me and sat on my leg.

"Well, first thing, you are way too heavy to sit on me like that. Let's go over to the sofa and you sit next to me. Although, I don't mind those long arms around my neck from such a beauty as you."

I got up, forcing her to tumble, with an exaggerated jump, onto the bison robe. She let out a screech that evidently was supposed to elicit my sympathy. "Get up here, you faker. I know your tricks and they won't work on me. Besides you're too young to be so seductive in your innocence."

She plopped down next to me and ran her fingers up my arm and curled my white hair around her finger. "What's the second thing?" she asked.

"Well, the third thing is you better not be acting that way with any young man just yet. And the second thing. Well, hell, I forgot what that was. You distracted me."

Valeri giggled and sat back on the sofa. "Are you getting senile?"

"Oh, I've been senile for years. That's what your grandma said for, well, a long time."

Val looked at me with large sad eyes. "You miss her, don't you?" Her eyes were dark blue-green, like her grandmother's.

"Yes, I do. A lot. But life goes on. I see a lot of her in you." I had to change the subject quickly. She did remind me of Sarah and it was too soon to be reminded of her in so vivid a way. I hadn't seen Valeri since Sarah's funeral the previous spring and the resemblance was scary.

"Oh, the second thing was don't call me grandpa. I have a name. Grandpa makes me feel old. When you were five years old, that was okay, but now you just call me Bert. You will never have permission to call me Bertrand. I'll have to shoot you if you do that."

"Oh Gran, "Valeri quickly stopped. "Oops. Oh, Bert. That makes you sound like a bear. Bertster. How's that?"

"Okay, Valerian." She hated her given name.

"Truce, I call you Bert, you call me Valeri. Better yet, Val. Why in the world did they name me Valerian?"

"I don't know. They didn't ask my advice. Maybe they were stoned or something. It is a beautiful flower."

"It's what you take to sleep instead of sleeping pills and it stinks."

"Probably you were squalling so much when you were born neither of them could get any sleep and they thought giving you that name might help them sleep. Well, you can give it a new meaning. One that smells and looks just wonderful."

Valeri pulled her knees up against her chest, and took a deep breath. "Bert, I need advice."

"Yeah, you said that. You know I am an expert on just about anything. Well, almost anything. But certainly not teenage man-killers."

"Get serious." Valeri changed her mood almost instantly. She looked at me and frowned.

I looked at her and squinted, putting on my most serious scowl.

"I mean it. I can't talk to Mom or Dad. They sound like a recording: be good—be patient—don't fool around—be a virgin the rest of my life."

"Whoa, this isn't about boys and…"

"Oh god no. I got the sex lecture years ago. I'm careful and appropriately chaste. This isn't about boys. Most are jerks anyway."

"My, you are smarter than I realized. And for my own protection, I'm not going to ask you to define 'appropriately chaste'." I got up to close the drapes. It was dark outside now, but it was still snowing.

"Bert, California is so different. The kids think they are grown up and sophisticated. But they are so immature and shallow. I guess I lived a pretty sheltered life so far, but I feel like I live in a different world out there. How do I deal with it?"

I looked at her. She was a beauty. Long, dark brown, almost black hair. She was at that age where her last spurt of growth had added inches to her height, but the rest of the body hadn't yet caught up. She had the ability her mother had, to look at you sideways with a twist to her face that combined pout with an innocent, yet seductive look. She also had the brains and self-confidence to go with her looks. This kid was definitely going to be a natural leader and I hoped she could handle it. I trusted her parents, both as solid in common sense as they were in what I called basic values. I was proud and I only wished Sarah could be here to enjoy the results of our lifelong parenting.

"You ask tough questions. You really think I have answers? How 'bout something easier like 'what is life all about?'"

"You are the smartest person I know. If you don't know,

then no one does." She snuggled even closer and gave me that pouty look again.

"You asking me for my Socrates-like opinions of life itself? Let's start with some specifics. Like?" I looked down at her with the expression that always got my students to open up.

"I don't know. Seems like life is so fast. Everyone is in a hurry. Do it now. Know everything immediately. People are just numbers. I didn't notice that in Montana."

I smiled. "I imagine you see a lot of things out there you didn't see in Montana. A lot can happen in a couple years. I've seen a lot of changes recently. And for California? Well, there are all those people for one. Weirdos with rings in their noses and who knows where else in their body."

Val laughed. "Oh, we had that back in Montana, but it was funny. Kids trying to be like, well, like California kids. I don't know. Maybe kind of..." She paused and looked at the fire flickering through the glass door of the stove. She seemed to be hypnotized by the fire. "Like that." She motioned with her head to the stove.

I spoke with a question in my comment. "The new kids are dancing and leaping around like that, with no purpose and no direction, but magnetically held in place by some fear? Or the old kids were based in solid values and slowly reached out, searching for meaning." I smiled at this esoteric thought.

She looked at me with that funny twist on her mouth and crinkled eyes. As she stared, I could see her mind sorting through meanings deeper than I even intended. "Sort of like when you look at the flame, there is really nothing there. What is flame? It's only an illusion. It's heat, but is it something that is really there? Can you touch it? I mean, so to speak."

"Good grief, Val, you are asking questions I've asked all my life. You find answers to those and I'll come to you for advice." I leaned back and thought about when I first wondered about fire. "I was probably in college before I asked that exact same question. What was fire?" I drifted into the past. Way back into the past.

As a kid, I liked to stack cardboard boxes in the garden, usually during the winter, and light them with a match. I pretended they were a house or building and the flames took out the rooms one by one, and the whole stack curled into black ash. One summer during college, I worked with a state park crew that was conscripted one day to fight a wildfire. As I savored my memories, I looked at Val. She was staring at me, knowing I was somewhere else. I decided to share my thoughts with her.

"I remember my first forest fire. When our crew drove up to it, I saw a line of flames creeping up a hillside covered in pine needles. I ran to it, shovel flying as I tried to beat out the flames. I thought the whole forest would ignite. I looked around and the rest of the crew was standing there laughing at me. 'Hold on, Bert,' they yelled. 'What's the hurry?' I stepped back and watched the flames. They were moving slowly up the hill, much slower than a person could walk. The colors were beautiful. They were dancing and waving, darting with each little gust of wind. Later that night, when we had a line around the fire, the night got cold and we actually huddled around a burning log to keep warm. We chunked pieces of wood into the little fire and told stories, watching the flames do the same dance and flicker. Same fire, different effects. Isn't that like life? One thing effects a person one way, another a different way. Montana kids. California kids."

Val held my hand. "Gram, er Bert, how do you come up with a comparison like that? Yeah, that might be true. I think the new kids, they are city kids. They don't know that the fire can be comforting. They only know the wild fire.

Only they don't know by experience, only by reputation. Country kids know it can be both ways. Yeah. Sweet."

"Fire is like life," I said. "Slow it down a little, it's nice and comforting. Speed it up, it gets to be a wild ride." That thought stirred more memories. I paused a few seconds, staring at the fire.

"Same thing with a river. Float a nice calm river, you can watch the scenery, admire the sounds and colors and wildlife. Your mind can wander. Float a whitewater torrent, it's hang on for dear life. The thrill and excitement is there, but you miss a lot of details. You are focused on one thing only, getting through the rough spots. Depends on what you want in life. To drift, or to hang on for a wild ride."

"It doesn't have to be just one or the other, does it?" Val shifted on the sofa and tucked her bare feet under one of Sarah's quilts.

"No, of course not. All of one or the other isn't good. You need a mix. Variety. We call it diversity of life. A good ecosystem contains a lot of edges. A meadow surrounded by forest. Water, cover, food. Most birds and animals need that mix. A deer is built to handle a sudden surge of adrenaline as she flees the cougar. But then she calmly forages in the meadow after the danger is past. Being chased by a cougar constantly, the adrenaline will kill her. Life is the same for us. We need a mix of drifting and racing. Meadows and forest. Fast water and slow. I think nowadays, maybe your California kids are too much into the racing, hanging on, and fast water."

Valeri stared into the fire again. "Awesome. Yeah, we need to drift a little." It sounded part question, part statement. We let it stand as a statement. She was thinking, maybe drifting a little.

I liked the term drifting. The river analogy sent me back to Idaho and my days at the University. I was not a city boy, not a country boy, but a small-town boy. My time at the University opened my eyes to many things. River rafting was one.

I bought a little yellow raft, my K-Mart special; cheap, not really fit for big whitewater. I took it on the nearby rivers, which were generally calm. Mostly the Clearwater east of Lewiston, a drifter except for springtime, which was when I floated it. Back in those days, you had to watch for logs floating to the Lewiston mill. That hasn't happened for decades.

I must have been smiling, because I came back to reality when Val tugged on my arm.

"You are back in time again aren't you, Bert?"

"Well you got me zooming around in my time machine. It's your fault."

"You might as well share it all with me. Is it the old stories I've heard a hundred times?"

"You think I remember which of the old stories I told you? You'd probably be bored to death."

"You kiddin'? You should write a book." She smiled and pushed her hair out of her face. A real tease I thought again. Those little gestures were going to drive some guy crazy. I just hoped it was a few more years before that happened.

"Val, I can tell you a few more stories. But let me warn you, I am at that point in life where I just don't tell the adventures. I put some kind of meaning to them. I use them to develop my philosophy of life. I don't know if you've heard me preach about consequences. Cause and effect. That's what real wisdom is. It is not just knowing facts; it is taking facts and attaching consequences to them. Attaching cause and effect. Abe Lincoln was a master at this. He told stories to make a point all the time."

The wisdom and meaning of life, how to get by, what my elders learned from their experiences—those were the things I wish I had heard from my father. I never knew my grandparents. They were dead before I was born. Val had something I never had. I heard my dad's stories a hundred times, but they were just stories. Maybe he didn't think too much about meanings. They were just his fishing and hunting adventures. Not much else. I never heard stories of his growing up, his learning about life. I'm not even sure he thought much about it. Maybe he did, but his life seemed simple and straightforward. I often thought that would make life easier and less complicated, but my mind didn't work that way. I was curious. I needed answers. I had too many questions carrying me to exotic places. By the look on Val's face, she had questions, too.

"Mom and Dad haven't really talked to me like this. I've overheard them in many discussions. They tend to get pretty—what term did you use, esoteric? Not sure exactly what that means, but I guess it's something like weird?"

Her hair had flopped over her left eye again. I brushed it back behind her ear. "You going to make me define all the terms I toss out? I may not know what they mean. I just repeat them. Or make them up."

"Oh, Bert, you know them." She jumped up off the sofa and went into the kitchen, dragging her hand along the log wall. She loved the log house. She was always feeling the logs, putting her face and hands up to their smooth rounded surfaces. In a minute, she returned with a bottle of juice and a bag of chips. "If we are going to exercise our brain cells, we need to feed them as well."

"Is that good brain food?" I asked her. I knew her folks were more health conscious than Sarah ever was. I had regressed in my food habits lately.

"The juice is good. The chips? Well, if we are going to be

couch potatoes tonight, then what better than chips?" She opened the bag and offered it to me first. Polite as well as smart, I thought.

"I used the term drifting. I like that term. It means to let your mind explore on its own. We don't use our brains anymore. We let machines do our thinking for us. Are you afraid to be alone? To be out in the forest, or standing along a river by yourself? Where it's safe, like it was near your house outside Bozeman?"

"You know the answer to that. I used to love to go sit on my favorite rock and watch the river flow by. I loved to listen to the birds, the sound of the water. It was so peaceful, so relaxing."

"Yeah, I think you are different. Do you know any others your age who would enjoy the same thing?"

"You kiddin'? Debbie or Elaine or Britney, I can't think of anyone who would be caught dead like that. They'd at least have a cell phone in their ear. They have to talk to someone. They are always in a crowd."

"Why?" Her blank look answered my question. So I tried again. "How creative are these people? Would any of them be sitting here asking the type questions you ask?"

"No way, dude." She frowned as she said that. She took a swig from the juice jug, then handed it to me.

"You're going to give me some horrible disease doing that. Who taught you proper manners?" I took a drink myself, then handed her the jug. She wiped the top with an exaggerated gesture and took another drink herself.

"We die together. I've seen you do this."

"Well I live alone. That's different."

"Any hypocrisy involved here?"

I picked up a chip that broke and fell out of my mouth. "How can I deal with you? You catch me on anything I try. Wish I had a few more students like you."

"Wish I had a few more teachers like you!" she shot right

back at me. "Where were we?"

"For someone as senile as me, you think I can remember after you keep interrupting me?" I hesitated. "Oh yes, creativity. Something we always tried to teach, your grandmother and me. After we started the Foundation, we wanted to let people know that solitude is necessary. Like the deer resting after the adrenaline surge. We need to be by ourselves and think. When you can recharge like that, then you open up your creative thoughts. You can't be creative if you are always in a crowd. Look at all the great thinkers, artists, writers, anyone who created things or thoughts. They needed time alone."

"Then a hermit should be creative."

"No, you're not thinking. What did I say about too much of anything? Some time alone, some with others. You should share your thoughts, your creative results. I don't see people alone anymore. Tell me something. What is so important that every kid driving to school has a cell phone in their ear? What do you talk about?"

"I don't talk about anything. I don't have a cell phone. They won't let me have one." She emphasized the word "they." "But everyone else in the universe, they have to stay connected. Gossip. Who did what last night? Who will do what tonight. If you are alone, you are out of the loop." Val got up to throw another chunk into the stove. We could hear the wind swirling outside. Once in a while it would force a puff of smoke out the stove door. Val walked over to the patio door and opened it. Snow blew into the room. She quickly shut it and flipped on the outside light. "Mom and Dad are going to have a tough trip back. You think they are all right?"

"You think a little snow will hurt them? If they stayed in town, it wouldn't be because of a little snow. Might be in order to foist you on me all evening and give them some peace and quiet."

"I'm not bothering you. You love this and you know it." She flipped her shoulders back and thrust up her chin.

"You asked for it. Where were we? Did I tell you about my rides down the Clearwater? When I was in college?"

"No. Never heard them." She gave me a puzzled look. "Is this a fire story?"

"No, it's a drifting story."

I took a deep breath. "I would drive down to Lewiston, then upstream along the Clearwater. I usually took one of my roommates, or if I was lucky, a girl I could convince this wasn't a date, but just an adventure. We would drive to a spot along the river, then put the raft in and float down a couple miles or so, then one of us hitch a ride back to the truck and do it again. Most of the time, it was just a leisurely float, but we had to be on the lookout for logs floating a little faster than a rubber raft. The loggers far upstream would stack their decks of logs all winter along the riverbank, then come springtime during high water, push them in and let them float to the mill at Lewiston. It wasn't dangerous, but you had to be on the lookout for the logs.

"One time, my roommate Danny and I floated a stretch of river, but we hit one standing wave sideways. We tipped. Next thing I knew, I was floating in the water, still holding onto the paddle. I looked around and Danny was climbing back in the raft about fifty feet behind me. The water was ice cold and I figured I would just swim to shore. I couldn't break out of the current. The river was carrying me down the middle and I couldn't make an inch towards shore. Luckily there were no logs right there. If one of them had hit me, it would have been all over."

I continued to stare at the fire, although I could tell Val was looking at me wide-eyed. "I looked at my paddle, wondered why I was still holding onto it, then tossed it aside. I turned back towards Danny who was still arranging himself in the raft. Then I started screaming for help. I really thought I was going to drown."

"Grandpa!" Valerie exclaimed, but I kept talking.

"The water was so cold, I was turning numb. It was then that Danny realized I was in trouble and started paddling with his hands. He reached me about the time we went under the bridge outside Orofino. I could see a group of people standing on the bridge waving their arms at me. They had stopped their cars in the middle of the bridge and they looked scared and were yelling but I couldn't hear them. They knew they couldn't help me. Danny pulled me into the raft and somehow we caught an eddy and were able to get ourselves to shore. There was a middle-aged lady stopped nearby who came over and helped us ashore. She was almost crying she was so scared. She said she knew I was going to drown but she prayed and suddenly we were okay.

"She drove us to a Dairy Queen to get a hot drink. I was shaking so hard I couldn't even talk. I'm sure it was hypothermia."

I looked down at Val and smiled. "You almost didn't exist. I came very close to not living past that day." Val rubbed her eyes and finally closed her mouth. "I never heard about that! What was your lesson on that one?"

"No lesson. Just that you can be full of life and having fun one second and the next, you can be gone. That is probably the first lesson in life. It is so tenuous and fragile. You can think you are just drifting and let your mind relax. Just don't mix drifting and racing too closely. You can drown."

"Wow. Did you think about death?" Val was still on the edge of her seat.

"No time to. It happened within a few seconds. I thought about it later, but not at the time. Even later, I didn't think about being dead. I just relived the cold water and the thought that why was I still holding onto that stupid paddle, and thankful we wore life vests. I didn't want to let go of the paddle even though it certainly wasn't going to help me. Maybe a lesson there. Be careful what you hold onto. Sometimes you need to throw something away if it cannot help you." I thought about Sarah. I was still holding onto her, but I couldn't let her go yet. Maybe never. She was my lifesaver many times.

"So did you sell the raft and stay off the rivers?"

"Of course not. If a horse throws you, you don't stay off. You get right back on. You need to prove to yourself you can do it. I was back floating the next week. Actually, I think the next week was my big date with Monica."

I looked at the wood stove, knowing this little bit of silence would drive Val crazy. She would have to ask about Monica.

She squirmed, almost afraid to ask, but I could tell she was dying to hear more. Finally, she couldn't stand it. "Well! Well? Tell me!" She pulled on my hand, making me spill the chips.

"I didn't think you'd care about that. You know, that yucky boy girl stuff."

"You can bite my ass," Val blurted before she realized what she said. "Oops," she said just as quickly, throwing her hand over her mouth and raising her eyebrows.

I laughed. "If you weren't my granddaughter and were a few decades older, I might be tempted, but no thanks."

"Bert!" she yelled in mock shock. "I'm learning more about you all the time. I'd tell you not to tell Mom I said that, but I guess I've told her the same thing. You better hope I don't tell her what you said."

She reached over and hugged me again. "Oh Bert, you are so fun to talk to. I wish I didn't live so far away."

"Yeah Sugarplum, me too." I ruffled her hair, then straightened it. Val slid off the sofa and sprawled on the bison robe on the floor. "Oh," she looked up at me and sat up quickly. "Monica. You left off at Monica. Grandma know about her?"

"No, that was before I met your grandmother. Nothing special. There was this really cute girl I met at the rec room where I worked on campus. In the basement of a big residence hall complex. I was part janitor, part person-in-charge several evenings a week. One of those student jobs. This gal kept coming in to play pool or something and we kept making eye contact but only a few pleasantries, like 'hi, how ya doing' type thing. Finally, I got up my nerve and asked her one night if she'd like to go rafting with me. Sounded better than 'do you wanna go to a movie'."

Val laughed, "Yeah, that would do it for me. More original than most come ons."

"I was shy and I didn't date much."

"You, shy? Yeah, like I believe that."

"Believe what you want. So we drove up to one of my favorite spots on the Clearwater and we floated down and hitch-hiked back a few times. I thought I could get a little action, so we pulled onto a sandy shore on the opposite side of the river. She knows what I'm doing. So she sits there with her knees pulled up—a good defensive posture. Well about that time it starts to rain. We hadn't even noticed the sky. A real downpour. I upend the raft and use it as a tent. Of course, I lean over and try to kiss Monica and she pulls away real quick and I fall flat on my face. Got a mouthful of sand. She starts laughing so I grab for her and she runs and I chase and, well, the rest be best left unsaid."

Val was staring intently. "So, you get any?"

"I think that falls into the category of 'that is none of your damn business young lady and you're not too old to...'"

She quickly interrupted, "Well you brought it up."

The telephone rang, interrupting us both at just the

right time. Val jumped up to answer it. It was her folks. They wondered what the weather was up here. They said it was snowing a blizzard in town and the sheriff was advising no travel anywhere. Roads were being closed. Val walked over and opened the door and a blast of wind and snow almost knocked her over. She talked a little more, then hung up.

"Folks are staying in town. Roads closed. Big blizzard. They got the last room at the motel."

I got up and opened the door and walked out. Val followed, holding onto my shirt. The wind felt good on my face. Snow was drifting against the house. I couldn't see the driveway. I closed the door and flipped off the outside light. We both walked over and stood by the wood stove. It felt good after that arctic blast. "Looks like you and me tonight, kiddo."

"Isn't that what was happening anyway. You and me? I didn't notice anyone else."

"Val, we've talked about my adventures. I want to hear more about what you are doing."

"You think I can compete with your adventures? You got a whole bookful there."

I rubbed my head. "See these white hairs? Each one comes with a price. I happen to have just a few more years' experience than you. That's the only difference between us. Your experiences are yet to happen. I know you've done some pretty exciting things. Didn't you write something that got published?"

"That was back in Montana. One of those things in grade school. They select poems from kids all over the state and print a book. Only the parents of those selected even buy the book. Half of those only read their own kid's poem."

"How many kids in your school had one selected?"

Val squirmed. She didn't take praise well. "Just me. But the poem was really stupid."

"Obviously someone didn't think so. By the way, go over there and look on the shelf. Remember, you autographed the book for me. Christmas four years ago."

"Oh," Val jumped up, then plopped down on her knees in front of me. "I gave a presentation to the City Council last month. It was awesome. I was on the local cable TV channel. Mom taped it."

"Wow, I'm impressed. Stop and think about it. That's more awesome than floating a river and getting dumped. What did you talk about?"

"I read a petition that I started and got three hundred signatures to have a reading program for immigrant farm workers. A lot of them can't read English and there was a big cutback on English as a second language in the schools. We got the school board to support us and the city agreed to start a program using students to volunteer. I got a letter and certificate from the Governor."

I reached out to shake Val's hand. She did some weird thing with my fingers, saying it was a secret handshake. I pulled her back over on the sofa and hugged her. "That type thing is more important than my stories."

"You're just saying that. Yours are much more exciting."

"But yours have more impact. Val, you are going to run for Governor yourself someday. I can sense it."

Val giggled and went down the hall and into the bathroom.

I leaned back on the sofa and thought about this granddaughter of mine. I had to remind myself she was only sixteen. She showed so much enthusiasm. She was the future and I smiled at that thought.

A pine branch slapped into the picture window. I didn't have nearby trees that touched the house. It must have broken off and the wind blew it against the building. My mind shifted back to the snowstorm raging outside. Probably a good idea for Vanessa and Alex to stay in town.

The snow reminded me of one time I was cross-country skiing near Rogers Pass, by myself except for my dog Gander. We had gone several miles on an old road and I decided it was time to turn back. Gander's long white hair collected ice balls as he waded in the snow. He clicked as he walked and kept stopping to chew off the ice. It started snowing as I turned around and headed back. I thought I would detour through a big meadow rather than following the road around the edge. About the time we reached the middle of the meadow, it was snowing and blowing a real whiteout. Within a few minutes, the snow was coming almost horizontal, stinging my eyes. I couldn't see anything. Gander was following on my heels, stepping on my skis with every step he took. My tracks were obliterated within seconds. I stopped for a minute to regain my bearings, and check the compass keychain clipped to the zipper-pull of my parka. We were headed in the right direction, right into the wind, but couldn't see a thing. When I paused a moment to catch my breath, Gander struggled past me and started barking. He kept on going, which was odd, considering the deep snow and the twenty pounds of ice and snow on his legs and belly. I hurried to catch up and as I reached the protection of the trees, saw old ski tracks in the lee of a tree. Mine from an hour before. From here it was easy to reach the road and follow it another mile to my pickup, now half-covered with snow. Gander alternated barking at the truck door and laying down to pull off ice balls. Fortunately, the door lock was not iced, and I quickly boosted Gander in, got in myself, and was able to back out of the snowdrifts to the unplowed highway just a few feet away. I somehow managed to make it down off the pass and into lighter snow. I don't know if Gander saved my life, but it had been touch and go for me.

When I came back from my memory, Val was standing

there staring at me.

"You were off again weren't you? Where to this time? Is this something I should worry about?"

"No, these snowy nights in front of a warm fire just take me away sometimes."

"Do I get to go on this ride? I'd love to hear about it. But it has to have a moral."

"I don't know about morals other than be prepared. Same as with Monica. I had planned the rain. Made it happen right when I wanted."

"Seriously," Val said. It was then I noticed she had put on what passed for her pajamas. Oversized, fire-engine red sweat shirt and sweat pants. Might as well be comfortable I thought.

"Even though I was a Cub Scout dropout, the Boy Scouts have a good motto: Be prepared. When I would go out in the woods, I would carry things like compass, a whistle, water, food, a map, things like that. Always think of what could go wrong, then hope it didn't. Simple concept. I would suggest the same to you. I call it defensive planning. Think of the worst and what you would do if it happened. When you do that, you can save yourself."

Before I began telling her the story, I reached over the back of the sofa where my jacket was, pulled it around and showed her the high-tech commercial zipper-pull compass I wear now. She was round-eyed and shivering when I got to the "in a whiteout with a white, ice-covered dog" part of the story.

"Were you always living on the edge?" she asked with amazement. "How many more times did you almost kill yourself?"

"The time as a little kid my brother left me on an island in a big lake and I was so scared I almost started swimming a mile across the lake? The time I got stranded on a cliff by myself? The time the bear chased me across a meadow? The time—"

"All right. All right. I give up. Not tonight. I should say a prayer of thanks I am even here. It's amazing Dad was even born. It's amazing you are here." Val plopped on the rug again after poking at the fire in the stove.

"You asked."

"Did Grandma know all this?"

I nodded yes. "That's why she married me."

"Yeah, like I believe that. You are lucky she put up with you."

"A lot of that was before she even met me." I thought a second, then added, "But then, she shared a few of them, too. Like the time we both—"

"No, I refuse to hear any more." She put her hands over her ears, then lowered them and put them on my knee. "I wanted to hear nice stories that you could add some of your "consequences wisdom" to. Just adventures, not death-defying feats of courage. Or stupidity."

The lights flickered and went out. But for the glow from the wood stove, we were in the dark. It didn't surprise me that the power had gone off, the way the wind was howling. Val seemed to shimmer in the flickering yellow firelight as she turned on the bison rug and looked at me. "Time for one more? Good opportunity for ghost stories."

"No ghost stories. But have you ever heard how I met your grandma?"

"Oh, Bert, no I haven't. I know how Dad met Mom, but they never told me about you. Was it romantic?" Val sat up and hugged her knees again.

"Guess it depends on your definition of romantic. Seemed pretty normal to me, but I think it was fate." I stared into the fire and thought. The memories came much easier than saying them out loud.

"I was on the trail crew at Rocky Mountain National Park. It was after my junior year in college. We had a crew apartment complex outside of Estes Park at the Ranger station. None of that is there now. Torn down years ago. We had been working a tough trail near Longs Peak. I was beat. Really tired. I could hardly walk. We drove into the ranger station and I literally stumbled out of the truck. There was this really cute girl standing next to a car pulling a travel trailer that was parked in the parking lot. Turns out she was staying with the family of a seasonal ranger from Reno. He had just arrived for the summer and it turns out they were in the apartment right next to mine.

"This girl was staring at me with a frown. I found out later she thought I was drunk. I was so tired I could hardly stand and this little blonde immediately thinks I'm soused. After they moved in, she avoided me for a week. Wouldn't even talk to me. I was her neighbor and she ignored me. I finally walked up to her one time after our nightly volleyball game and introduced myself. She had a wicked serve and was always on the team I wasn't on. She said something snotty like "I don't talk to drinkers." That really threw me since I hadn't had a drink since I met her that first day. Only thing I would drink anyway was an occasional beer on the weekend. We worked too hard to be hindered by a hangover.

"By going out of my way all summer to be polite to her, I finally broke through her misconception. I knew I turned the corner when she and the daughter of the ranger she was staying with somehow unlocked the door between our apartments and came in during the day while I was at work and cleaned my apartment. It was pretty dirty—dishes in the sink, dirty clothes on the floor, the standard for a summer time apartment. The apartment was spic and span when I got off work and walked in the room. I just stood there with my mouth open. I could hear the laughter from next door. At the end of the summer, I took her to a fancy restaurant outside Estes. That night, I thought I would do my usual Mr. Cool routine and take her out and park and make out. We sat there in the truck and she started crying. Really sad. Turns out her dad was an alcoholic and she didn't want to go home.

"I tried to talk her into transferring to my college since she only had two years to go and I had one. She wouldn't do it, but she did come back to Estes the next year where we worked together. She worked as a seasonal ranger at the Entrance station most of the time and I was on the trail crew again. We shacked up all summer in an apartment in Loveland. How's that for romance? Loveland. That summer was magic. We hiked and picked wildflowers and walked along the streams and climbed Longs Peak. We got married the next year."

"I never knew that. That was romantic. Sweet!" She reached over and hit me on the leg. "I don't care how romantic that is. It's hypocritical. You and Mom preach to me about being chaste and pure and you shack up with this teen-age girl. Don't tell me you didn't sleep with her."

"Well first, miss none-of-your-business, she was 20 years old. How old are you?" I reached down and flicked Val on the head with my finger. "Second, I can do what I want but you can't and you will never ever know what we did and anyway it is none of your business. Whatever we did, you wouldn't be here if we didn't do it, so there, smarty."

"Oh, is that lame. That is the lamest thing I heard ever. You just ruined a sweet story, dude." Val looked again at the fire. "But it is sweet. You rescued her. Knight in shining armor and all. I wish I had known that when Grandma was here." She dropped her eyes and lay back down. I could see a tear run down her cheek.

I sat back and closed my eyes. This entire evening had been peaceful. I looked at the fire, then at the shadows dancing along the log walls. Then I looked down at my granddaughter and smiled. I started drifting again. The CD had long ago stopped, but I continued to play the music in my mind. I thought back to more adventures, more rivers, more snowstorms. I wondered if I would have any more. Without Sarah, I wondered if they would have any meaning. For months after Sarah left, I doubted if life had any meaning at all.

I opened my eyes to see Val sprawled on her side, her eyes shut, right hand lying on my stocking foot. Her steady breathing indicated she was asleep. I thought about how fortunate she was and how incredibly smart and perceptive as well. She had the whole world in front of her. I could coach her a little bit, but she was well on her way all by herself. The only thing I could add to the scene was to have Sarah sitting beside me, huddled close, watching the soft flickering light of the fire, smiling at her granddaughter. After talking with Val, I realized that maybe life had meaning for me after all.

Maybe we all need more drifting than racing. Drifting allows time to reflect and remember as well as think about meanings. Yeah, life has meanings, but it also has no meaning sometimes. Drifting down the river or drifting with memories. Life just happens. Fate is really there, waiting in the wings. You can blank out the world except for the birds, the blue of the sky, the passing clouds, the ripple of the water lapping on the shore. You let the snow howl outside and drift the world into a formless soft heap. You watch the dancing fire as its reflections bounce off the walls, and cast a halo on a sleeping young girl in whom rests the future. I drifted into sleep with a smile on my face, my right arm resting beside me on the sofa, around someone existing then only in my memory.

I awoke on the sofa as the sun came glaring through the window, bouncing off a million diamonds sparkling on the new snow. The bison robe was wrapped around me. Val was sitting at the kitchen table staring at me.

"Good morning, Bert," she said as she smiled. "Would you like some breakfast? Then we can go for a walk. The snow is so beautiful."

WHITE BUFFALO

One winter night, the shaman went under a full moon to say a prayer for him. He was lying under a gnarled ancient pine tree. They both knew his time was up. The shaman lay down next to him and patted the massive head. The bison grunted, slumped over, and never moved again.

Bert was comfortable on a pine bench. Dancing yellow light reflected off his white hair and beard. The Hunter Moon shown down on a waning Indian summer, two nights to full. Golden leaves were a memory in the high country. A dusting of snow powdered elevations above 10,000 feet, heralding a winter he wondered might be his last. His granddaughter Val sat cross-legged across the fire circle on another pine bench. At her side was her son Bridger. Ten years old now, he could still remember his father, but just barely. A tragic accident three years earlier stunned the family and forever altered Val's life, depriving Bridger of a father and cut the heart out of Val. Bert thought back to the day he lost his beloved wife, but he had shared a lifetime of memories. Val and Bridger could never have that. They were still struggling.

Bert laid another chunk of pinyon on the fire. The fragrance always rekindled youthful memories, nights in clear desert air where shooting stars always seemed to aim directly at the coyotes singing on the next ridge. He told Val when she was young that the perfume of burning pinyon would stay with her forever, and she would never forget those rare nights when she and her parents shared a campfire. Now, she shared them whenever she could with her grandfather and son. She knew there would not be very many left, and she wanted Bridger to make these memories a part of his life.

A great horned owl hooted from the split top pine down by the pond. Since Val and Bridger came to live with Bert two years ago, the owl—they named her Chip, after Chief Ouray's wife Chipeta—had nested in that Owl Tree. Bert often reminded Val and Bridger that Chip and her feathered ancestors had used it for decades. Sometimes the nest was vacant for a year or two, but it was rebuilt and reused again and again. Val's parents worried about Bert, now approaching 90. He had lived alone quite well for twenty years as a widower. But a few years ago, he had a mild stroke and started losing shreds of memory. Nothing serious, he said, but he was out here a mile from the nearest neighbor, slowing down but still thinking he could walk his trails and do his chores. They tried to talk him into moving into town, but knew it was a futile effort. He would not leave his home and his lifestyle. After Val was widowed, she asked Bert about living with him in his roomy lodge-style home. She could still write her novels—now moving up on the best seller lists—surreptitiously look after him, and raise her son the way she was raised, next to nature and with a role model who adored them both. Bridger tossed on a small branch and asked, "Grandpa Bert, will you tell a story? You tell such fun stories."

Bert thought for a minute. He slowly looked up from the flames and nodded. "Have I ever told you about the white buffalo?"

"A white buffalo? You mean white hair all over? Like your hair?"

Bert chuckled. "You think I look like an old buffalo? You know white buffalo were rare. And sacred."

"Why were they sacred?"

"You have to understand the natives' way of life." Bert always struggled with what to call the people who lived here millennia before the Europeans. They were Americans. He avoided the word Indian since that term had been misused so badly. Cowboys and Indians. Indians from south Asia India. And it was tragic how an ancient American way of life was destroyed and the true Americans humiliated.

"Around here, buffalo, or more correctly bison, were the mainstay of their way of life. They provided food, clothing, housing, tools, medicine. The shamans, the holy men, could talk to the bison, calling them when the People needed them. When an albino or white bison showed up, the People knew their gods were sending a protector. The white bison was sacred to them. They protected it and said prayers that it would look after them. They would not kill it for any reason."

Bridger looked at his mom. "I heard about buffalo jumps where they killed way more than they needed." Val smiled.

"Sometimes. You remember that buffalo jump we visited in Wyoming? They were people just like us. Sometimes they got greedy and took advantage of a situation. But remember what the Lakota called bison: 'Tatanka.' Very similar to their name for their god: 'Wakan Tanka.'" Bert seemed to be talking to himself.

"When I first moved here, I visited with an elder from the Ute nation. They used to live here. He told me the story of a white bison living in the valley. It hung out in the trees at the edge of the valley, and would come down to the meadows to eat, then move into the trees at night. Bison are not like the cattle nowadays. Cows will camp down on the creek and eat everything down to the roots, muddying up the stream, eroding the streambanks. The bison were always on the move. Like deer and elk. You don't see them hanging out.

One minute they are there, the next they are gone—just like ghosts. Same with bison, and especially the white one. He stayed with the herd, but hung out by himself. Almost like an outcast. But the People always knew where he was. He stayed in this valley for years, even times when the rest of the herd moved across the mountains for a few months."

Bert stopped to listen to the owl. The fire cracked and popped. No one spoke. Val savored moments like this. Making a memory she called it. She hoped Bridger was making his own memory.

Bridger fidgeted, waiting for more of the story. "Well, what happened to the white buffalo?"

"He was old. Ancient as bison go. He was going blind and couldn't walk very well. The People would bring him gifts, tokens of their respect. One winter night, the shaman went under a full moon to say a prayer for him. He was lying under a gnarled ancient pine tree. They both knew his time was up. The shaman lay down next to him and patted the massive head. The bison grunted, slumped over, and never moved again. The People came to say goodbye, each walking by touching the horns. No one dared to take anything. His robe would have been priceless, the horns would be a crown worthy of the greatest of the tribe. But no one disturbed the body. They lay branches and limbs over the body, and covered it with rocks. The People say the rock pile is still there, but no one will say exactly where. The site is sacred, guarding the spirit forever."

Bert turned his head so neither would see the tears in his eyes. He was always moved by the respect the People showed for sacred things. It wasn't just another bison, but it was symbolic of something special.

"Are there any white buffalo anywhere now?" Bridger asked, jumping up to dodge a breeze that blew smoke in his face.

"What do you think?" Bert reached over to pick up another branch for the fire.

"I think you sort of look like a white buffalo, but you don't have any horns." He stepped over to Bert and threw his arms around him. "You may look like a buffalo, but don't you ever go off to lay down and die. Never…" He let out a cry and hugged Bert tighter.

Val choked back a sob as she got up and put her arms around Bridger. She wanted to say she agreed. Bridger's father was taken away by death and she knew Bert probably wasn't very many years behind. She cherished Bert's mentoring and love, and wanted some of that for her own son.

Bert was surprised by their show of emotion. As he had told the story, he hadn't realized the symbolism they might see. Sure, he had given some thought recently to his going off like the white bison, but was that being selfish—could he do that to his granddaughter and great-grandson?

"Oh Bridger, I am tough like all those other bison. I will stay with you as long as I can. But remember, the rest of the herd didn't like him around. By the way, I am not sacred, but you can bring me gifts if you want." Bert chuckled.

Bridger eased out of the hug. "They were jealous of him, weren't they? He was better than them."

"We don't want to think of things that way. That is a judgement. Better than them? No one is better than anyone else. He was different, just like I am different from your mother. And your grandfather is different from me. And your mother is different from everyone." He dodged as Val let out an "Oh Gran!"

"I think, with that unnecessary comment, it is time for Bridger to go in to bed before he sees me pour a glass of water on you." As Bridger got up to walk inside, the breeze shifted, briefly engulfing him with smoke again. Coughing, he tried to yell 'goodnight' as he opened the door and disappeared inside.

"I sure know what it is like to get a mouthful of smoke. Happened to me many times on fires," Bert started to continue, but Val cut him off.

"Okay, I cry 'Uncle'. I have heard those fire stories so often, I could tell them. As I've told you many times, I don't know how you survived, and why Dad and I even exist."

Bert stared into the dancing flames. "Smoke is just as interesting as flames."

"Listen, old man, I know you and your stories. They all have meanings. What was the meaning of the white bison? You make that one up?"

"Probably not. In ten thousand years, I'm sure something like that happened."

"Oh lord. What are we going to do with you?" Val sighed in an exaggerated exclamation. "But you do worry me. Are you comparing yourself to that white bison?"

"We all grow old. We all die. I certainly am not any symbol. Or anything sacred. No one is going to come touch my white hair and fondle my horns."

"You know what I mean. I am here living with you. And don't tell anyone, but I enjoy it. I even consider it an honor. But you do realize few saints were honored during their life. Only when they were gone did they gain fame. And your time is not up yet. You will continue to harass us for a long time."

"Good try sweetie." Bert coughed as another shift in the breeze sent smoke his way. "Saints didn't get choked by the smoke gods, did they?"

"No, but the goddess of frustration did smack old men in the face when they harassed their grand-daughters."

"Harassed? Who is harassing whom? Life is harassing me. I am old. You deny that?"

"I am here to love and take care of you. I depend on you. Bridger needs you to be a surrogate father." Val got up and stood behind her grandfather, caressed his neck and she kissed the top of his shaggy white-haired head.

"Old white bison going off to die. Really, Bert. I saw the look in your eyes. The flames reflected off them, but I saw that look. I have seen it more and more lately. It is starting to worry me. A lot. If I lose another love of my life so soon, I may just have to go off and find that bison and join him. You want to do that to me?"

"You remember the story of...?" Bert started to say, but she cut him off.

"No, no more stories. Not now. I want to know what you are thinking. Your mind is still good. So you forget a few things once in a while. Want to know how often I forget something? Like yesterday, I couldn't find my car keys. I looked for an hour. Last week, I forgot to get the bag of rice from the store. That was why I drove into town and I forgot the friggin' bag of rice I went in to get. You think you get sympathy for a little forgetfulness?"

She sat back down and threw a chunk of pinyon into the fire.

Bert frowned at her. "Now we will have to sit here another hour waiting for that to burn down."

"Oh, good grief. Bert, I am serious. I am worrying about you. I can't do that right now. Bridge is getting to be the age he needs a male influence. And I'm starting research on my new novel."

"Well young lady, go out and socialize and find a new man. You are still very smart and attractive."

"Oh, sometimes I could throw a bucket of water on you!" Val got up and walked around the fire. "No wonder the old white bison spent so much time by himself. The rest of the herd probably kicked him out for being an old snot head."

"He wanted a story. I told him one. Now that makes me a snot head?"

"Goodnight. I am going to bed." With that, she stomped off through the darkness. Bert couldn't hold back a laugh when he heard her trip over a chair by the back door.

"Nighty night. Don't hurt yourself."

Bert was frustrated. She was right. She and Bridger needed him, but he was getting too old. His time was up, just like the old bison. They would have to understand that. Their world was different. His world was almost gone, disappearing like the fog on a sunny autumn morning.

He let the fire burn down as the moon rose higher in the brightening sky. The Milky Way slowly faded as the moon-glow out-shown the stars. He had always been fascinated by the stars and moon and infinite blackness. Nowadays, he was mesmerized.

"I know you are out there," he whispered to the moon as it turned his world ghostly. "Is my ticket ready? Am I being selfish? Am I supposed to do something else or be someone I never was before?"

He got up and slowly walked to the huge old pine standing sentinel at the edge of his unkempt lawn. He knew this giant was hundreds of years old. What had it seen in its long life? Its world was not disappearing. He eased down, first leaning against the trunk, then sliding down to lie against it. He knew how the white bison felt. It was so comfortable and welcoming. He heard familiar voices as he closed his eyes. They were talking to him. He recognized them as friends and loved ones long gone. They were calling to him. Did they want him to come with them?

Was he dreaming? Was he seeing another world open up? He felt hands on his face. He opened his eyes to see Val shining a flashlight in his eyes.

"What the..." he mumbled.

"I was worried you didn't come inside," she said. "I heard you talking and wondered what was going on. You were reaching out. Were you dreaming? Or were you reaching for the bison?" Bert closed his eyes again. What would he see when he next opened them?

About the Author

Joseph Colwell has worked and lived across the west for over fifty years. During his college years at the University of Idaho, he spent summers working in Idaho state parks, Mt. Rainier National Park, and Grand Canyon National Park. With his degree in wildlife management, he spent the next twenty-seven years with the US Forest Service, working on five different national forests. In each location, he spent much time exploring the adjacent forests, grasslands, and canyons, expanding his knowledge of the natural world. Retiring from his Forest Service career, he continued work on wildland fires as a fire information officer, assisting the general public and homeowners in understanding wildfires. He has authored two books of nature essays: *Canyon Breezes: Exploring Magical Places in Nature* and *The Zephyr of Time: Meditations on Time and Nature*. Both were published by Lichen Rock Press. His first novel, *Sands of Time: A Flight of Discovery and Search for Meanings of Time,* will be published by Page Publishing in 2018. Joseph and his artist wife, Katherine, now live on their forty acre nature preserve overlooking the North Fork Gunnison River Valley of western Colorado. They created Colwell Cedars Retreat, which offers a peaceful secluded haven for guests as well as wildlife. It is also a great place for thinking about geologic time. He can be reached at ColwellCedars.com.